SEVEN SEAS ENTERTAINMENT PRESENTS

The Saint's Magic Power is Omnipotent VOLUME 1

story by **YUKA TACHIBANA**   art by **FUJIAZUKI**   character design by **YASUYUKI SYURI**

TRANSLATION
Kumar Sivasubramanian

ADAPTATION
Ysabet Reinhardt MacFarlane

LETTERING AND RETOUCH
Jennifer Skarupa

COVER DESIGN
Nicky Lim

PROOFREADER
Danielle King
Dawn Davis

EDITOR
J.P. Sullivan

PREPRESS TECHNICIAN
Rhiannon Rasmussen-Silverstein

PRODUCTION MANAGER
Lissa Pattillo

MANAGING EDITOR
Julie Davis

ASSOCIATE PUBLISHER
Adam Arnold

PUBLISHER
Jason DeAngelis

SEIJO NO MARYOKU HA BANNO DESU Vol.1
©Fujiazuki 2018
©Yuka Tachibana, Yasuyuki Syuri 2018
First published in Japan in 2018 by KADOKAWA CORPORATION, Tokyo.
English translation rights arranged with KADOKAWA CORPORATION, Tokyo.

Seven Seas press and purchase enquiries can be sent to Marketing Manager Lianne Sentar at press@gomanga.com. Information regarding the distribution and purchase of digital editions is available from Digital Manager CK Russell at digital@gomanga.com.

Seven Seas and the Seven Seas logo are trademarks of Seven Seas Entertainment. All rights reserved.

ISBN: 978-1-64505-853-3

Printed in Canada

First Printing: December 2020

10 9 8 7 6 5 4 3 2 1

FOLLOW US ONLINE: *www.sevenseasentertainment.com*

READING DIRECTIONS

This book reads from *right to left*, Japanese style. If this is your first time reading manga, you start reading from the top right panel on each page and take it from there. If you get lost, just follow the numbered diagram here. It may seem backwards at first, but you'll get the hang of it! Have fun!!

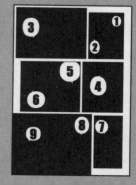

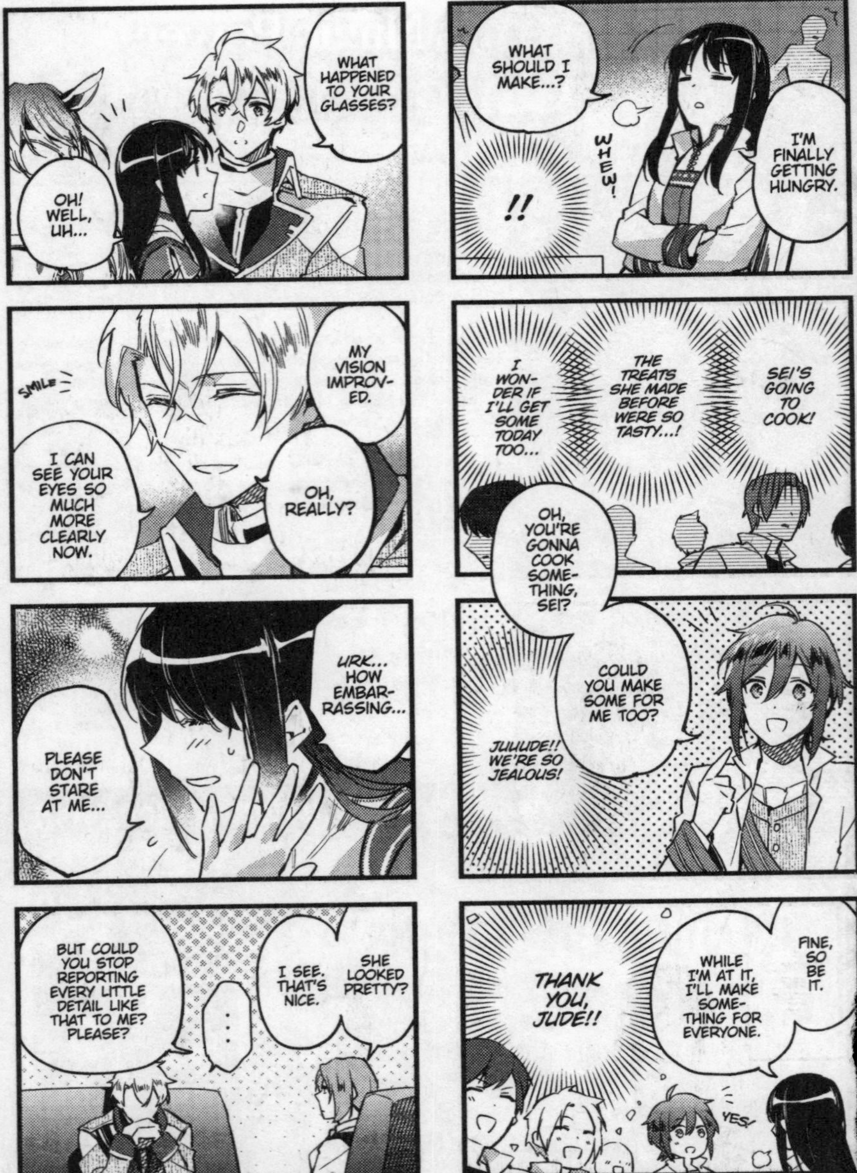
WHAT SHOULD I MAKE...?
I'M FINALLY GETTING HUNGRY.
WHEW!
!!
SEI'S GOING TO COOK!
THE TREATS SHE MADE BEFORE WERE SO TASTY...!
I WONDER IF I'LL GET SOME TODAY TOO...
OH, YOU'RE GONNA COOK SOMETHING, SEI?
COULD YOU MAKE SOME FOR ME TOO?
JUUUDE!! WE'RE SO JEALOUS!
FINE, SO BE IT.
WHILE I'M AT IT, I'LL MAKE SOMETHING FOR EVERYONE.
THANK YOU, JUDE!!
YES!
WHAT HAPPENED TO YOUR GLASSES?
OH! WELL, UH...
MY VISION IMPROVED.
SMILE
OH, REALLY?
I CAN SEE YOUR EYES SO MUCH MORE CLEARLY NOW.
URK... HOW EMBARRASSING...
PLEASE DON'T STARE AT ME...
SHE LOOKED PRETTY?
I SEE. THAT'S NICE.
...
BUT COULD YOU STOP REPORTING EVERY LITTLE DETAIL LIKE THAT TO ME? PLEASE?

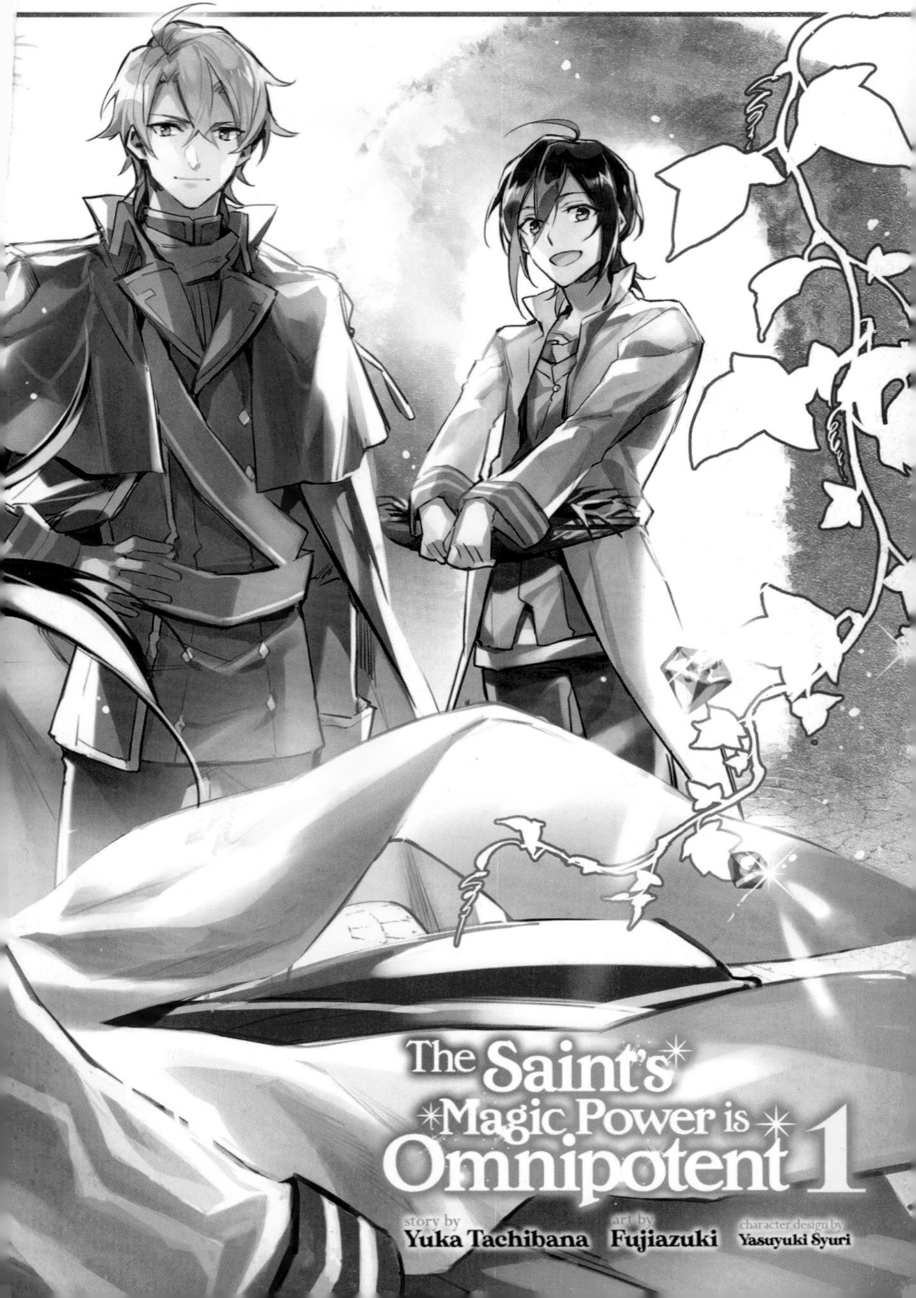
The Saint's Magic Power is Omnipotent 1
story by
Yuka Tachibana
art by
Fujiazuki
character design by
Yasuyuki Syuri

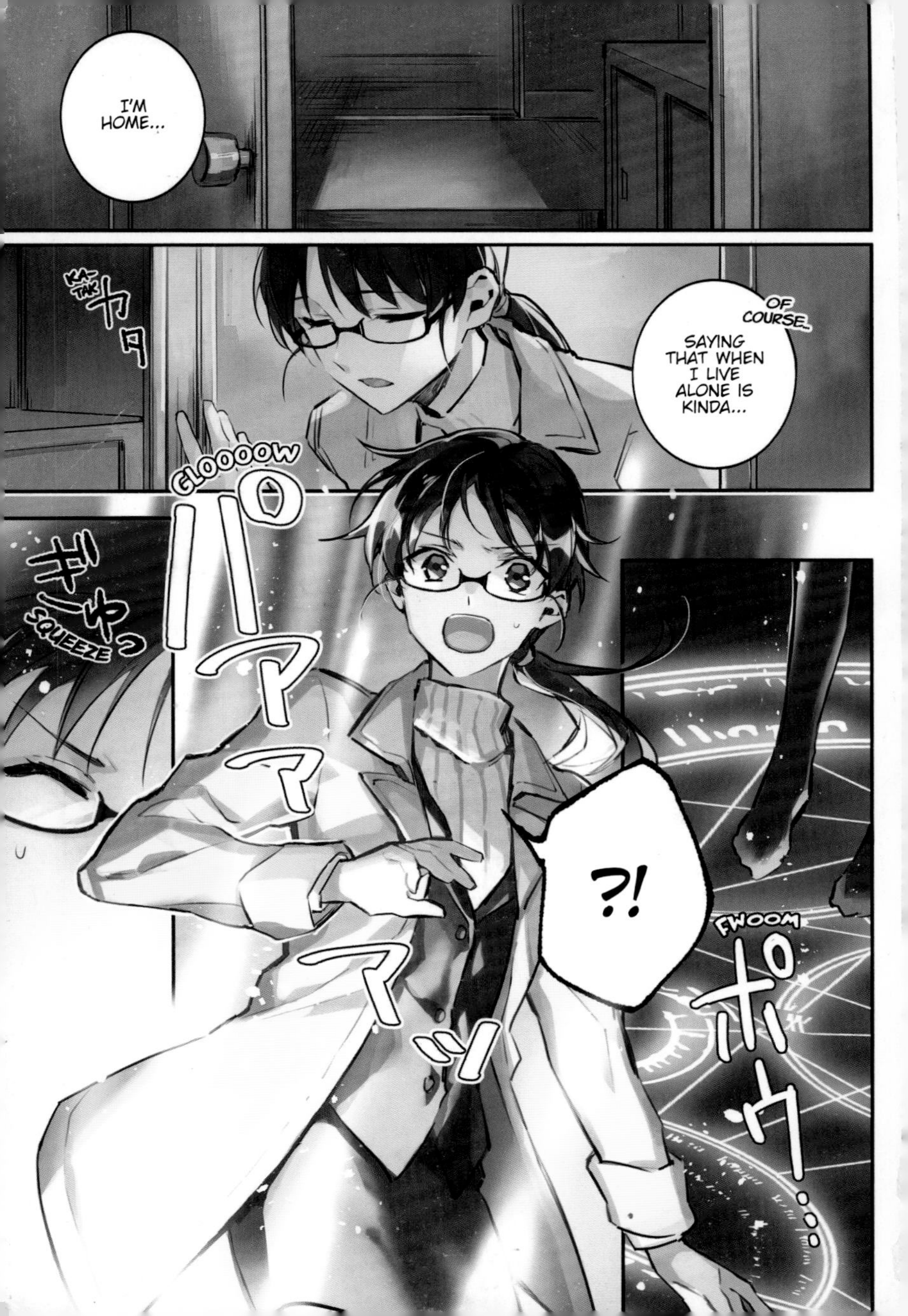
I'M HOME...
OF COURSE.. SAYING THAT WHEN I LIVE ALONE IS KINDA...
KA-TAK
FWOOM
GLOOOOW
SQUEEZE
?!

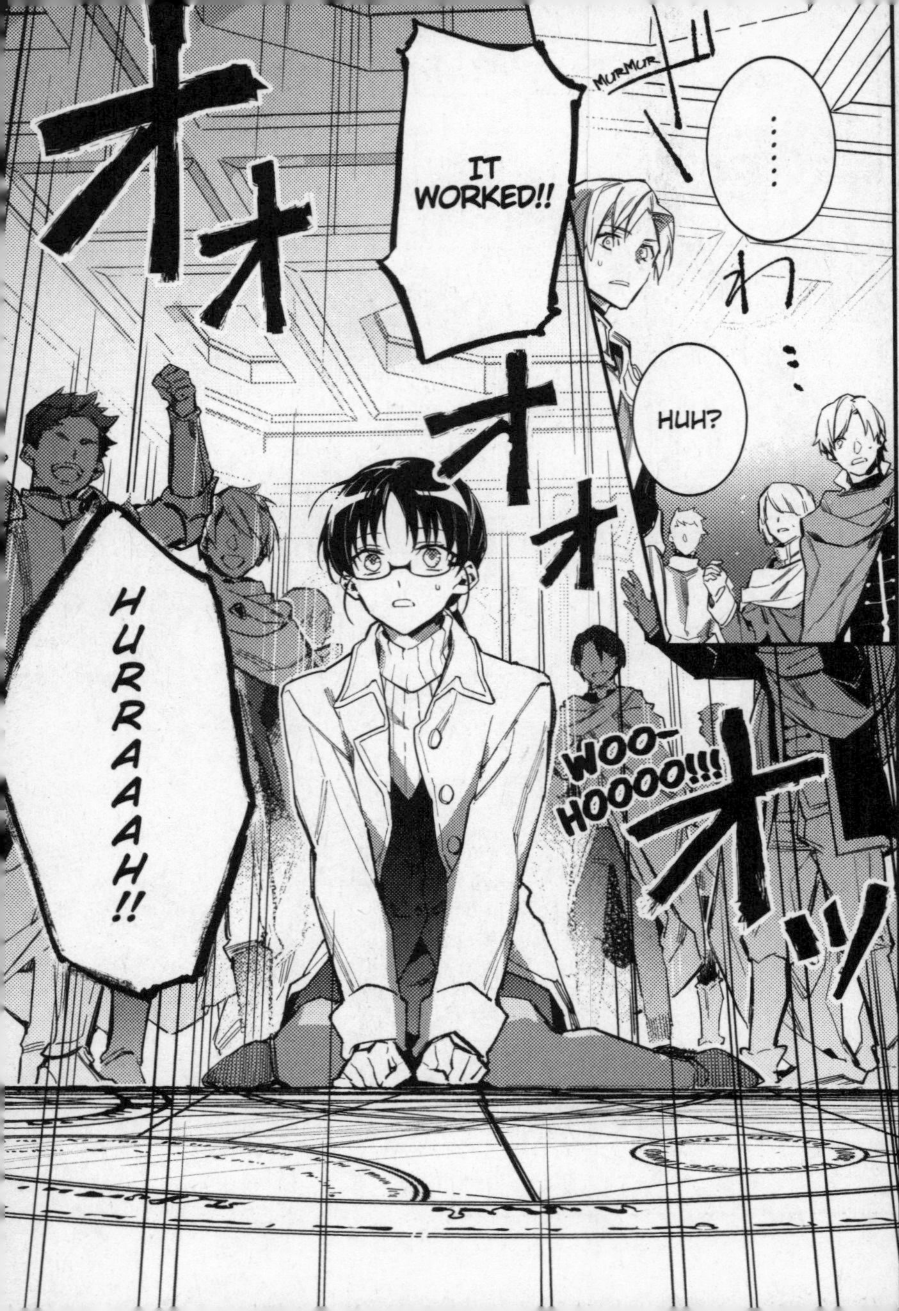
MURMUR
......
HUH?
IT WORKED!!
WOO-HOOOO!!!
HURRAAAAH!!

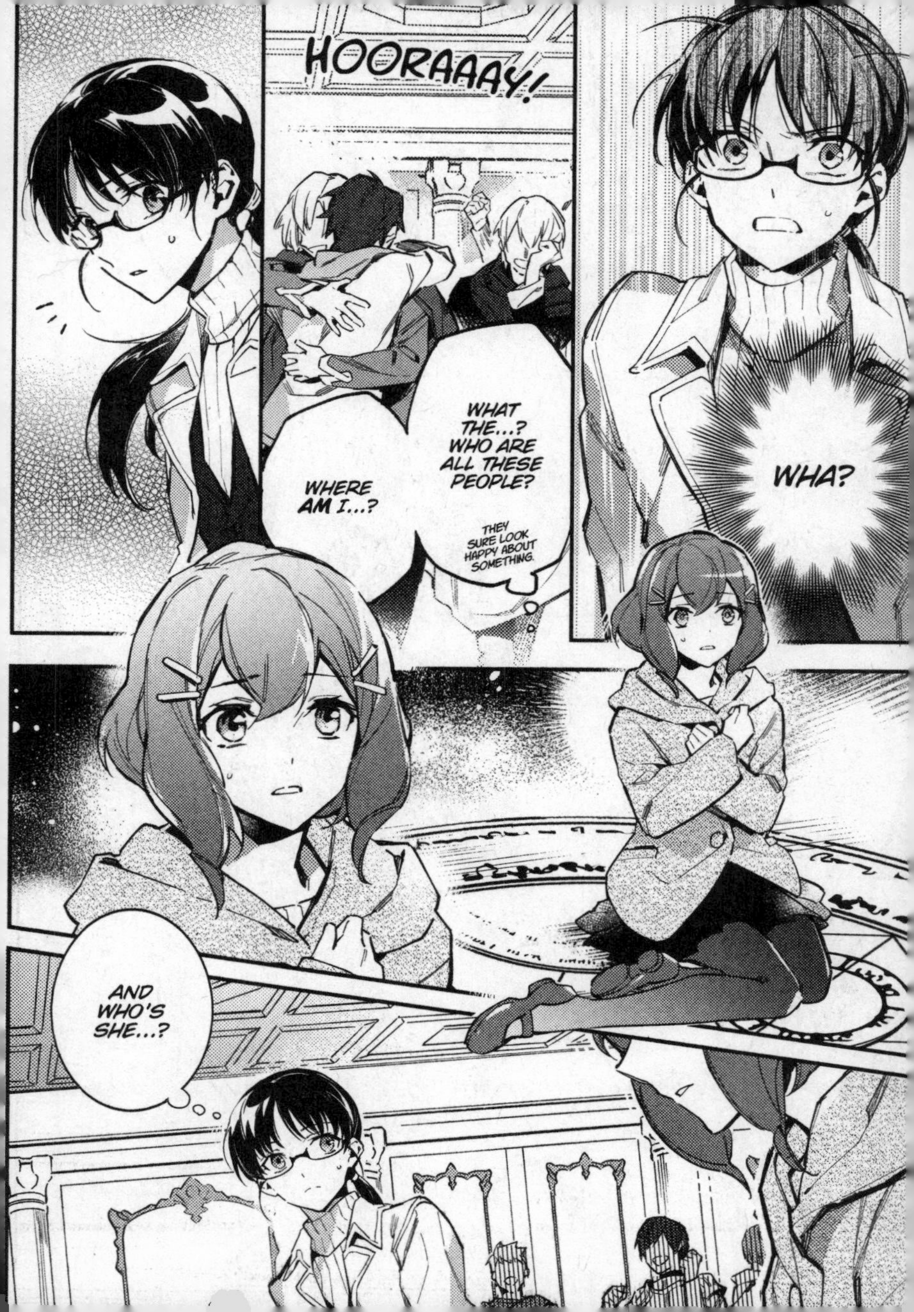
WHA?
HOORAAAY!
WHAT THE...? WHO ARE ALL THESE PEOPLE?
WHERE AM I...?
THEY SURE LOOK HAPPY ABOUT SOMETHING.
AND WHO'S SHE...?

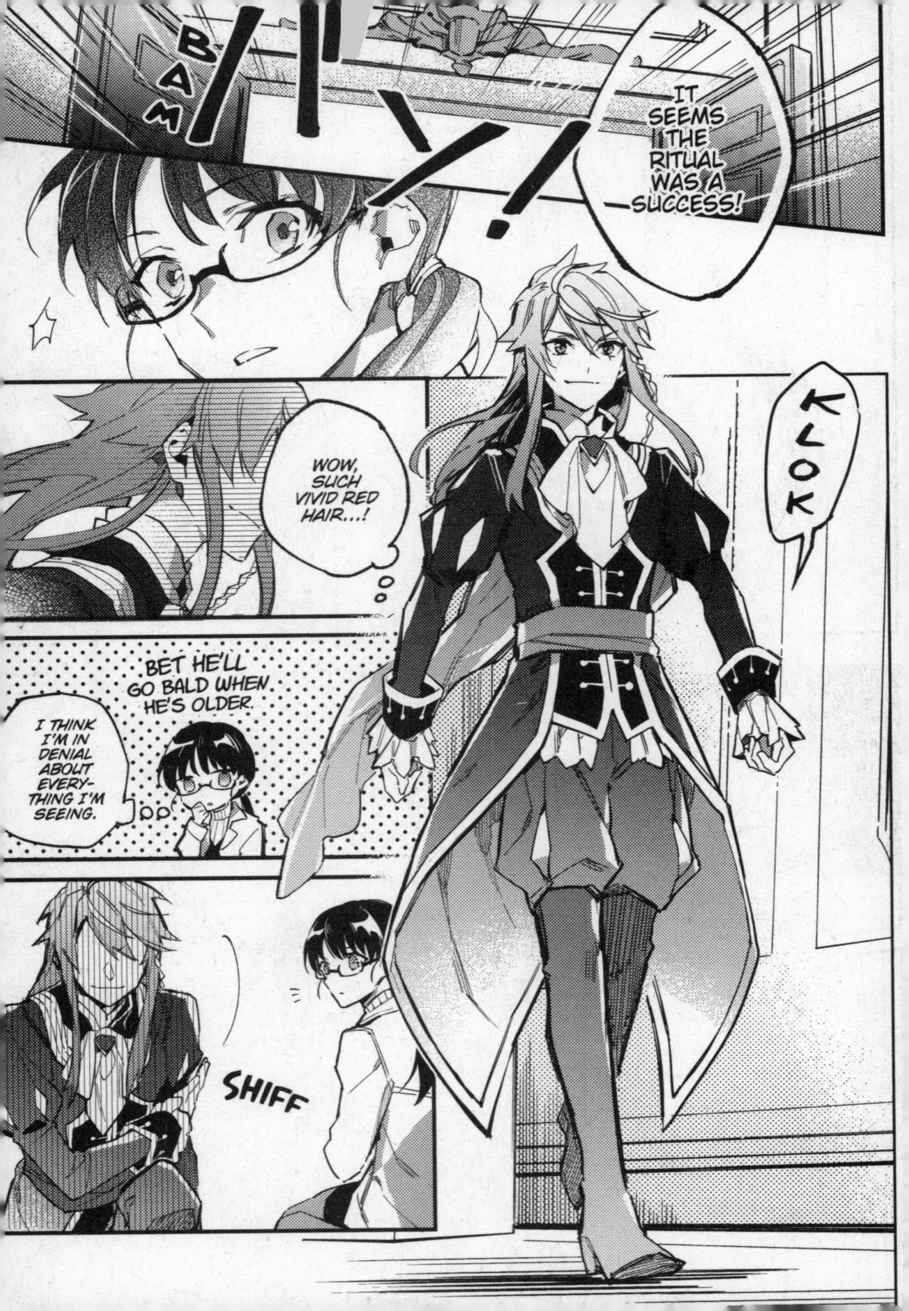
IT SEEMS THE RITUAL WAS A SUCCESS!
BAM
KLOK
WOW, SUCH VIVID RED HAIR...!
BET HE'LL GO BALD WHEN HE'S OLDER.
I THINK I'M IN DENIAL ABOUT EVERYTHING I'M SEEING.
SHIFF

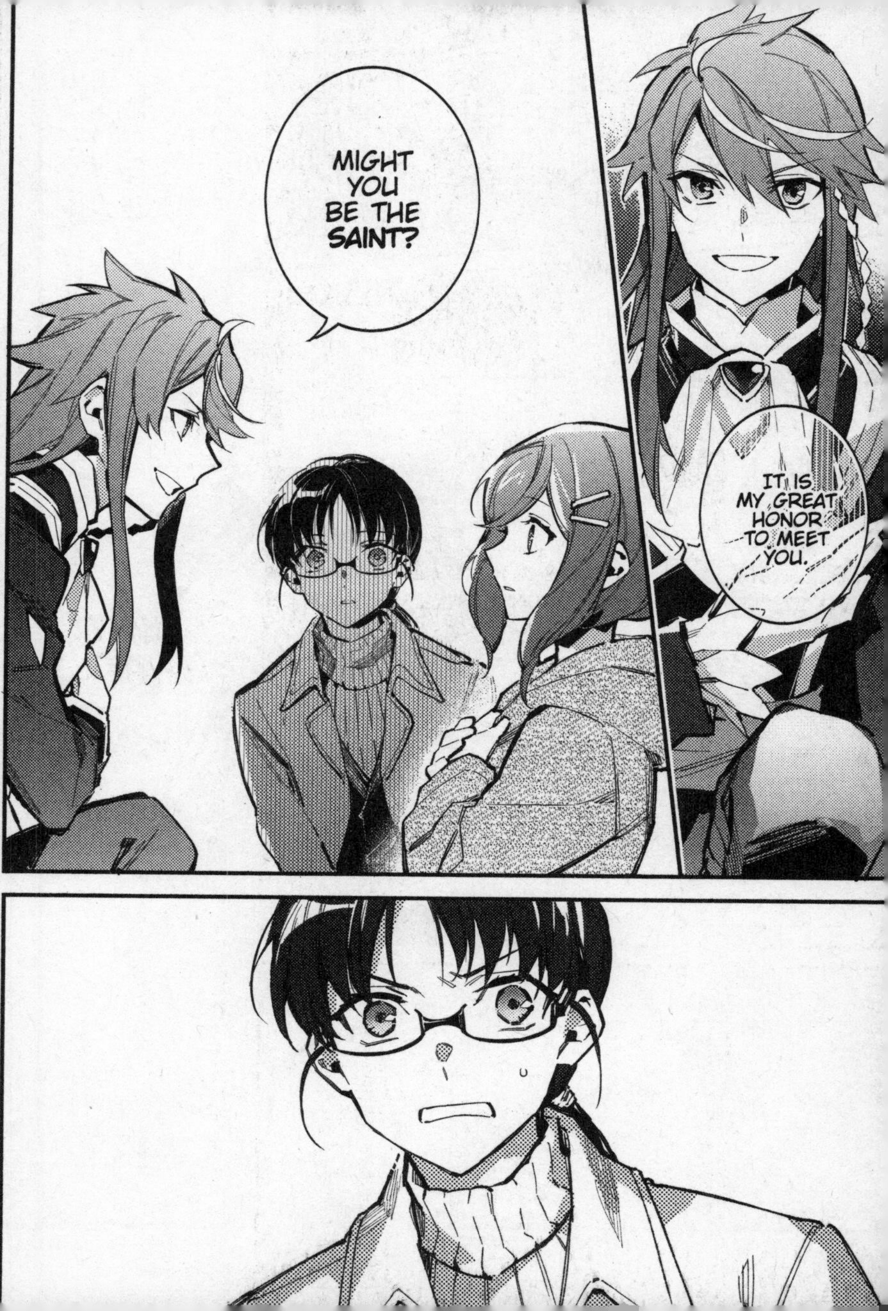
IT IS MY GREAT HONOR TO MEET YOU.
MIGHT YOU BE THE SAINT?

WAIT, WHAT...?

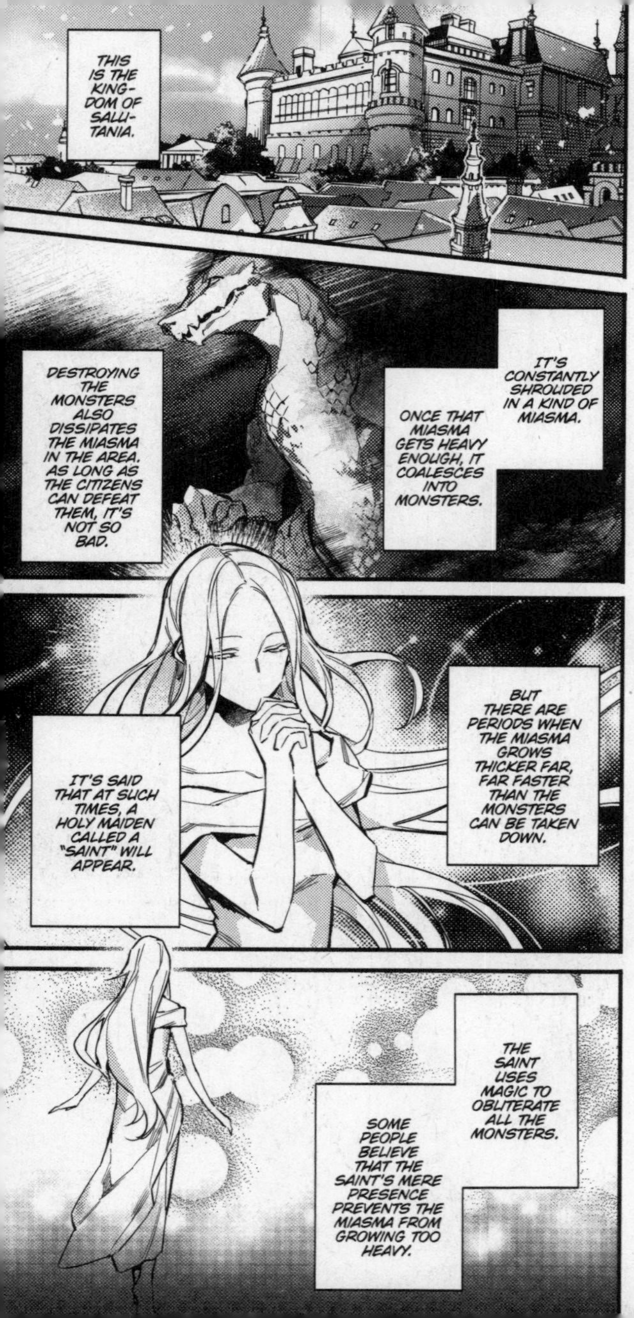
THIS IS THE KINGDOM OF SALUTANIA.
IT'S CONSTANTLY SHROUDED IN A KIND OF MIASMA.
ONCE THAT MIASMA GETS HEAVY ENOUGH, IT COALESCES INTO MONSTERS.
DESTROYING THE MONSTERS ALSO DISSIPATES THE MIASMA IN THE AREA. AS LONG AS THE CITIZENS CAN DEFEAT THEM, IT'S NOT SO BAD.
BUT THERE ARE PERIODS WHEN THE MIASMA GROWS THICKER FAR, FAR FASTER THAN THE MONSTERS CAN BE TAKEN DOWN.
IT'S SAID THAT AT SUCH TIMES, A HOLY MAIDEN CALLED A "SAINT" WILL APPEAR.
THE SAINT USES MAGIC TO OBLITERATE ALL THE MONSTERS.
SOME PEOPLE BELIEVE THAT THE SAINT'S MERE PRESENCE PREVENTS THE MIASMA FROM GROWING TOO HEAVY.

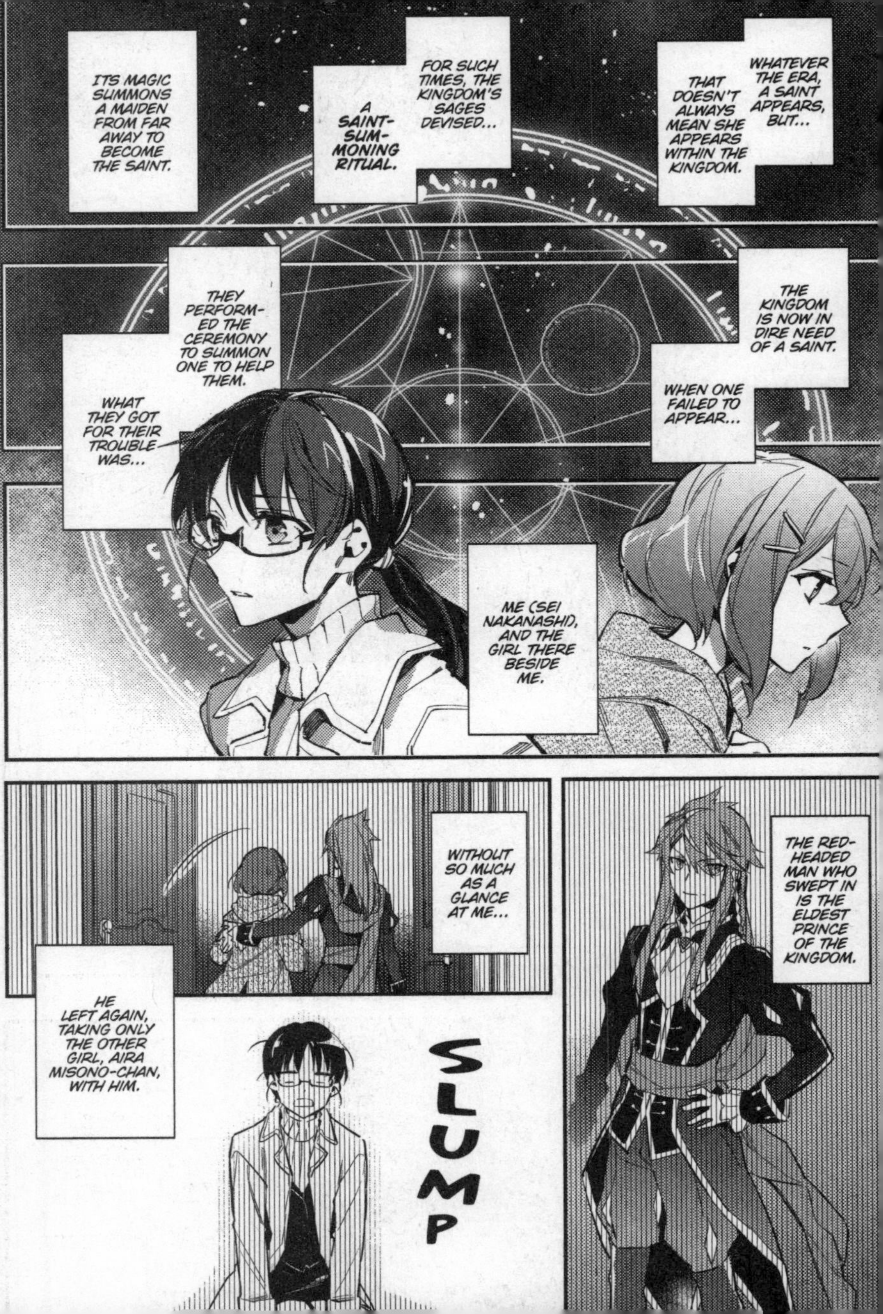
WHATEVER THE ERA, A SAINT APPEARS, BUT...
THAT DOESN'T ALWAYS MEAN SHE APPEARS WITHIN THE KINGDOM.
FOR SUCH TIMES, THE KINGDOM'S SAGES DEVISED...
A SAINT-SUMMONING RITUAL.
ITS MAGIC SUMMONS A MAIDEN FROM FAR AWAY TO BECOME THE SAINT.
THE KINGDOM IS NOW IN DIRE NEED OF A SAINT.
WHEN ONE FAILED TO APPEAR...
THEY PERFORMED THE CEREMONY TO SUMMON ONE TO HELP THEM.
WHAT THEY GOT FOR THEIR TROUBLE WAS...
ME (SEI NAKANASHI), AND THE GIRL THERE BESIDE ME.
THE RED-HEADED MAN WHO SWEPT IN IS THE ELDEST PRINCE OF THE KINGDOM.
WITHOUT SO MUCH AS A GLANCE AT ME...
HE LEFT AGAIN, TAKING ONLY THE OTHER GIRL, AIRA MISONO-CHAN, WITH HIM.
SLUMP

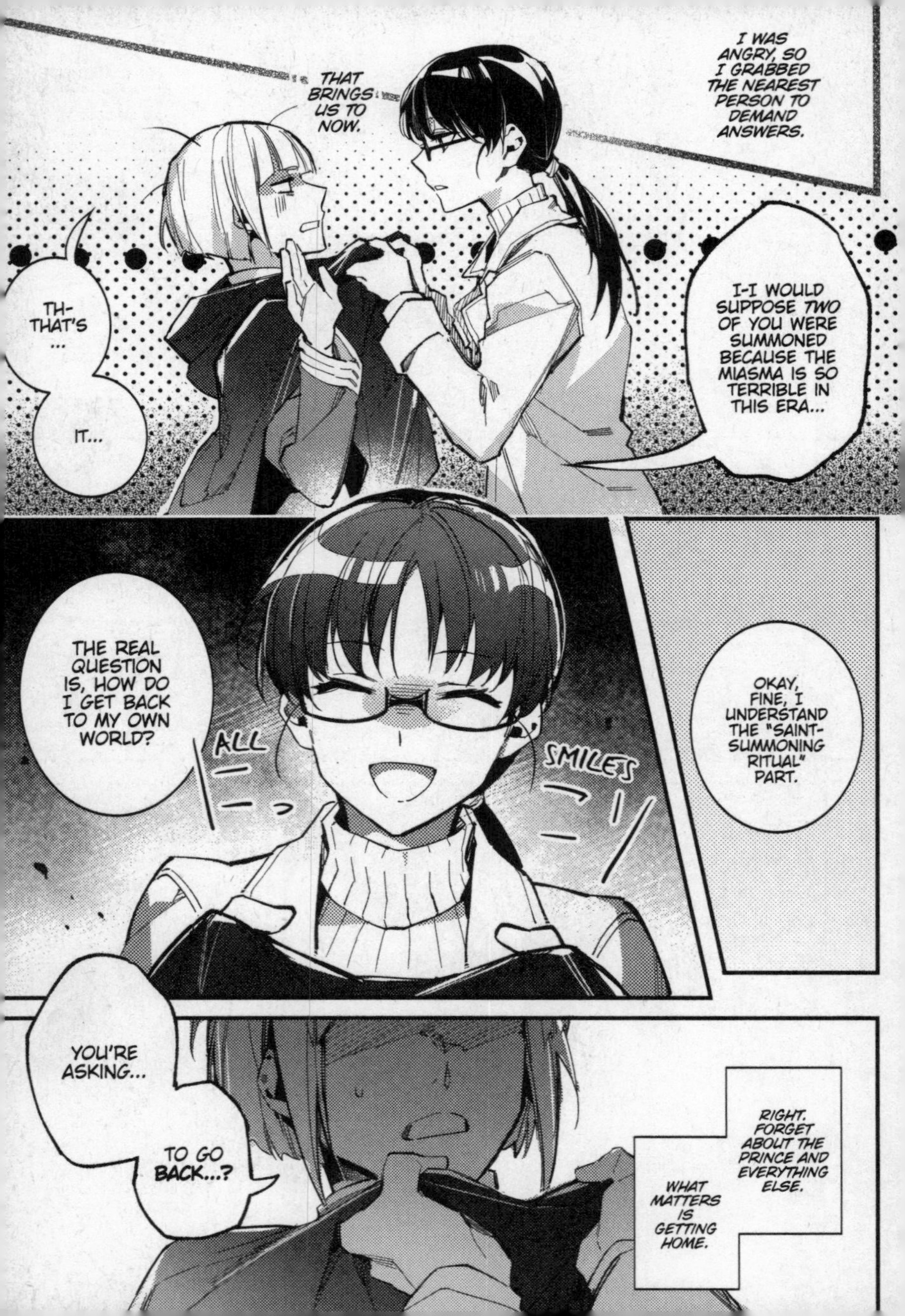
I WAS ANGRY, SO I GRABBED THE NEAREST PERSON TO DEMAND ANSWERS.
THAT BRINGS US TO NOW.
I-I WOULD SUPPOSE *TWO* OF YOU WERE SUMMONED BECAUSE THE MIASMA IS SO TERRIBLE IN THIS ERA...
TH-THAT'S ... IT...
OKAY, FINE, I UNDERSTAND THE "SAINT-SUMMONING RITUAL" PART.
ALL SMILES
THE REAL QUESTION IS, HOW DO I GET BACK TO MY OWN WORLD?
RIGHT. FORGET ABOUT THE PRINCE AND EVERYTHING ELSE.
WHAT MATTERS IS GETTING HOME.
YOU'RE ASKING... TO GO **BACK**...?

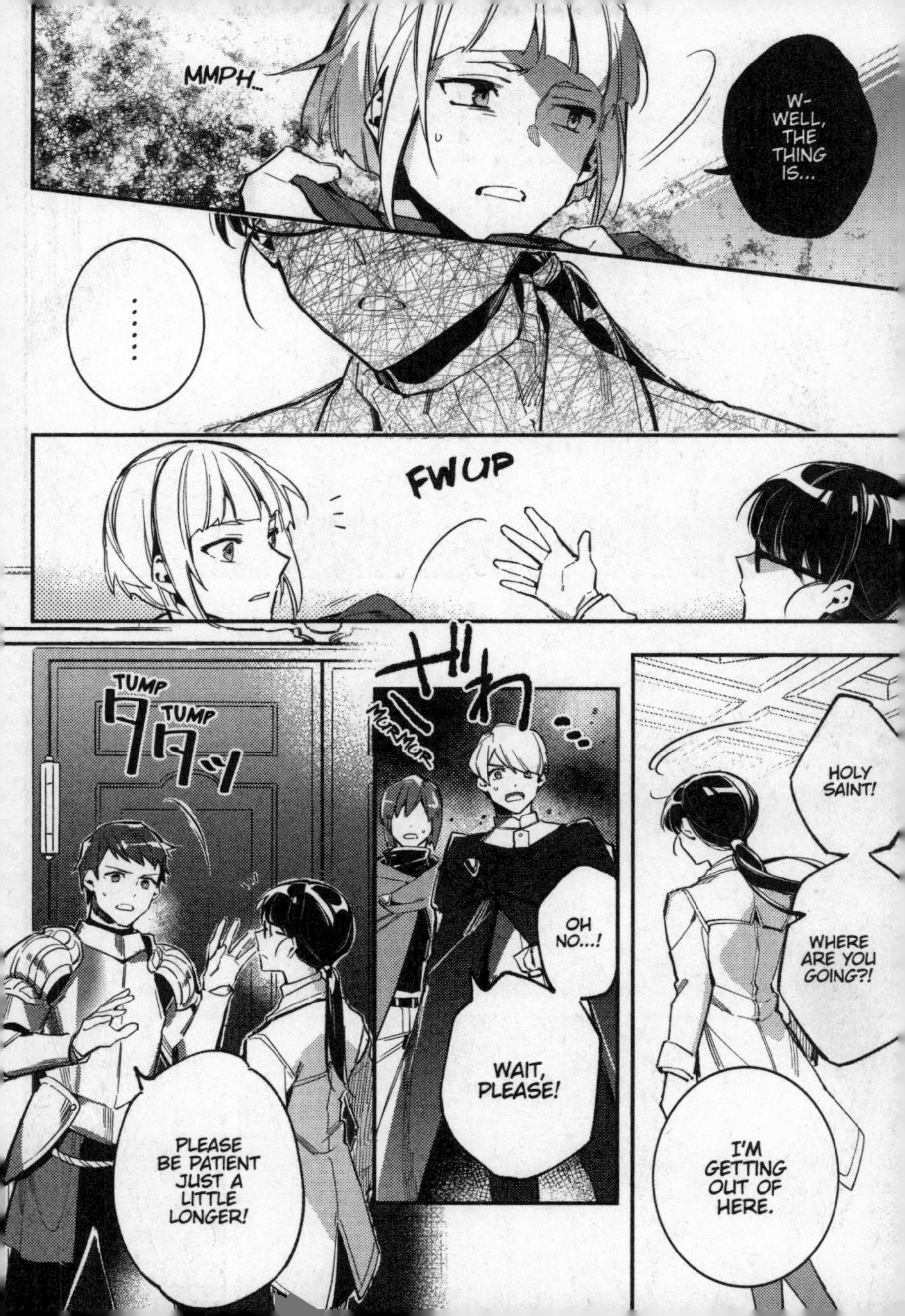
W-WELL, THE THING IS...
MMPH...
......
FWUP
HOLY SAINT!
WHERE ARE YOU GOING?!
I'M GETTING OUT OF HERE.
ざわ
MORMUR
OH NO...!
WAIT, PLEASE!
TUMP TUMP
タタッ
PLEASE BE PATIENT JUST A LITTLE LONGER!

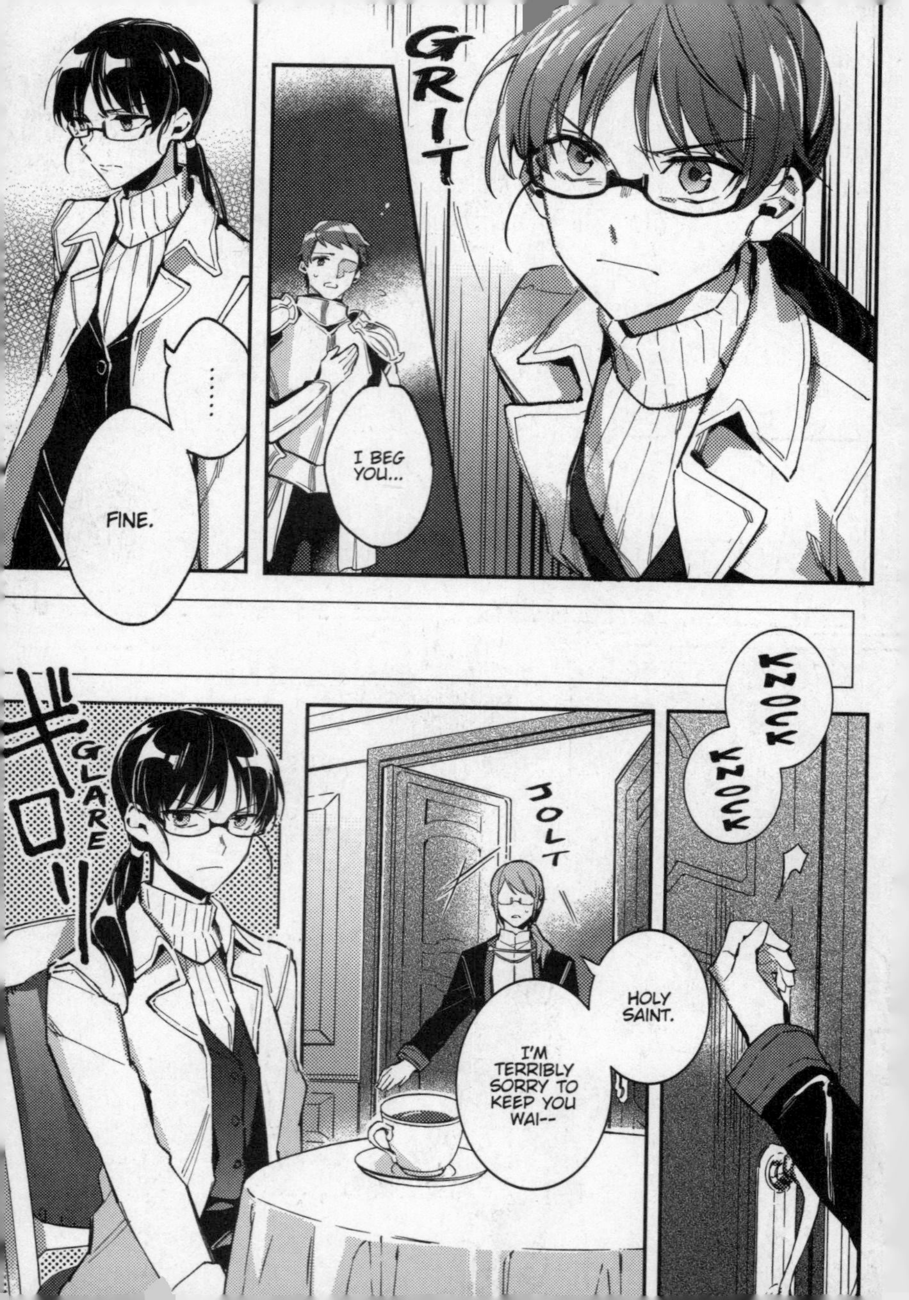
GRIT
I BEG YOU...
......
FINE.
KNOCK KNOCK
JOLT
HOLY SAINT.
I'M TERRIBLY SORRY TO KEEP YOU WAI--
GLARE

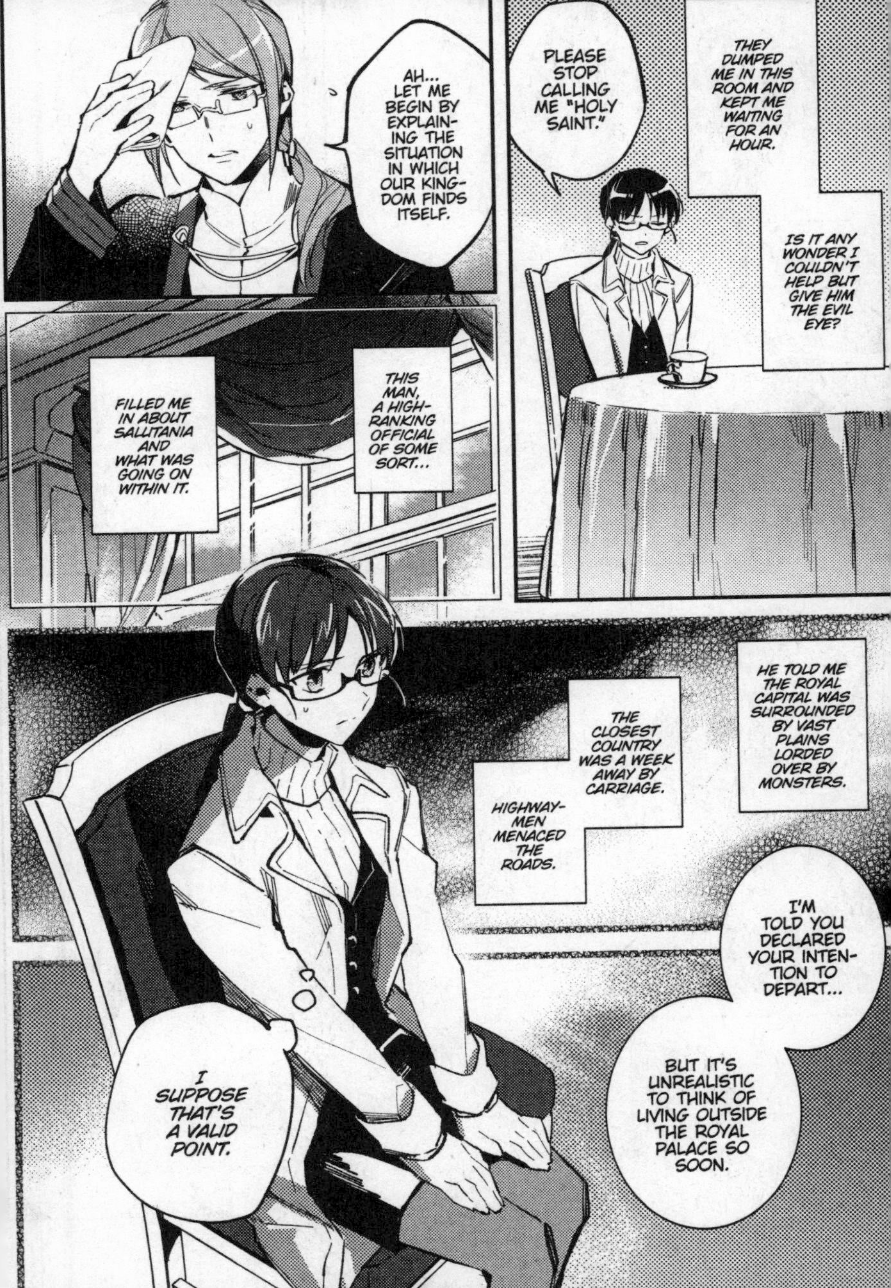
THEY DUMPED ME IN THIS ROOM AND KEPT ME WAITING FOR AN HOUR.
PLEASE STOP CALLING ME "HOLY SAINT."
IS IT ANY WONDER I COULDN'T HELP BUT GIVE HIM THE EVIL EYE?
AH... LET ME BEGIN BY EXPLAIN-ING THE SITUATION IN WHICH OUR KING-DOM FINDS ITSELF.
THIS MAN, A HIGH-RANKING OFFICIAL OF SOME SORT...
FILLED ME IN ABOUT SALUTANIA AND WHAT WAS GOING ON WITHIN IT.
HE TOLD ME THE ROYAL CAPITAL WAS SURROUNDED BY VAST PLAINS LORDED OVER BY MONSTERS.
THE CLOSEST COUNTRY WAS A WEEK AWAY BY CARRIAGE.
HIGHWAY-MEN MENACED THE ROADS.
I'M TOLD YOU DECLARED YOUR INTEN-TION TO DEPART...
BUT IT'S UNREALISTIC TO THINK OF LIVING OUTSIDE THE ROYAL PALACE SO SOON.
I SUPPOSE THAT'S A VALID POINT.

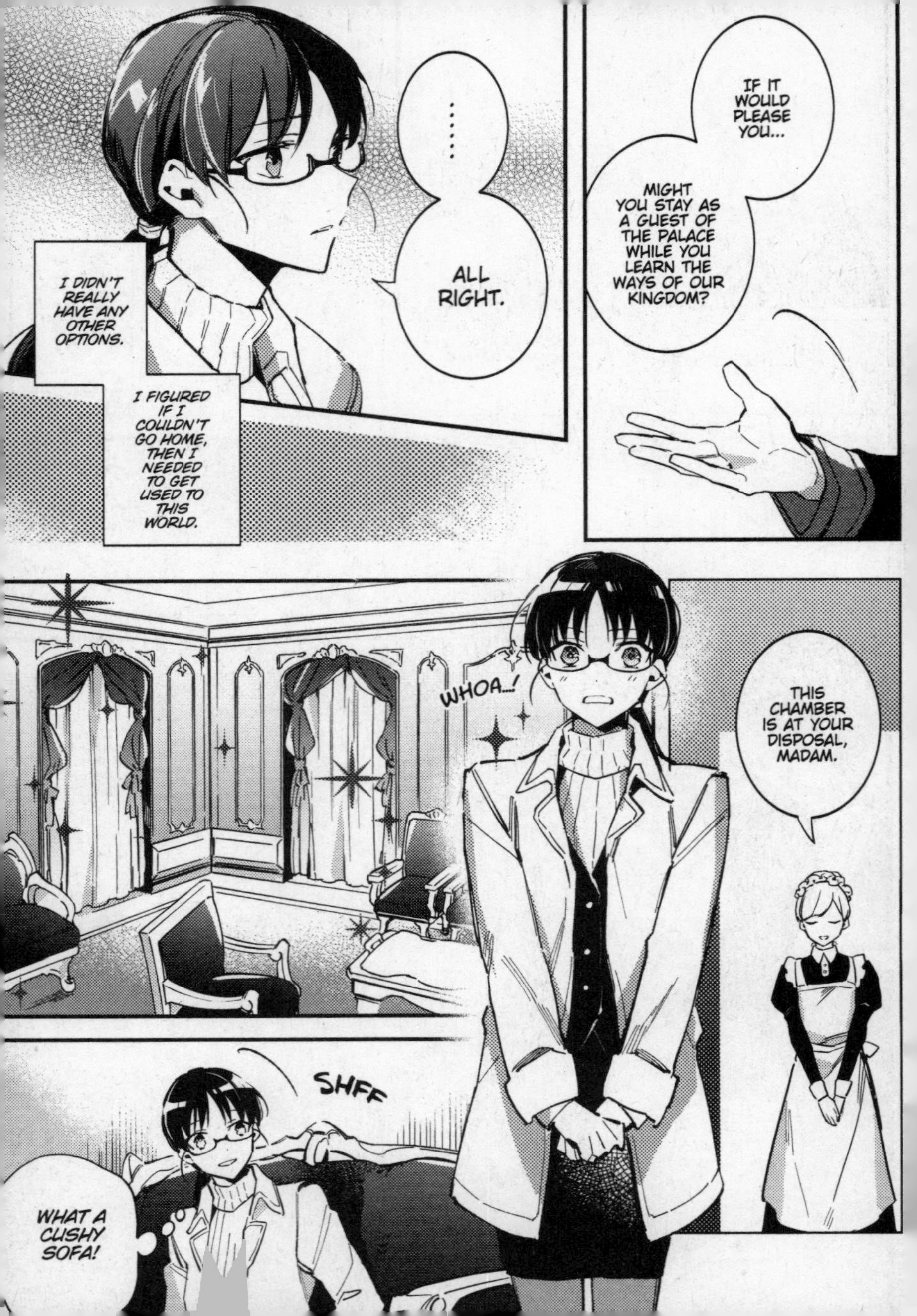
IF IT WOULD PLEASE YOU...
MIGHT YOU STAY AS A GUEST OF THE PALACE WHILE YOU LEARN THE WAYS OF OUR KINGDOM?
......
ALL RIGHT.
I DIDN'T REALLY HAVE ANY OTHER OPTIONS.
I FIGURED IF I COULDN'T GO HOME, THEN I NEEDED TO GET USED TO THIS WORLD.
THIS CHAMBER IS AT YOUR DISPOSAL, MADAM.
WHOA...!
SHFF
WHAT A CUSHY SOFA!

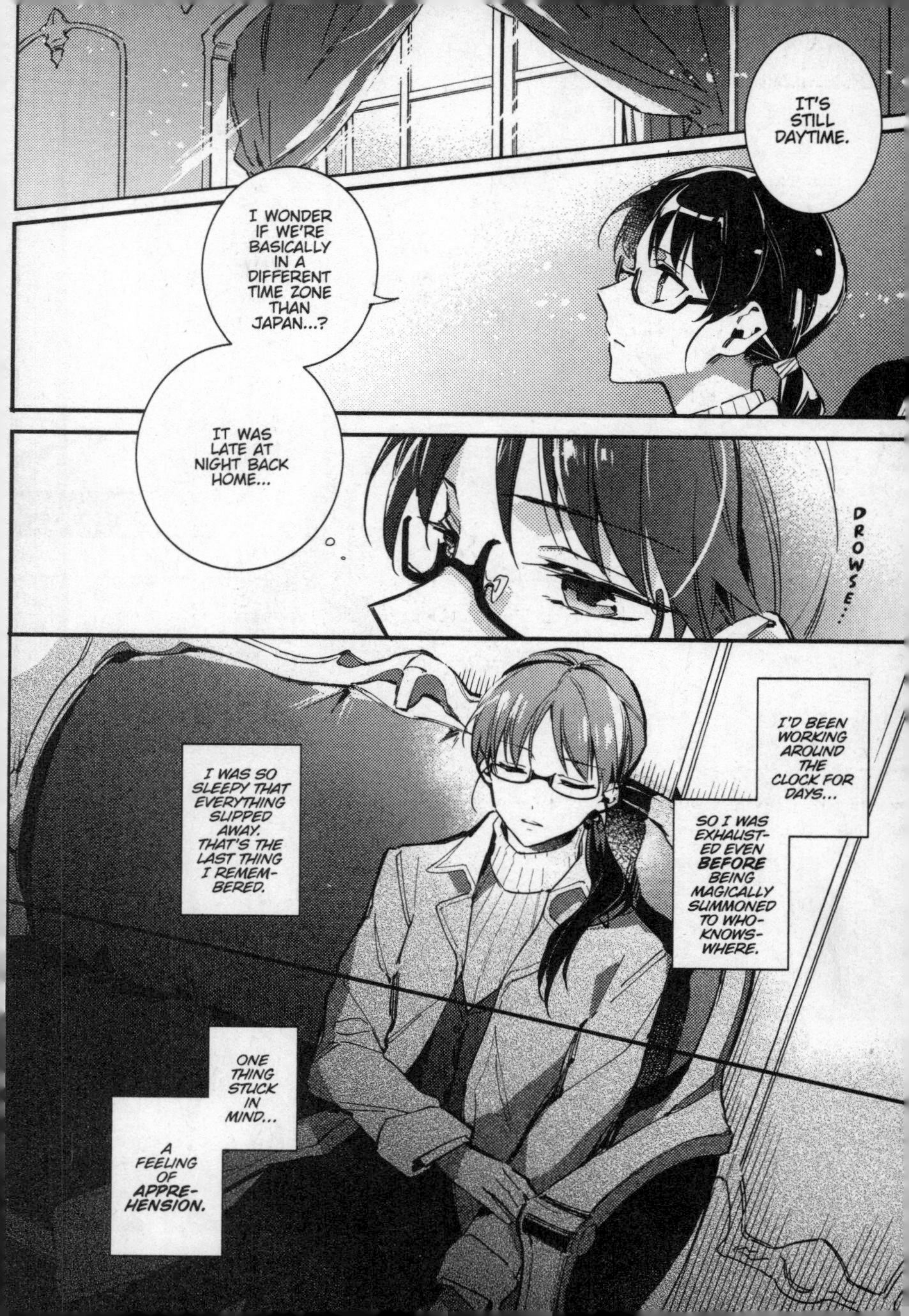
IT'S STILL DAYTIME.
I WONDER IF WE'RE BASICALLY IN A DIFFERENT TIME ZONE THAN JAPAN...?
IT WAS LATE AT NIGHT BACK HOME...
DROWSE...
I'D BEEN WORKING AROUND THE CLOCK FOR DAYS...
SO I WAS EXHAUSTED EVEN BEFORE BEING MAGICALLY SUMMONED TO WHO-KNOWS-WHERE.
I WAS SO SLEEPY THAT EVERYTHING SLIPPED AWAY. THAT'S THE LAST THING I REMEMBERED.
ONE THING STUCK IN MIND...
A FEELING OF APPREHENSION.

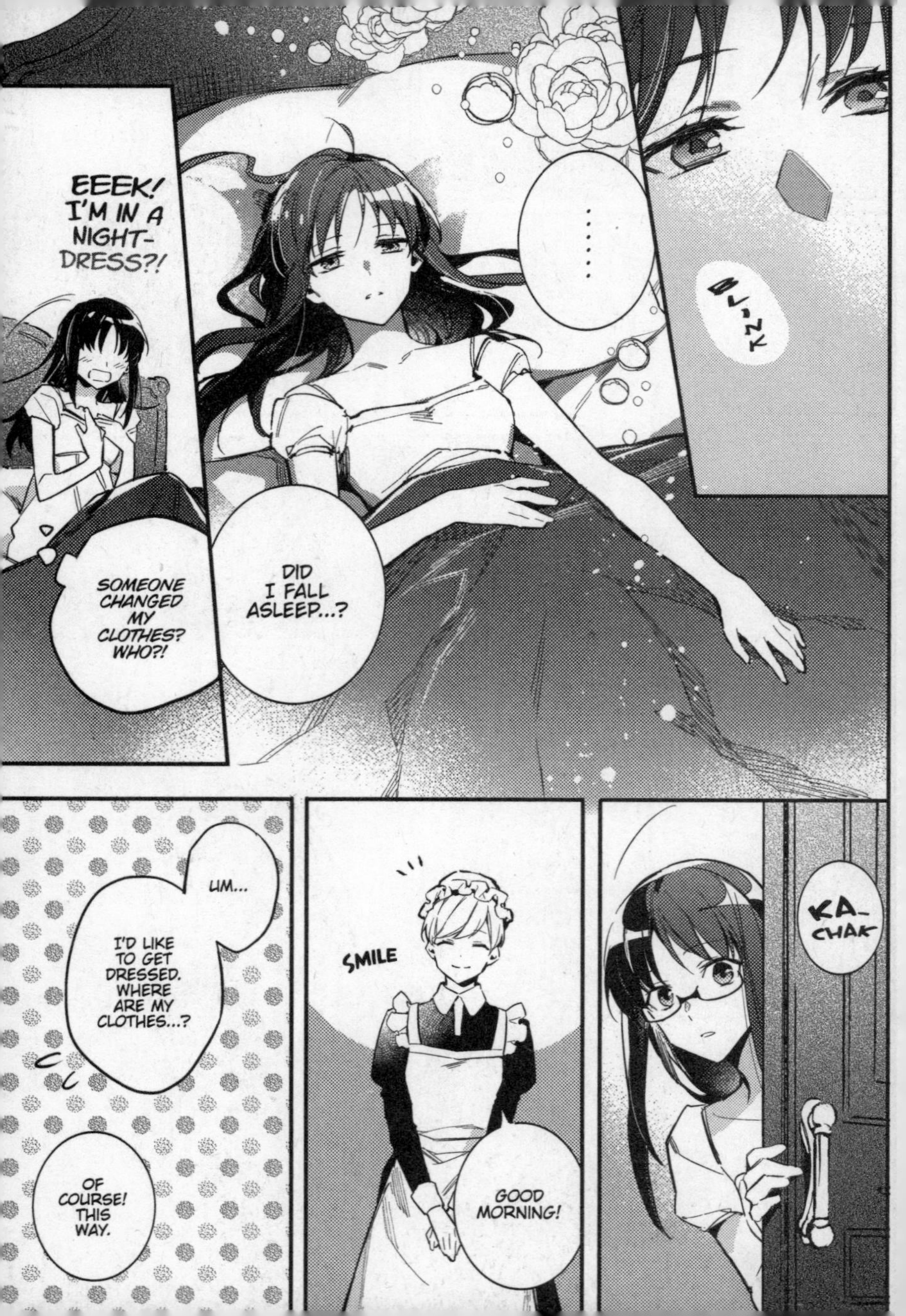
BLINK
......
DID I FALL ASLEEP...?
EEEK! I'M IN A NIGHT-DRESS?!
SOMEONE CHANGED MY CLOTHES? WHO?!
KA-CHAK
SMILE
GOOD MORNING!
UM...
I'D LIKE TO GET DRESSED. WHERE ARE MY CLOTHES...?
OF COURSE! THIS WAY.

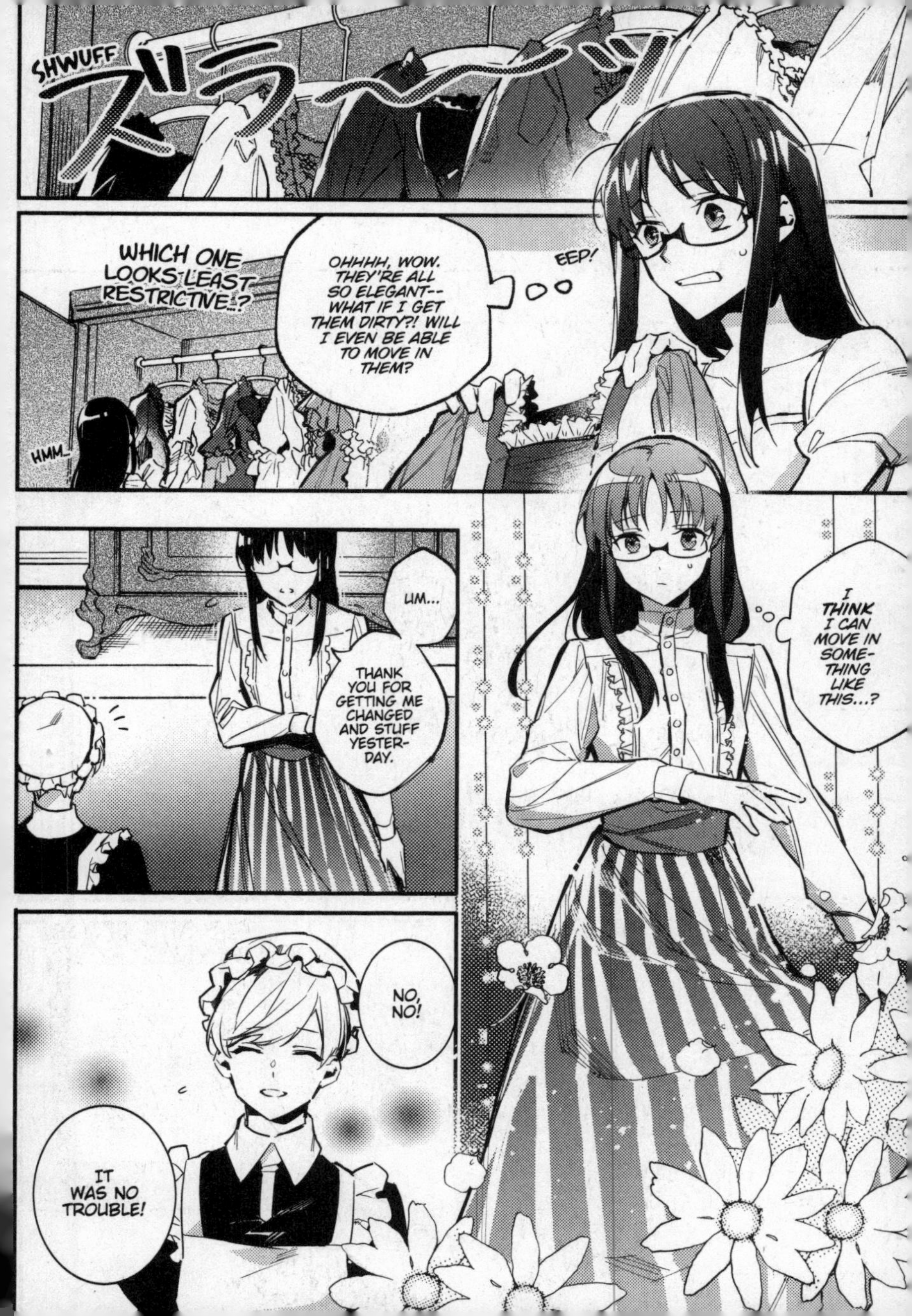
SHWUFF
ズラ〜〜ッ
EEP!
OHHHH, WOW. THEY'RE ALL SO ELEGANT-- WHAT IF I GET THEM DIRTY?! WILL I EVEN BE ABLE TO MOVE IN THEM?
WHICH ONE LOOKS LEAST RESTRICTIVE...?
HMM...
I THINK I CAN MOVE IN SOMETHING LIKE THIS...?
UM...
THANK YOU FOR GETTING ME CHANGED AND STUFF YESTERDAY.
NO, NO!
IT WAS NO TROUBLE!

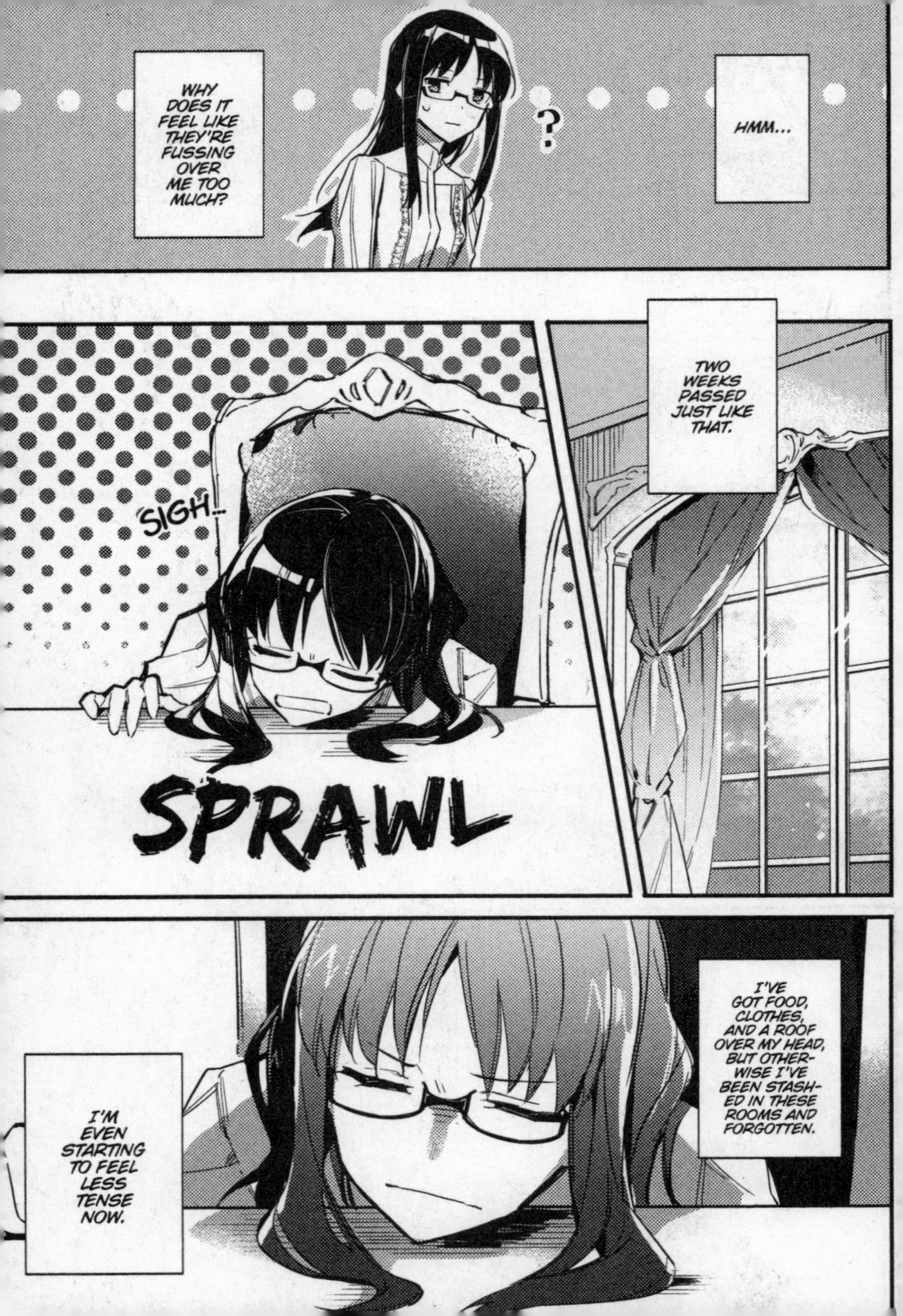
HMM...
?
WHY DOES IT FEEL LIKE THEY'RE FUSSING OVER ME TOO MUCH?
TWO WEEKS PASSED JUST LIKE THAT.
SIGH...
SPRAWL
I'VE GOT FOOD, CLOTHES, AND A ROOF OVER MY HEAD, BUT OTHER-WISE I'VE BEEN STASH-ED IN THESE ROOMS AND FORGOTTEN.
I'M EVEN STARTING TO FEEL LESS TENSE NOW.

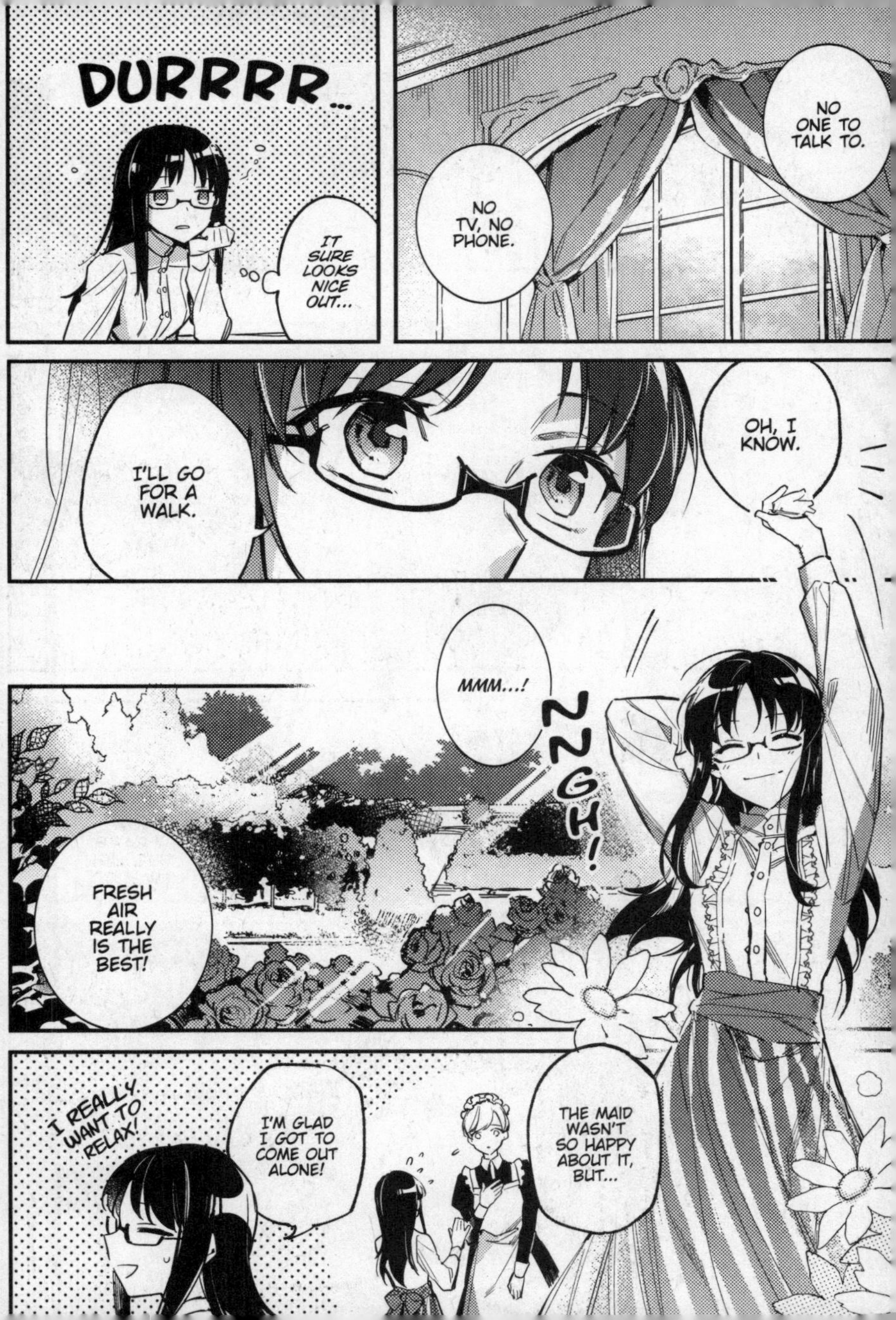
NO ONE TO TALK TO.
NO TV, NO PHONE.
DURRRR...
IT SURE LOOKS NICE OUT...
OH, I KNOW.
I'LL GO FOR A WALK.
MMM...!
NNGH!
FRESH AIR REALLY IS THE BEST!
THE MAID WASN'T SO HAPPY ABOUT IT, BUT...
I'M GLAD I GOT TO COME OUT ALONE!
I REALLY WANT TO RELAX!

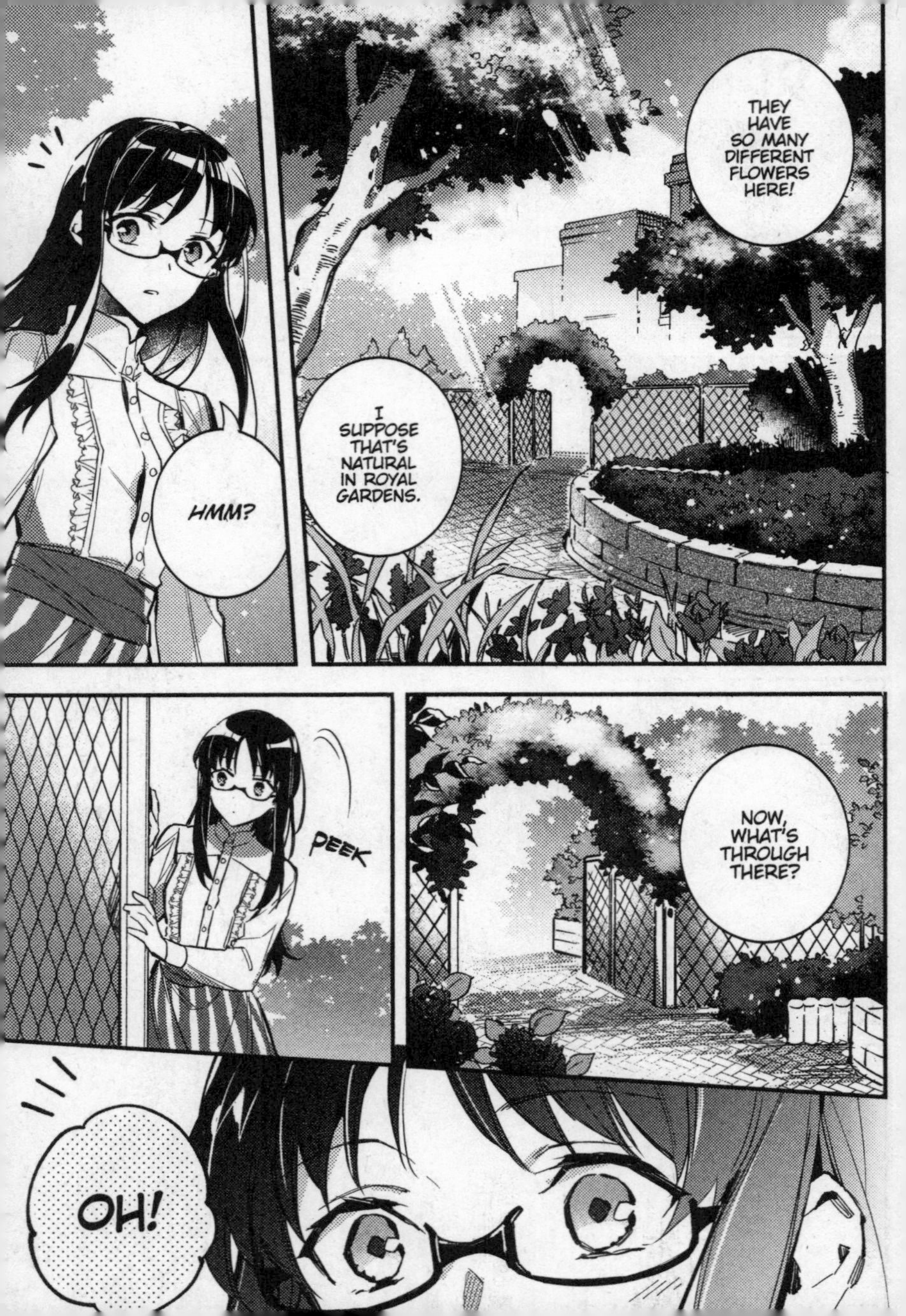
THEY HAVE SO MANY DIFFERENT FLOWERS HERE!
I SUPPOSE THAT'S NATURAL IN ROYAL GARDENS.
HMM?
NOW, WHAT'S THROUGH THERE?
PEEK
OH!

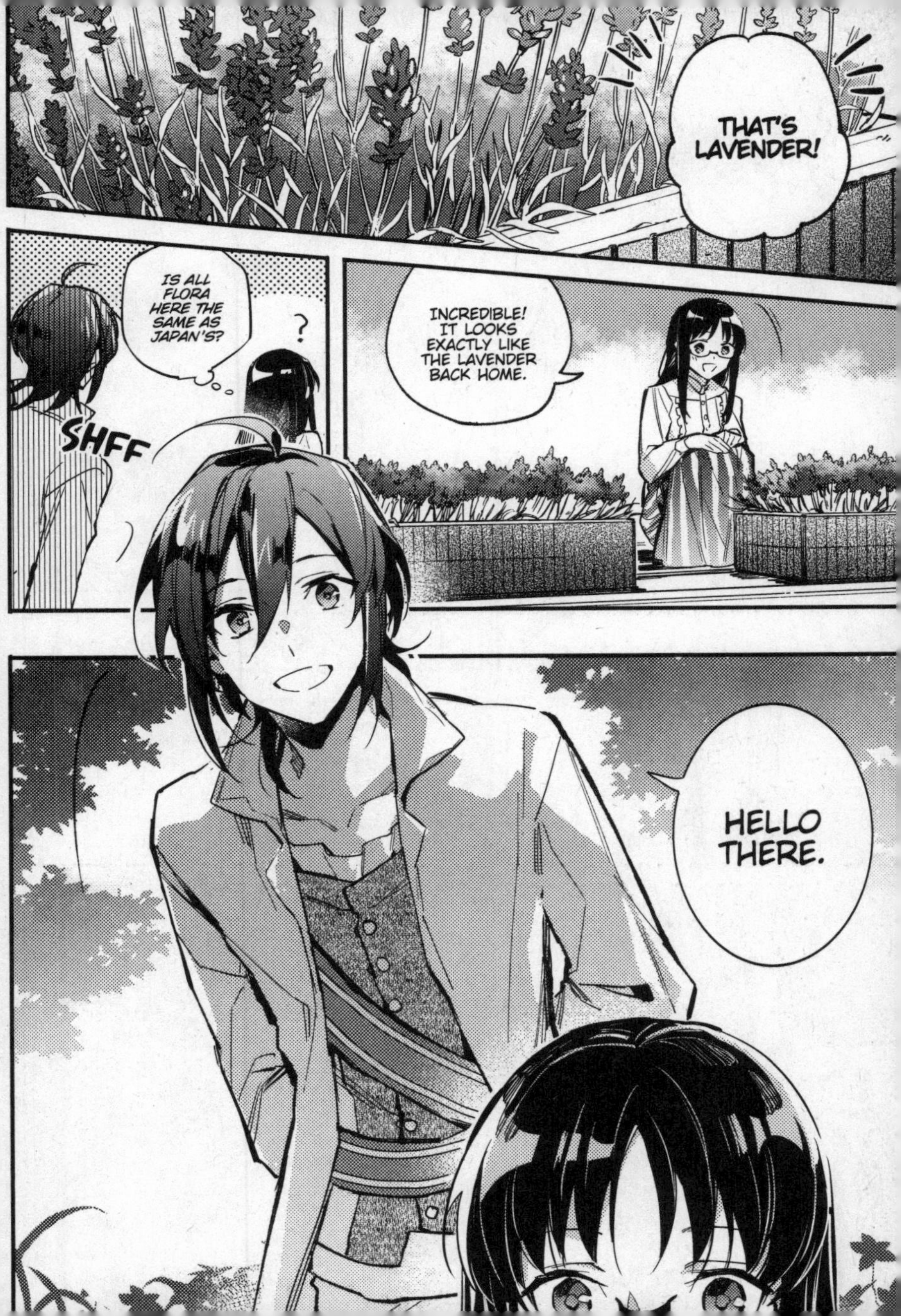
THAT'S LAVENDER!
INCREDIBLE! IT LOOKS EXACTLY LIKE THE LAVENDER BACK HOME.
IS ALL FLORA HERE THE SAME AS JAPAN'S?
?
SHFF
HELLO THERE.

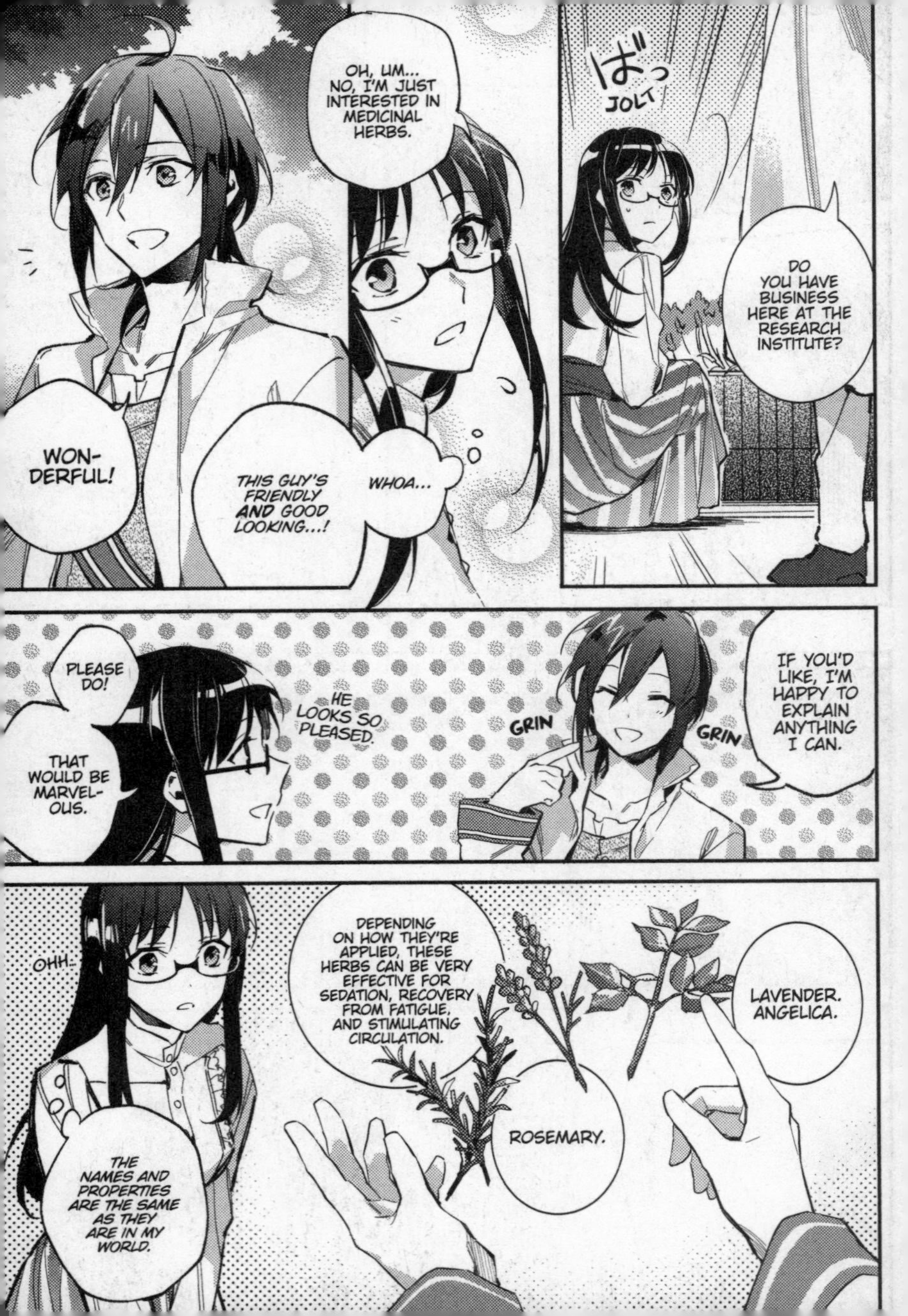
ばっ
JOLT
DO YOU HAVE BUSINESS HERE AT THE RESEARCH INSTITUTE?
OH, UM... NO, I'M JUST INTERESTED IN MEDICINAL HERBS.
WHOA...
THIS GUY'S FRIENDLY AND GOOD LOOKING...!
WON-DERFUL!
IF YOU'D LIKE, I'M HAPPY TO EXPLAIN ANYTHING I CAN.
GRIN
GRIN
HE LOOKS SO PLEASED.
PLEASE DO!
THAT WOULD BE MARVEL-OUS.
LAVENDER. ANGELICA.
ROSEMARY.
DEPENDING ON HOW THEY'RE APPLIED, THESE HERBS CAN BE VERY EFFECTIVE FOR SEDATION, RECOVERY FROM FATIGUE, AND STIMULATING CIRCULATION.
OHH...
THE NAMES AND PROPERTIES ARE THE SAME AS THEY ARE IN MY WORLD.

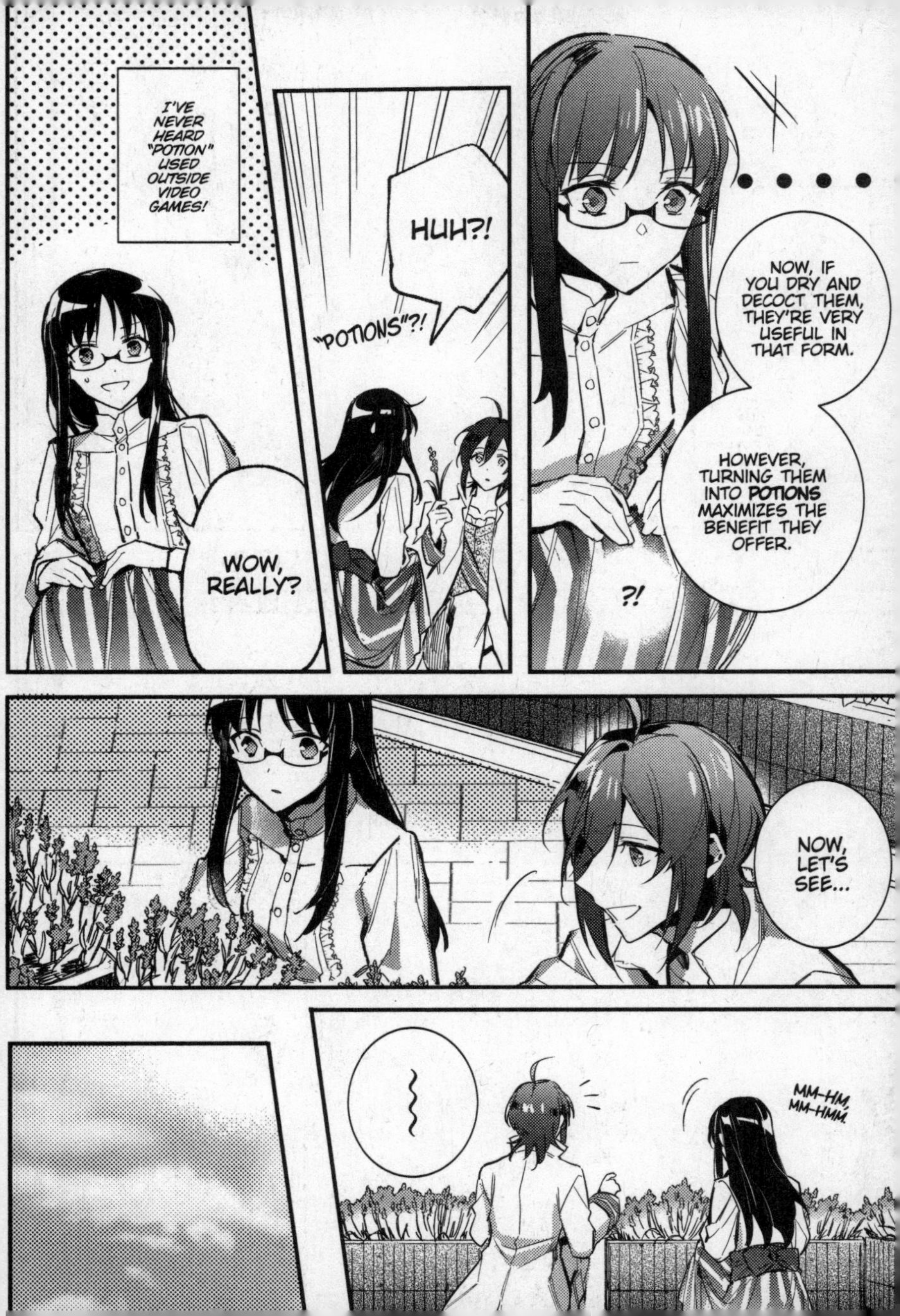
• • • •
NOW, IF YOU DRY AND DECOCT THEM, THEY'RE VERY USEFUL IN THAT FORM.
HOWEVER, TURNING THEM INTO **POTIONS** MAXIMIZES THE BENEFIT THEY OFFER.
?!
HUH?!
"POTIONS"?!
I'VE NEVER HEARD "POTION" USED OUTSIDE VIDEO GAMES!
WOW, REALLY?
NOW, LET'S SEE...
MM-HM, MM-HMM.

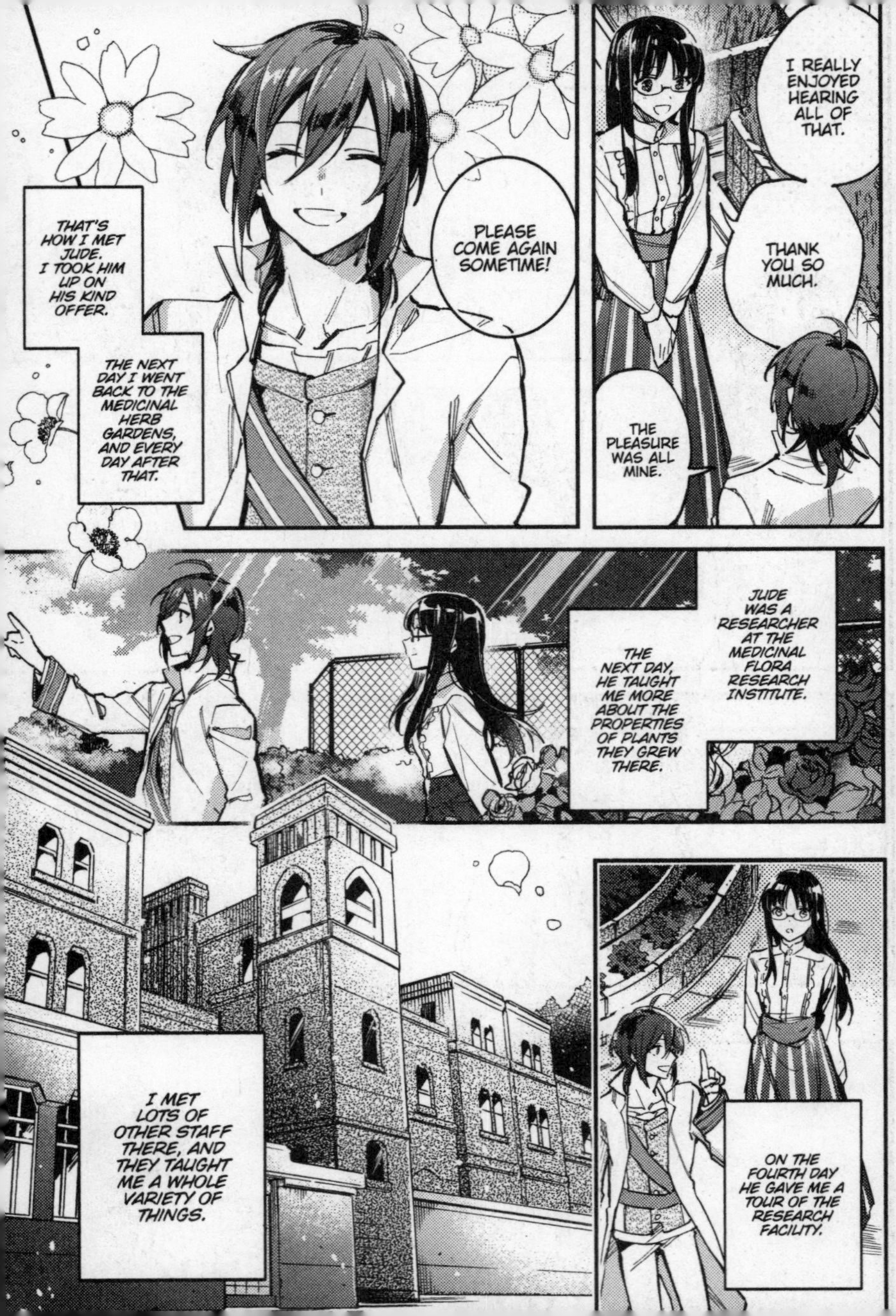
I REALLY ENJOYED HEARING ALL OF THAT.
THANK YOU SO MUCH.
THE PLEASURE WAS ALL MINE.
PLEASE COME AGAIN SOMETIME!
THAT'S HOW I MET JUDE. I TOOK HIM UP ON HIS KIND OFFER.
THE NEXT DAY I WENT BACK TO THE MEDICINAL HERB GARDENS, AND EVERY DAY AFTER THAT.
JUDE WAS A RESEARCHER AT THE MEDICINAL FLORA RESEARCH INSTITUTE.
THE NEXT DAY, HE TAUGHT ME MORE ABOUT THE PROPERTIES OF PLANTS THEY GREW THERE.
ON THE FOURTH DAY HE GAVE ME A TOUR OF THE RESEARCH FACILITY.
I MET LOTS OF OTHER STAFF THERE, AND THEY TAUGHT ME A WHOLE VARIETY OF THINGS.

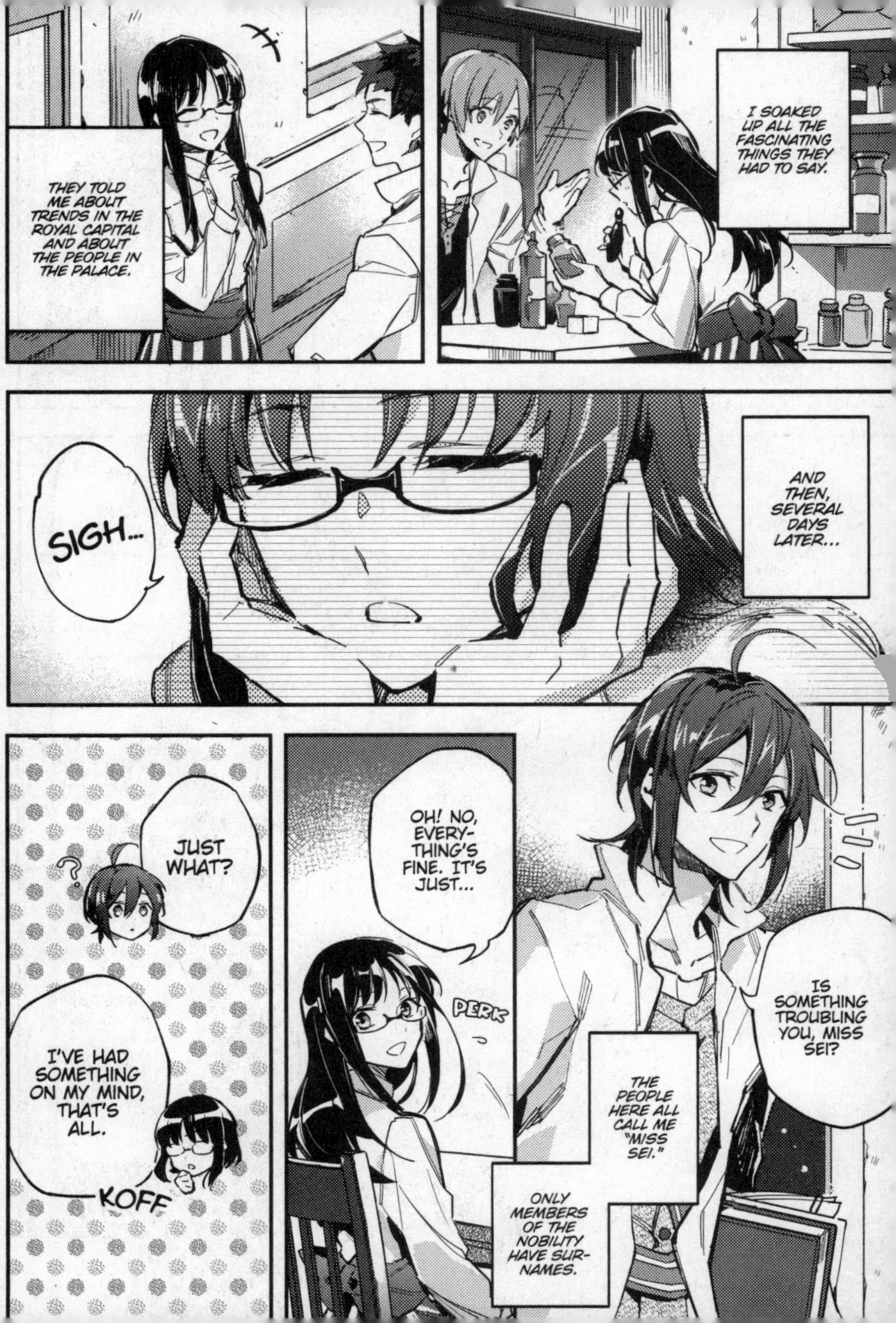
I SOAKED UP ALL THE FASCINATING THINGS THEY HAD TO SAY.
THEY TOLD ME ABOUT TRENDS IN THE ROYAL CAPITAL AND ABOUT THE PEOPLE IN THE PALACE.
AND THEN, SEVERAL DAYS LATER...
SIGH...
IS SOMETHING TROUBLING YOU, MISS SEI?
THE PEOPLE HERE ALL CALL ME "MISS SEI."
ONLY MEMBERS OF THE NOBILITY HAVE SURNAMES.
PERK
OH! NO, EVERYTHING'S FINE. IT'S JUST...
JUST WHAT?
I'VE HAD SOMETHING ON MY MIND, THAT'S ALL.
KOFF

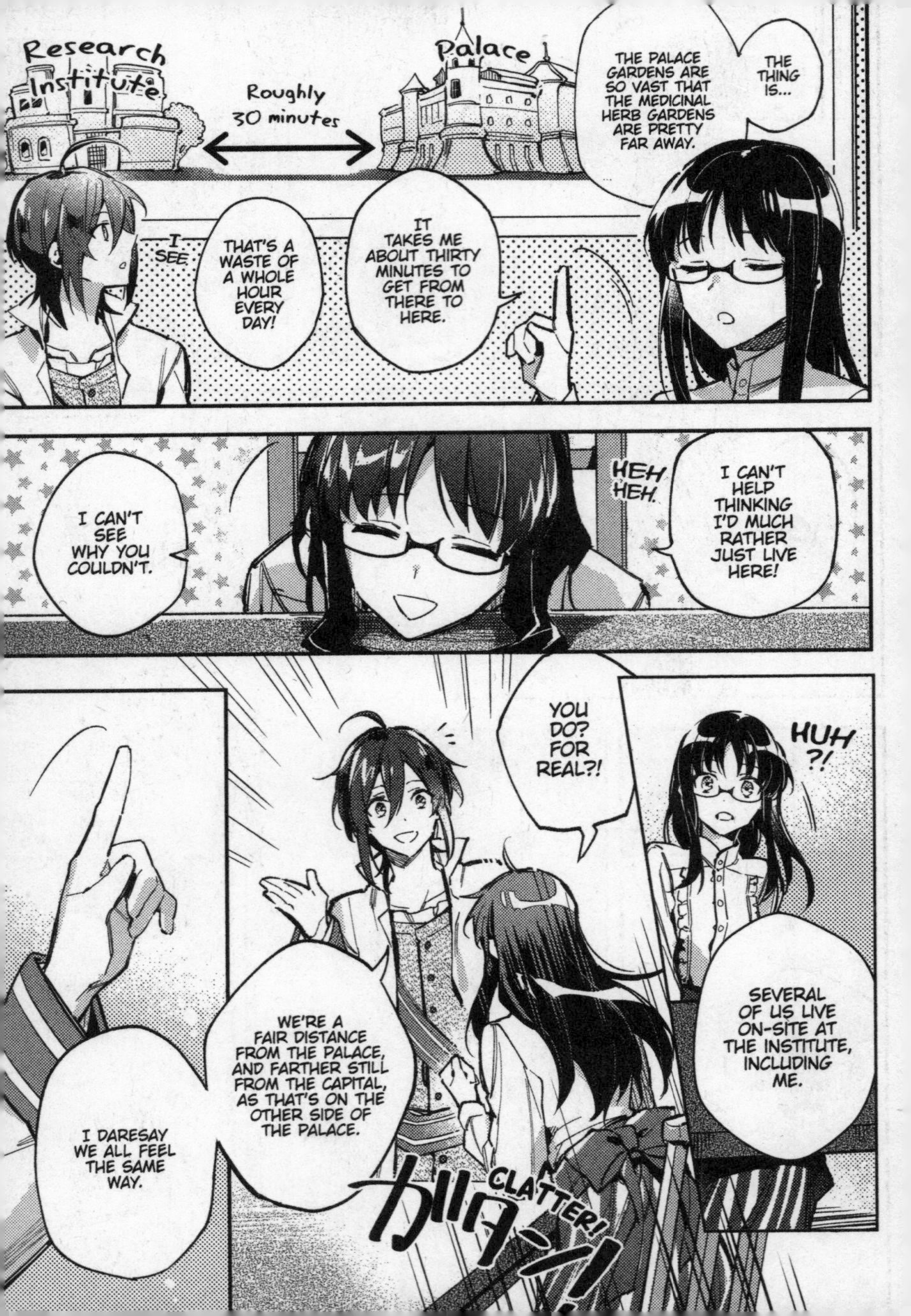
THE THING IS...
THE PALACE GARDENS ARE SO VAST THAT THE MEDICINAL HERB GARDENS ARE PRETTY FAR AWAY.
Palace
Roughly 30 minutes
Research Institute
IT TAKES ME ABOUT THIRTY MINUTES TO GET FROM THERE TO HERE.
THAT'S A WASTE OF A WHOLE HOUR EVERY DAY!
I SEE
I CAN'T HELP THINKING I'D MUCH RATHER JUST LIVE HERE!
HEH HEH.
I CAN'T SEE WHY YOU COULDN'T.
HUH?!
YOU DO? FOR REAL?!
SEVERAL OF US LIVE ON-SITE AT THE INSTITUTE, INCLUDING ME.
WE'RE A FAIR DISTANCE FROM THE PALACE, AND FARTHER STILL FROM THE CAPITAL, AS THAT'S ON THE OTHER SIDE OF THE PALACE.
I DARESAY WE ALL FEEL THE SAME WAY.
CLATTER!

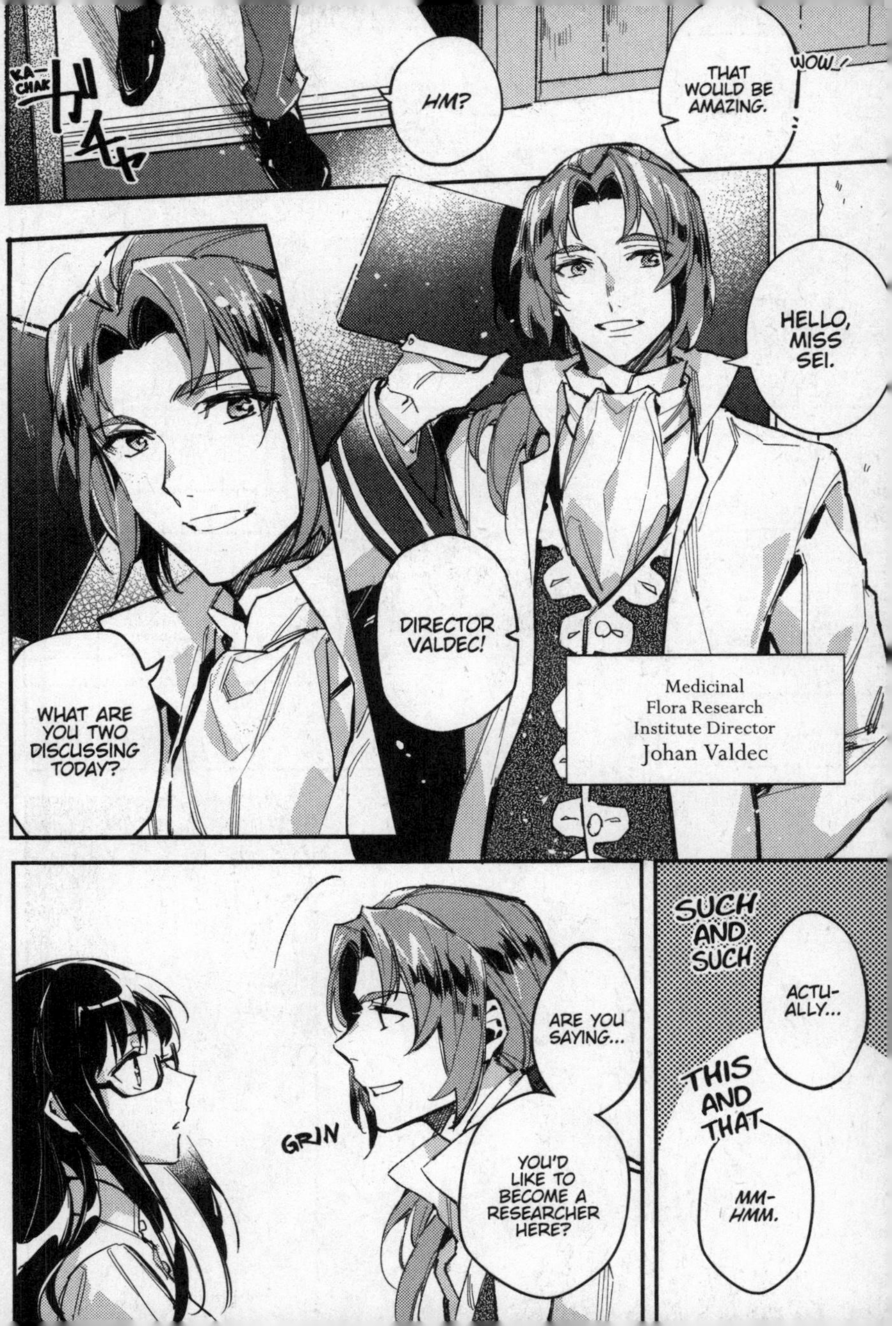
WOW..!
THAT WOULD BE AMAZING.
HM?
KA-CHAK
HELLO, MISS SEI.
Medicinal Flora Research Institute Director Johan Valdec
DIRECTOR VALDEC!
WHAT ARE YOU TWO DISCUSSING TODAY?
SUCH AND SUCH
ACTU-ALLY...
THIS AND THAT
MM-HMM.
ARE YOU SAYING...
GRIN
YOU'D LIKE TO BECOME A RESEARCHER HERE?

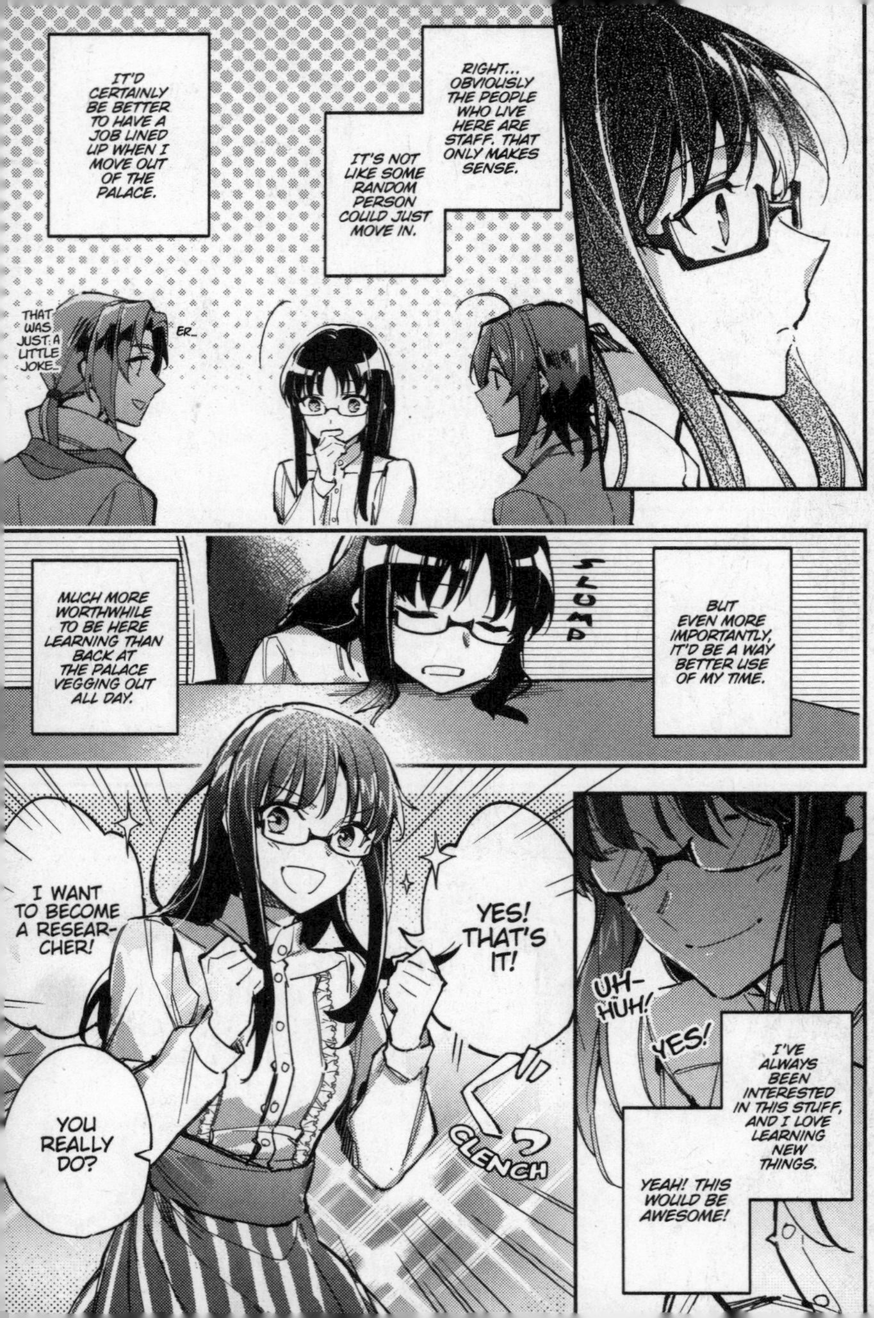
RIGHT... OBVIOUSLY THE PEOPLE WHO LIVE HERE ARE STAFF. THAT ONLY MAKES SENSE.
IT'S NOT LIKE SOME RANDOM PERSON COULD JUST MOVE IN.
IT'D CERTAINLY BE BETTER TO HAVE A JOB LINED UP WHEN I MOVE OUT OF THE PALACE.
ER...
THAT WAS JUST A LITTLE JOKE...
BUT EVEN MORE IMPORTANTLY, IT'D BE A WAY BETTER USE OF MY TIME.
SLUMP
MUCH MORE WORTHWHILE TO BE HERE LEARNING THAN BACK AT THE PALACE VEGGING OUT ALL DAY.
UH-HUH!
YES!
I'VE ALWAYS BEEN INTERESTED IN THIS STUFF, AND I LOVE LEARNING NEW THINGS.
YEAH! THIS WOULD BE AWESOME!
YES! THAT'S IT!
I WANT TO BECOME A RESEARCHER!
CLENCH
YOU REALLY DO?

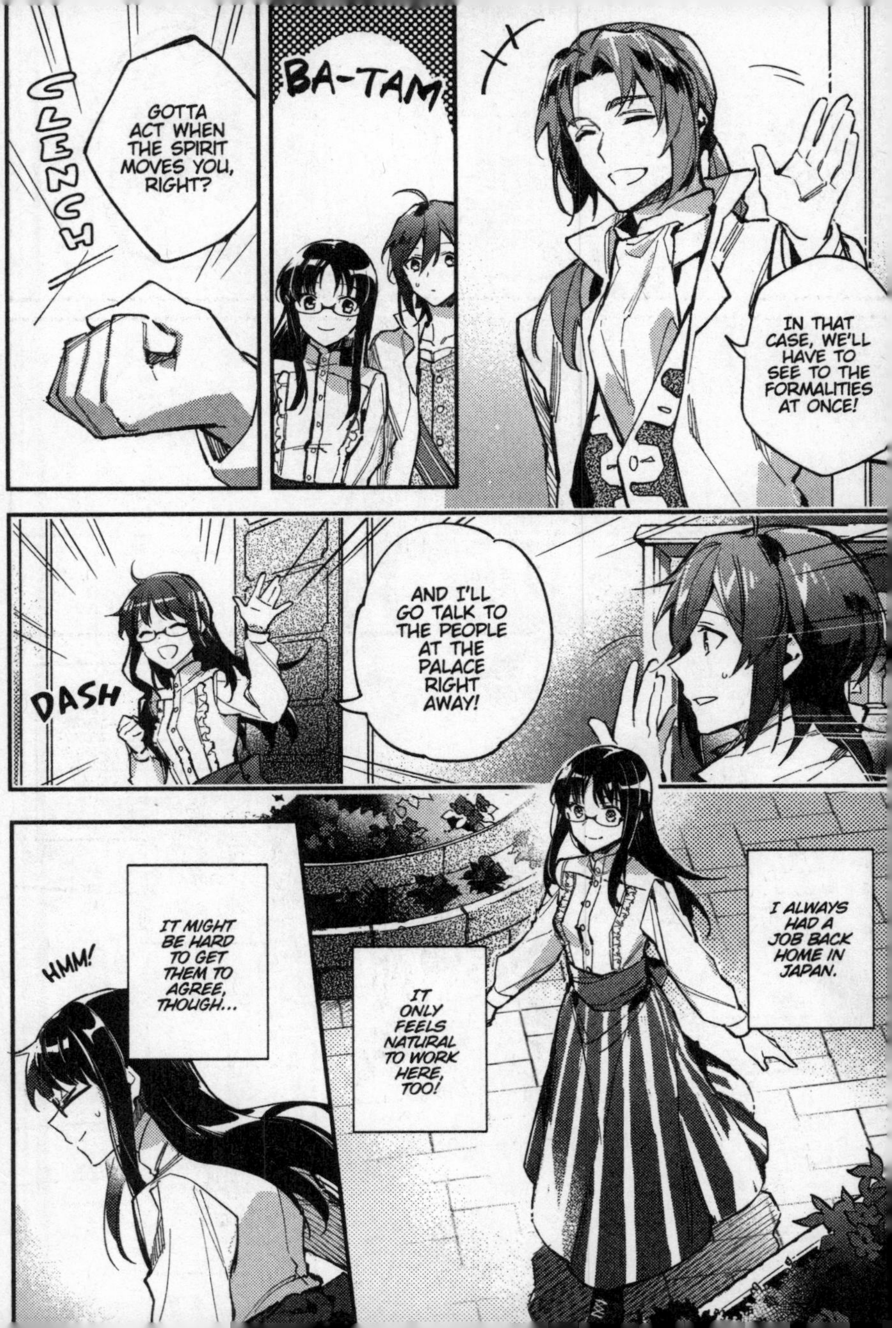
IN THAT CASE, WE'LL HAVE TO SEE TO THE FORMALITIES AT ONCE!
BA-TAM
GOTTA ACT WHEN THE SPIRIT MOVES YOU, RIGHT?
CLENCH
AND I'LL GO TALK TO THE PEOPLE AT THE PALACE RIGHT AWAY!
DASH
I ALWAYS HAD A JOB BACK HOME IN JAPAN.
IT ONLY FEELS NATURAL TO WORK HERE, TOO!
IT MIGHT BE HARD TO GET THEM TO AGREE, THOUGH...
HMM!

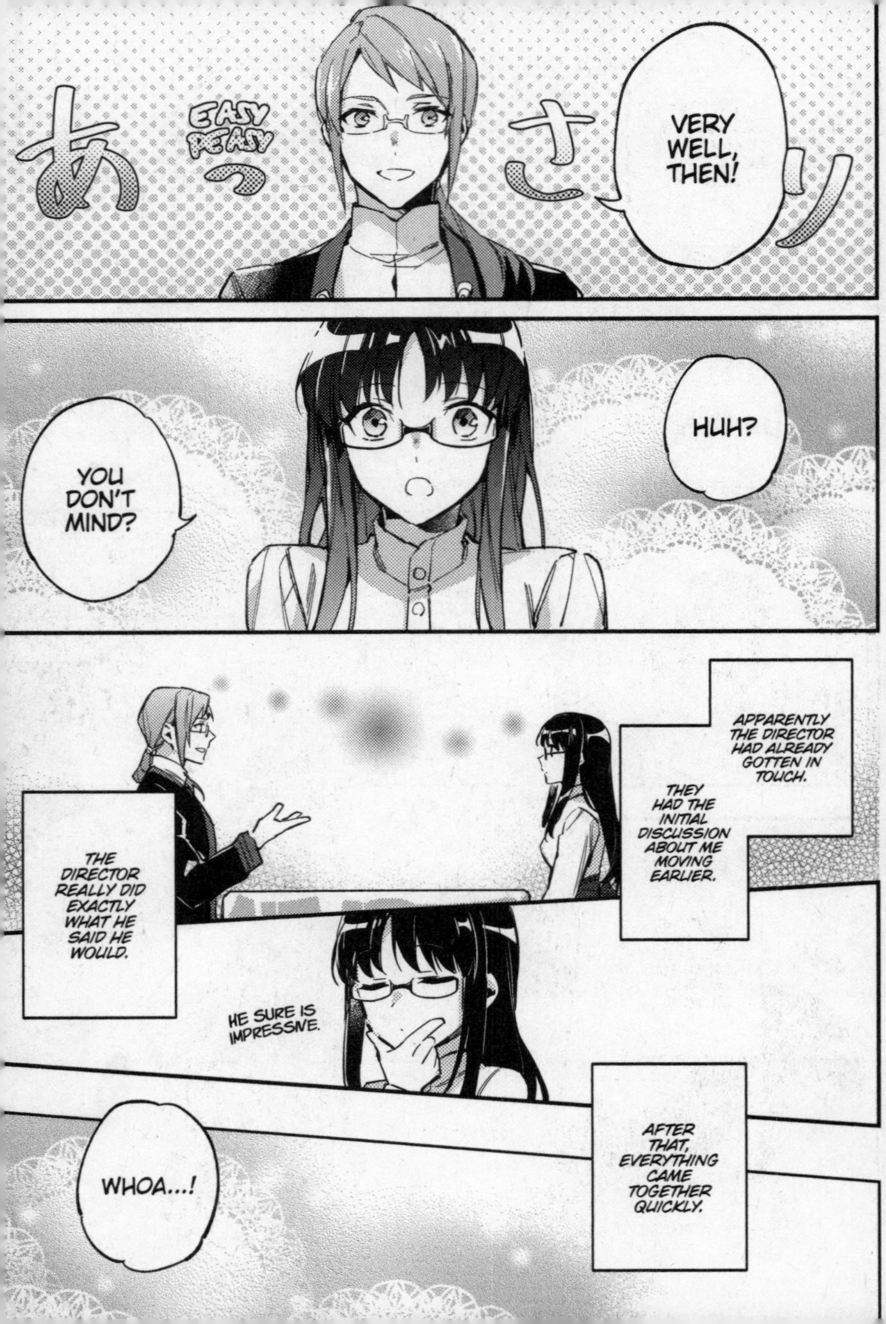
VERY WELL, THEN!
あっさり
EASY PEASY
HUH?
YOU DON'T MIND?
APPARENTLY THE DIRECTOR HAD ALREADY GOTTEN IN TOUCH.
THEY HAD THE INITIAL DISCUSSION ABOUT ME MOVING EARLIER.
THE DIRECTOR REALLY DID EXACTLY WHAT HE SAID HE WOULD.
HE SURE IS IMPRESSIVE.
AFTER THAT, EVERYTHING CAME TOGETHER QUICKLY.
WHOA...!

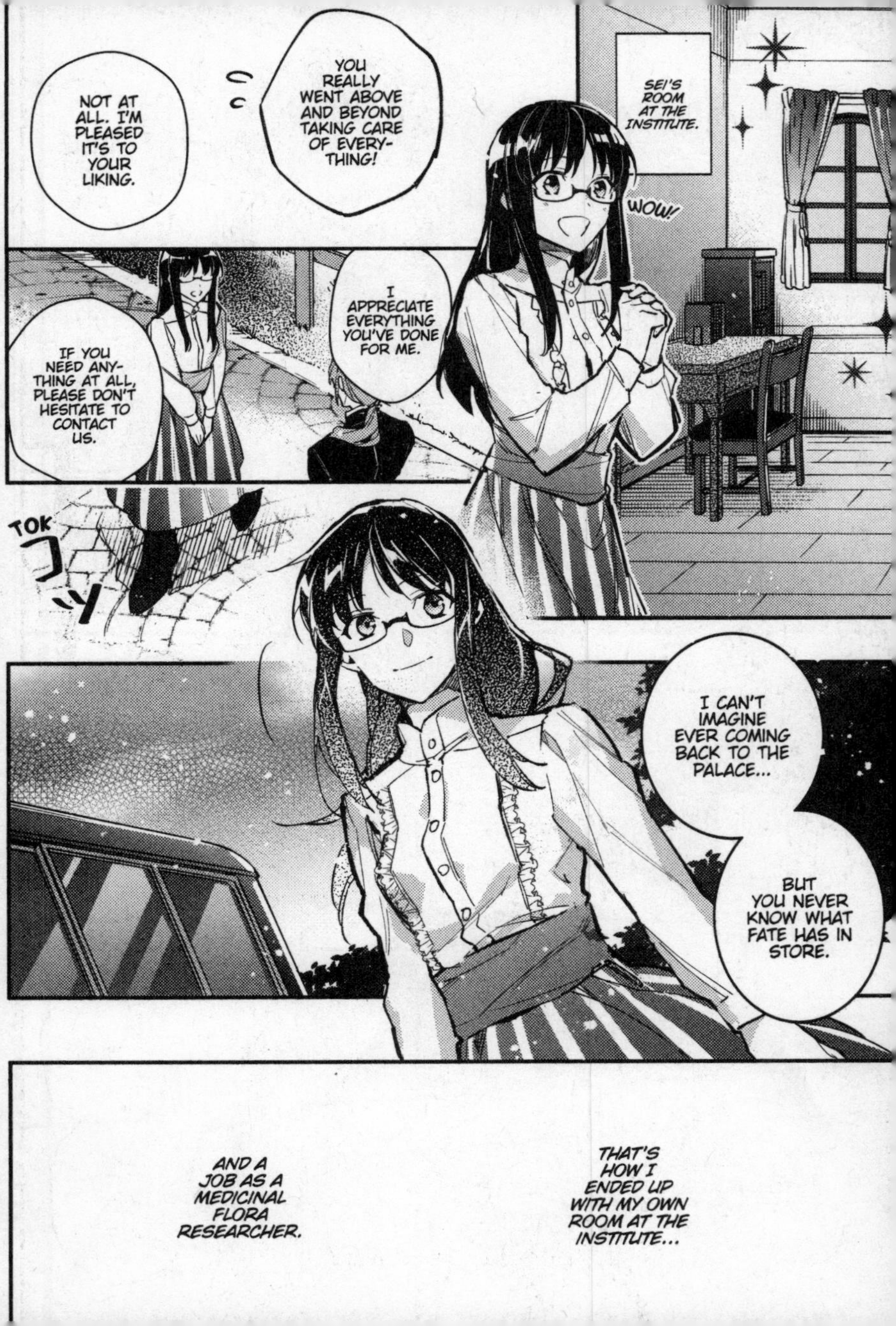

SEI'S ROOM AT THE INSTITUTE.
WOW!
YOU REALLY WENT ABOVE AND BEYOND TAKING CARE OF EVERY-THING!
NOT AT ALL. I'M PLEASED IT'S TO YOUR LIKING.
I APPRECIATE EVERYTHING YOU'VE DONE FOR ME.
IF YOU NEED ANY-THING AT ALL, PLEASE DON'T HESITATE TO CONTACT US.
TOK
I CAN'T IMAGINE EVER COMING BACK TO THE PALACE...
BUT YOU NEVER KNOW WHAT FATE HAS IN STORE.
THAT'S HOW I ENDED UP WITH MY OWN ROOM AT THE INSTITUTE...
AND A JOB AS A MEDICINAL FLORA RESEARCHER.

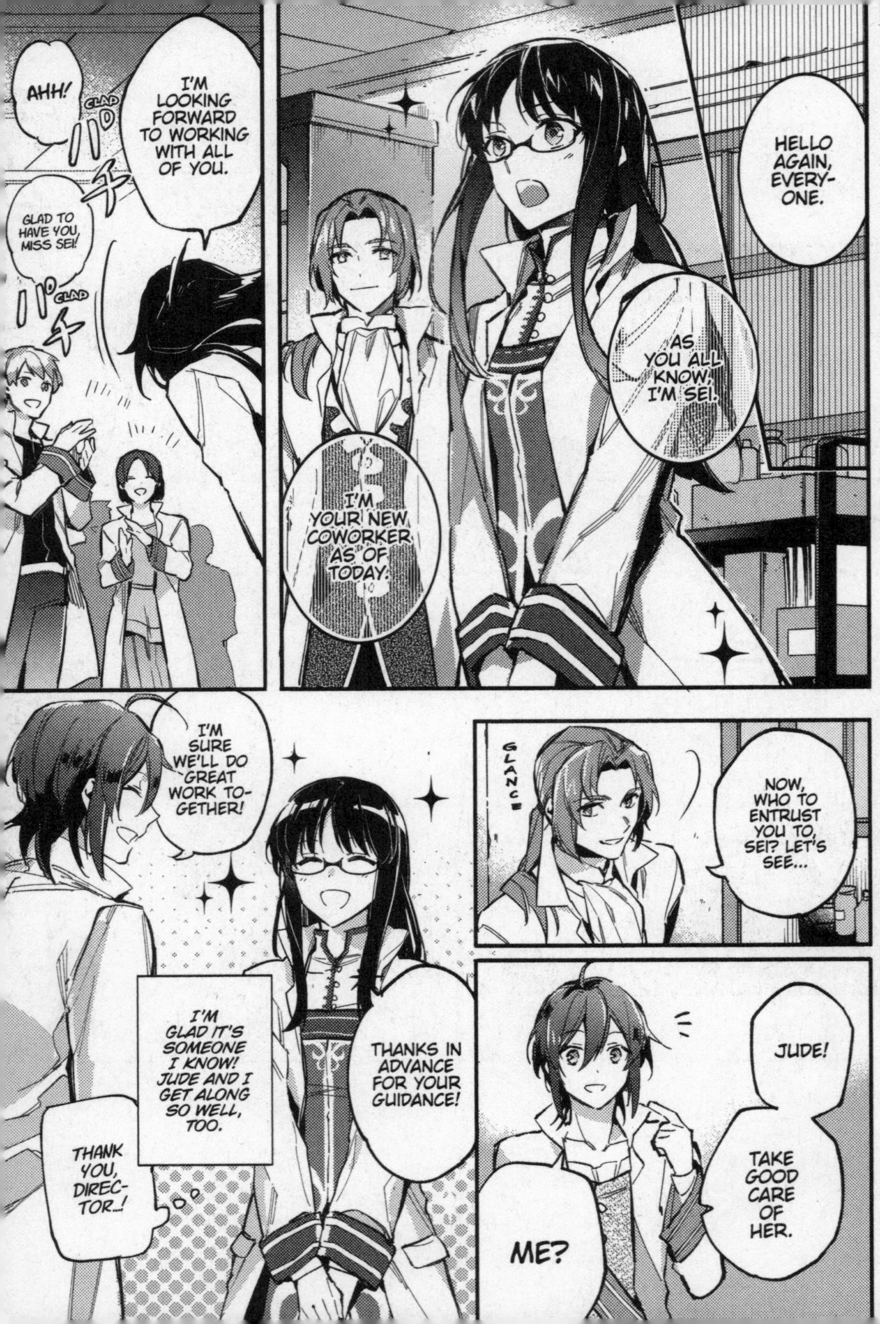
HELLO AGAIN, EVERY-ONE.
AS YOU ALL KNOW, I'M SEI.
I'M YOUR NEW COWORKER AS OF TODAY.
I'M LOOKING FORWARD TO WORKING WITH ALL OF YOU.
AHH!
GLAD
GLAD TO HAVE YOU, MISS SEI!
GLAD
NOW, WHO TO ENTRUST YOU TO, SEI? LET'S SEE...
GLANCE
JUDE!
TAKE GOOD CARE OF HER.
ME?
THANKS IN ADVANCE FOR YOUR GUIDANCE!
I'M SURE WE'LL DO GREAT WORK TO-GETHER!
I'M GLAD IT'S SOMEONE I KNOW! JUDE AND I GET ALONG SO WELL, TOO.
THANK YOU, DIREC-TOR...!

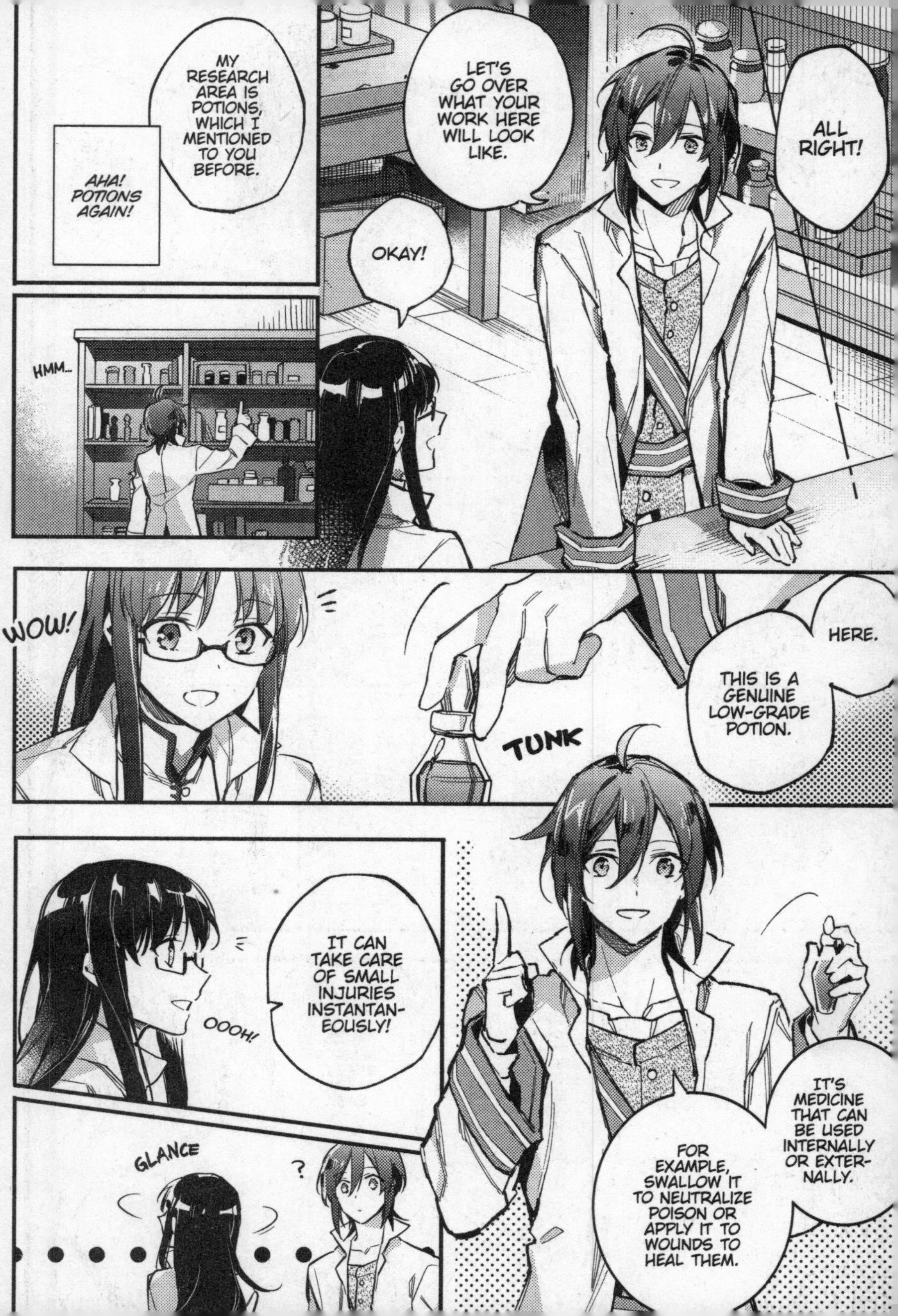
ALL RIGHT!
LET'S GO OVER WHAT YOUR WORK HERE WILL LOOK LIKE.
OKAY!
MY RESEARCH AREA IS POTIONS, WHICH I MENTIONED TO YOU BEFORE.
AHA! POTIONS AGAIN!
HMM..
HERE.
THIS IS A GENUINE LOW-GRADE POTION.
TUNK
WOW!
IT'S MEDICINE THAT CAN BE USED INTERNALLY OR EXTERNALLY.
FOR EXAMPLE, SWALLOW IT TO NEUTRALIZE POISON OR APPLY IT TO WOUNDS TO HEAL THEM.
IT CAN TAKE CARE OF SMALL INJURIES INSTANTANEOUSLY!
OOOH!
?
GLANCE
......

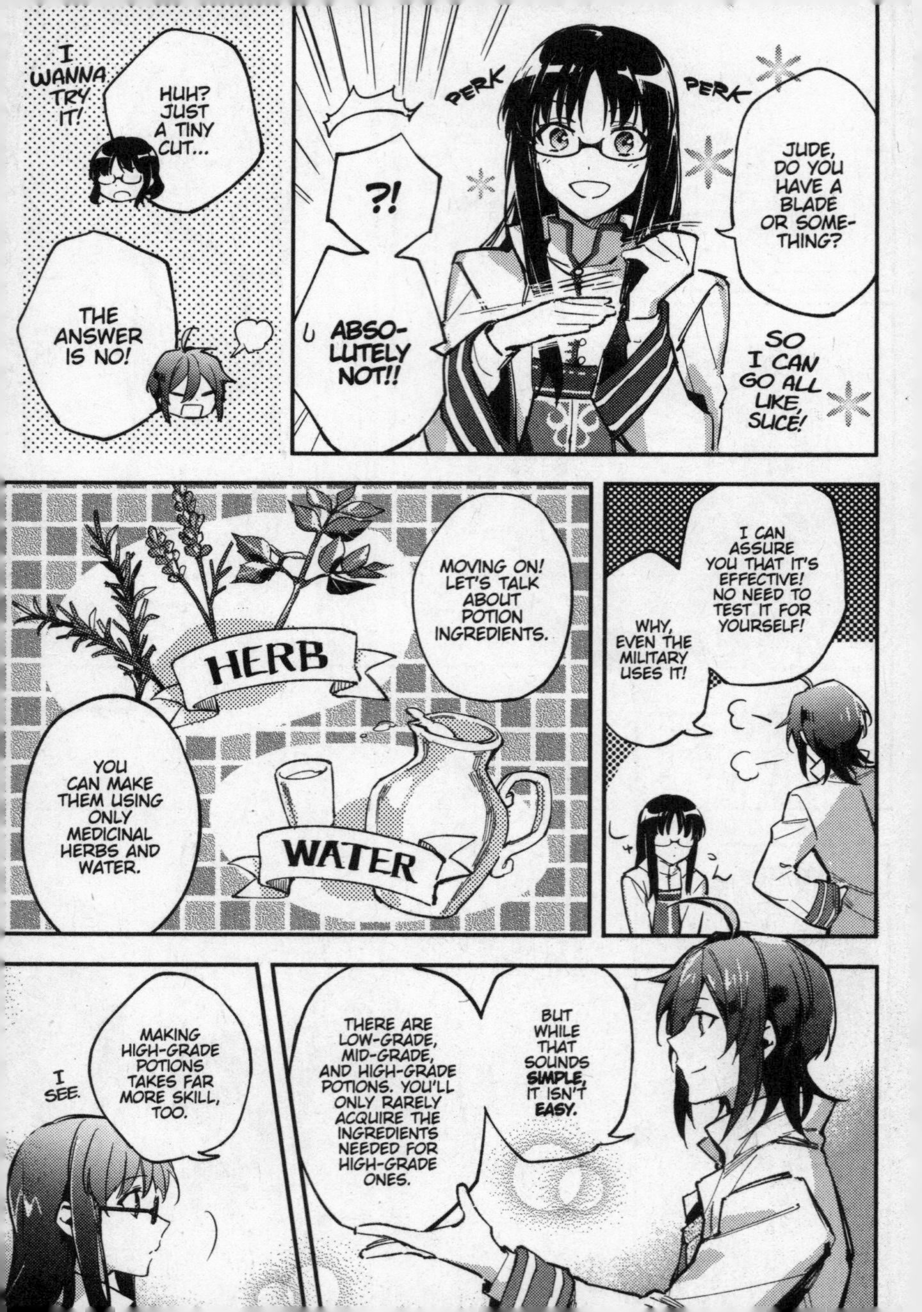
PERK
PERK
JUDE, DO YOU HAVE A BLADE OR SOMETHING?
SO I CAN GO ALL LIKE, SLICE!
?!
ABSOLUTELY NOT!!
HUH? JUST A TINY CUT...
I WANNA TRY IT!
THE ANSWER IS NO!
I CAN ASSURE YOU THAT IT'S EFFECTIVE! NO NEED TO TEST IT FOR YOURSELF!
WHY, EVEN THE MILITARY USES IT!
MOVING ON! LET'S TALK ABOUT POTION INGREDIENTS.
HERB
WATER
YOU CAN MAKE THEM USING ONLY MEDICINAL HERBS AND WATER.
BUT WHILE THAT SOUNDS SIMPLE, IT ISN'T EASY.
THERE ARE LOW-GRADE, MID-GRADE, AND HIGH-GRADE POTIONS. YOU'LL ONLY RARELY ACQUIRE THE INGREDIENTS NEEDED FOR HIGH-GRADE ONES.
MAKING HIGH-GRADE POTIONS TAKES FAR MORE SKILL, TOO.
I SEE.

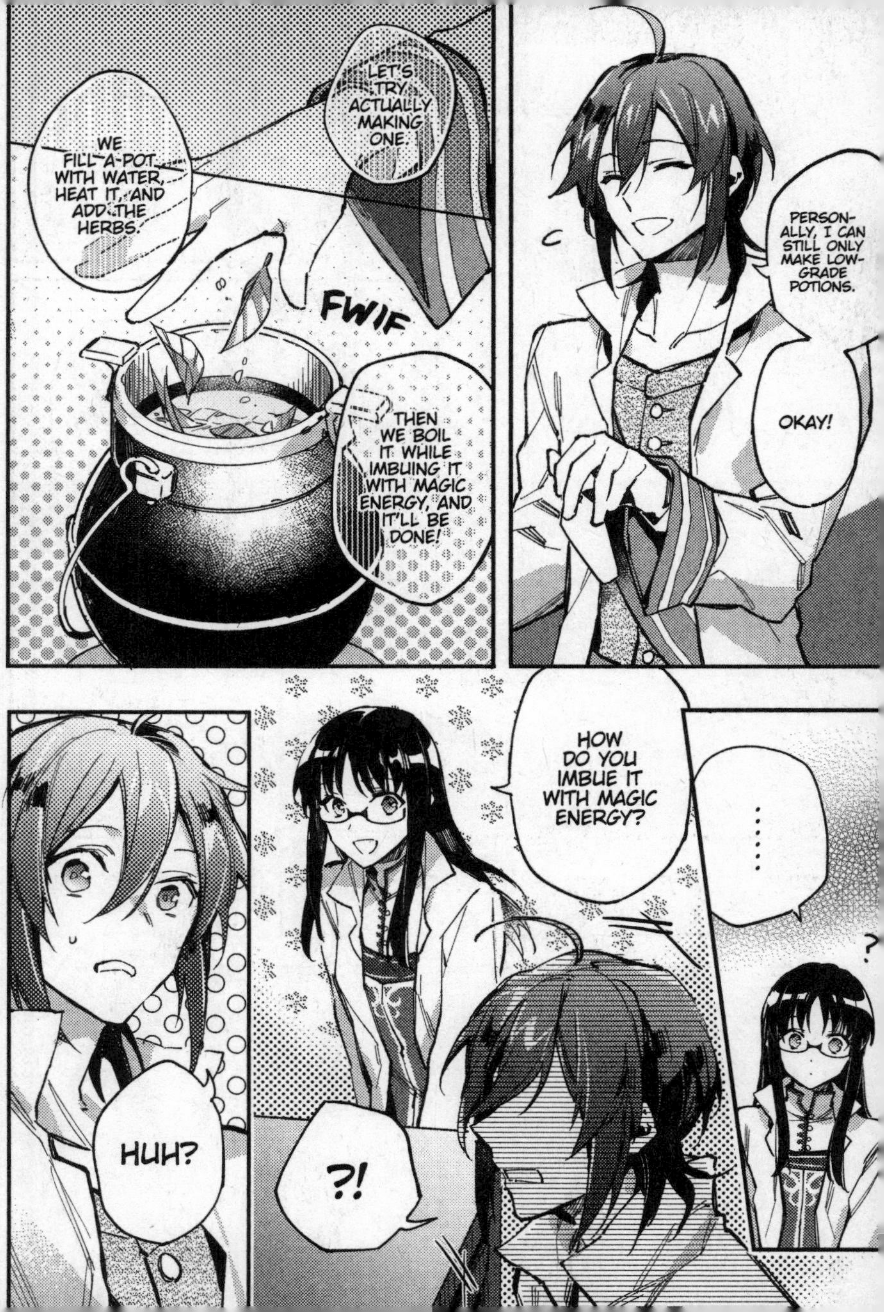
PERSONALLY, I CAN STILL ONLY MAKE LOW-GRADE POTIONS.
OKAY!
LET'S TRY ACTUALLY MAKING ONE.
WE FILL A POT WITH WATER, HEAT IT, AND ADD THE HERBS.
FWIF
THEN WE BOIL IT WHILE IMBUING IT WITH MAGIC ENERGY, AND IT'LL BE DONE!
......
?
HOW DO YOU IMBUE IT WITH MAGIC ENERGY?
?!
HUH?

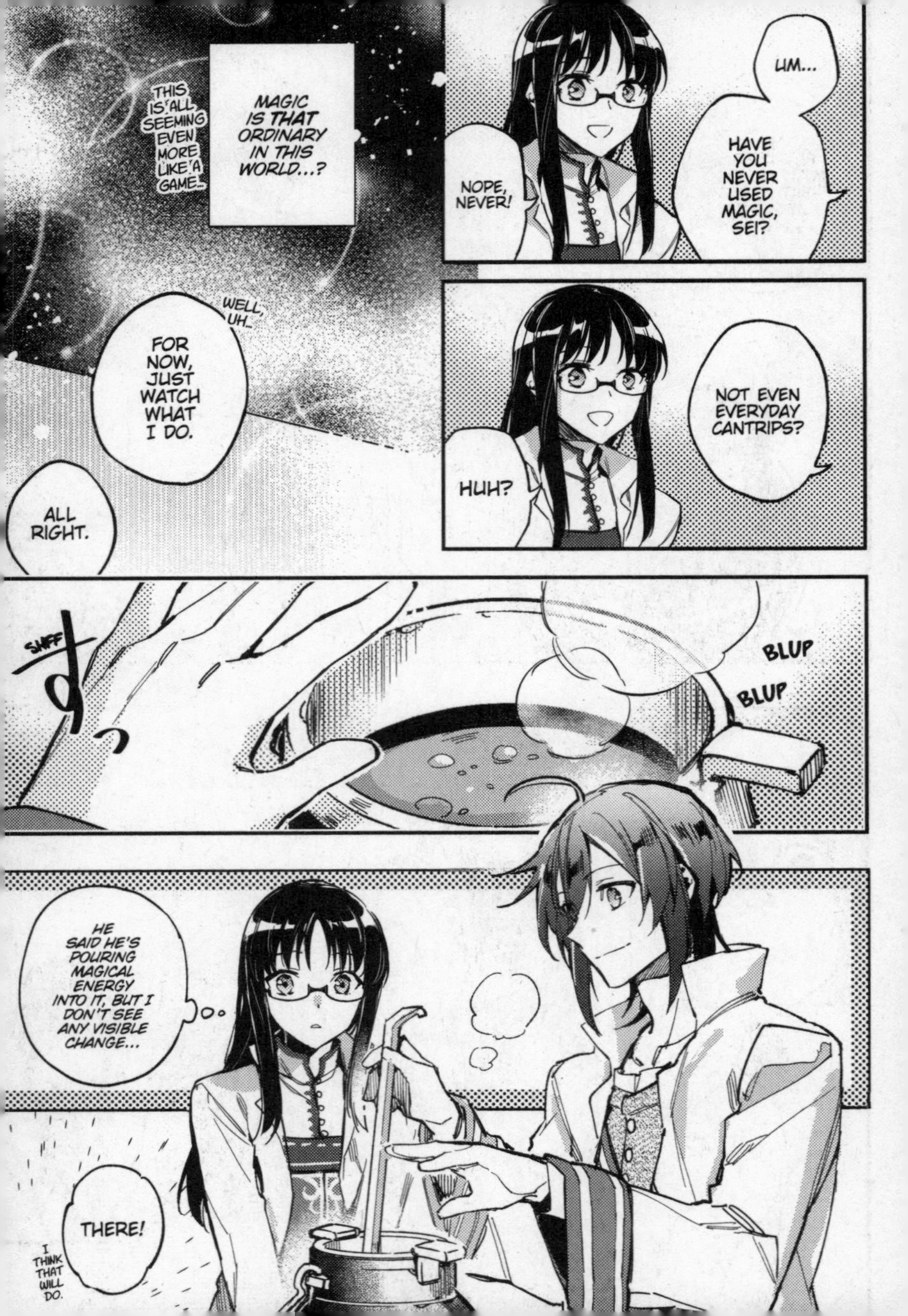
UM...
HAVE YOU NEVER USED MAGIC, SEI?
NOPE, NEVER!
NOT EVEN EVERYDAY CANTRIPS?
HUH?
MAGIC IS THAT ORDINARY IN THIS WORLD...?
THIS IS ALL SEEMING EVEN MORE LIKE A GAME...
WELL, UH...
FOR NOW, JUST WATCH WHAT I DO.
ALL RIGHT.
BLUP
BLUP
SHFF
HE SAID HE'S POURING MAGICAL ENERGY INTO IT, BUT I DON'T SEE ANY VISIBLE CHANGE...
THERE!
I THINK THAT WILL DO.

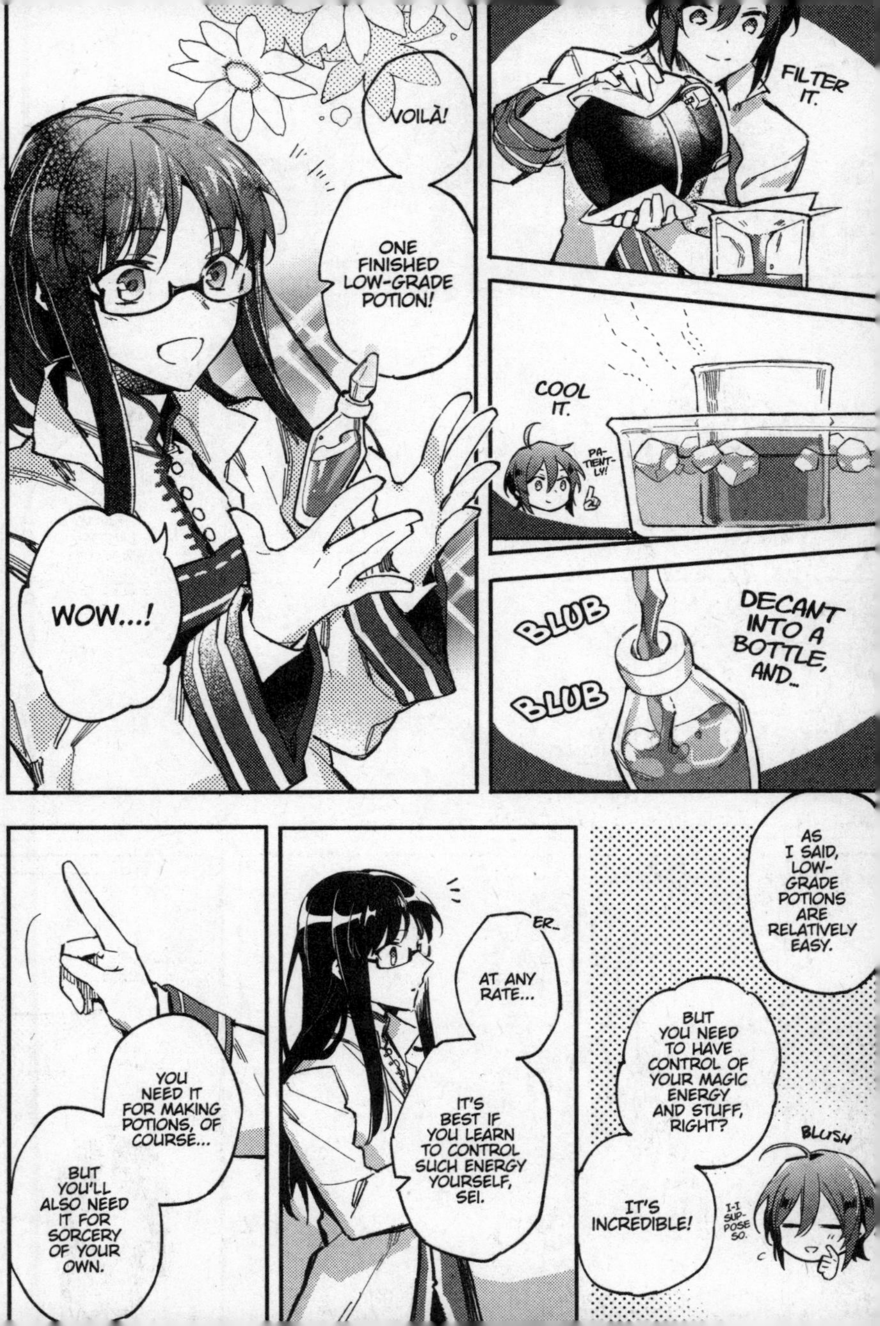
FILTER IT.
COOL IT.
PATIENTLY!
BLUB
BLUB
DECANT INTO A BOTTLE, AND...
VOILÀ!
ONE FINISHED LOW-GRADE POTION!
WOW...!
AS I SAID, LOW-GRADE POTIONS ARE RELATIVELY EASY.
BUT YOU NEED TO HAVE CONTROL OF YOUR MAGIC ENERGY AND STUFF, RIGHT?
IT'S INCREDIBLE!
BLUSH
I-I SUPPOSE SO.
ER...
AT ANY RATE...
IT'S BEST IF YOU LEARN TO CONTROL SUCH ENERGY YOURSELF, SEI.
YOU NEED IT FOR MAKING POTIONS, OF COURSE...
BUT YOU'LL ALSO NEED IT FOR SORCERY OF YOUR OWN.

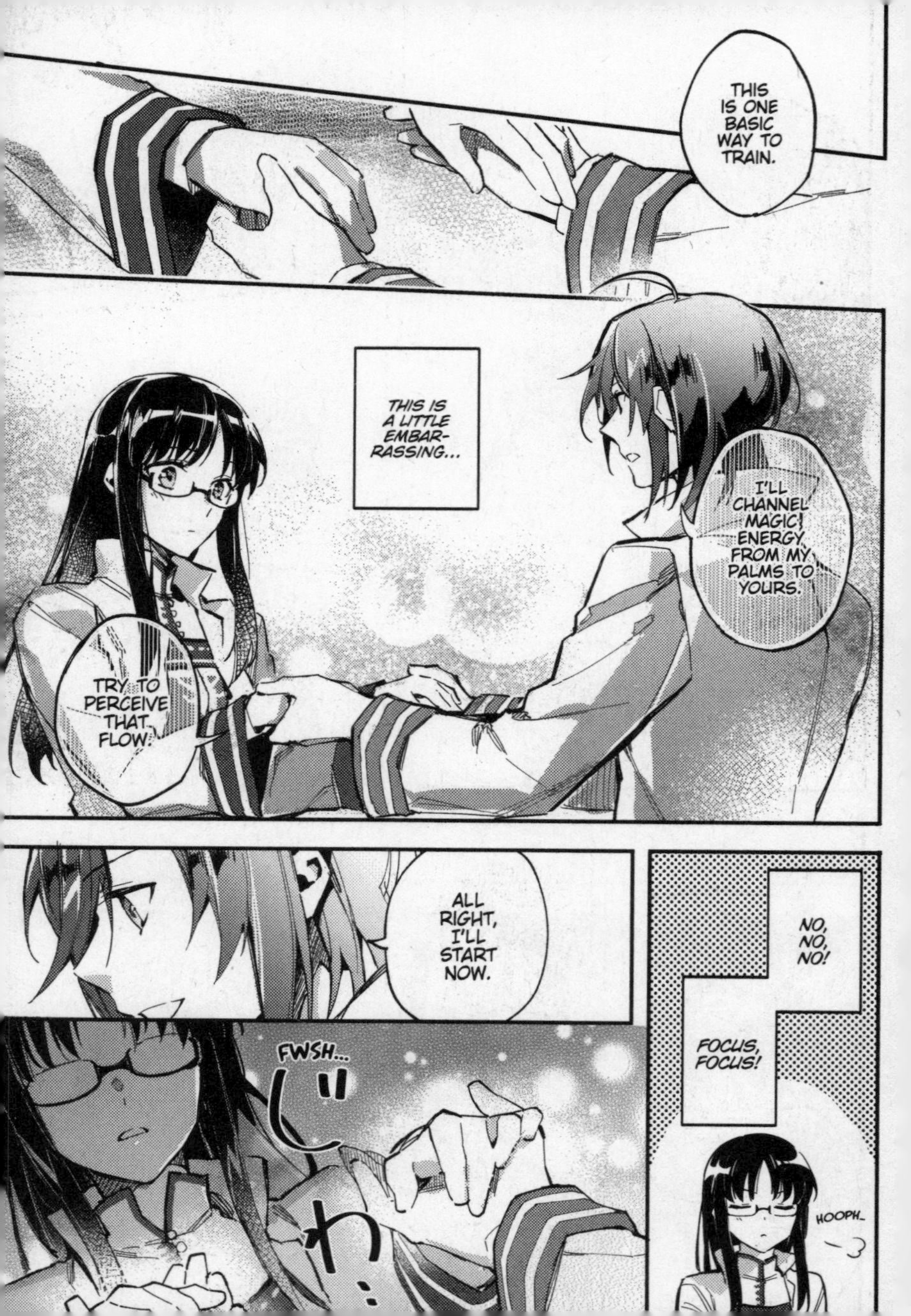
THIS IS ONE BASIC WAY TO TRAIN.
I'LL CHANNEL MAGIC ENERGY FROM MY PALMS TO YOURS.
THIS IS A LITTLE EMBARRASSING...
TRY TO PERCEIVE THAT FLOW.
NO, NO, NO!
FOCUS, FOCUS!
HOOPH_
ALL RIGHT, I'LL START NOW.
FWSH...

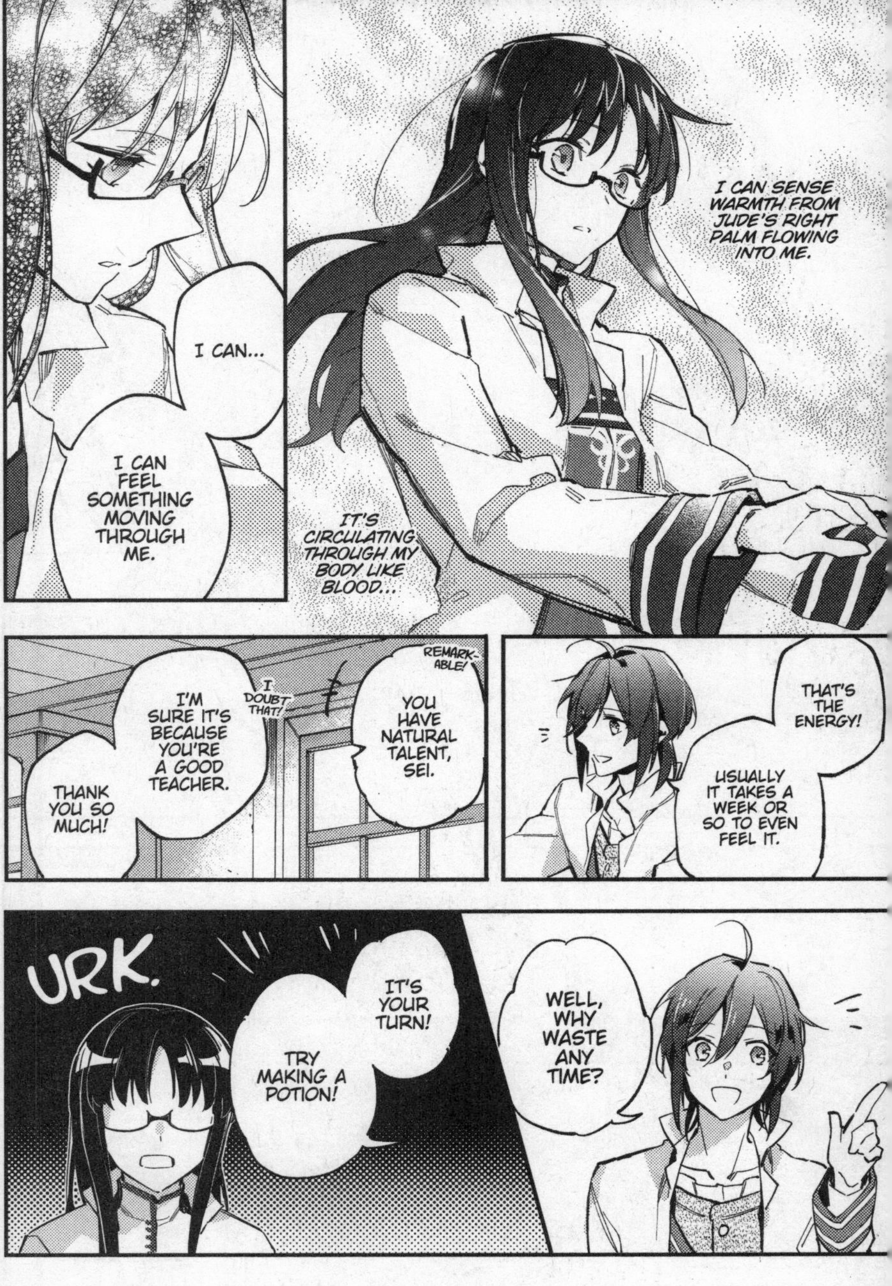
I CAN SENSE WARMTH FROM JUDE'S RIGHT PALM FLOWING INTO ME.
IT'S CIRCULATING THROUGH MY BODY LIKE BLOOD...
I CAN...
I CAN FEEL SOMETHING MOVING THROUGH ME.
THAT'S THE ENERGY!
USUALLY IT TAKES A WEEK OR SO TO EVEN FEEL IT.
REMARKABLE!
YOU HAVE NATURAL TALENT, SEI.
I DOUBT THAT!
I'M SURE IT'S BECAUSE YOU'RE A GOOD TEACHER.
THANK YOU SO MUCH!
WELL, WHY WASTE ANY TIME?
IT'S YOUR TURN!
TRY MAKING A POTION!
URK.

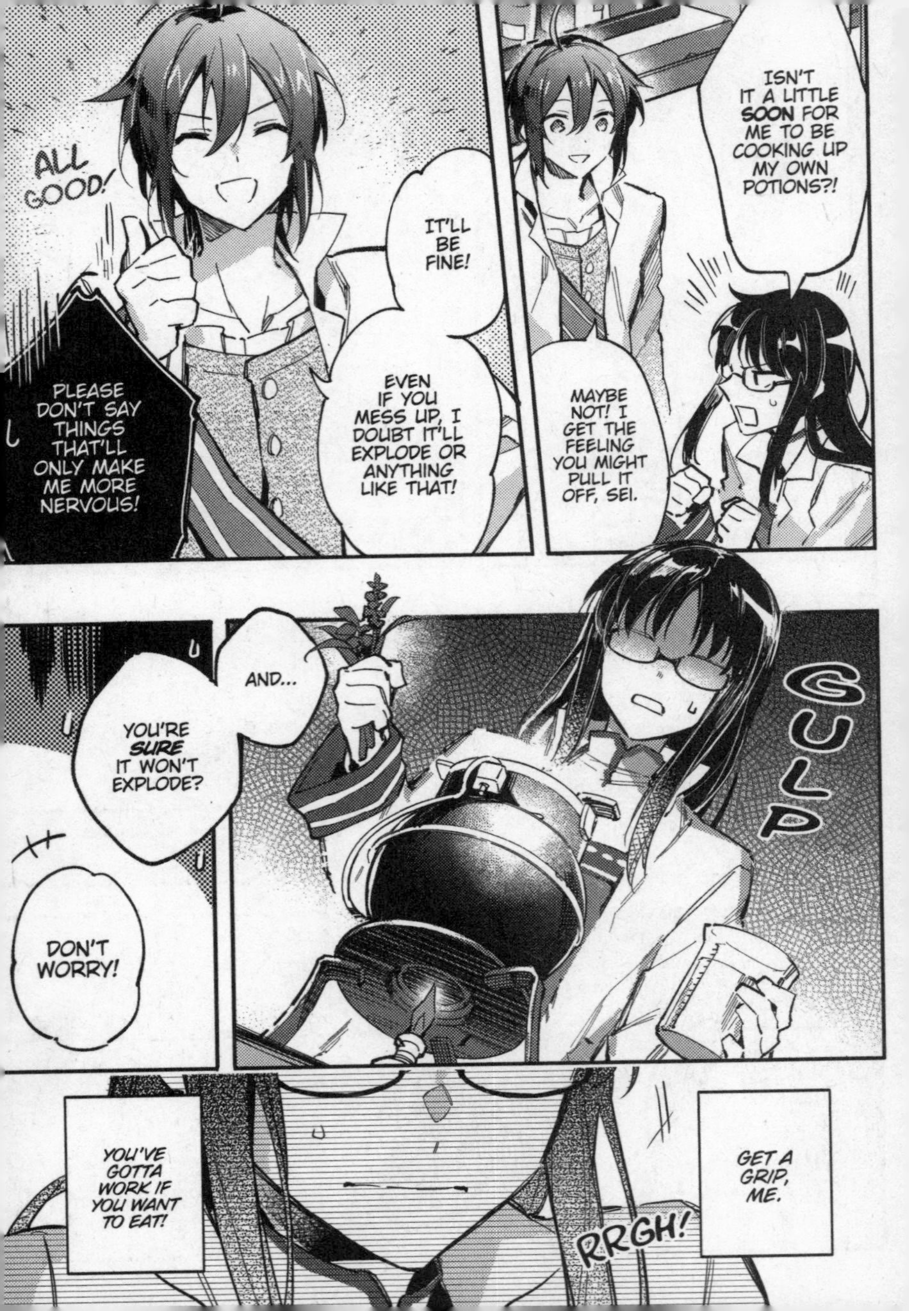
ISN'T IT A LITTLE SOON FOR ME TO BE COOKING UP MY OWN POTIONS?!
MAYBE NOT! I GET THE FEELING YOU MIGHT PULL IT OFF, SEI.
IT'LL BE FINE!
ALL GOOD!
EVEN IF YOU MESS UP, I DOUBT IT'LL EXPLODE OR ANYTHING LIKE THAT!
PLEASE DON'T SAY THINGS THAT'LL ONLY MAKE ME MORE NERVOUS!
GULP
AND...
YOU'RE SURE IT WON'T EXPLODE?
DON'T WORRY!
GET A GRIP, ME.
RRGH!
YOU'VE GOTTA WORK IF YOU WANT TO EAT!

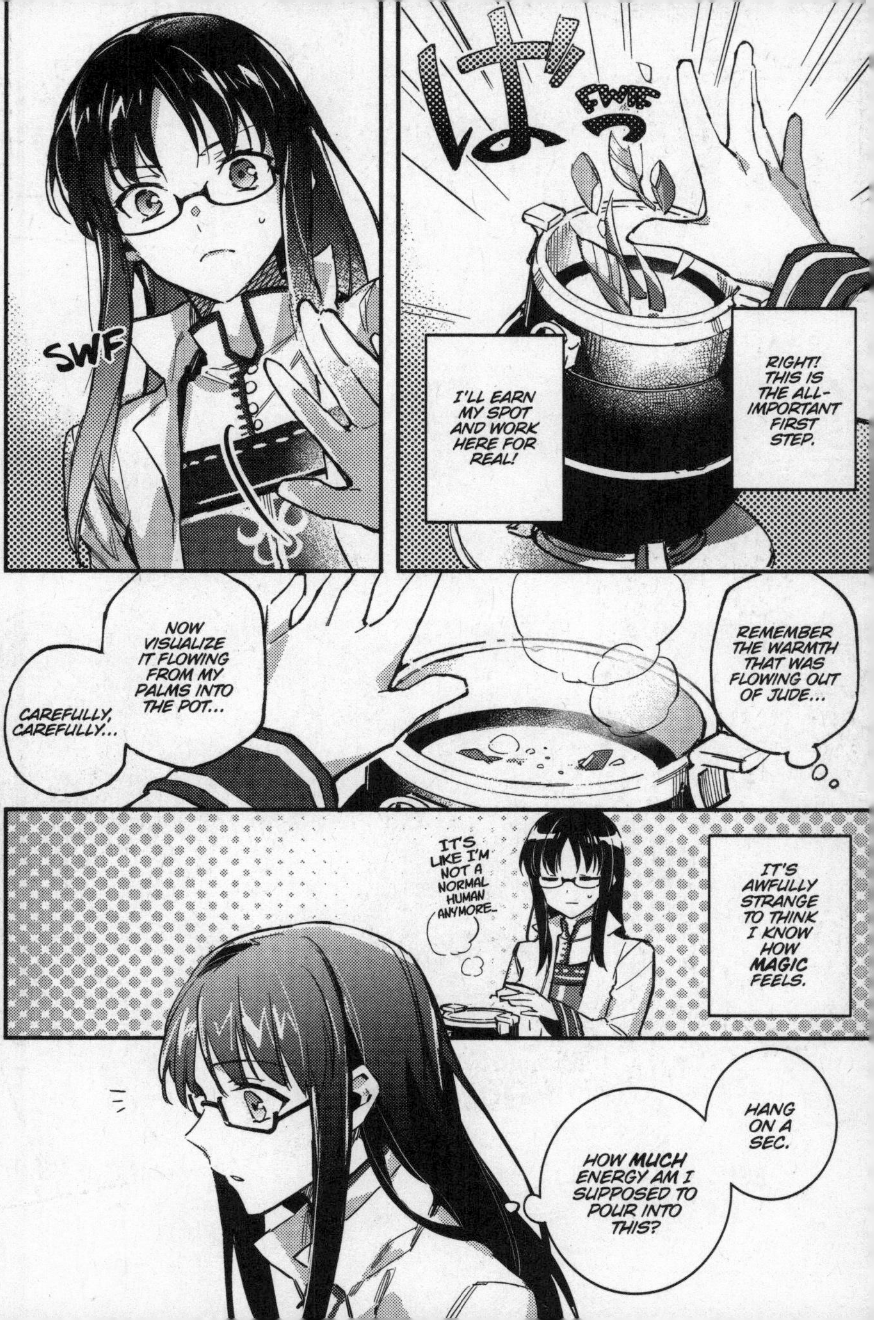
ぱっ
FWF
RIGHT! THIS IS THE ALL-IMPORTANT FIRST STEP.
I'LL EARN MY SPOT AND WORK HERE FOR REAL!
SWF
REMEMBER THE WARMTH THAT WAS FLOWING OUT OF JUDE...
NOW VISUALIZE IT FLOWING FROM MY PALMS INTO THE POT...
CAREFULLY, CAREFULLY...
IT'S AWFULLY STRANGE TO THINK I KNOW HOW MAGIC FEELS.
IT'S LIKE I'M NOT A NORMAL HUMAN ANYMORE...
HANG ON A SEC.
HOW MUCH ENERGY AM I SUPPOSED TO POUR INTO THIS?

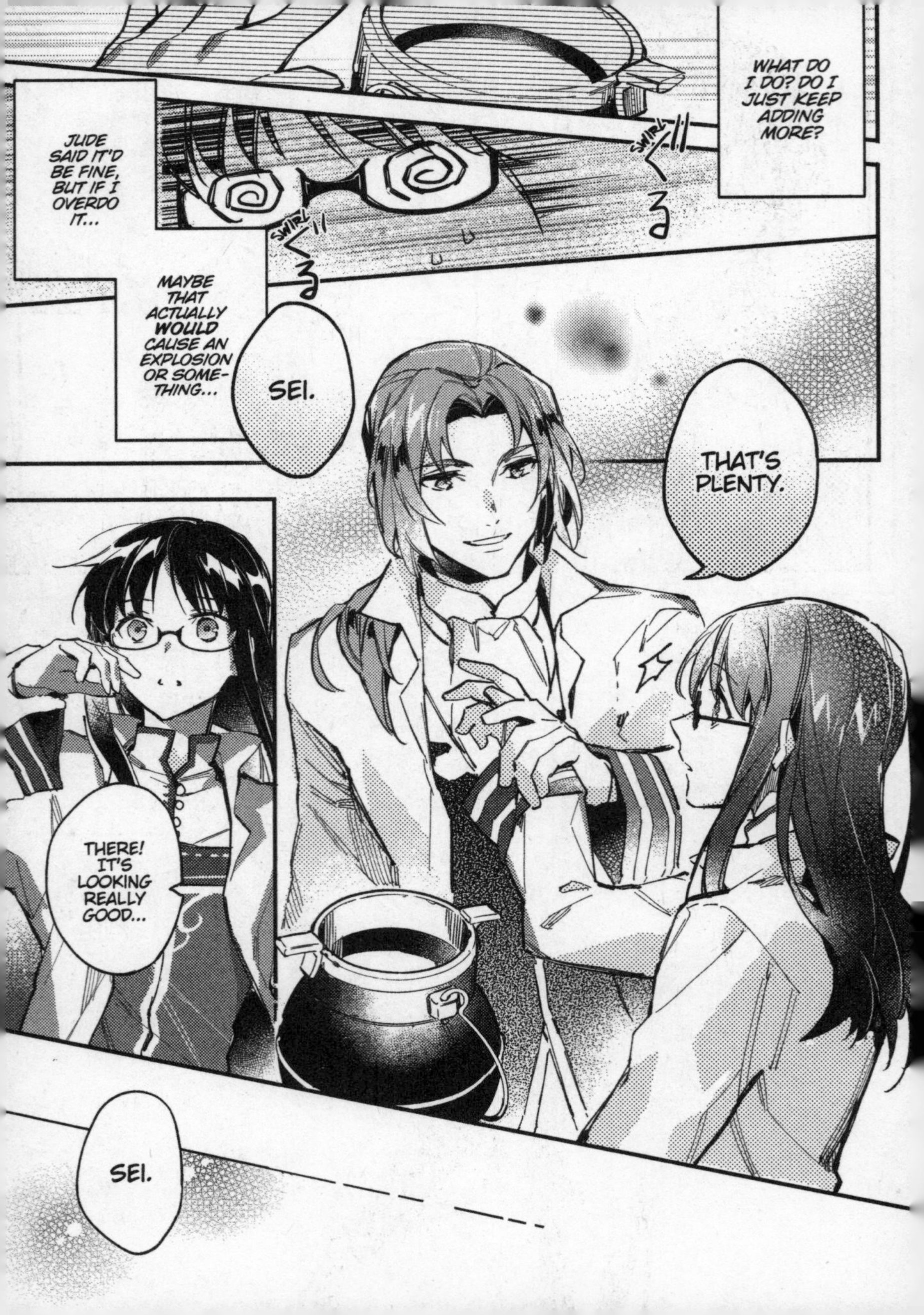
WHAT DO I DO? DO I JUST KEEP ADDING MORE?
SWIRL
JUDE SAID IT'D BE FINE, BUT IF I OVERDO IT...
SWIRL
MAYBE THAT ACTUALLY WOULD CAUSE AN EXPLOSION OR SOME-THING...
SEI.
THAT'S PLENTY.
THERE! IT'S LOOKING REALLY GOOD...
SEI.

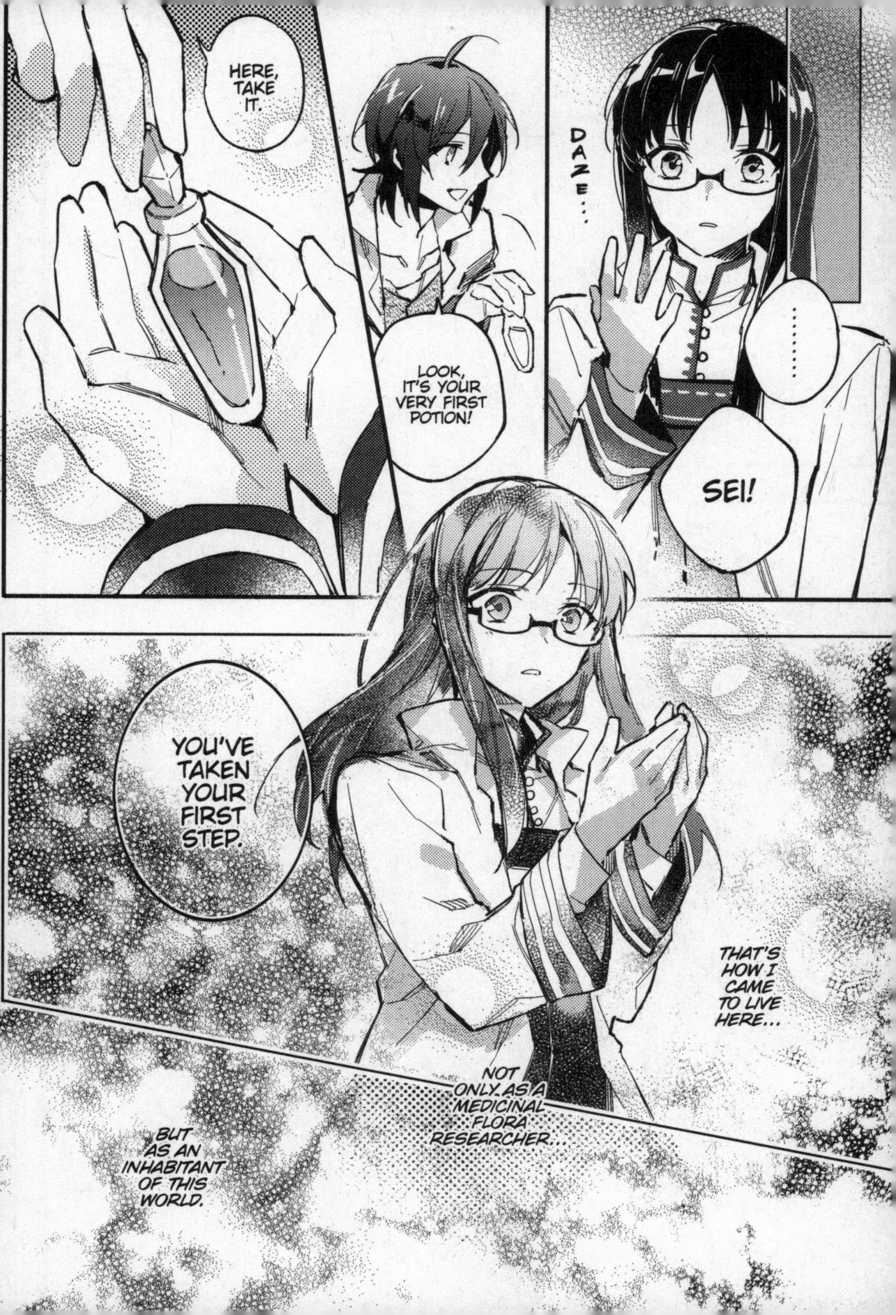
......
DAZE...
SEI!
HERE, TAKE IT.
LOOK, IT'S YOUR VERY FIRST POTION!
THAT'S HOW I CAME TO LIVE HERE...
YOU'VE TAKEN YOUR FIRST STEP.
NOT ONLY AS A MEDICINAL FLORA RESEARCHER...
BUT AS AN INHABITANT OF THIS WORLD.

The Saint's
Magic Power is
Omnipotent

The Saint's*
*Magic Power is *
Omnipotent

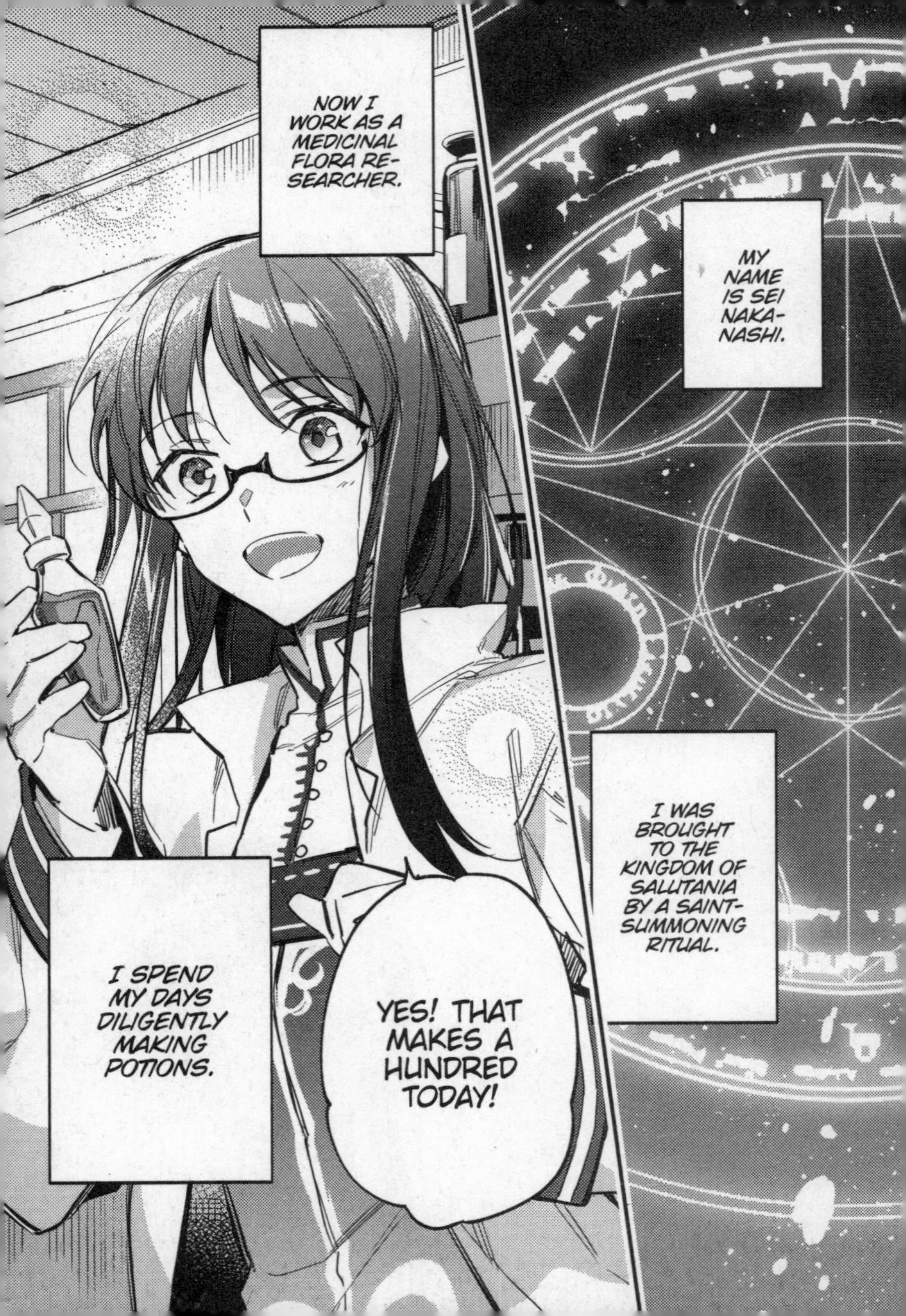
MY NAME IS SEI NAKA-NASHI.
I WAS BROUGHT TO THE KINGDOM OF SALUTANIA BY A SAINT-SUMMONING RITUAL.
NOW I WORK AS A MEDICINAL FLORA RE-SEARCHER.
YES! THAT MAKES A HUNDRED TODAY!
I SPEND MY DAYS DILIGENTLY MAKING POTIONS.

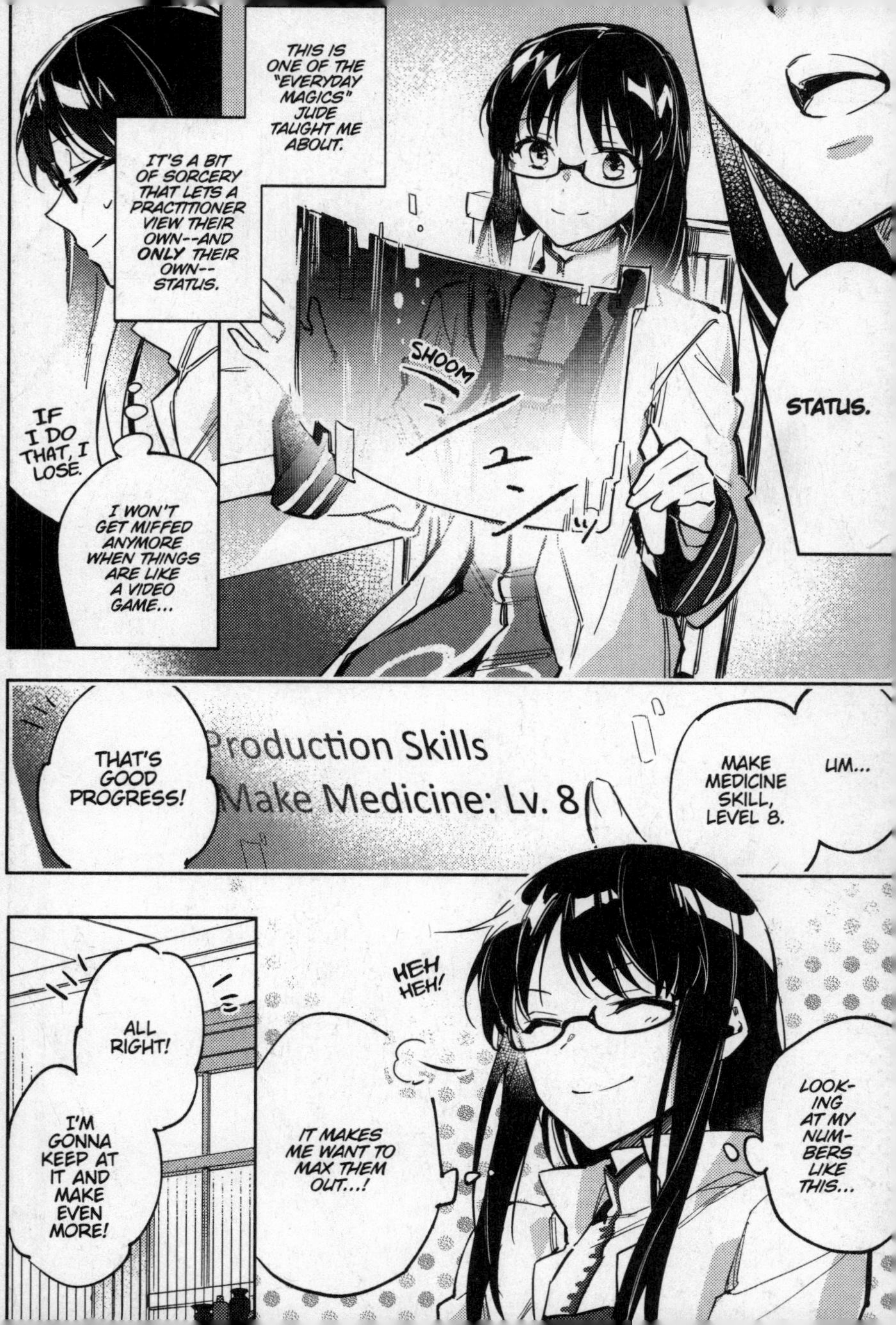
STATUS.
THIS IS ONE OF THE "EVERYDAY MAGICS" JUDE TAUGHT ME ABOUT.
IT'S A BIT OF SORCERY THAT LETS A PRACTITIONER VIEW THEIR OWN--AND ONLY THEIR OWN--STATUS.
SHOOM
IF I DO THAT, I LOSE.
I WON'T GET MIFFED ANYMORE WHEN THINGS ARE LIKE A VIDEO GAME...
UM...
MAKE MEDICINE SKILL, LEVEL 8.
Production Skills
Make Medicine: Lv. 8
THAT'S GOOD PROGRESS!
LOOKING AT MY NUMBERS LIKE THIS...
HEH HEH!
IT MAKES ME WANT TO MAX THEM OUT...!
ALL RIGHT!
I'M GONNA KEEP AT IT AND MAKE EVEN MORE!

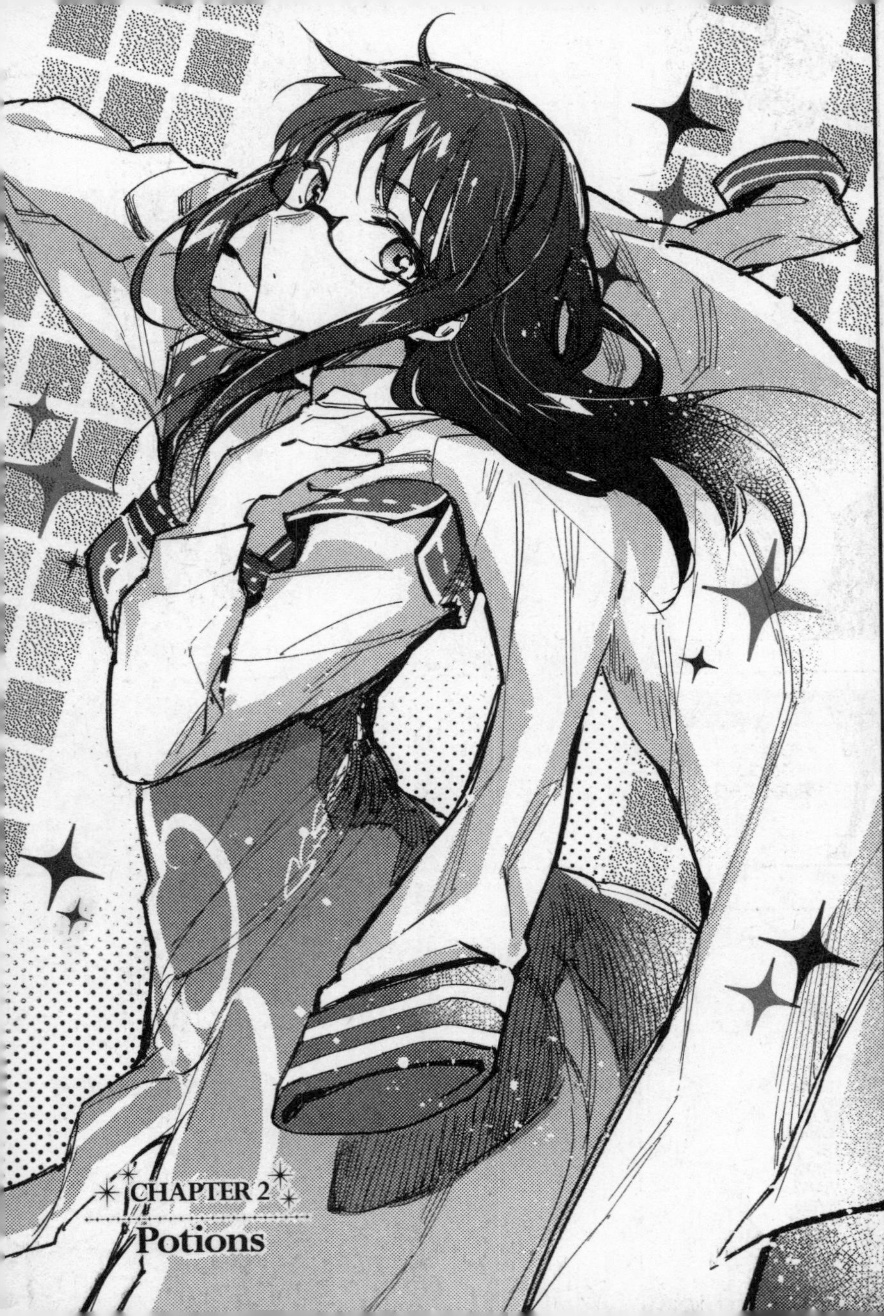
CHAPTER 2
Potions

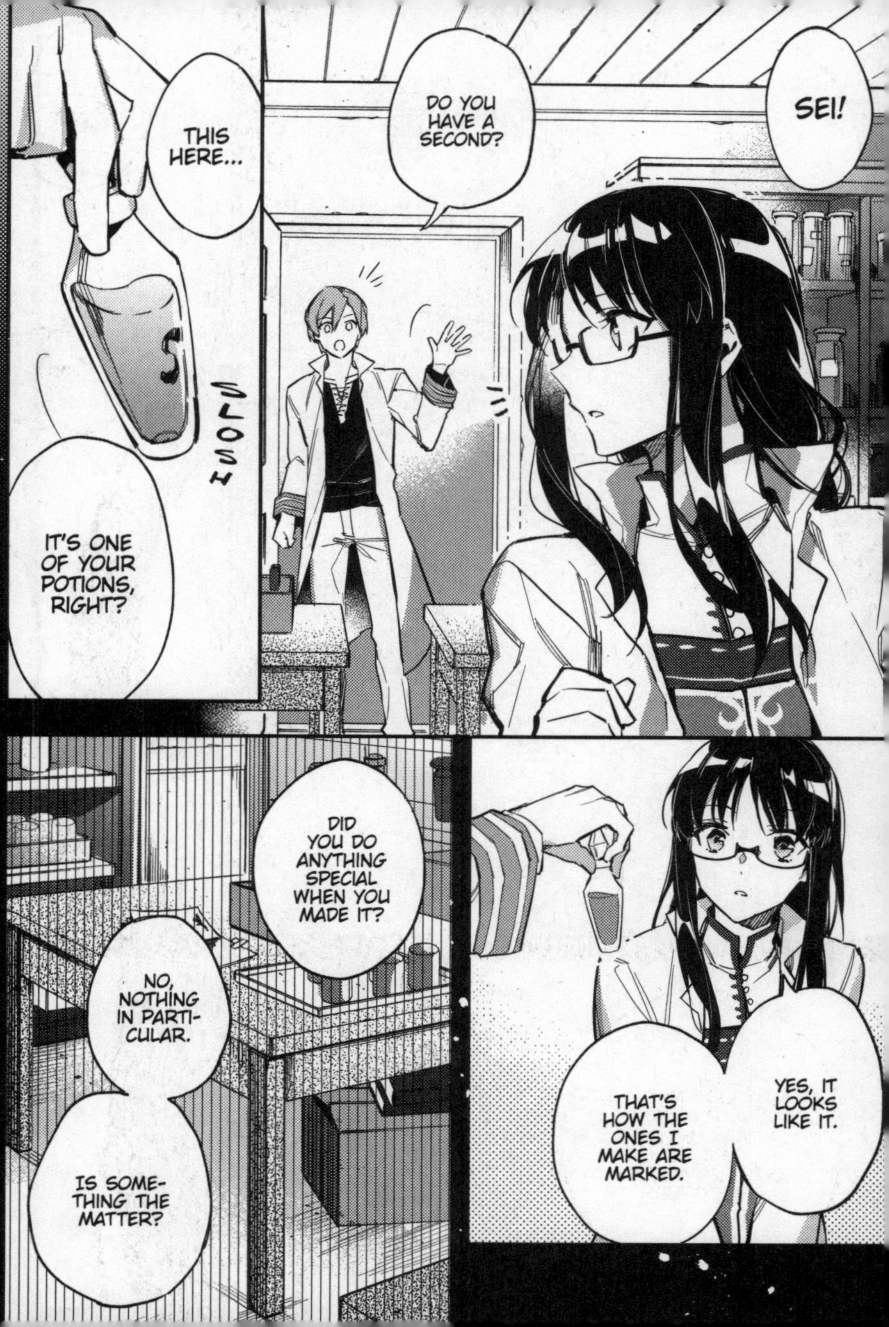
SEI!
DO YOU HAVE A SECOND?
THIS HERE...
SLOSH
IT'S ONE OF YOUR POTIONS, RIGHT?
YES, IT LOOKS LIKE IT.
THAT'S HOW THE ONES I MAKE ARE MARKED.
DID YOU DO ANYTHING SPECIAL WHEN YOU MADE IT?
NO, NOTHING IN PARTICULAR.
IS SOMETHING THE MATTER?

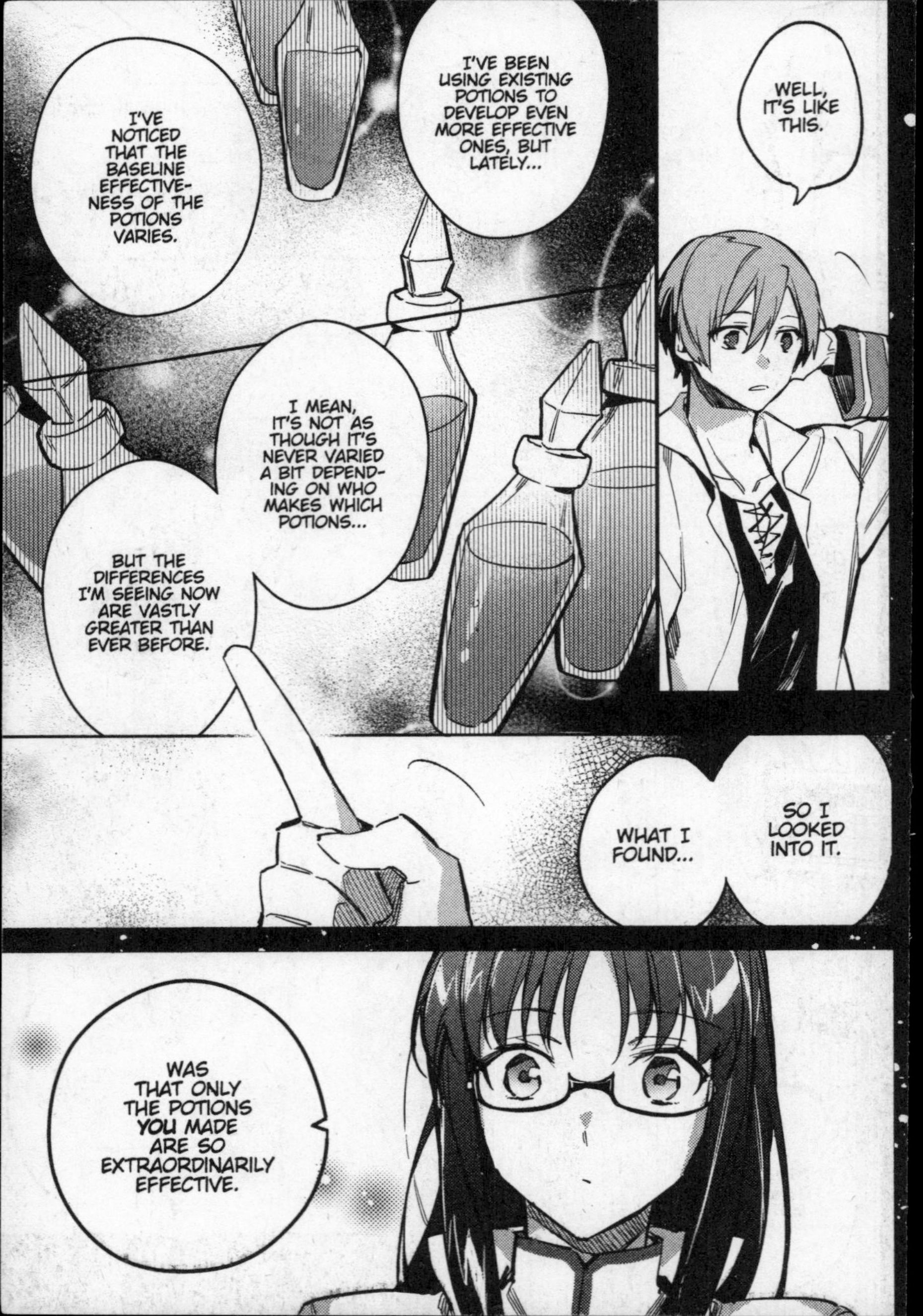
WELL, IT'S LIKE THIS.
I'VE BEEN USING EXISTING POTIONS TO DEVELOP EVEN MORE EFFECTIVE ONES, BUT LATELY...
I'VE NOTICED THAT THE BASELINE EFFECTIVE-NESS OF THE POTIONS VARIES.
I MEAN, IT'S NOT AS THOUGH IT'S NEVER VARIED A BIT DEPEND-ING ON WHO MAKES WHICH POTIONS...
BUT THE DIFFERENCES I'M SEEING NOW ARE VASTLY GREATER THAN EVER BEFORE.
SO I LOOKED INTO IT.
WHAT I FOUND...
WAS THAT ONLY THE POTIONS **YOU** MADE ARE SO EXTRAORDINARILY EFFECTIVE.

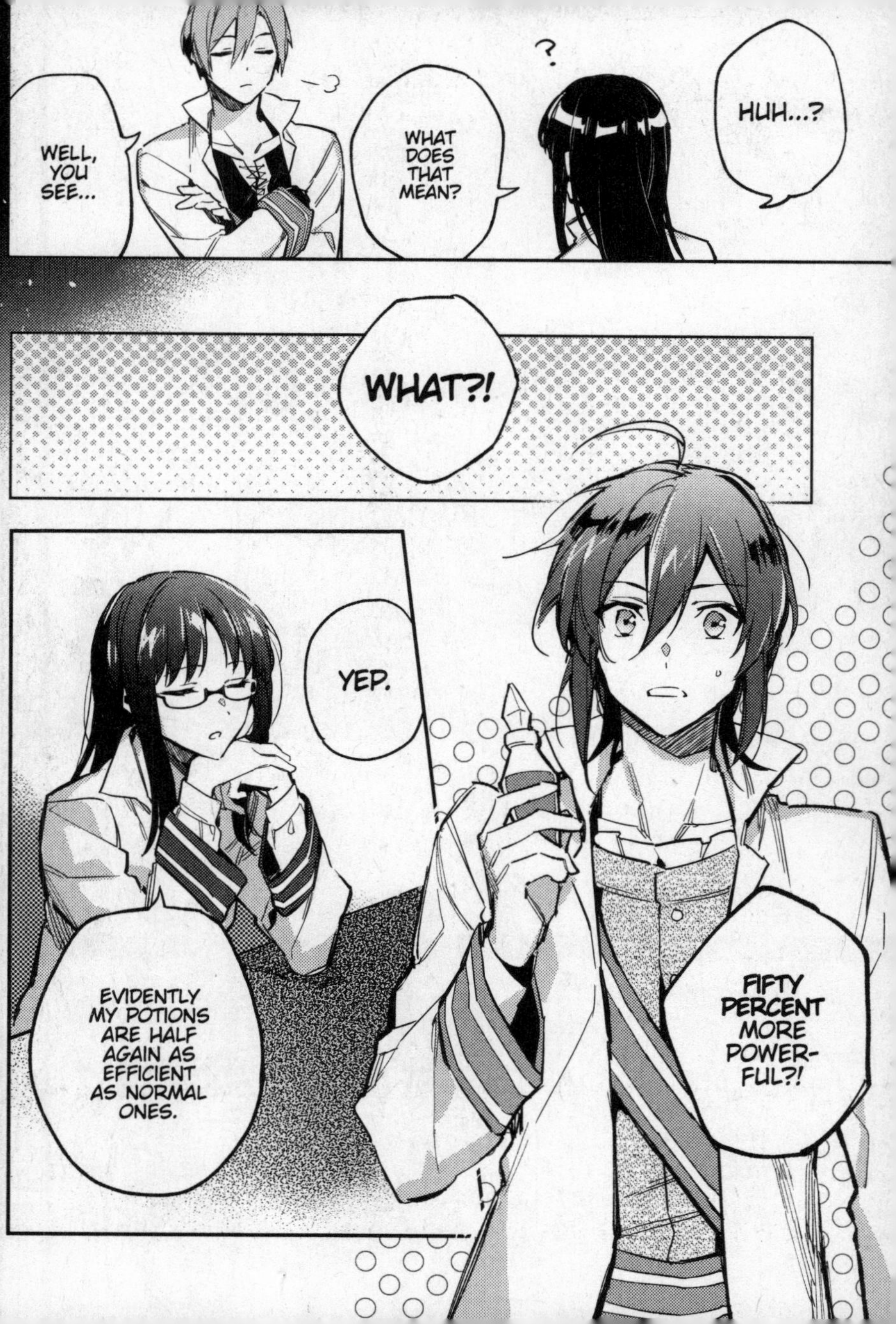
HUH...?
?
WHAT DOES THAT MEAN?
WELL, YOU SEE...
WHAT?!
FIFTY PERCENT MORE POWER-FUL?!
YEP.
EVIDENTLY MY POTIONS ARE HALF AGAIN AS EFFICIENT AS NORMAL ONES.

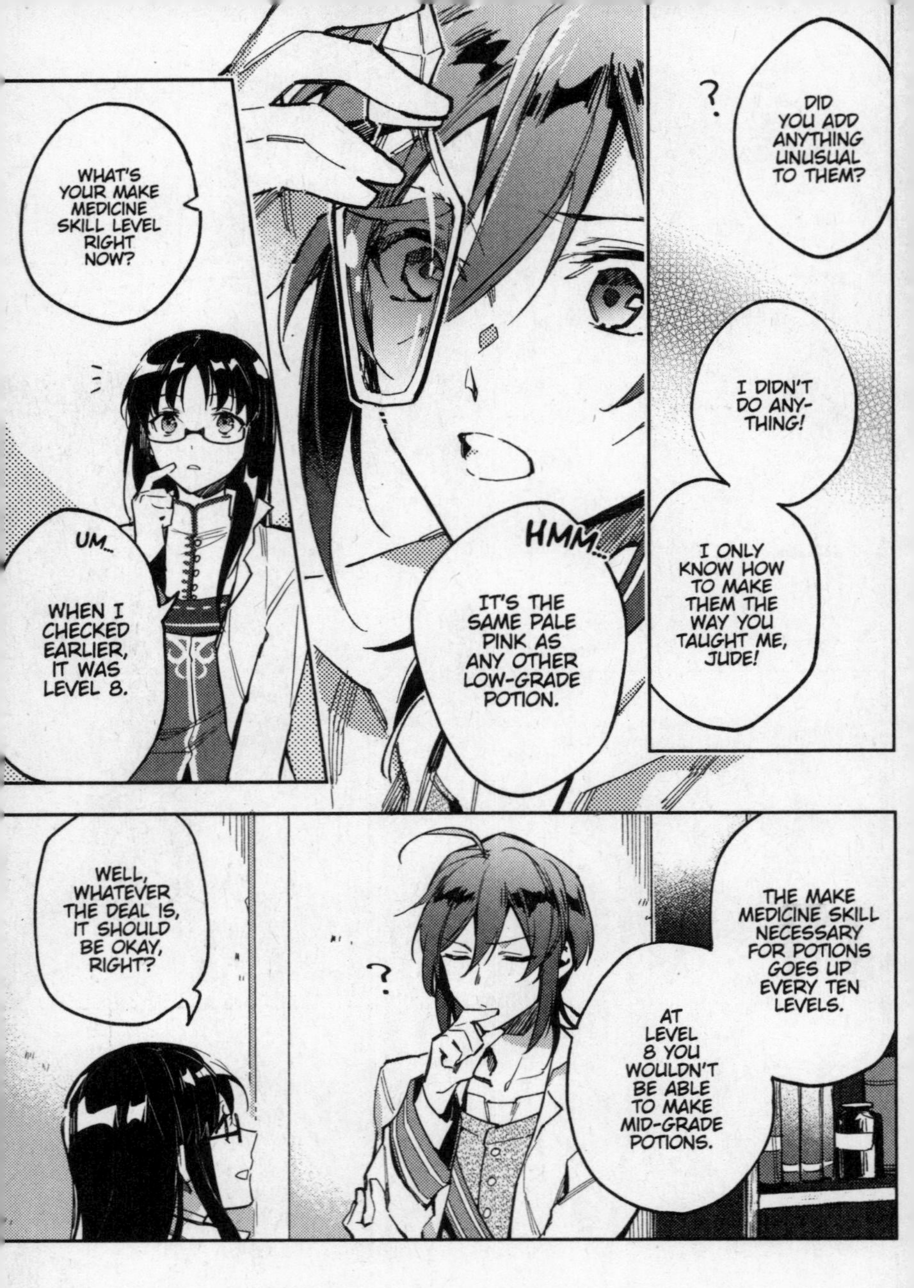
DID YOU ADD ANYTHING UNUSUAL TO THEM?
?
I DIDN'T DO ANY-THING!
I ONLY KNOW HOW TO MAKE THEM THE WAY YOU TAUGHT ME, JUDE!
HMM...
IT'S THE SAME PALE PINK AS ANY OTHER LOW-GRADE POTION.
WHAT'S YOUR MAKE MEDICINE SKILL LEVEL RIGHT NOW?
UM...
WHEN I CHECKED EARLIER, IT WAS LEVEL 8.
THE MAKE MEDICINE SKILL NECESSARY FOR POTIONS GOES UP EVERY TEN LEVELS.
AT LEVEL 8 YOU WOULDN'T BE ABLE TO MAKE MID-GRADE POTIONS.
?
WELL, WHATEVER THE DEAL IS, IT SHOULD BE OKAY, RIGHT?

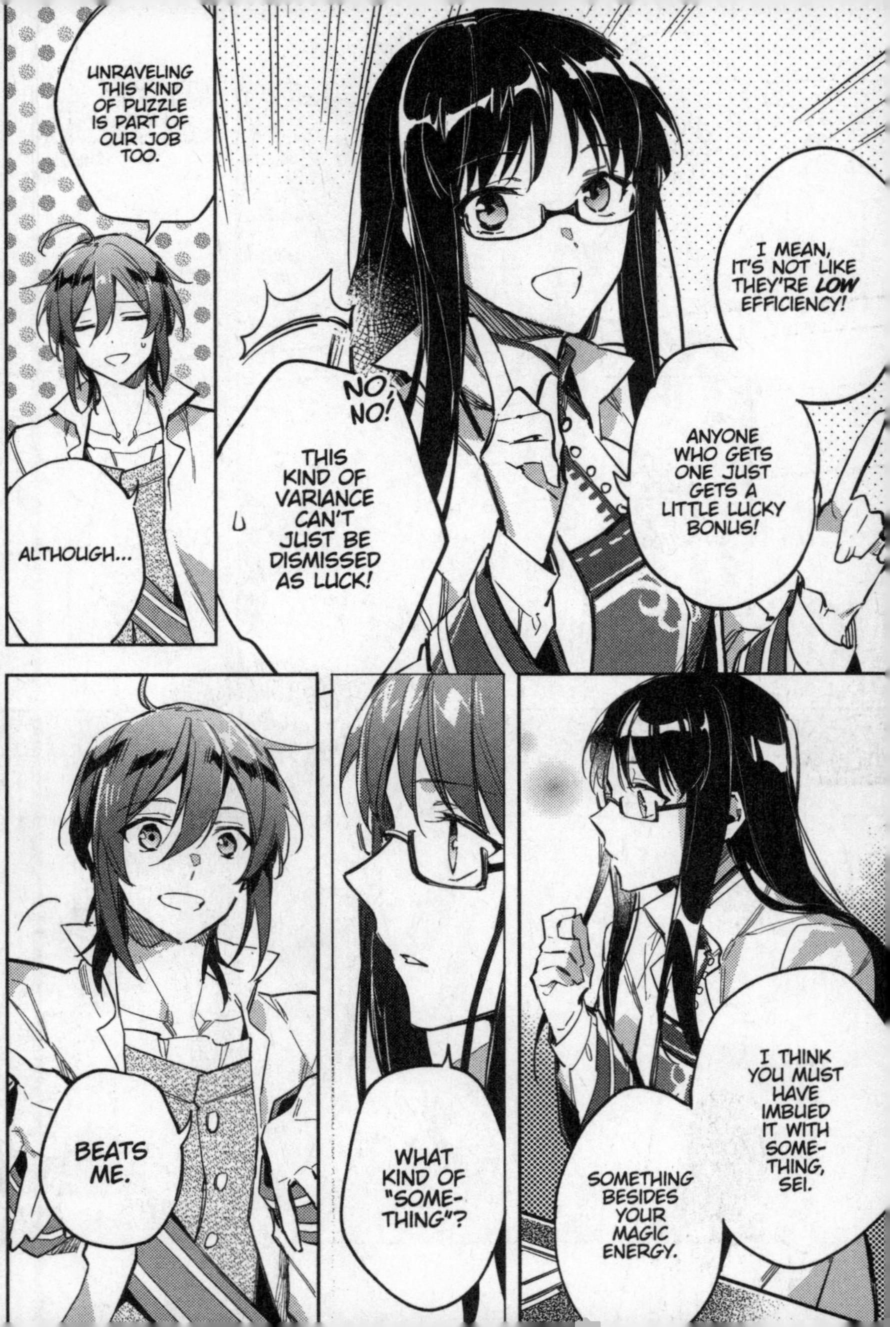
I MEAN, IT'S NOT LIKE THEY'RE ***LOW*** EFFICIENCY!
ANYONE WHO GETS ONE JUST GETS A LITTLE LUCKY BONUS!
NO, NO!
THIS KIND OF VARIANCE CAN'T JUST BE DISMISSED AS LUCK!
UNRAVELING THIS KIND OF PUZZLE IS PART OF OUR JOB TOO.
ALTHOUGH...
I THINK YOU MUST HAVE IMBUED IT WITH SOME-THING, SEI.
SOMETHING BESIDES YOUR MAGIC ENERGY.
WHAT KIND OF "SOME-THING"?
BEATS ME.

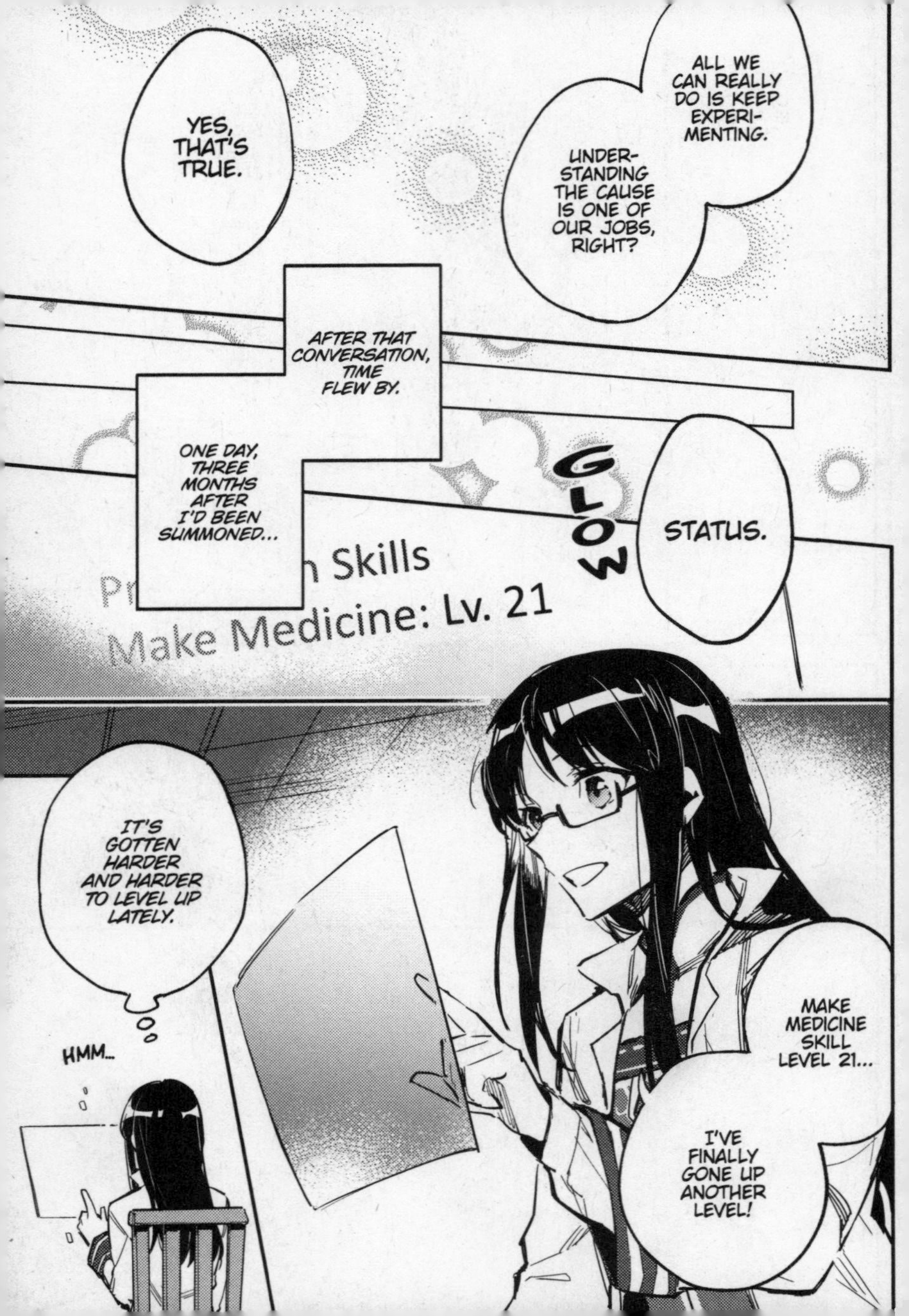
ALL WE CAN REALLY DO IS KEEP EXPERIMENTING.
UNDERSTANDING THE CAUSE IS ONE OF OUR JOBS, RIGHT?
YES, THAT'S TRUE.
AFTER THAT CONVERSATION, TIME FLEW BY.
ONE DAY, THREE MONTHS AFTER I'D BEEN SUMMONED...
STATUS.
GLOW
Make Medicine: Lv. 21
MAKE MEDICINE SKILL LEVEL 21...
I'VE FINALLY GONE UP ANOTHER LEVEL!
IT'S GOTTEN HARDER AND HARDER TO LEVEL UP LATELY.
HMM...

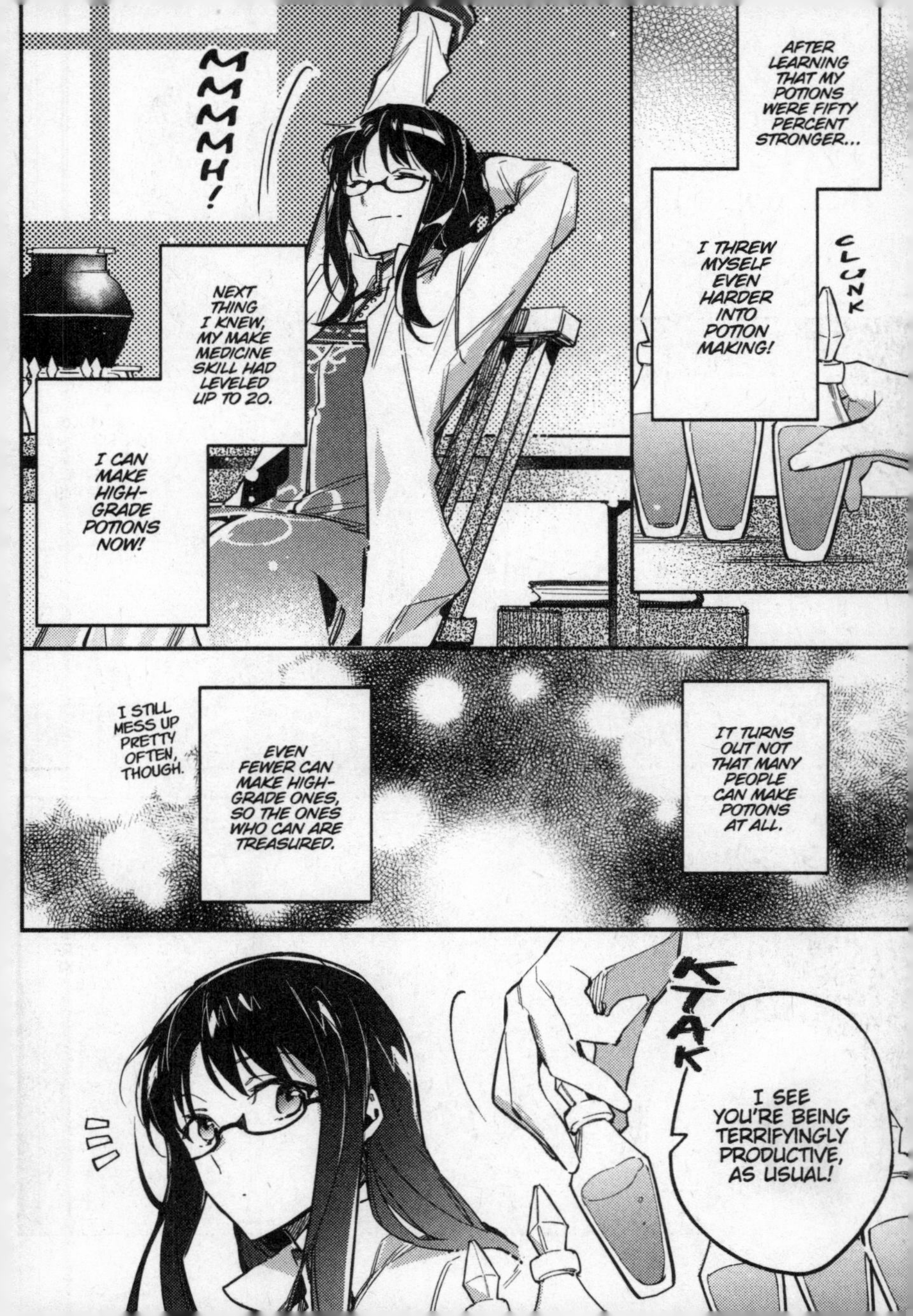
AFTER LEARNING THAT MY POTIONS WERE FIFTY PERCENT STRONGER...
I THREW MYSELF EVEN HARDER INTO POTION MAKING!
CLUNK
MMMMMH!
NEXT THING I KNEW, MY MAKE MEDICINE SKILL HAD LEVELED UP TO 20.
I CAN MAKE HIGH-GRADE POTIONS NOW!
IT TURNS OUT NOT THAT MANY PEOPLE CAN MAKE POTIONS AT ALL.
EVEN FEWER CAN MAKE HIGH-GRADE ONES, SO THE ONES WHO CAN ARE TREASURED.
I STILL MESS UP PRETTY OFTEN, THOUGH.
KTAK
I SEE YOU'RE BEING TERRIFYINGLY PRODUCTIVE, AS USUAL!

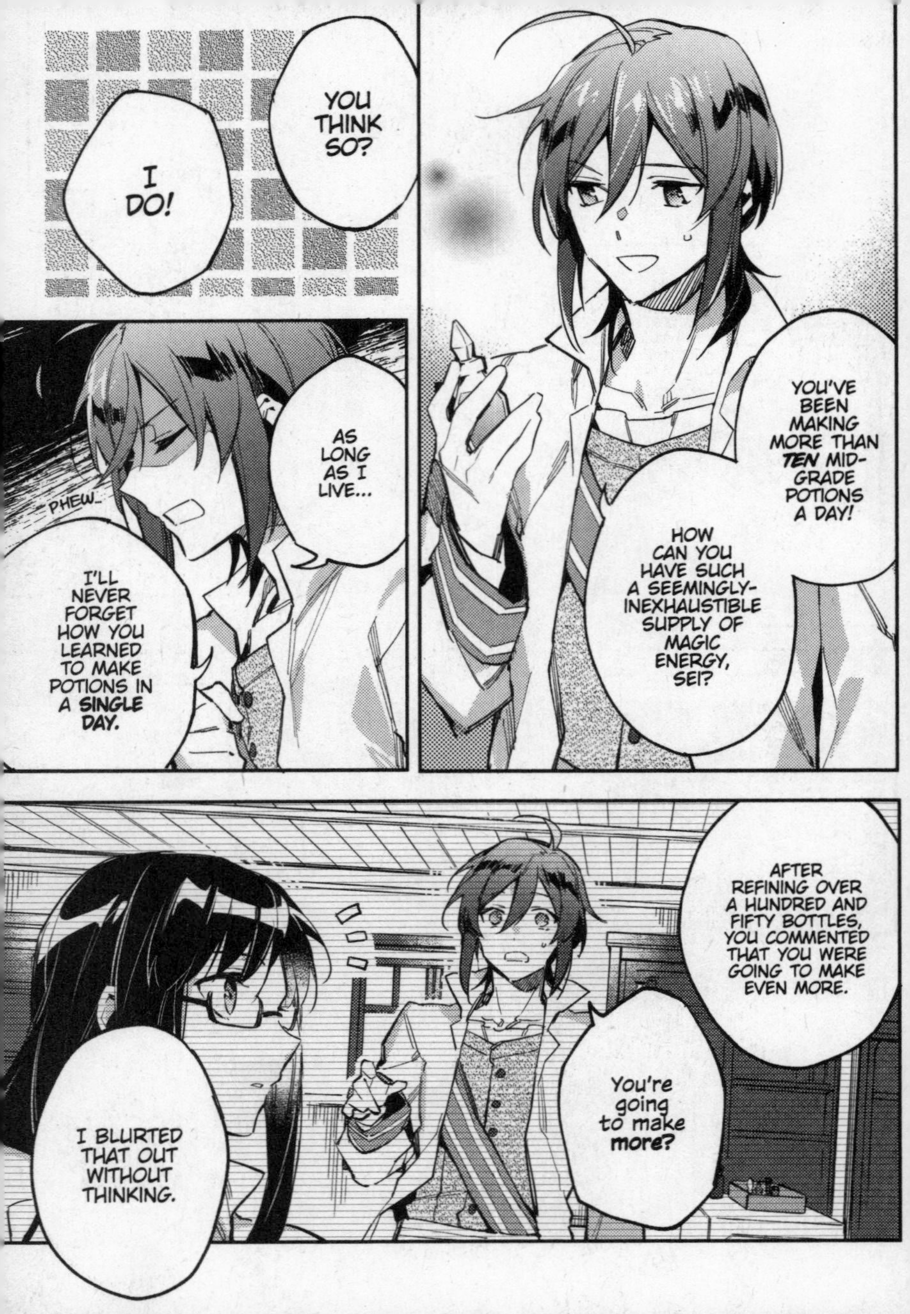
YOU'VE BEEN MAKING MORE THAN TEN MID-GRADE POTIONS A DAY!
HOW CAN YOU HAVE SUCH A SEEMINGLY-INEXHAUSTIBLE SUPPLY OF MAGIC ENERGY, SEI?
YOU THINK SO?
I DO!
AS LONG AS I LIVE...
PHEW...
I'LL NEVER FORGET HOW YOU LEARNED TO MAKE POTIONS IN A SINGLE DAY.
AFTER REFINING OVER A HUNDRED AND FIFTY BOTTLES, YOU COMMENTED THAT YOU WERE GOING TO MAKE EVEN MORE.
You're going to make more?
I BLURTED THAT OUT WITHOUT THINKING.

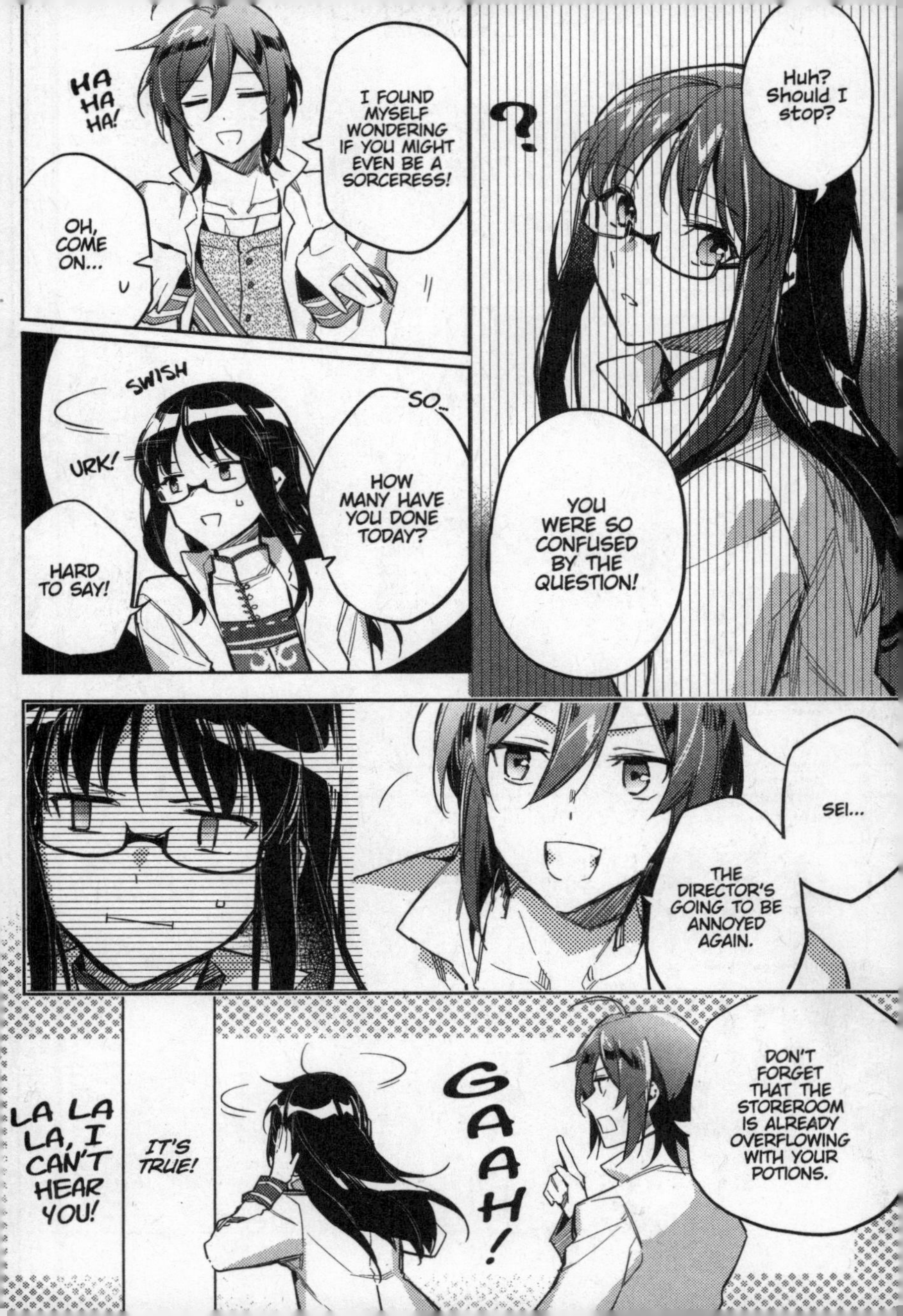
Huh? Should I stop?
?
YOU WERE SO CONFUSED BY THE QUESTION!
I FOUND MYSELF WONDERING IF YOU MIGHT EVEN BE A SORCERESS!
HA HA HA!
OH, COME ON...
SO...
HOW MANY HAVE YOU DONE TODAY?
SWISH
URK!
HARD TO SAY!
SEI...
THE DIRECTOR'S GOING TO BE ANNOYED AGAIN.
DON'T FORGET THAT THE STOREROOM IS ALREADY OVERFLOWING WITH YOUR POTIONS.
GAAH!
IT'S TRUE!
LA LA LA, I CAN'T HEAR YOU!

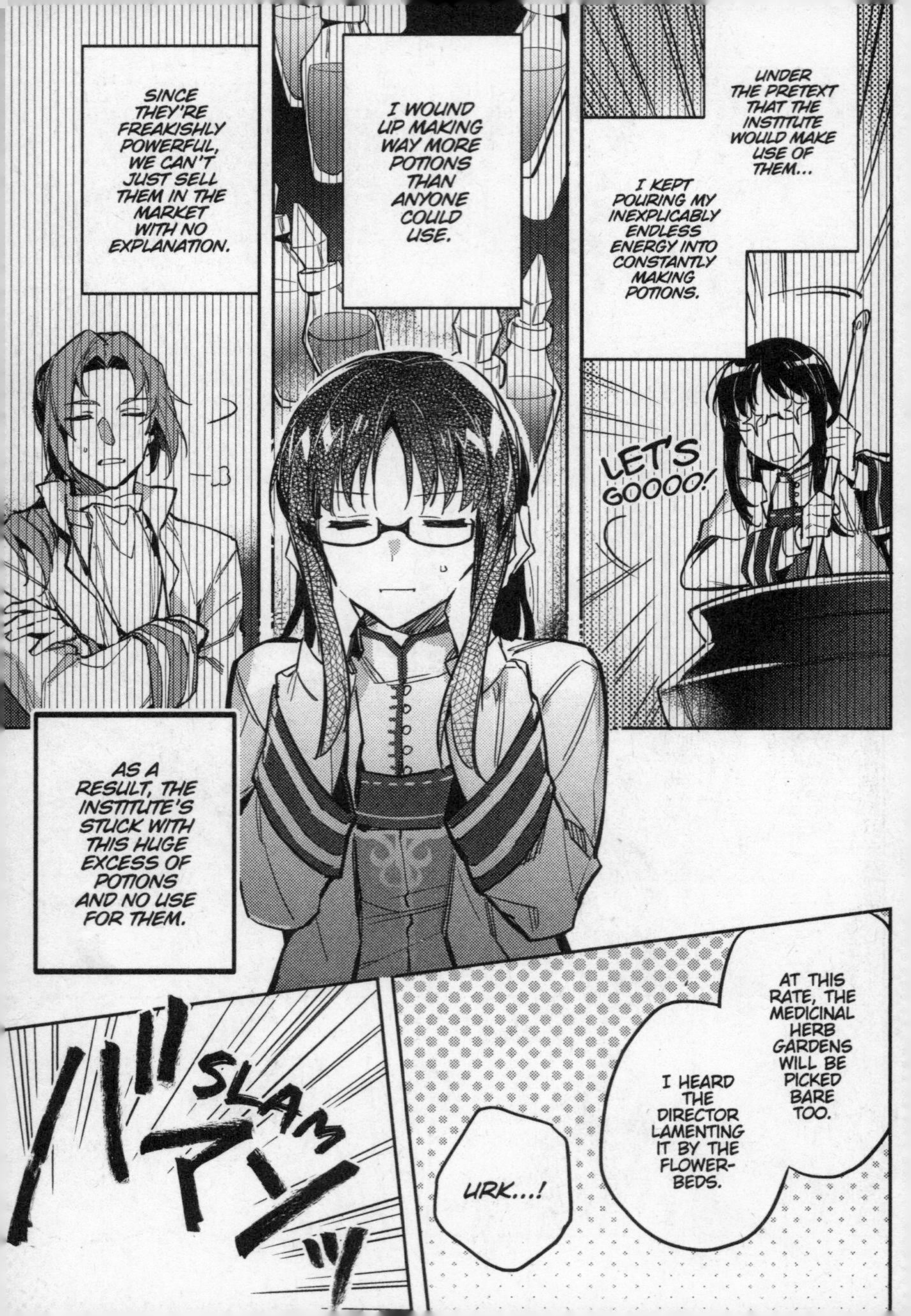
UNDER THE PRETEXT THAT THE INSTITUTE WOULD MAKE USE OF THEM...
I KEPT POURING MY INEXPLICABLY ENDLESS ENERGY INTO CONSTANTLY MAKING POTIONS.
LET'S GOOOO!
I WOUND UP MAKING WAY MORE POTIONS THAN ANYONE COULD USE.
SINCE THEY'RE FREAKISHLY POWERFUL, WE CAN'T JUST SELL THEM IN THE MARKET WITH NO EXPLANATION.
AS A RESULT, THE INSTITUTE'S STUCK WITH THIS HUGE EXCESS OF POTIONS AND NO USE FOR THEM.
AT THIS RATE, THE MEDICINAL HERB GARDENS WILL BE PICKED BARE TOO.
I HEARD THE DIRECTOR LAMENTING IT BY THE FLOWER-BEDS.
URK...!
SLAM

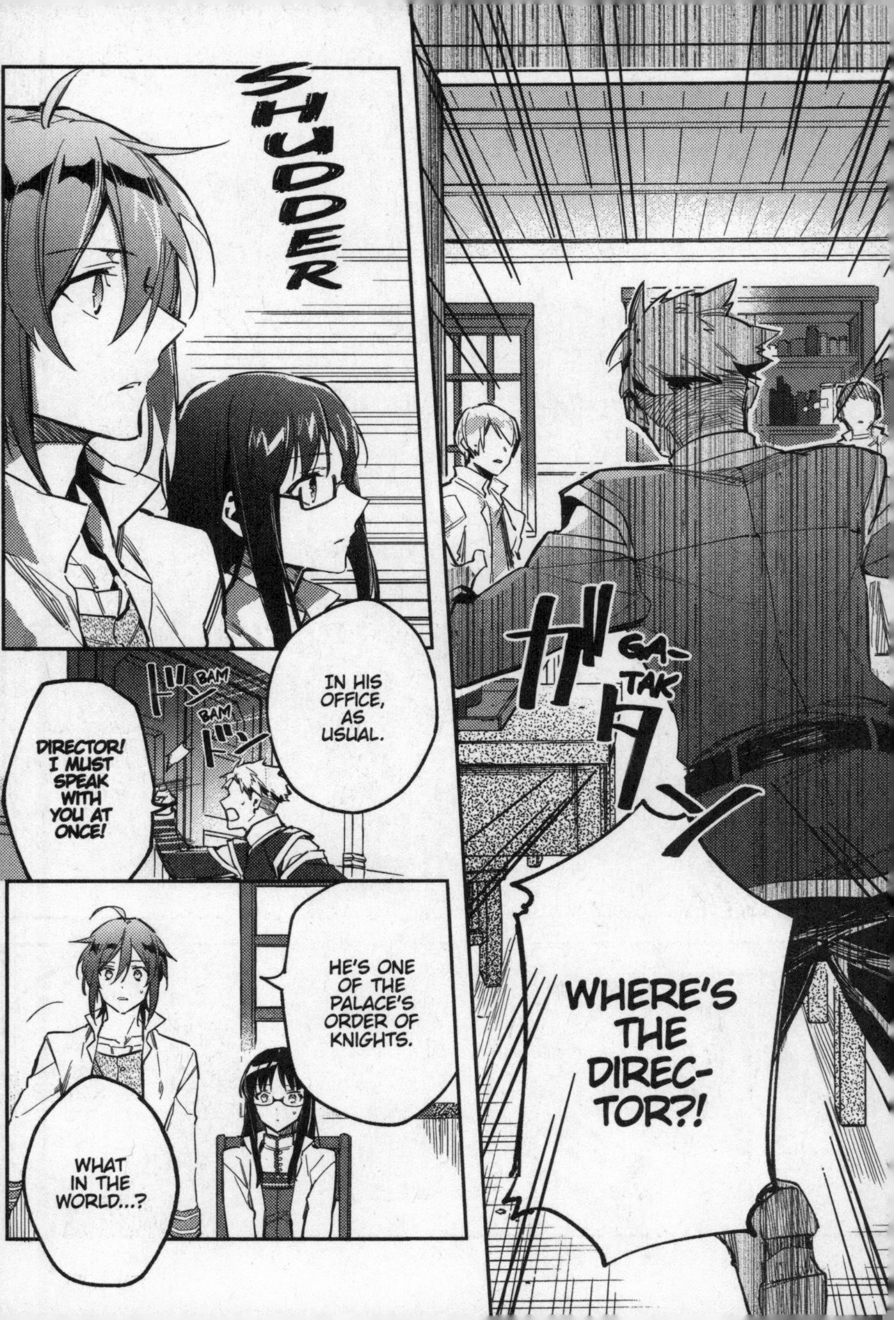
GA-TAK
WHERE'S THE DIREC-TOR?!
SHUDDER
IN HIS OFFICE, AS USUAL.
BAM BAM
DIRECTOR! I MUST SPEAK WITH YOU AT ONCE!
HE'S ONE OF THE PALACE'S ORDER OF KNIGHTS.
WHAT IN THE WORLD...?

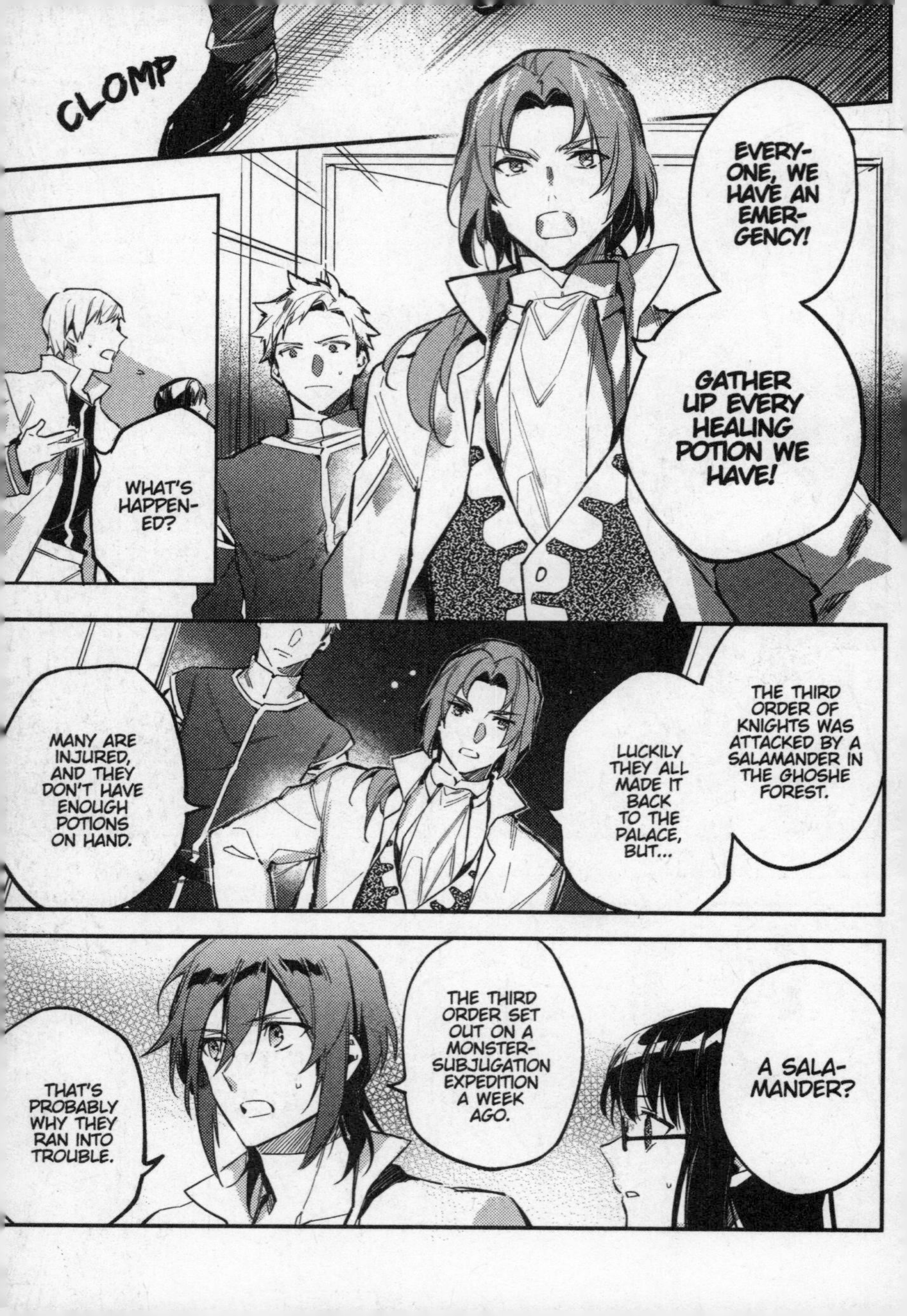
CLOMP
EVERYONE, WE HAVE AN EMERGENCY!
GATHER UP EVERY HEALING POTION WE HAVE!
WHAT'S HAPPENED?
THE THIRD ORDER OF KNIGHTS WAS ATTACKED BY A SALAMANDER IN THE GHOSHE FOREST.
LUCKILY THEY ALL MADE IT BACK TO THE PALACE, BUT...
MANY ARE INJURED, AND THEY DON'T HAVE ENOUGH POTIONS ON HAND.
A SALAMANDER?
THE THIRD ORDER SET OUT ON A MONSTER-SUBJUGATION EXPEDITION A WEEK AGO.
THAT'S PROBABLY WHY THEY RAN INTO TROUBLE.

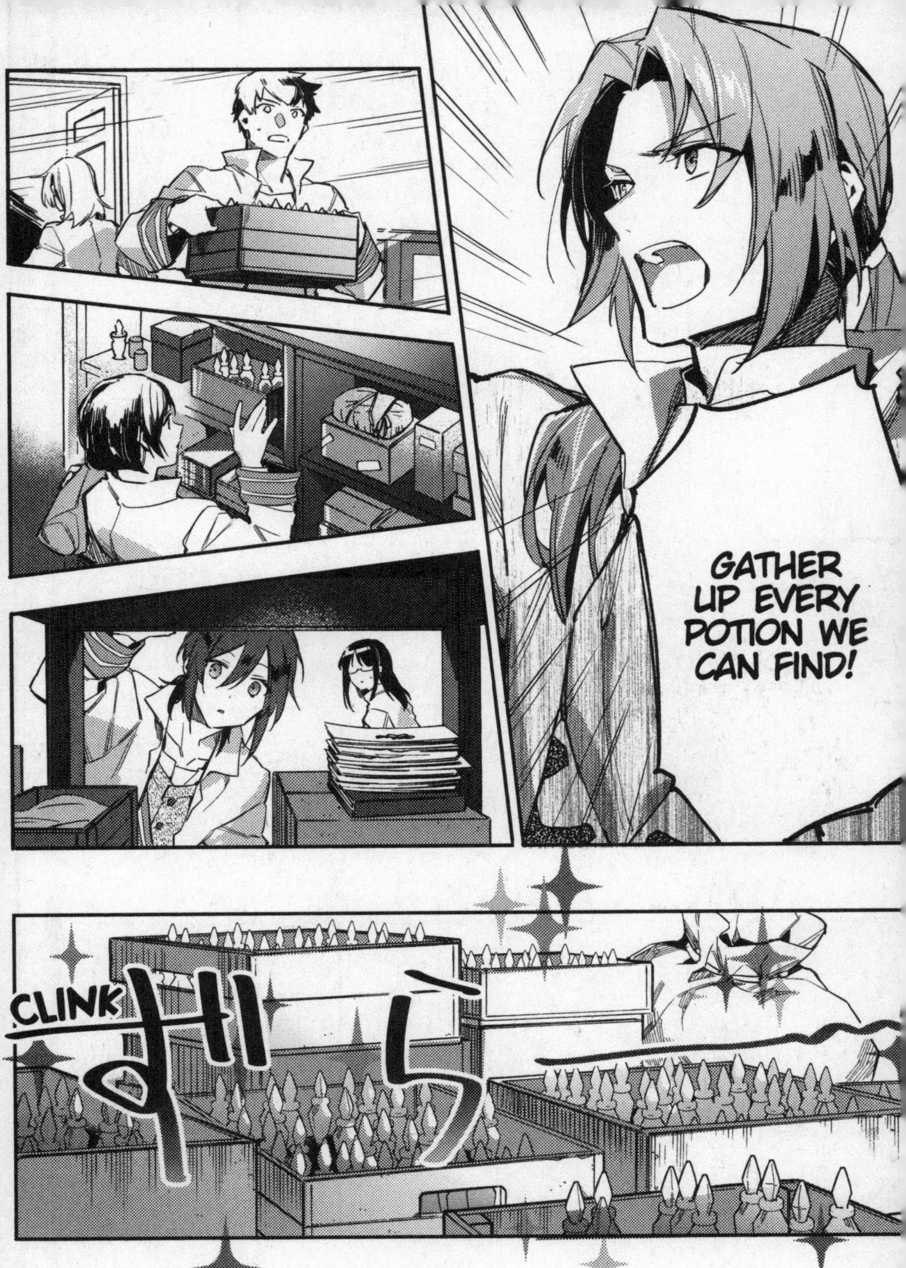
GATHER UP EVERY POTION WE CAN FIND!
CLINK

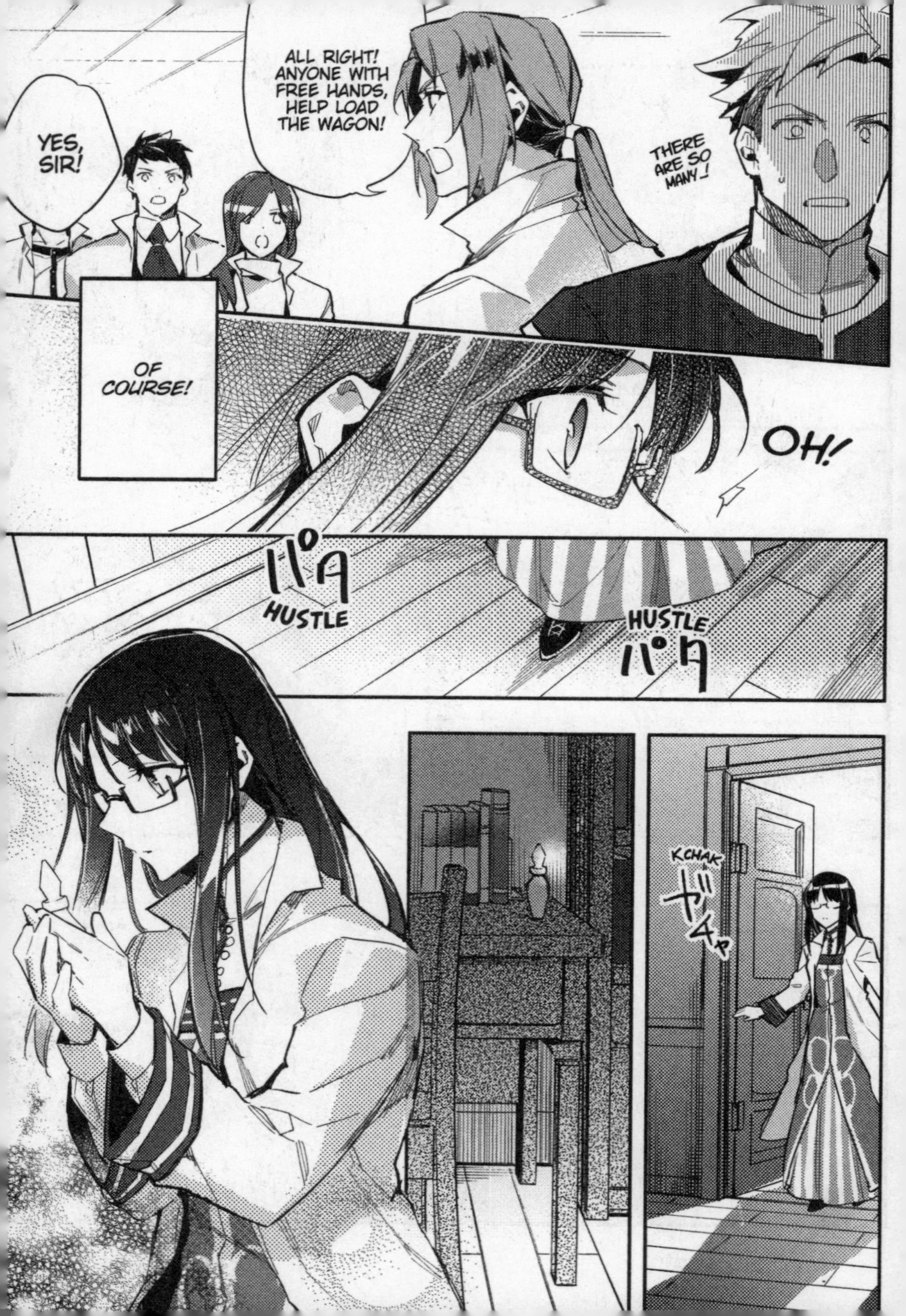
THERE ARE SO MANY...!
ALL RIGHT! ANYONE WITH FREE HANDS, HELP LOAD THE WAGON!
YES, SIR!
OH!
OF COURSE!
HUSTLE
パタ
パタ
HUSTLE
KCHAK
ガチャ

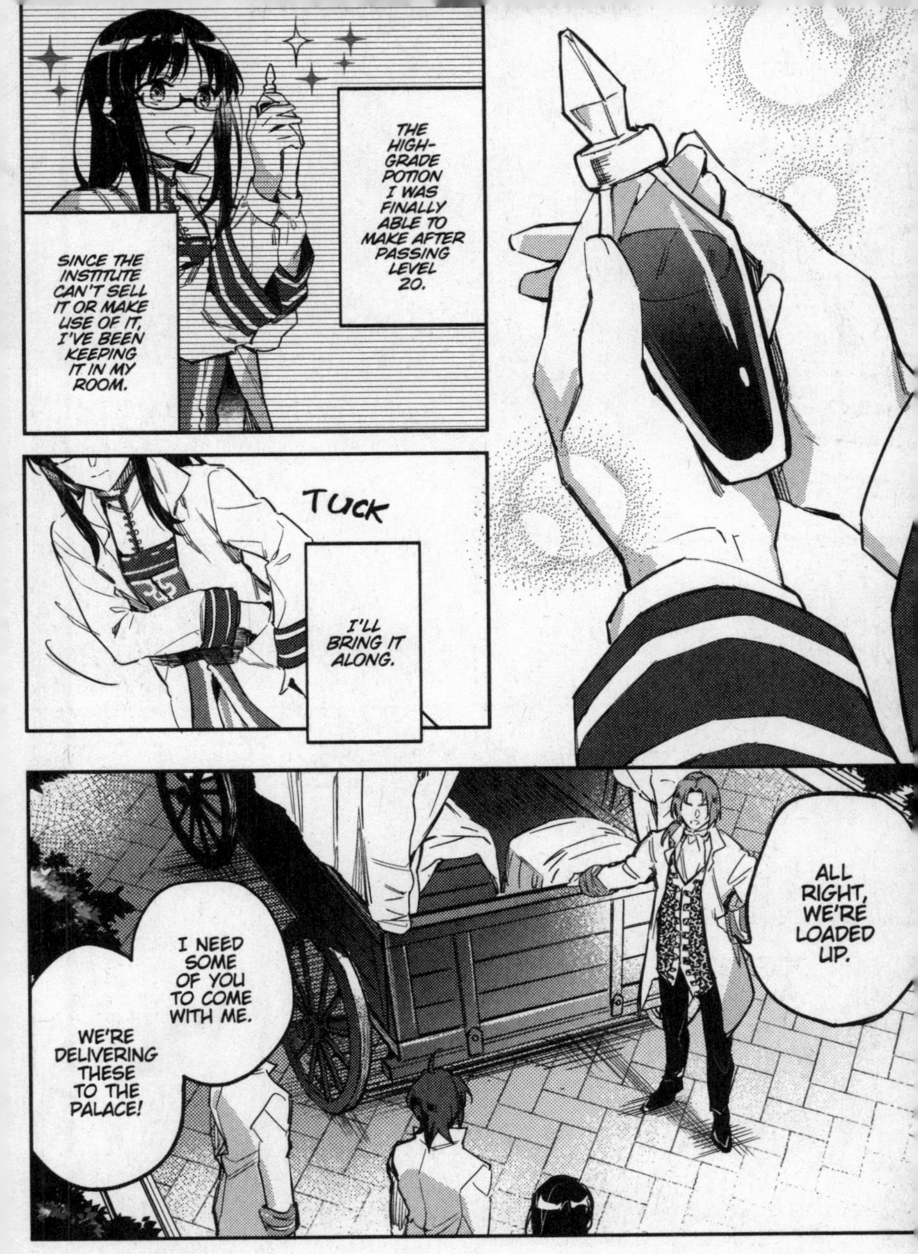
THE HIGH-GRADE POTION I WAS FINALLY ABLE TO MAKE AFTER PASSING LEVEL 20.
SINCE THE INSTITUTE CAN'T SELL IT OR MAKE USE OF IT, I'VE BEEN KEEPING IT IN MY ROOM.
TUCK
I'LL BRING IT ALONG.
ALL RIGHT, WE'RE LOADED UP.
I NEED SOME OF YOU TO COME WITH ME.
WE'RE DELIVERING THESE TO THE PALACE!

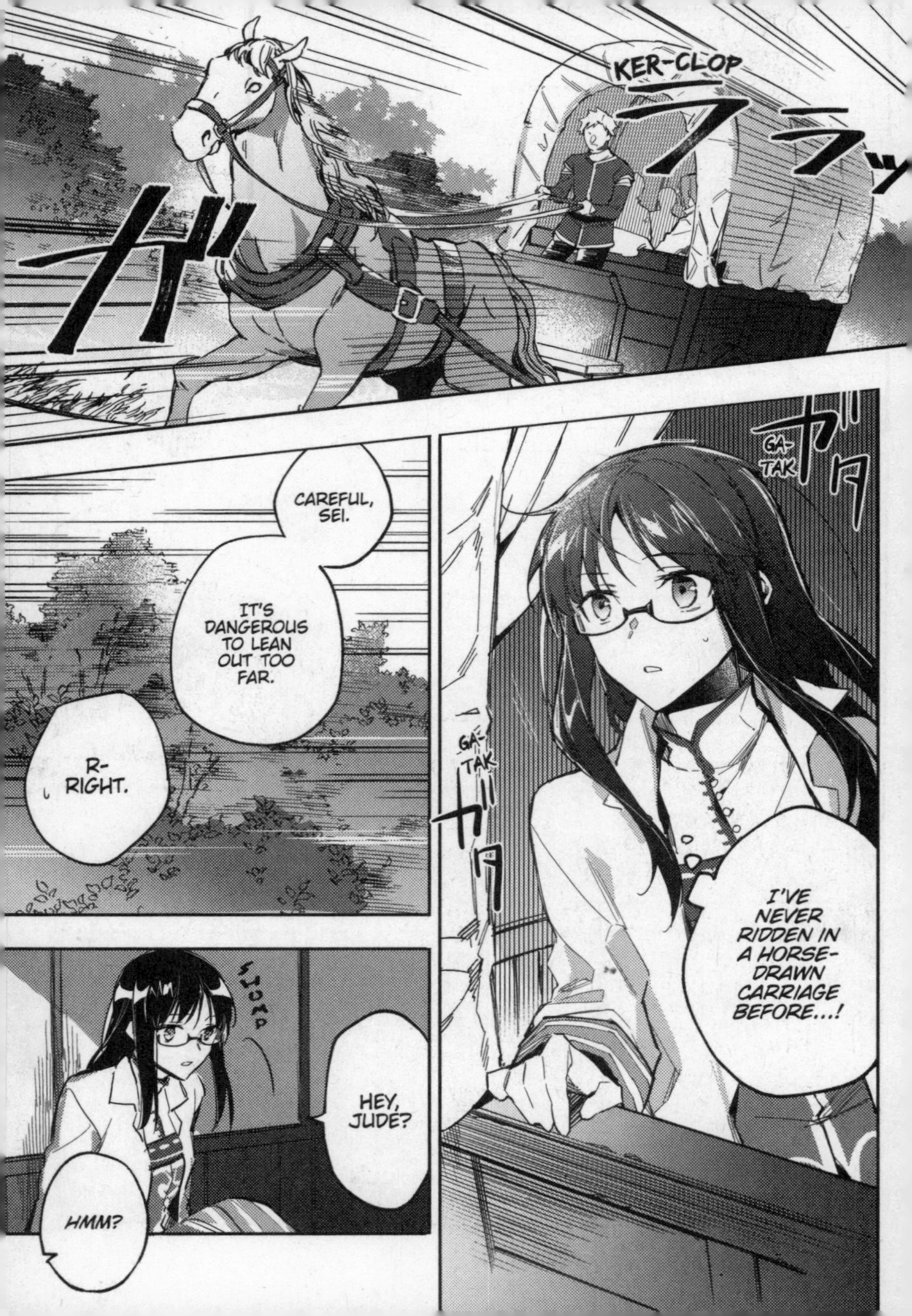
KER-CLOP
GA-TAK
GA-TAK
I'VE NEVER RIDDEN IN A HORSE-DRAWN CARRIAGE BEFORE...!
CAREFUL, SEI.
IT'S DANGEROUS TO LEAN OUT TOO FAR.
R-RIGHT.
HEY, JUDE?
HMM?

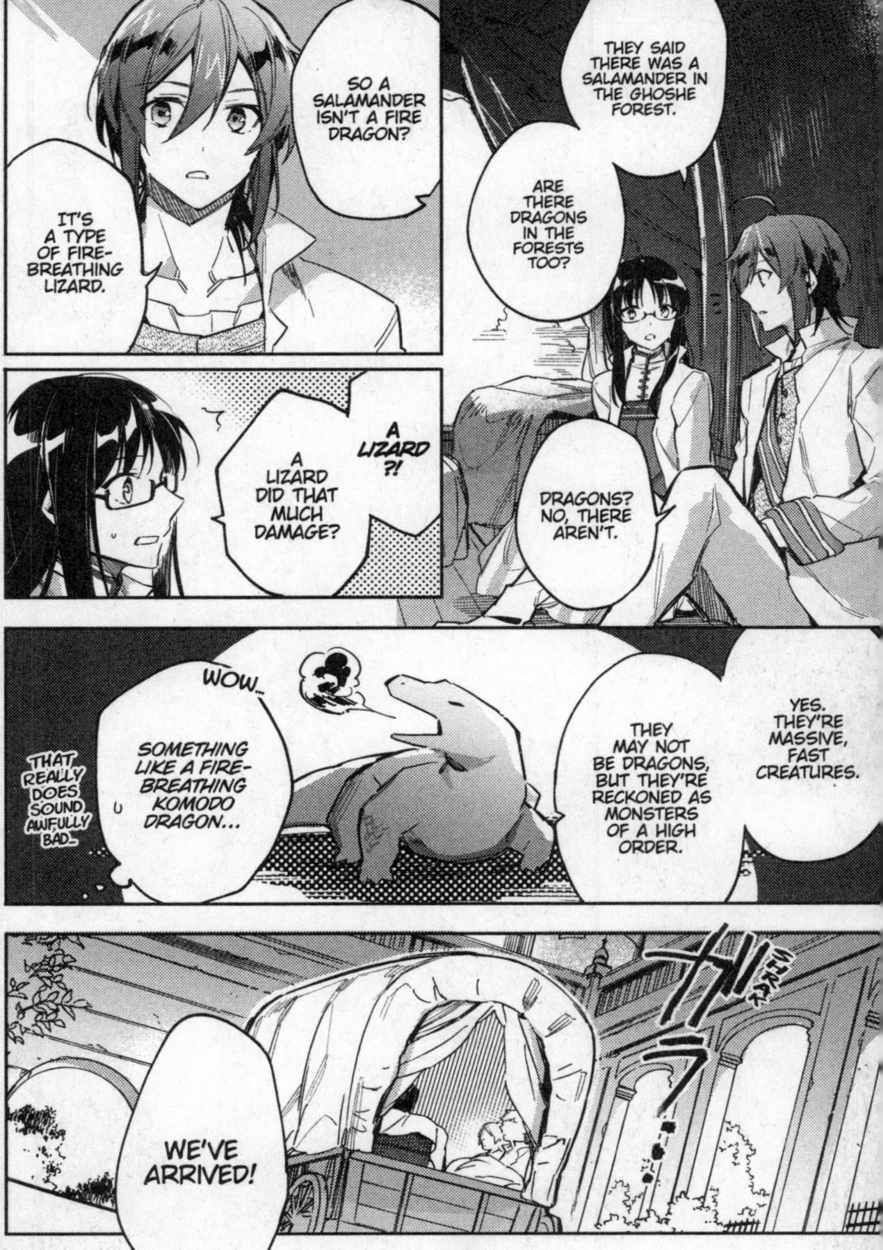
THEY SAID THERE WAS A SALAMANDER IN THE GHOSHE FOREST.
ARE THERE DRAGONS IN THE FORESTS TOO?
DRAGONS? NO, THERE AREN'T.
SO A SALAMANDER ISN'T A FIRE DRAGON?
IT'S A TYPE OF FIRE-BREATHING LIZARD.
A LIZARD?!
A LIZARD DID THAT MUCH DAMAGE?
YES. THEY'RE MASSIVE, FAST CREATURES.
THEY MAY NOT BE DRAGONS, BUT THEY'RE RECKONED AS MONSTERS OF A HIGH ORDER.
WOW...
SOMETHING LIKE A FIRE-BREATHING KOMODO DRAGON...
THAT REALLY DOES SOUND AWFULLY BAD...
SHRAK
WE'VE ARRIVED!

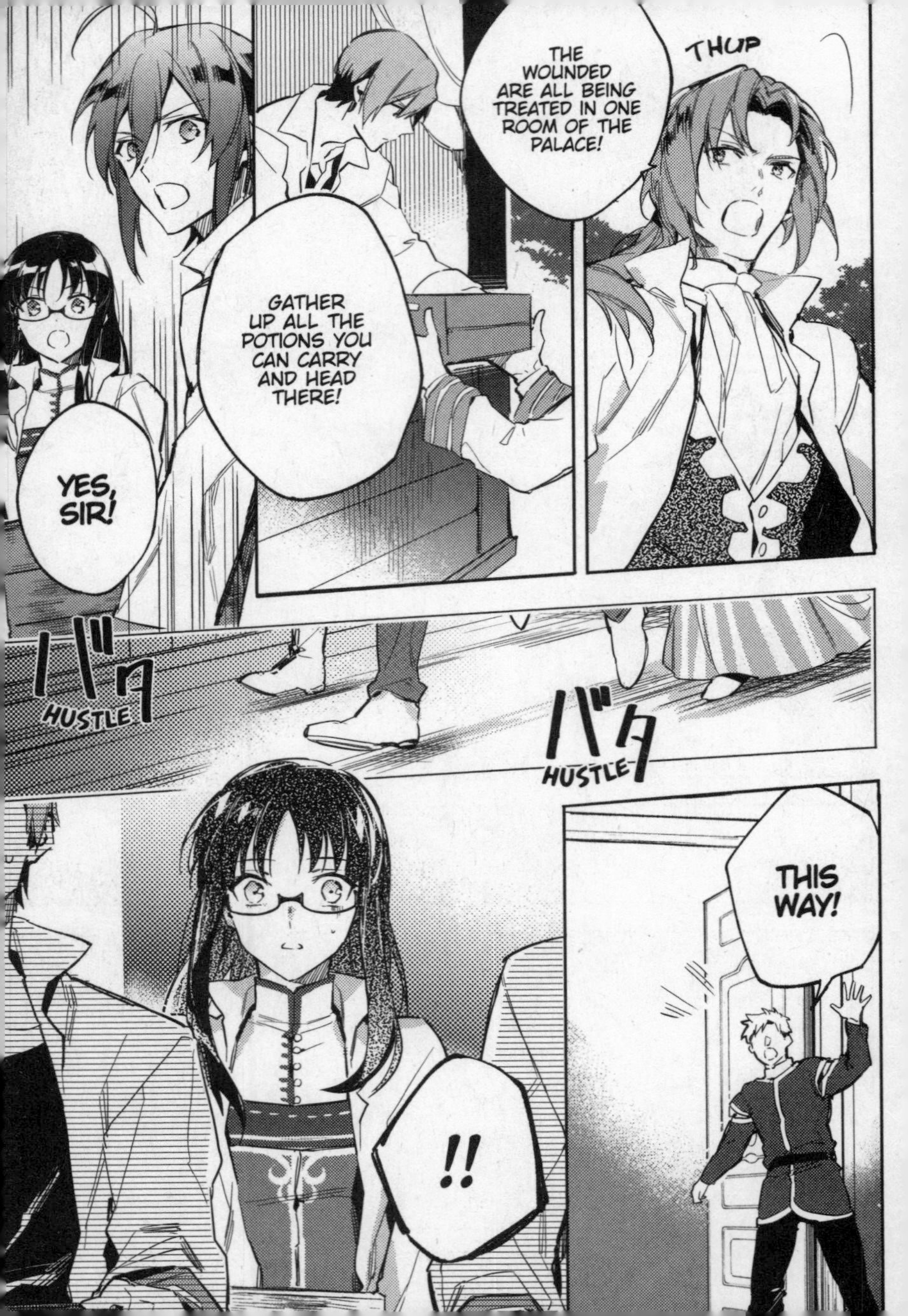
THUP
THE WOUNDED ARE ALL BEING TREATED IN ONE ROOM OF THE PALACE!
GATHER UP ALL THE POTIONS YOU CAN CARRY AND HEAD THERE!
YES, SIR!
バタ
HUSTLE
バタ
HUSTLE
THIS WAY!
!!

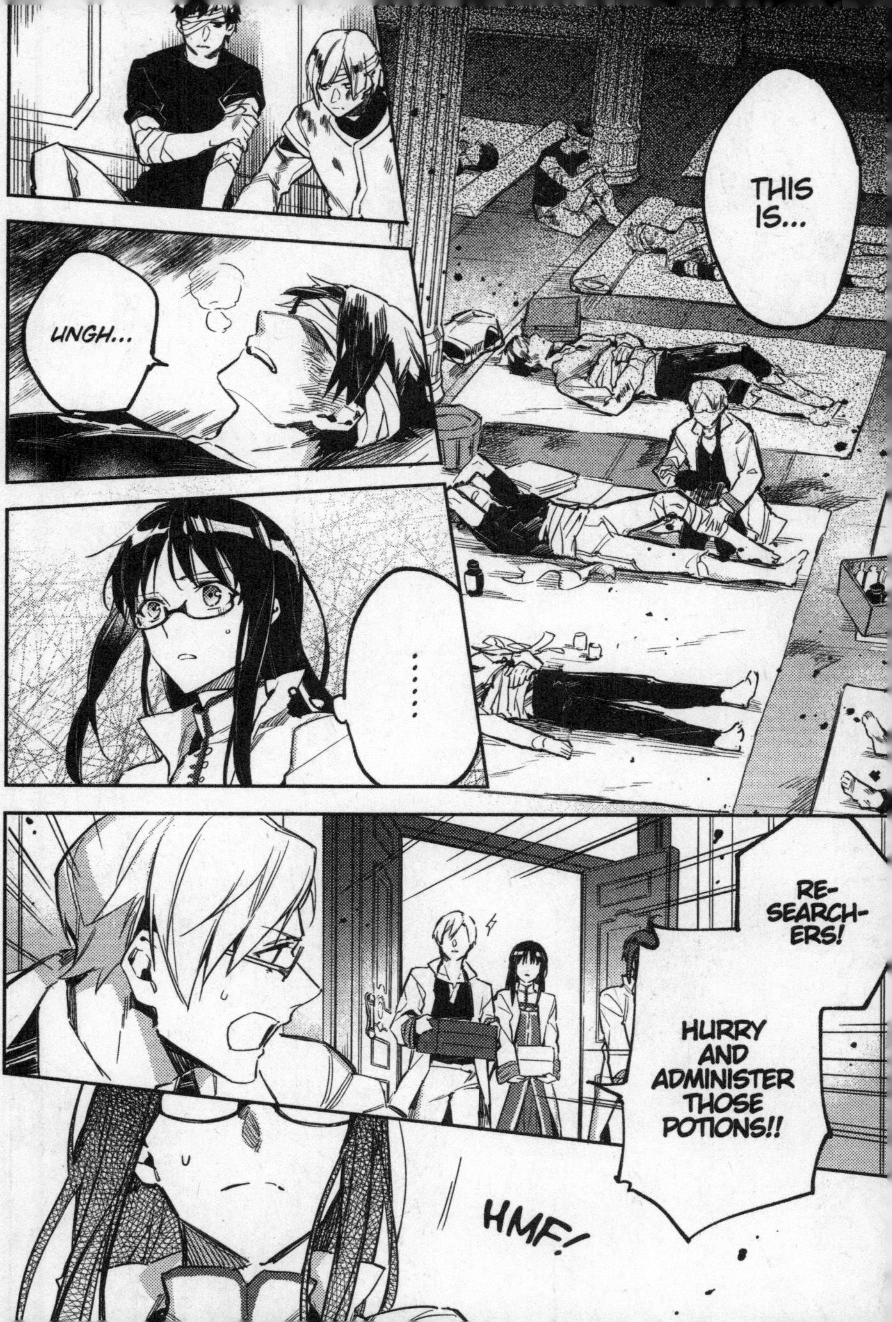
THIS IS...
UNGH...
......
RE-SEARCHERS!
HURRY AND ADMINISTER THOSE POTIONS!!
HMF!

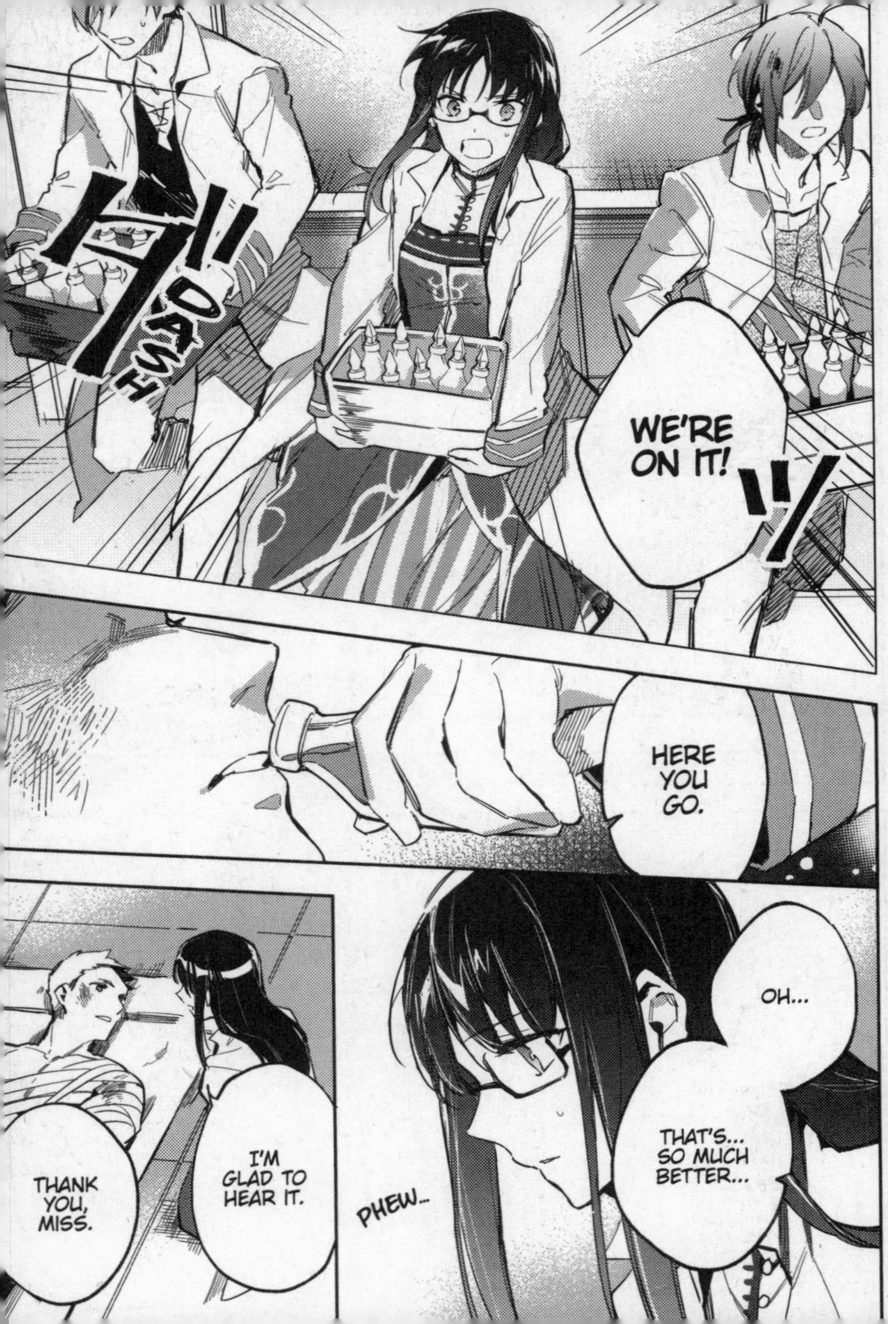
WE'RE ON IT!
DASH
HERE YOU GO.
OH...
THAT'S... SO MUCH BETTER...
PHEW...
I'M GLAD TO HEAR IT.
THANK YOU, MISS.

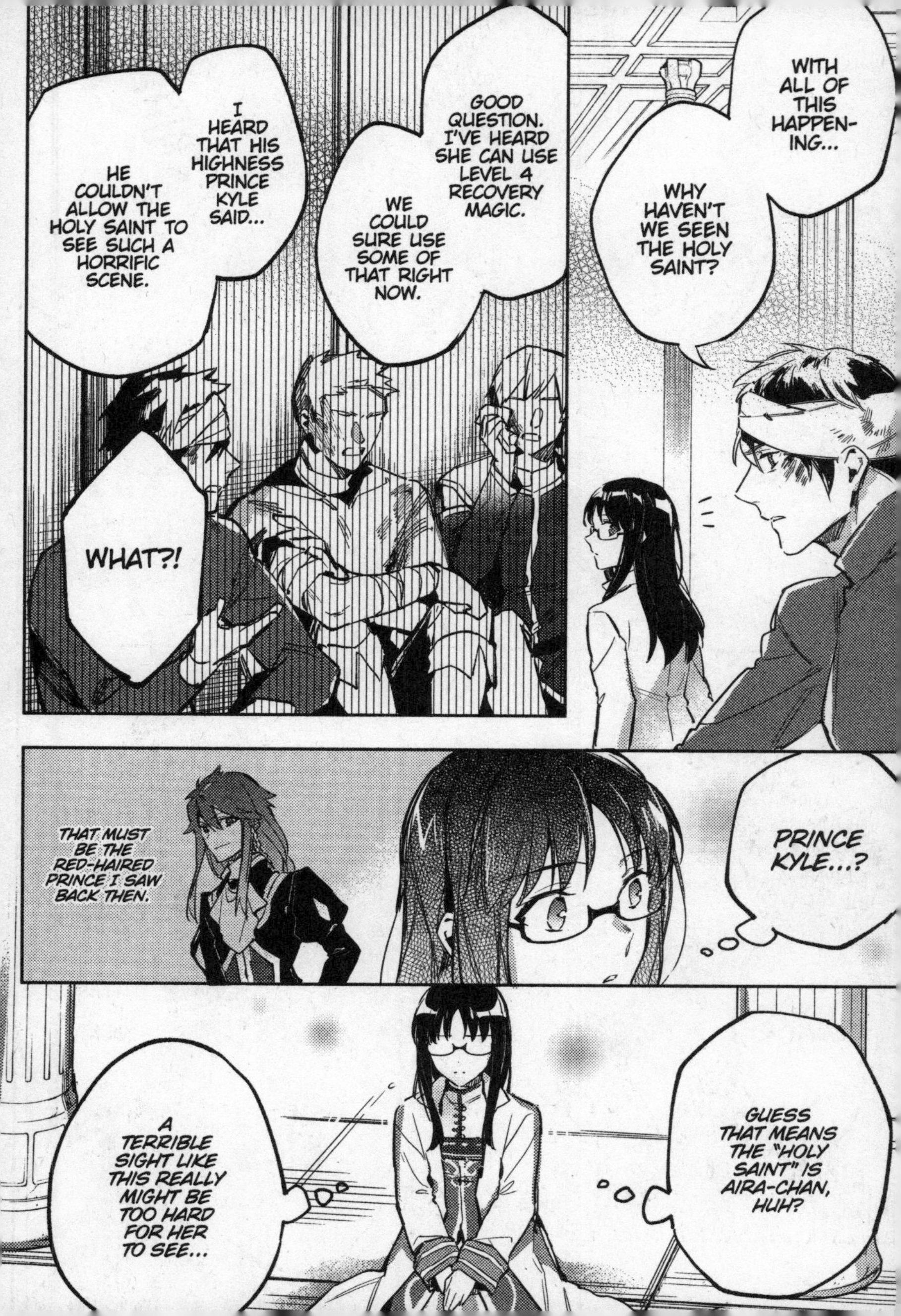
WITH ALL OF THIS HAPPENING...
WHY HAVEN'T WE SEEN THE HOLY SAINT?
GOOD QUESTION. I'VE HEARD SHE CAN USE LEVEL 4 RECOVERY MAGIC.
WE COULD SURE USE SOME OF THAT RIGHT NOW.
I HEARD THAT HIS HIGHNESS PRINCE KYLE SAID...
HE COULDN'T ALLOW THE HOLY SAINT TO SEE SUCH A HORRIFIC SCENE.
WHAT?!
PRINCE KYLE...?
THAT MUST BE THE RED-HAIRED PRINCE I SAW BACK THEN.
GUESS THAT MEANS THE "HOLY SAINT" IS AIRA-CHAN, HUH?
A TERRIBLE SIGHT LIKE THIS REALLY MIGHT BE TOO HARD FOR HER TO SEE...

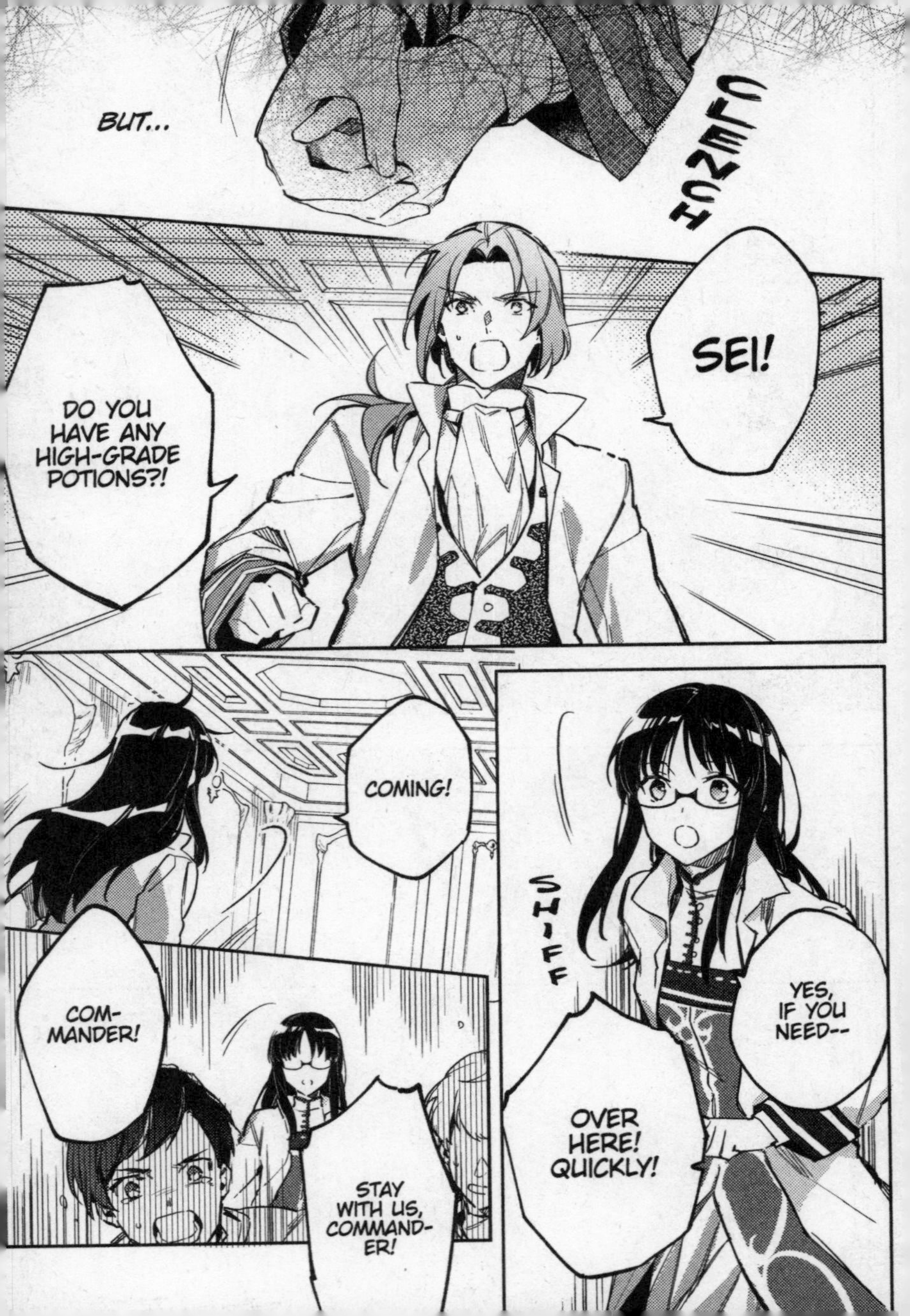

CLENCH
BUT...
SEI!
DO YOU HAVE ANY HIGH-GRADE POTIONS?!
YES, IF YOU NEED--
SHIFF
COMING!
OVER HERE! QUICKLY!
STAY WITH US, COMMANDER-ER!
COM-MANDER!

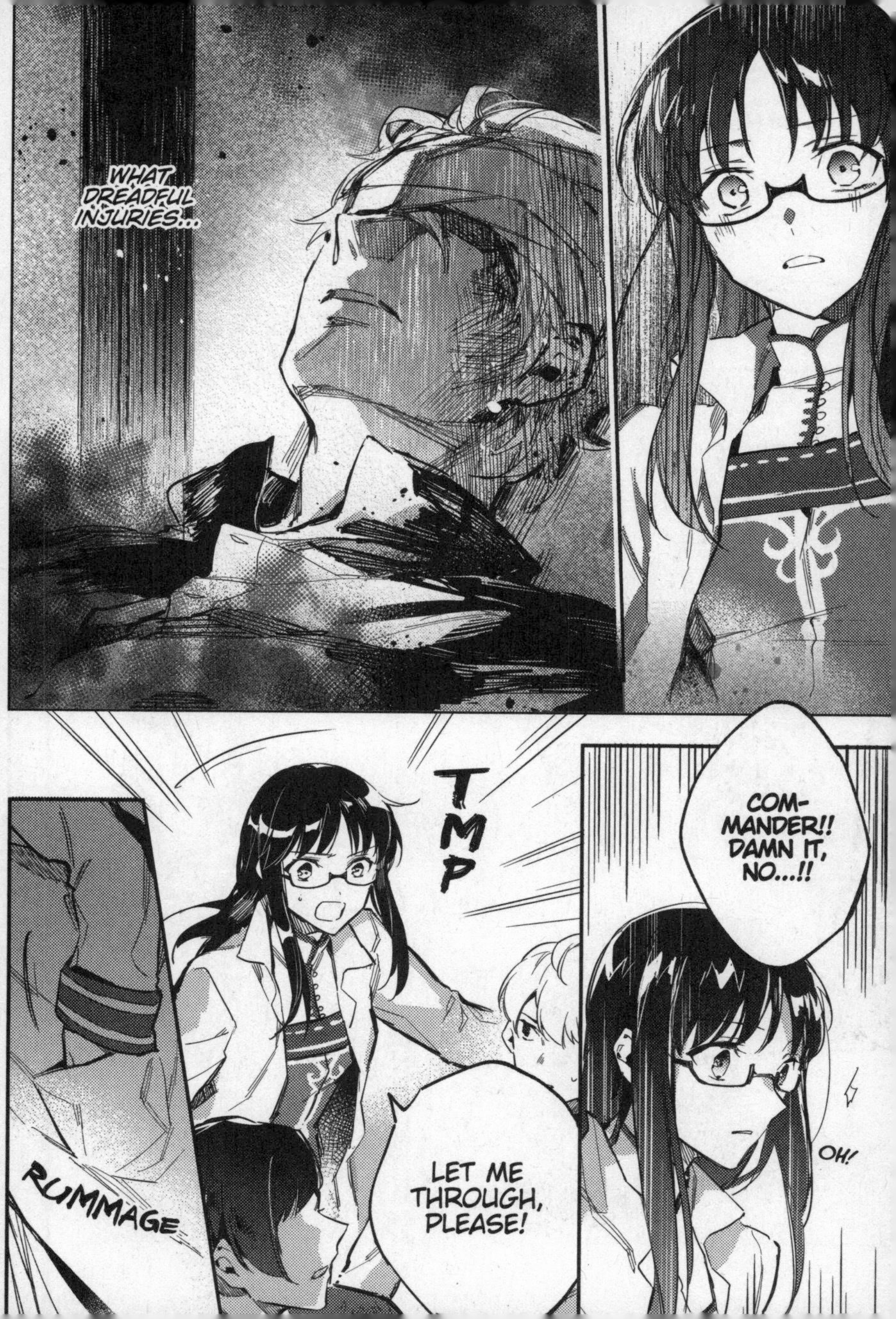
WHAT DREADFUL INJURIES...
COM-MANDER!! DAMN IT, NO...!!
OH!
TMP
LET ME THROUGH, PLEASE!
RUMMAGE

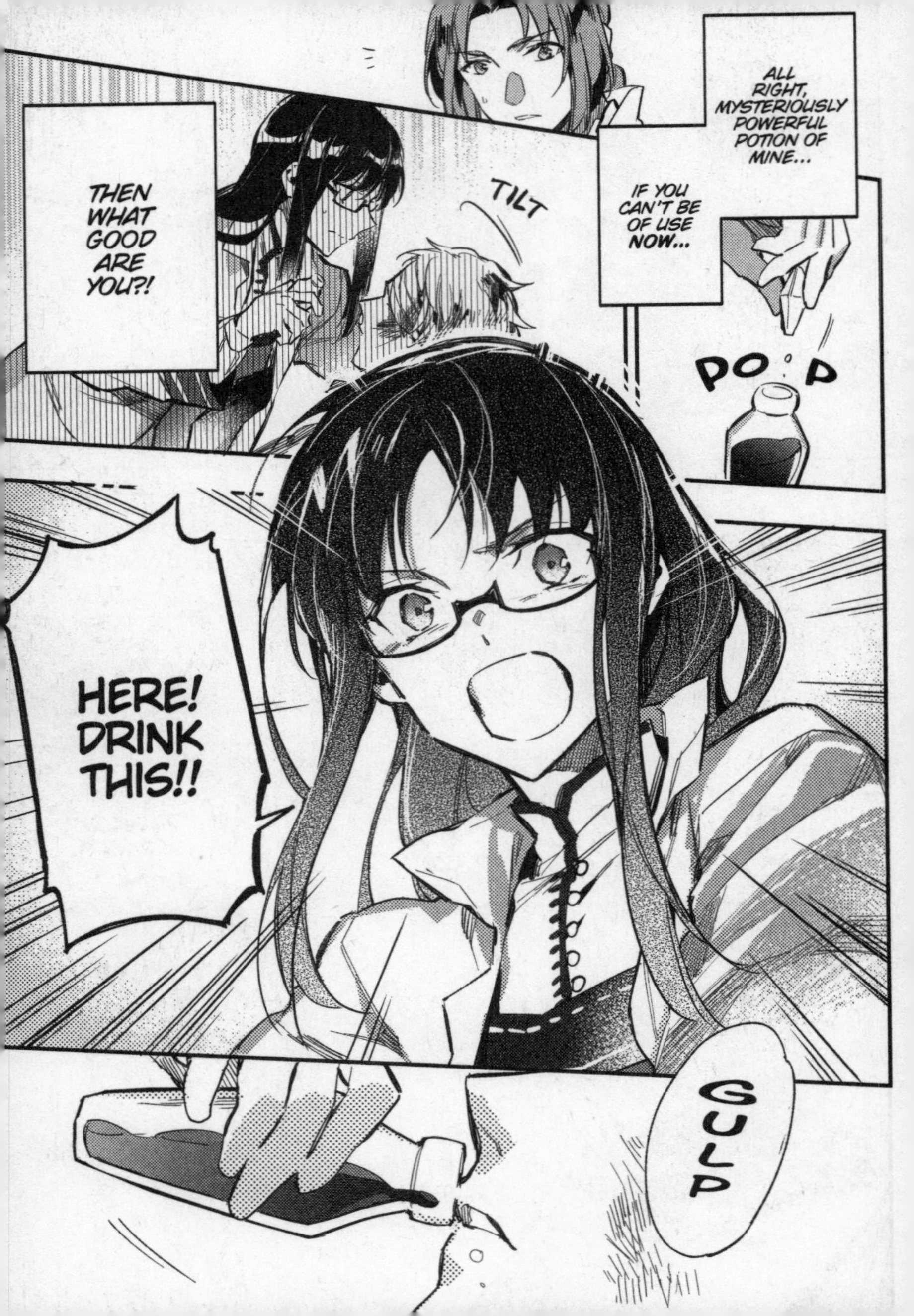
ALL RIGHT, MYSTERIOUSLY POWERFUL POTION OF MINE...
IF YOU CAN'T BE OF USE NOW...
POP
TILT
THEN WHAT GOOD ARE YOU?!
HERE! DRINK THIS!!
GULP

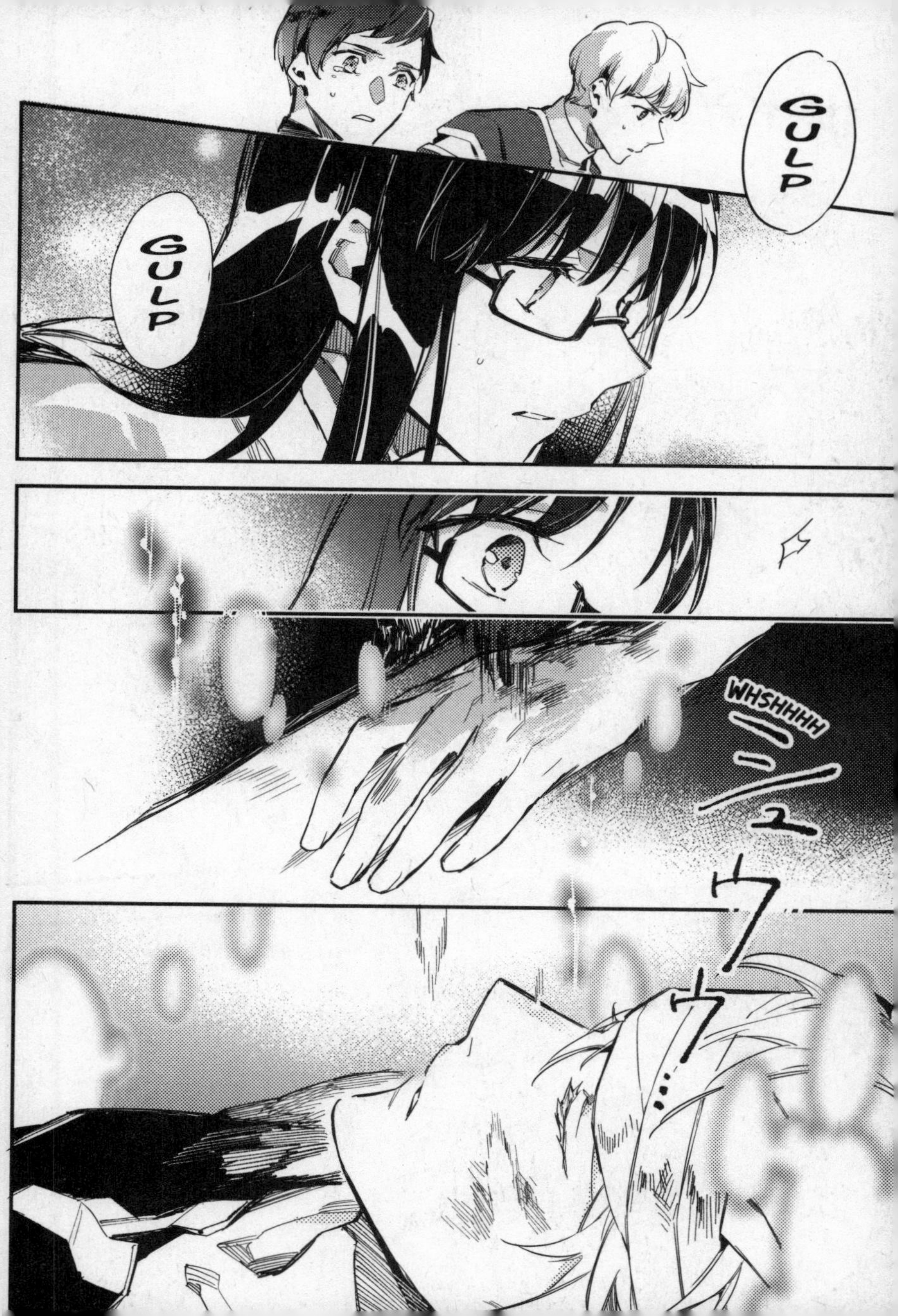
GULP
GULP
WHSHHHH

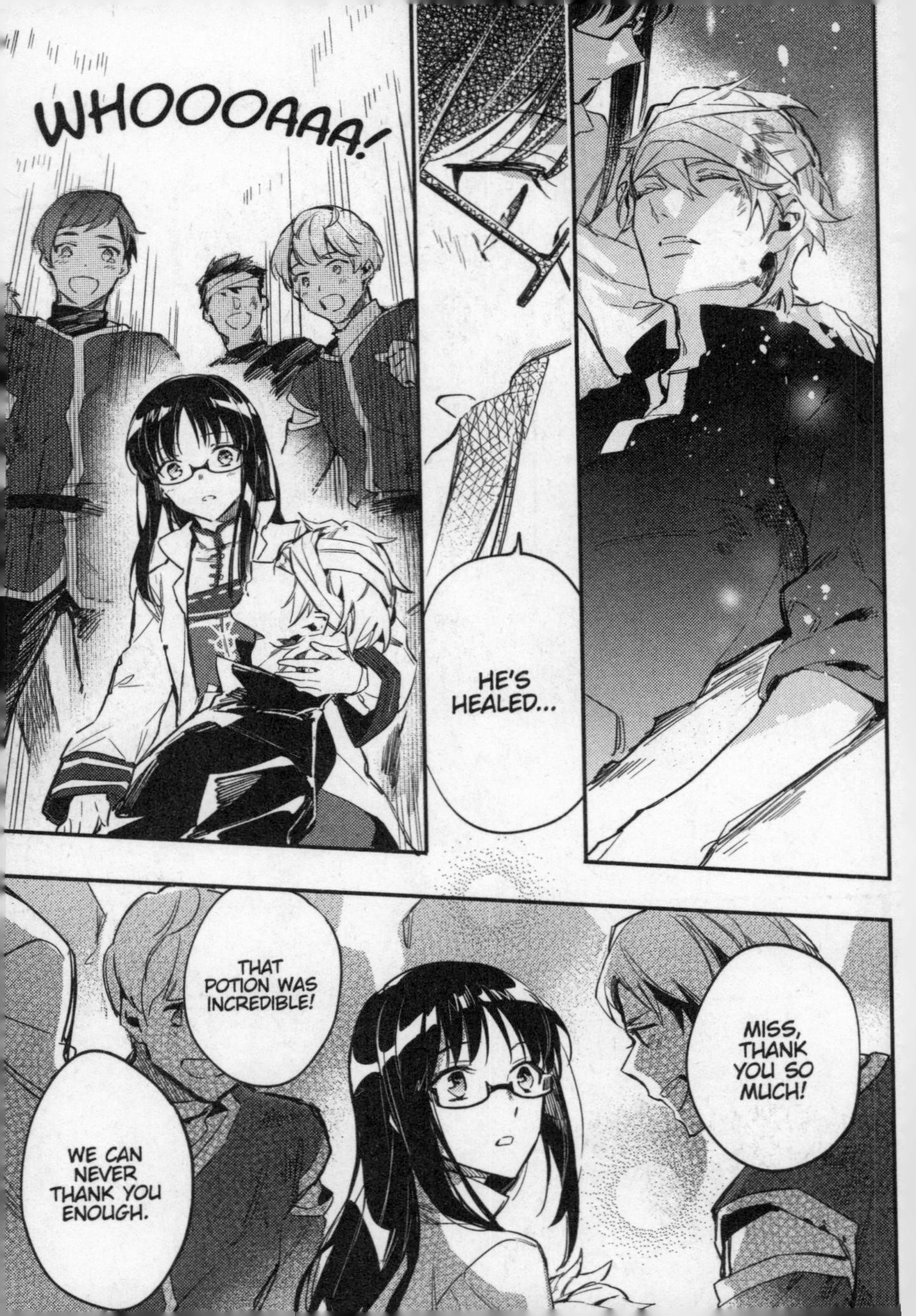
HE'S HEALED...
WHOOOAAA!
MISS, THANK YOU SO MUCH!
THAT POTION WAS INCREDIBLE!
WE CAN NEVER THANK YOU ENOUGH.

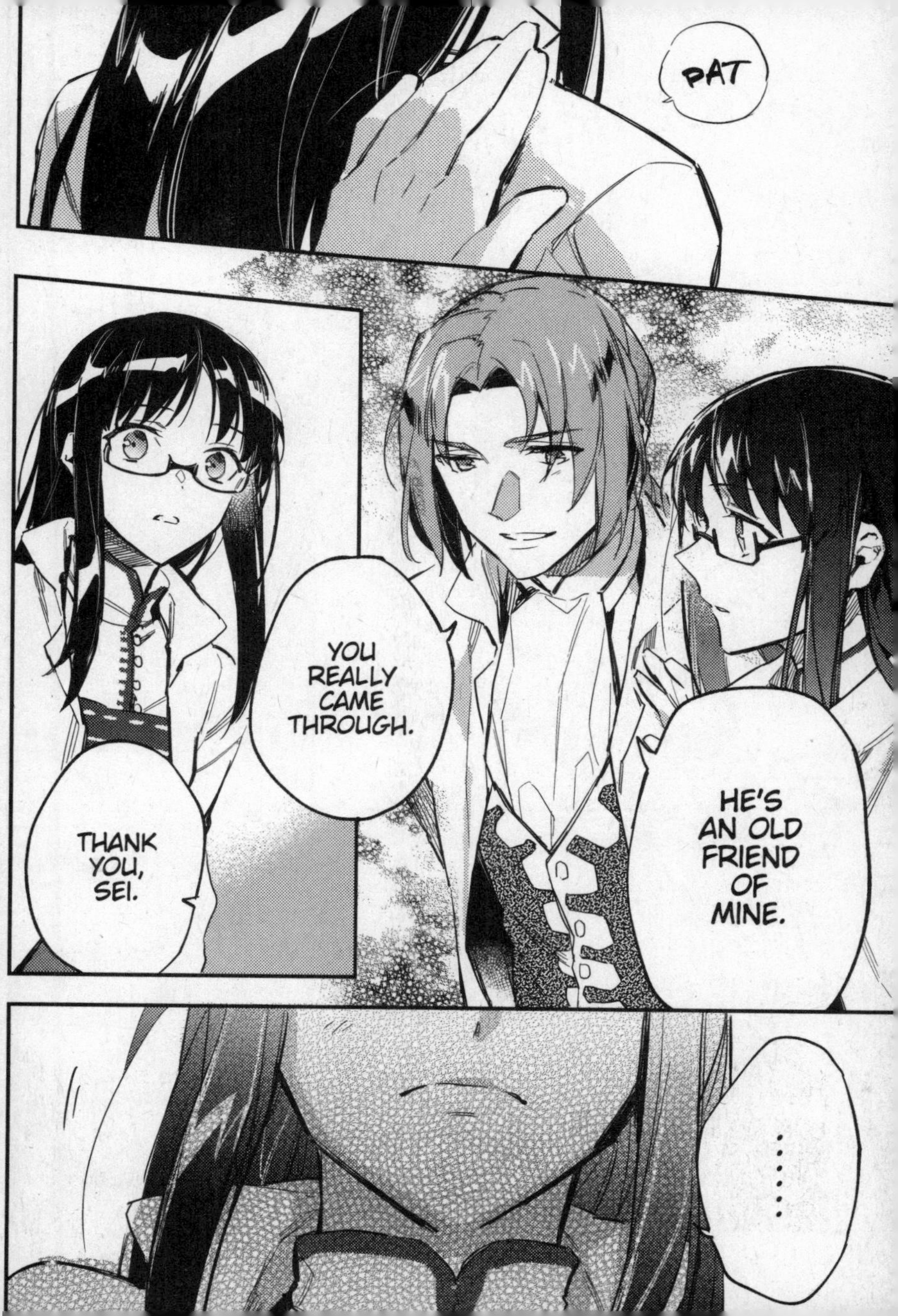
PAT
HE'S AN OLD FRIEND OF MINE.
YOU REALLY CAME THROUGH.
THANK YOU, SEI.
......

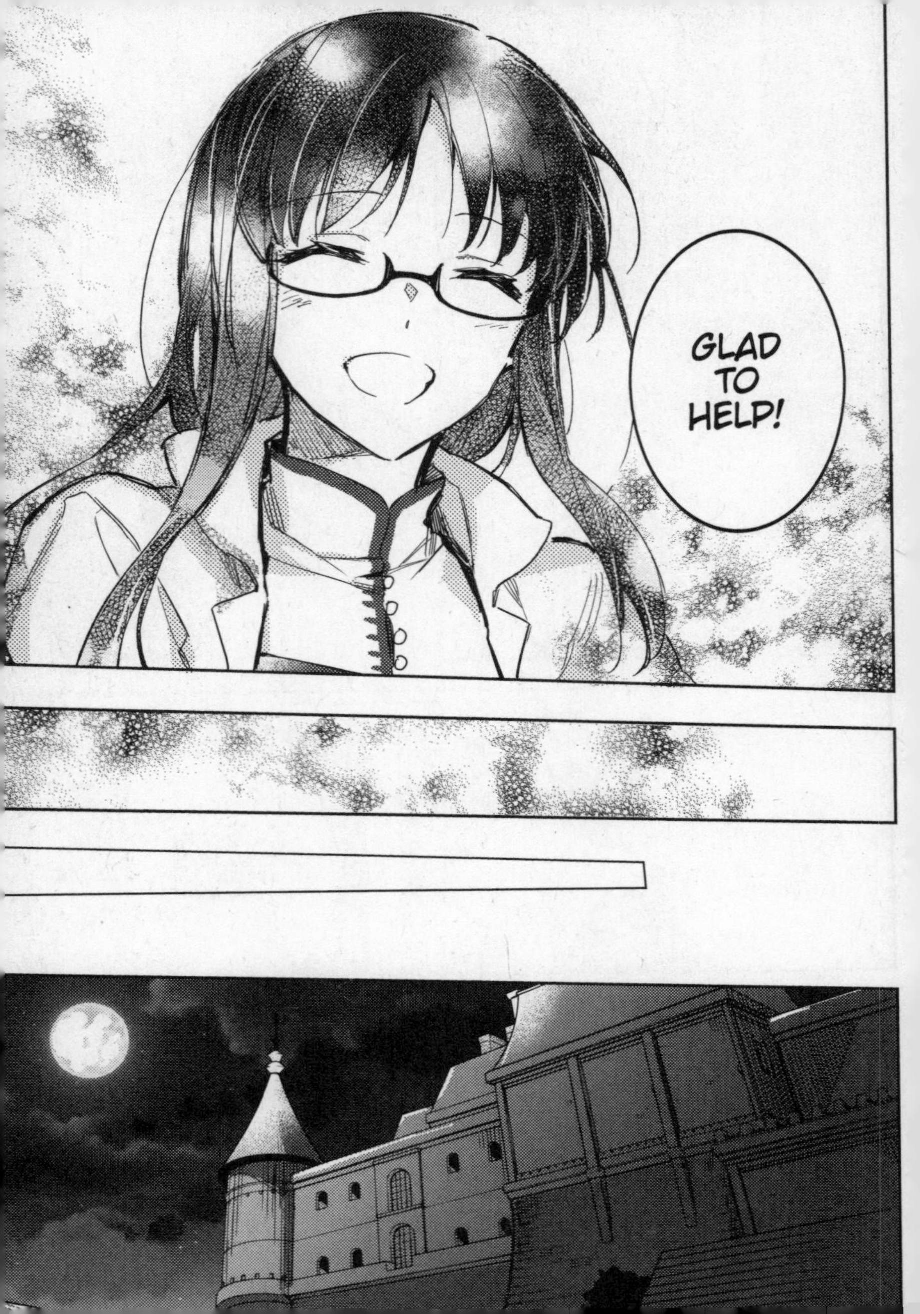
GLAD TO HELP!

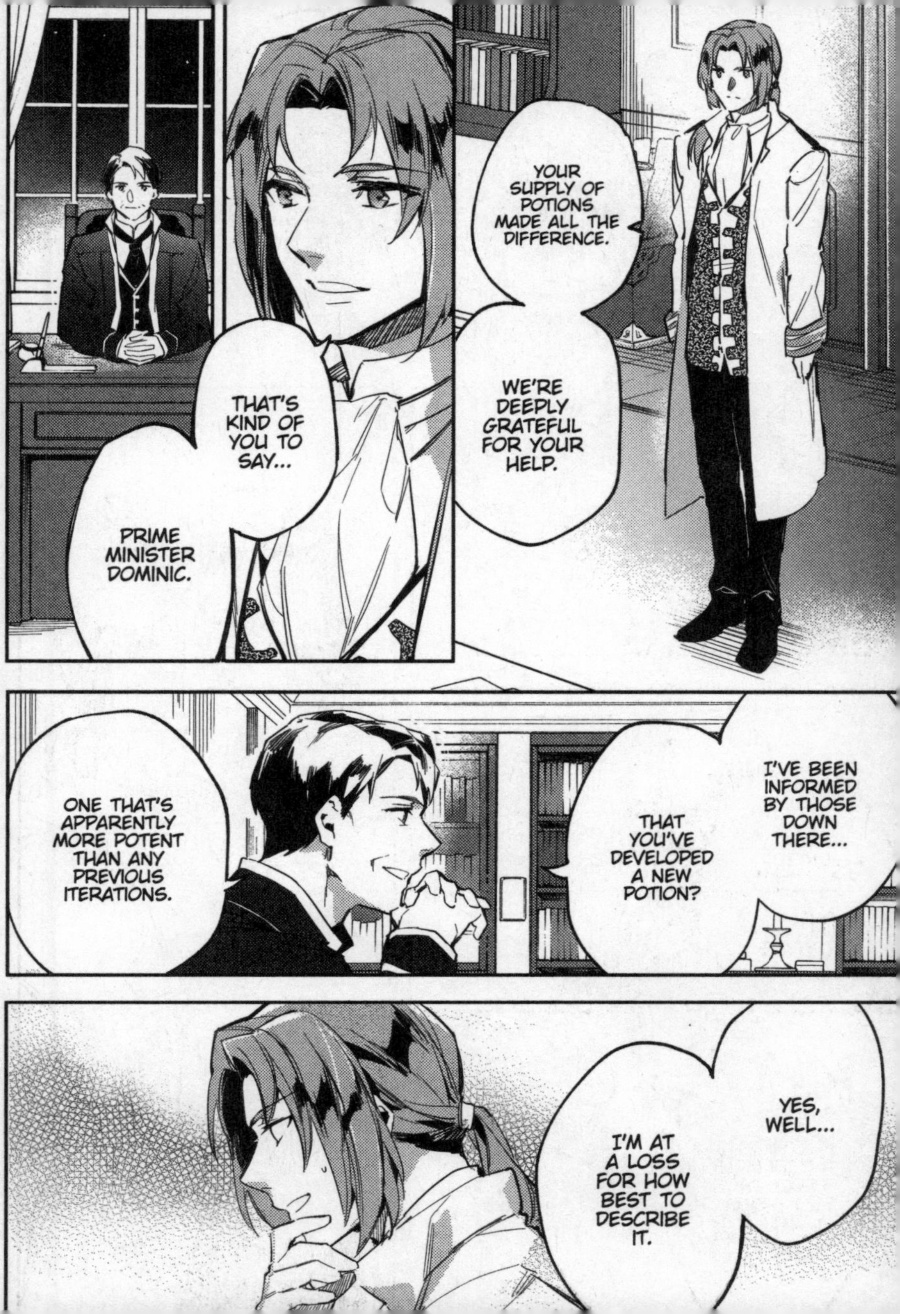
YOUR SUPPLY OF POTIONS MADE ALL THE DIFFERENCE.
WE'RE DEEPLY GRATEFUL FOR YOUR HELP.
THAT'S KIND OF YOU TO SAY...
PRIME MINISTER DOMINIC.
I'VE BEEN INFORMED BY THOSE DOWN THERE...
THAT YOU'VE DEVELOPED A NEW POTION?
ONE THAT'S APPARENTLY MORE POTENT THAN ANY PREVIOUS ITERATIONS.
YES, WELL...
I'M AT A LOSS FOR HOW BEST TO DESCRIBE IT.

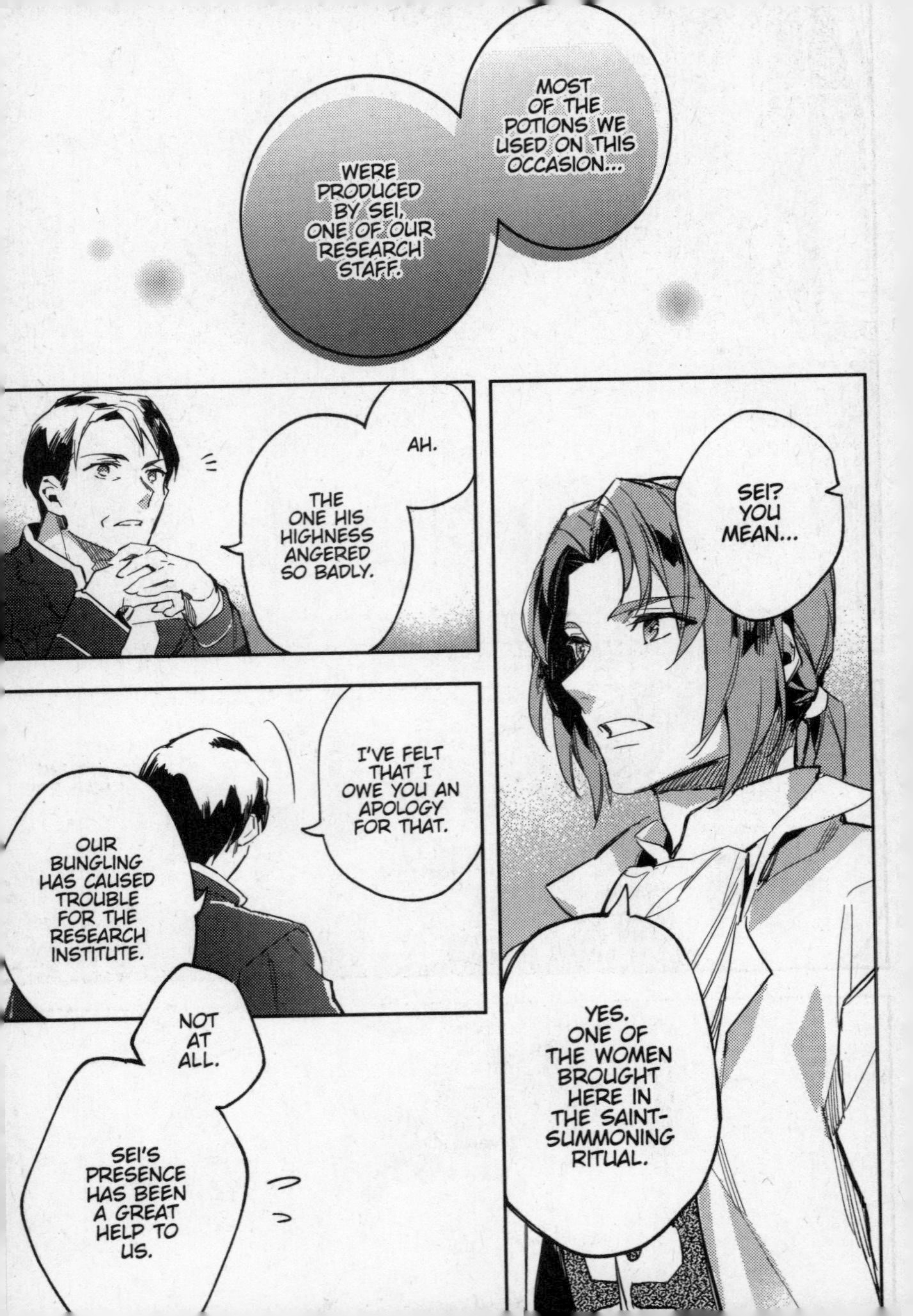
MOST OF THE POTIONS WE USED ON THIS OCCASION...
WERE PRODUCED BY SEI, ONE OF OUR RESEARCH STAFF.
SEI? YOU MEAN...
YES. ONE OF THE WOMEN BROUGHT HERE IN THE SAINT-SUMMONING RITUAL.
AH.
THE ONE HIS HIGHNESS ANGERED SO BADLY.
I'VE FELT THAT I OWE YOU AN APOLOGY FOR THAT.
OUR BUNGLING HAS CAUSED TROUBLE FOR THE RESEARCH INSTITUTE.
NOT AT ALL.
SEI'S PRESENCE HAS BEEN A GREAT HELP TO US.

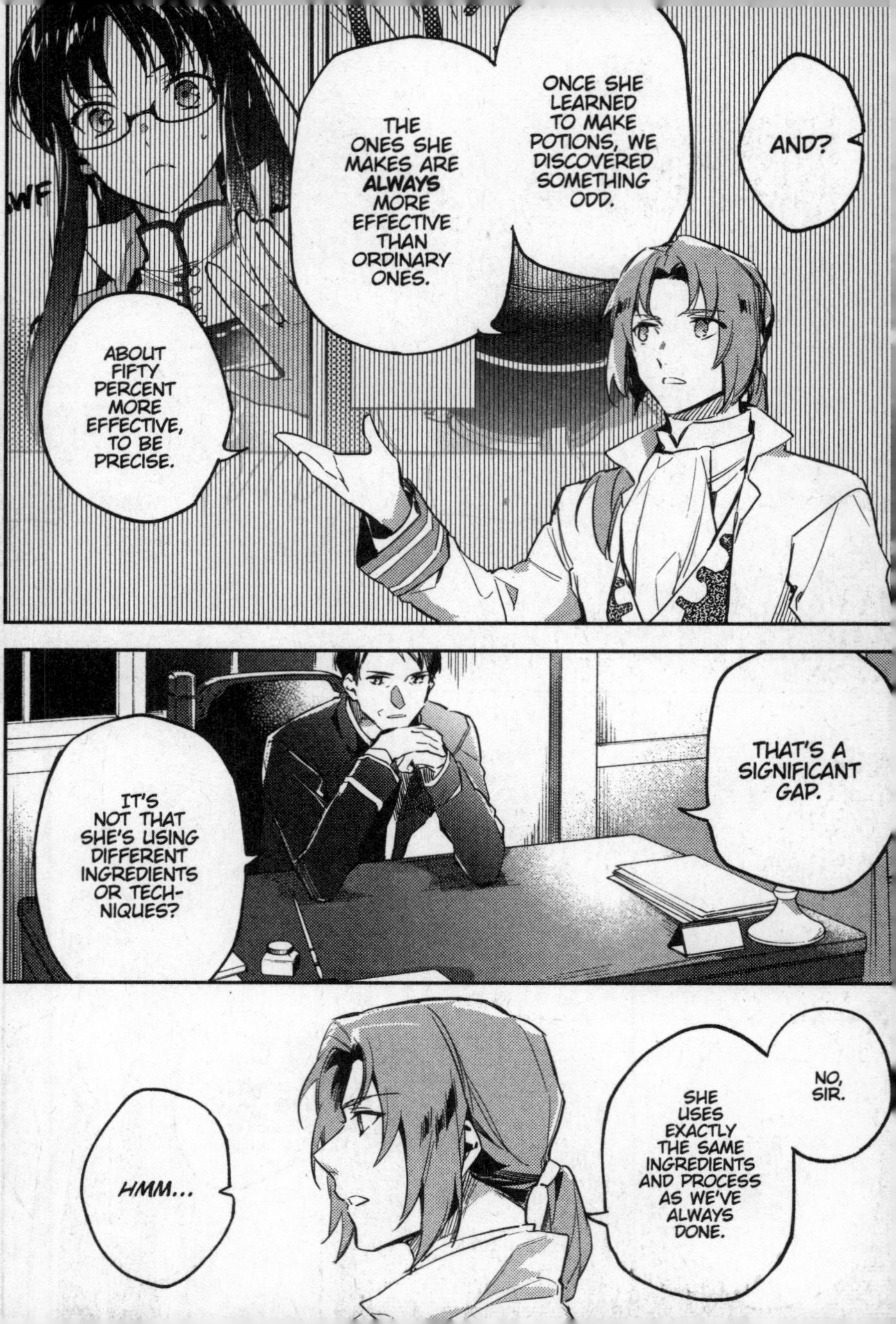
AND?
ONCE SHE LEARNED TO MAKE POTIONS, WE DISCOVERED SOMETHING ODD.
THE ONES SHE MAKES ARE **ALWAYS** MORE EFFECTIVE THAN ORDINARY ONES.
ABOUT FIFTY PERCENT MORE EFFECTIVE, TO BE PRECISE.
THAT'S A SIGNIFICANT GAP.
IT'S NOT THAT SHE'S USING DIFFERENT INGREDIENTS OR TECHNIQUES?
NO, SIR.
SHE USES EXACTLY THE SAME INGREDIENTS AND PROCESS AS WE'VE ALWAYS DONE.
HMM...

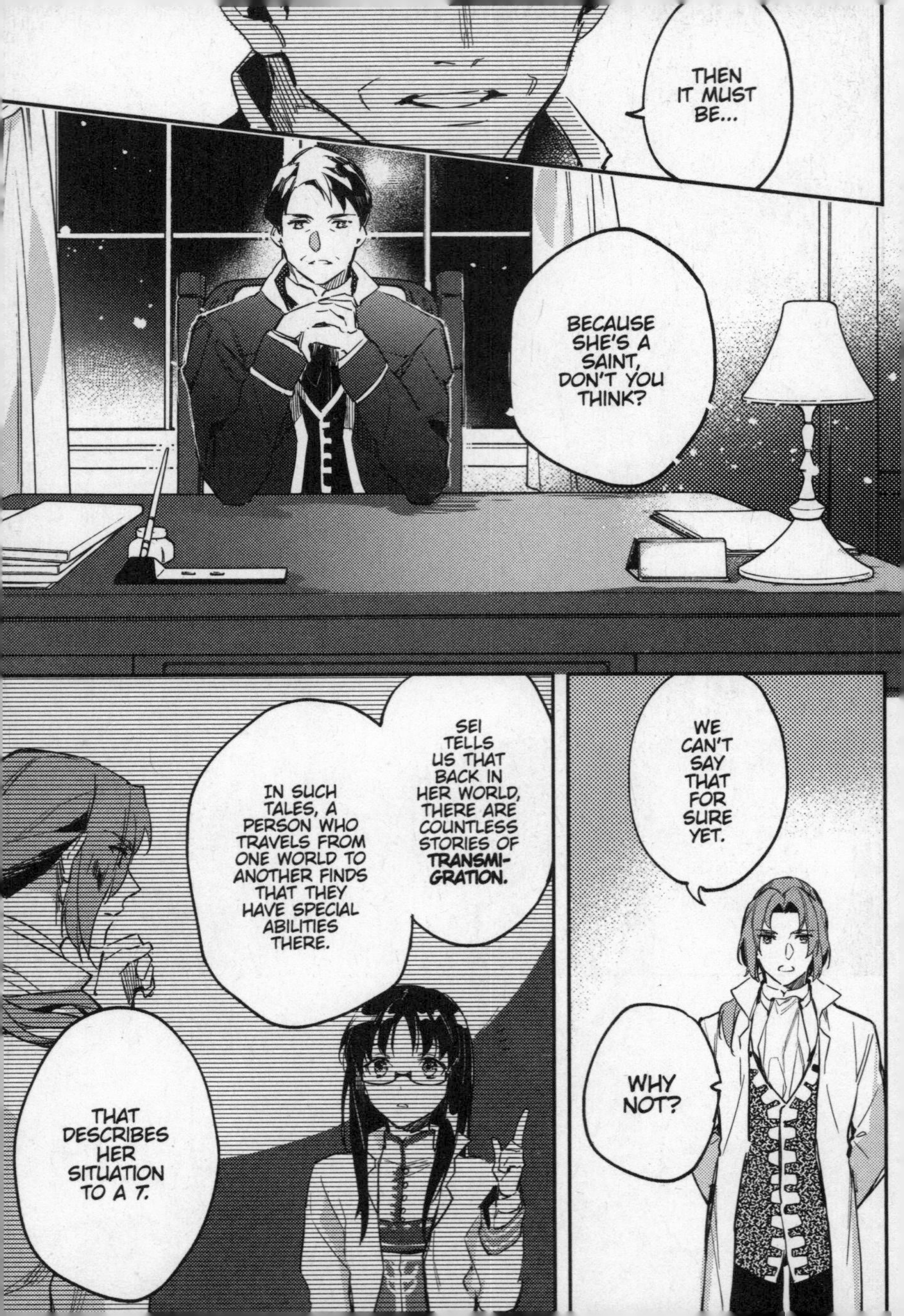
THEN IT MUST BE...
BECAUSE SHE'S A SAINT, DON'T YOU THINK?
WE CAN'T SAY THAT FOR SURE YET.
WHY NOT?
SEI TELLS US THAT BACK IN HER WORLD, THERE ARE COUNTLESS STORIES OF **TRANSMIGRATION**.
IN SUCH TALES, A PERSON WHO TRAVELS FROM ONE WORLD TO ANOTHER FINDS THAT THEY HAVE SPECIAL ABILITIES THERE.
THAT DESCRIBES HER SITUATION TO A *T*.

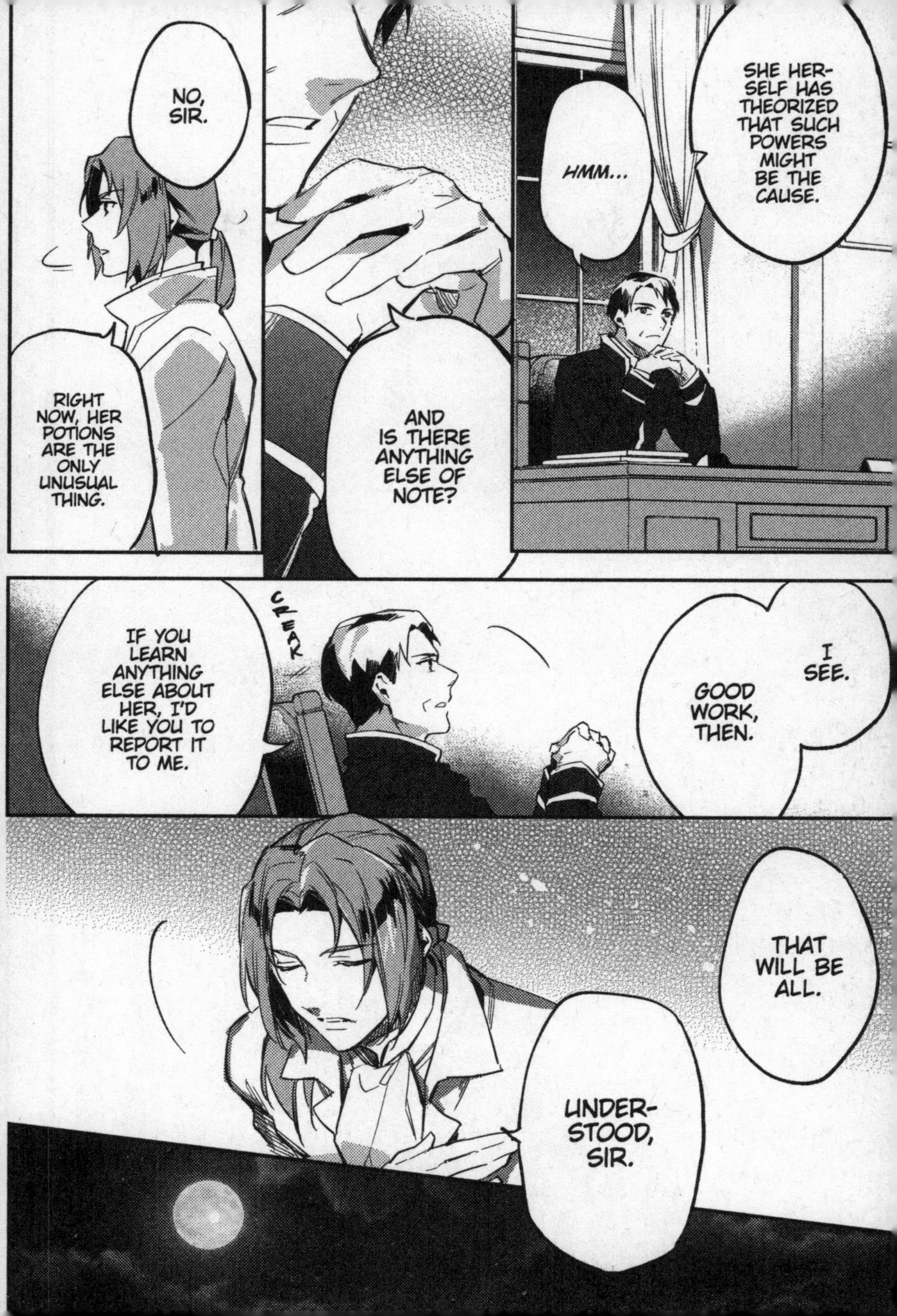
SHE HERSELF HAS THEORIZED THAT SUCH POWERS MIGHT BE THE CAUSE.
HMM...
AND IS THERE ANYTHING ELSE OF NOTE?
NO, SIR.
RIGHT NOW, HER POTIONS ARE THE ONLY UNUSUAL THING.
I SEE.
GOOD WORK, THEN.
CREAK
IF YOU LEARN ANYTHING ELSE ABOUT HER, I'D LIKE YOU TO REPORT IT TO ME.
THAT WILL BE ALL.
UNDERSTOOD, SIR.

The Saint's*
*Magic Power is *
Omnipotent

The Saint's*
*Magic Power is *
Omnipotent

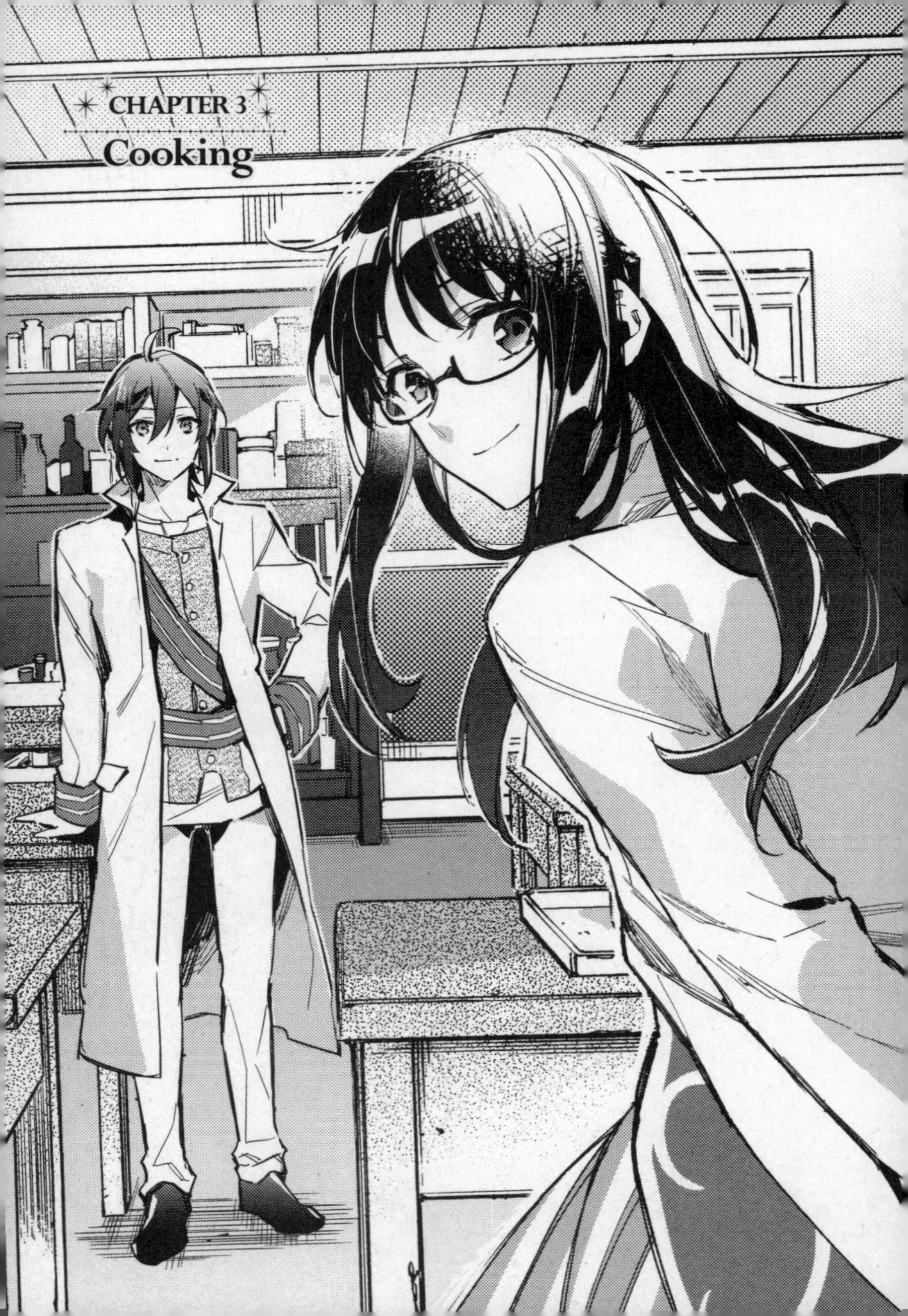
CHAPTER 3
Cooking

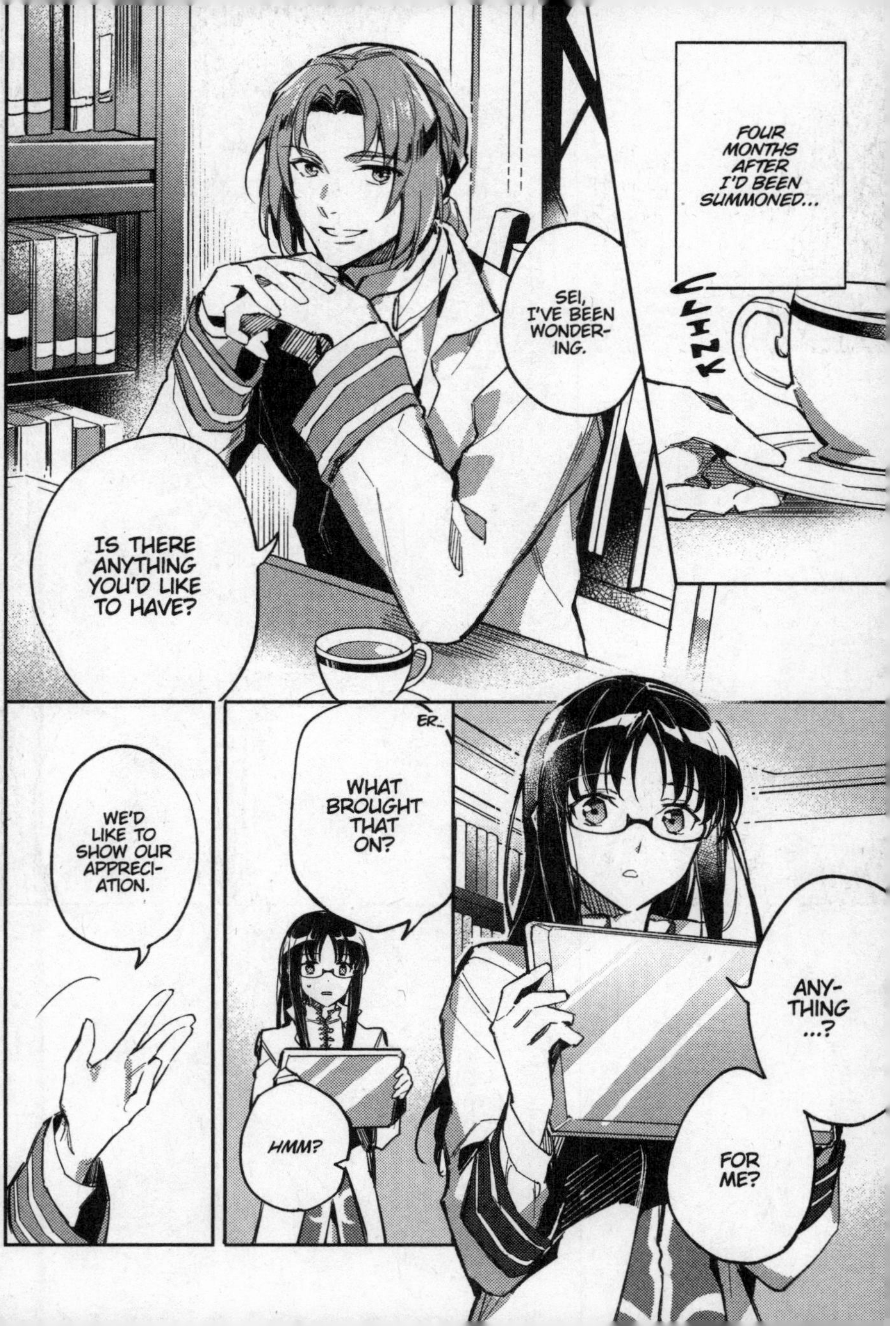
FOUR MONTHS AFTER I'D BEEN SUMMONED...
CLINK
SEI, I'VE BEEN WONDERING.
IS THERE ANYTHING YOU'D LIKE TO HAVE?
ANYTHING...?
FOR ME?
ER...
WHAT BROUGHT THAT ON?
HMM?
WE'D LIKE TO SHOW OUR APPRECIATION.

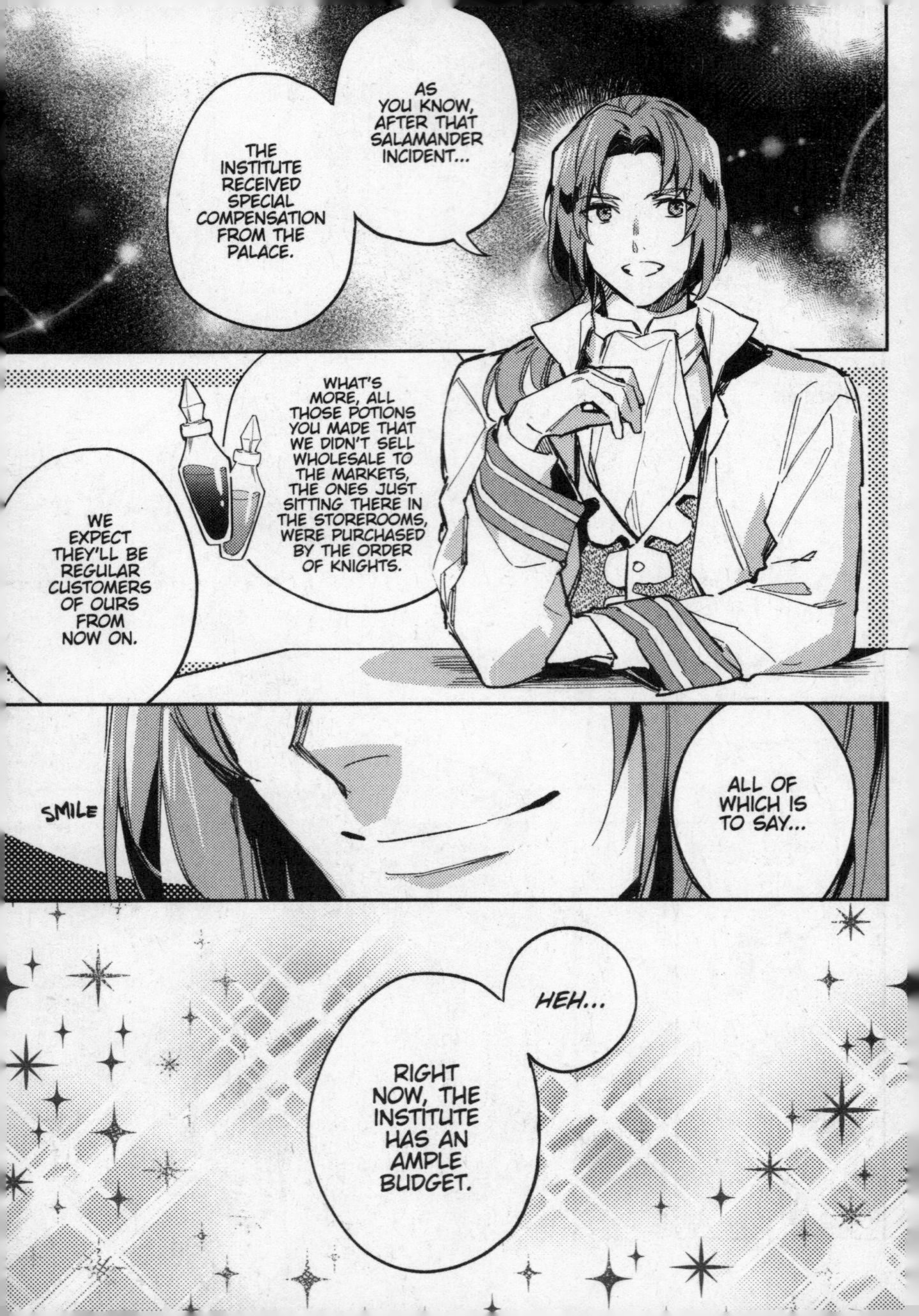
AS YOU KNOW, AFTER THAT SALAMANDER INCIDENT...
THE INSTITUTE RECEIVED SPECIAL COMPENSATION FROM THE PALACE.
WHAT'S MORE, ALL THOSE POTIONS YOU MADE THAT WE DIDN'T SELL WHOLESALE TO THE MARKETS, THE ONES JUST SITTING THERE IN THE STOREROOMS, WERE PURCHASED BY THE ORDER OF KNIGHTS.
WE EXPECT THEY'LL BE REGULAR CUSTOMERS OF OURS FROM NOW ON.
ALL OF WHICH IS TO SAY...
SMILE
HEH...
RIGHT NOW, THE INSTITUTE HAS AN AMPLE BUDGET.

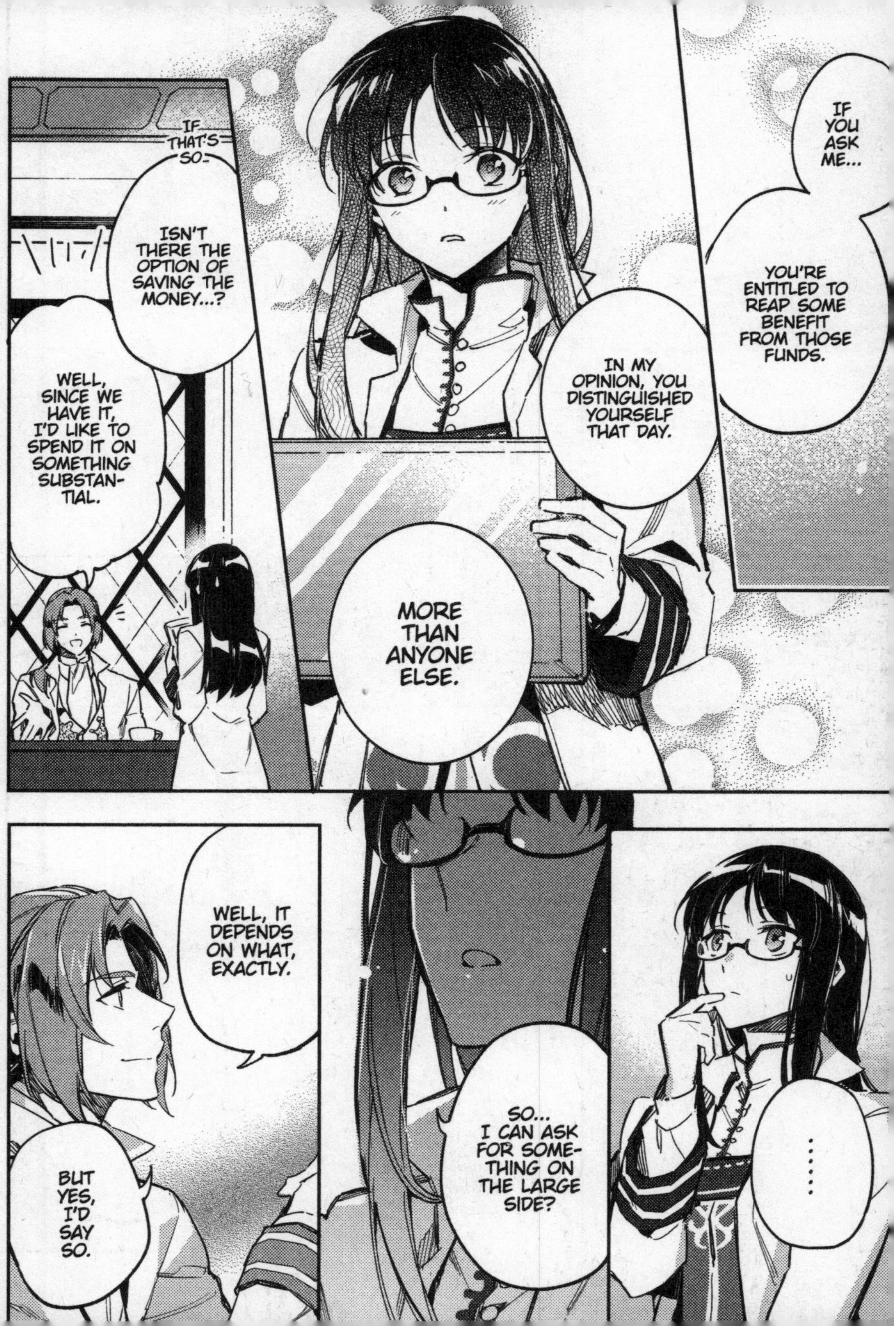
IF YOU ASK ME...
YOU'RE ENTITLED TO REAP SOME BENEFIT FROM THOSE FUNDS.
IN MY OPINION, YOU DISTINGUISHED YOURSELF THAT DAY.
MORE THAN ANYONE ELSE.
IF THAT'S SO...
ISN'T THERE THE OPTION OF SAVING THE MONEY...?
WELL, SINCE WE HAVE IT, I'D LIKE TO SPEND IT ON SOMETHING SUBSTAN-TIAL.
......
SO... I CAN ASK FOR SOME-THING ON THE LARGE SIDE?
WELL, IT DEPENDS ON WHAT, EXACTLY.
BUT YES, I'D SAY SO.

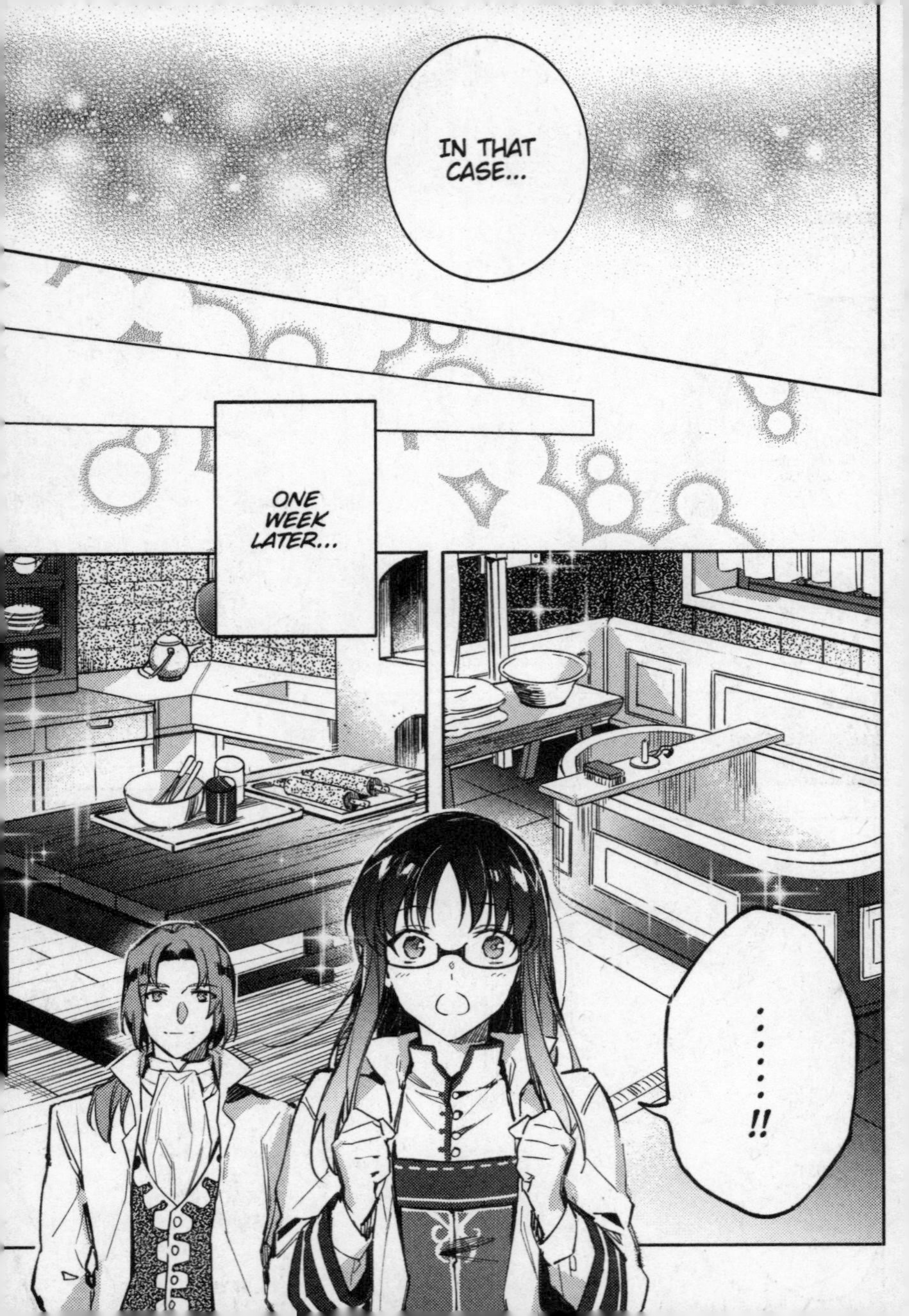
IN THAT CASE...
ONE WEEK LATER...
......!!

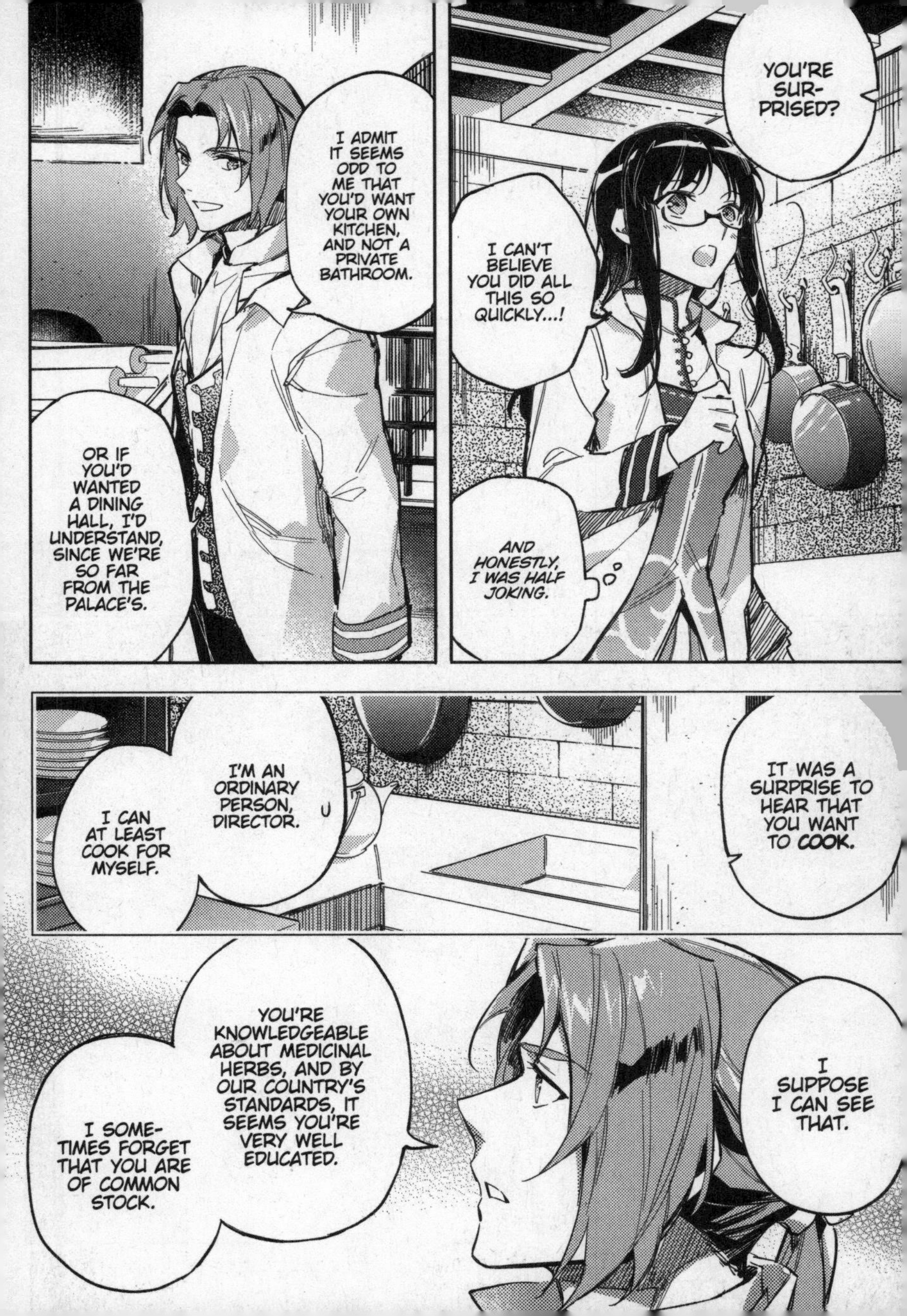
YOU'RE SUR-PRISED?
I CAN'T BELIEVE YOU DID ALL THIS SO QUICKLY...!
AND HONESTLY, I WAS HALF JOKING.
I ADMIT IT SEEMS ODD TO ME THAT YOU'D WANT YOUR OWN KITCHEN, AND NOT A PRIVATE BATHROOM.
OR IF YOU'D WANTED A DINING HALL, I'D UNDERSTAND, SINCE WE'RE SO FAR FROM THE PALACE'S.
IT WAS A SURPRISE TO HEAR THAT YOU WANT TO **COOK.**
I'M AN ORDINARY PERSON, DIRECTOR.
I CAN AT LEAST COOK FOR MYSELF.
I SUPPOSE I CAN SEE THAT.
YOU'RE KNOWLEDGEABLE ABOUT MEDICINAL HERBS, AND BY OUR COUNTRY'S STANDARDS, IT SEEMS YOU'RE VERY WELL EDUCATED.
I SOME-TIMES FORGET THAT YOU ARE OF COMMON STOCK.

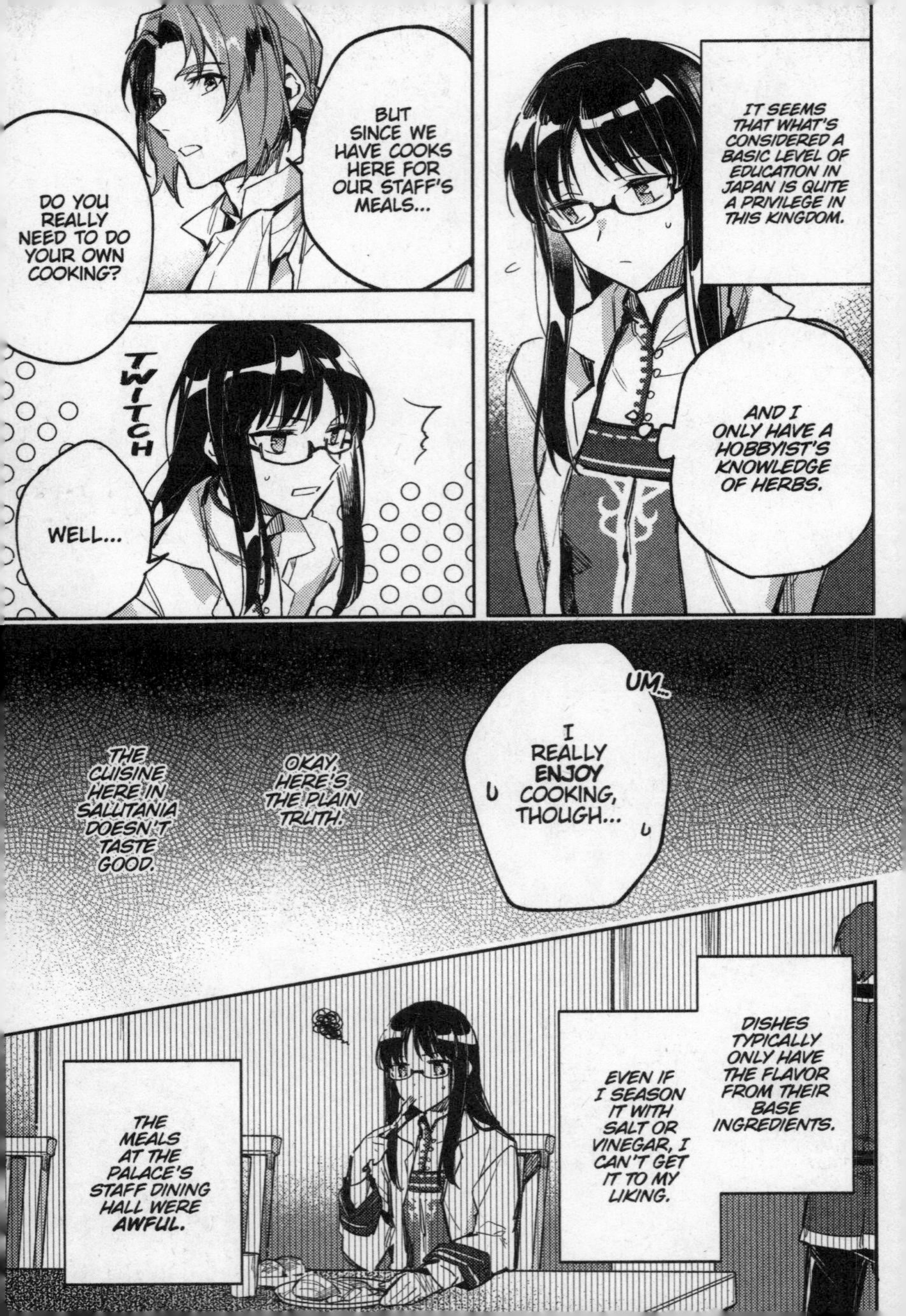
IT SEEMS THAT WHAT'S CONSIDERED A BASIC LEVEL OF EDUCATION IN JAPAN IS QUITE A PRIVILEGE IN THIS KINGDOM.
AND I ONLY HAVE A HOBBYIST'S KNOWLEDGE OF HERBS.
BUT SINCE WE HAVE COOKS HERE FOR OUR STAFF'S MEALS...
DO YOU REALLY NEED TO DO YOUR OWN COOKING?
TWITCH
WELL...
UM...
I REALLY ENJOY COOKING, THOUGH...
OKAY, HERE'S THE PLAIN TRUTH.
THE CUISINE HERE IN SALUTANIA DOESN'T TASTE GOOD.
DISHES TYPICALLY ONLY HAVE THE FLAVOR FROM THEIR BASE INGREDIENTS.
EVEN IF I SEASON IT WITH SALT OR VINEGAR, I CAN'T GET IT TO MY LIKING.
THE MEALS AT THE PALACE'S STAFF DINING HALL WERE AWFUL.

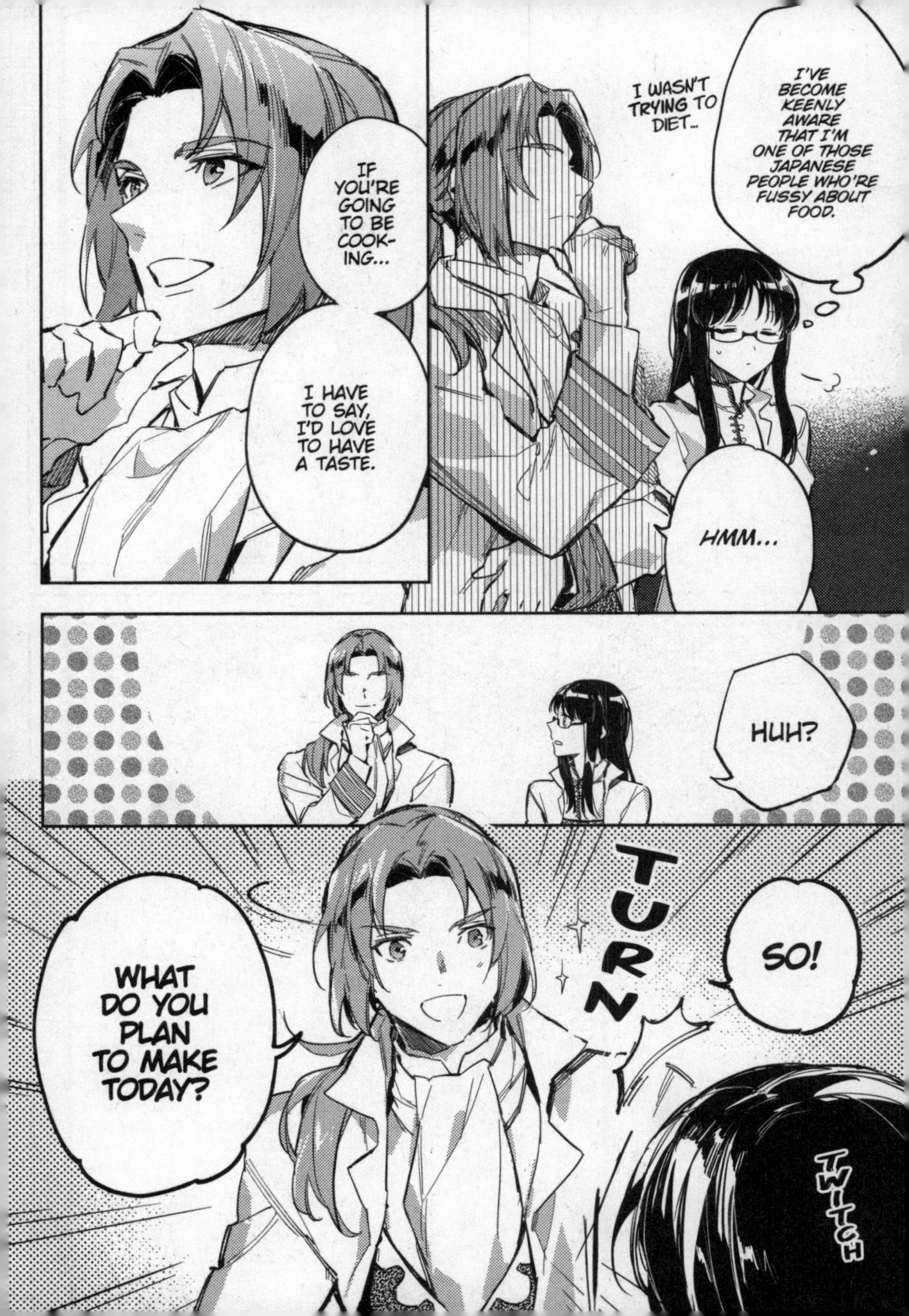
I'VE BECOME KEENLY AWARE THAT I'M ONE OF THOSE JAPANESE PEOPLE WHO'RE FUSSY ABOUT FOOD.
I WASN'T TRYING TO DIET...
HMM...
IF YOU'RE GOING TO BE COOKING...
I HAVE TO SAY, I'D LOVE TO HAVE A TASTE.
HUH?
SO!
TURN
WHAT DO YOU PLAN TO MAKE TODAY?
TWITCH

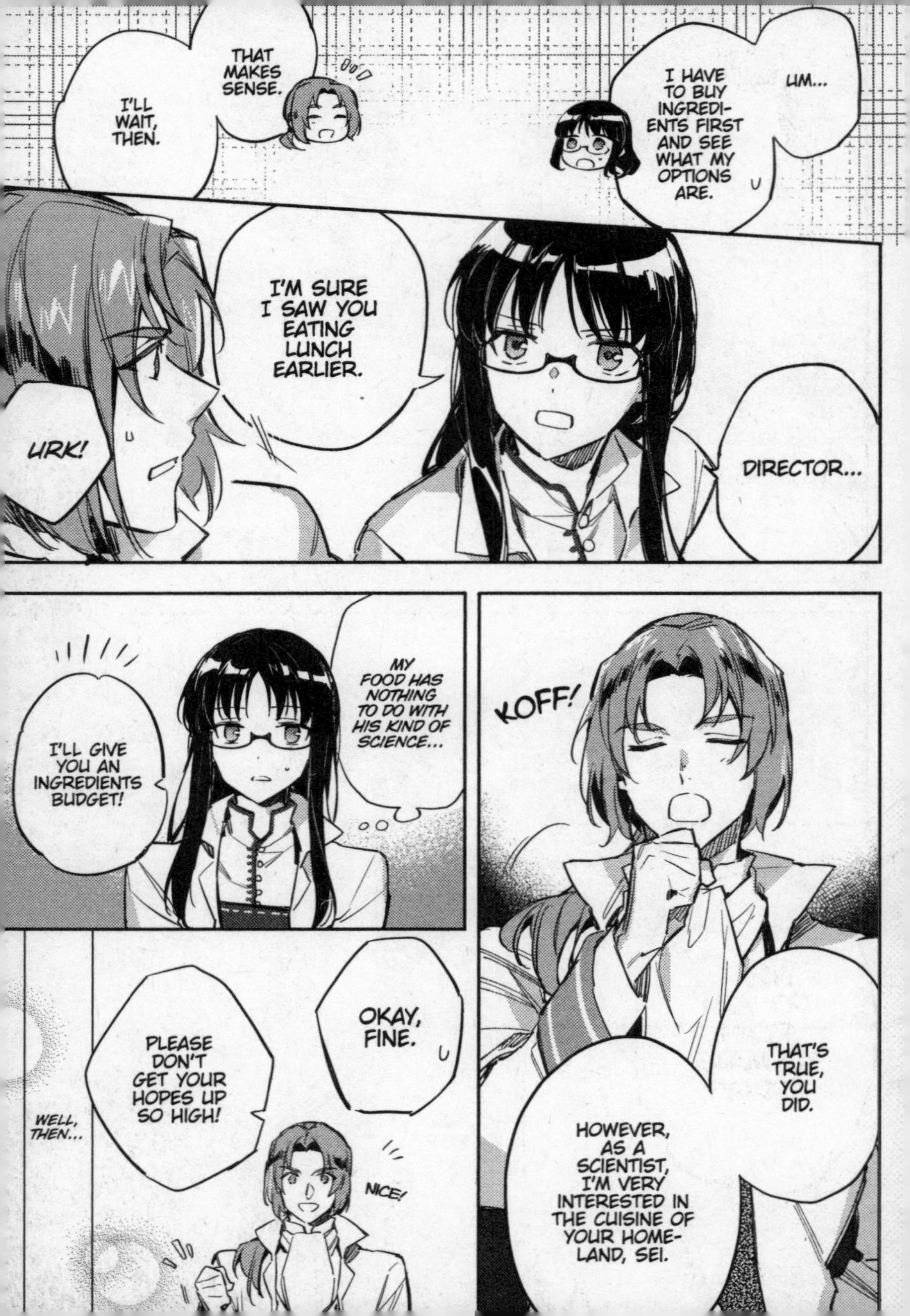
UM...
I HAVE TO BUY INGREDIENTS FIRST AND SEE WHAT MY OPTIONS ARE.
THAT MAKES SENSE.
I'LL WAIT, THEN.
DIRECTOR...
I'M SURE I SAW YOU EATING LUNCH EARLIER.
URK!
KOFF!
THAT'S TRUE, YOU DID.
HOWEVER, AS A SCIENTIST, I'M VERY INTERESTED IN THE CUISINE OF YOUR HOME-LAND, SEI.
MY FOOD HAS NOTHING TO DO WITH HIS KIND OF SCIENCE...
I'LL GIVE YOU AN INGREDIENTS BUDGET!
OKAY, FINE.
PLEASE DON'T GET YOUR HOPES UP SO HIGH!
NICE!
WELL, THEN...

HMPH!

IF HE'S GOING THAT FAR...

I GUESS I'M DOING THIS!

ROLL

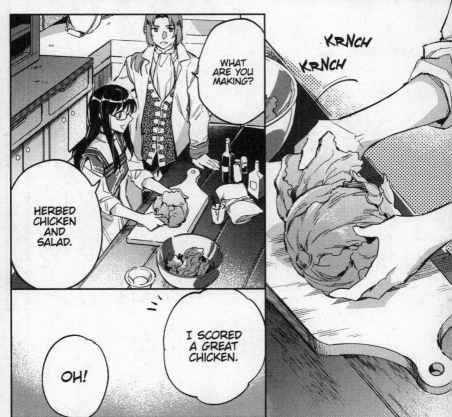

WHAT ARE YOU MAKING?

KRNCH

KRNCH

HERBED CHICKEN AND SALAD.

I SCORED A GREAT CHICKEN.

OH!

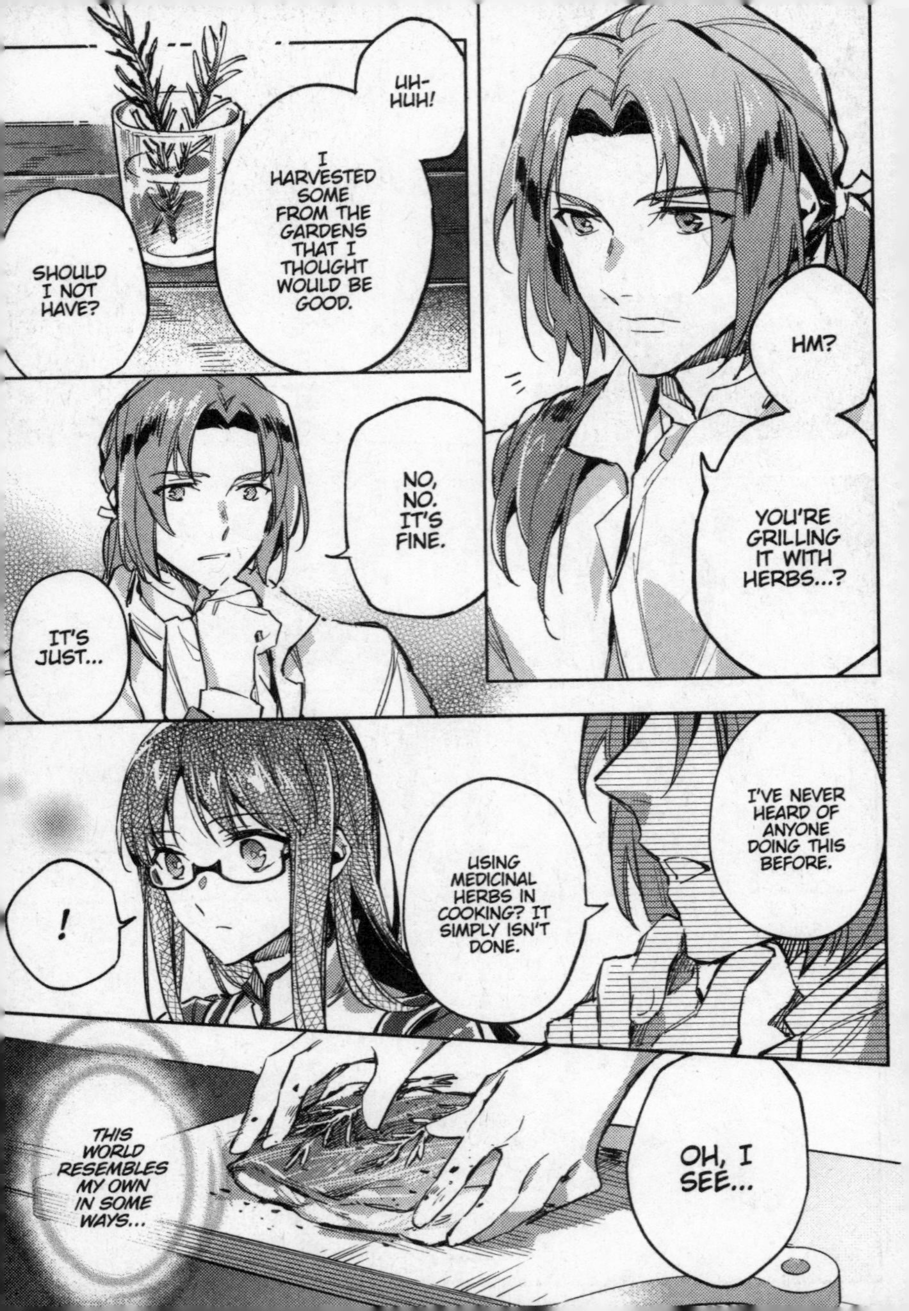
HM?
YOU'RE GRILLING IT WITH HERBS...?
UH-HUH!
I HARVESTED SOME FROM THE GARDENS THAT I THOUGHT WOULD BE GOOD.
SHOULD I NOT HAVE?
NO, NO. IT'S FINE.
IT'S JUST...
I'VE NEVER HEARD OF ANYONE DOING THIS BEFORE.
USING MEDICINAL HERBS IN COOKING? IT SIMPLY ISN'T DONE.
!
OH, I SEE...
THIS WORLD RESEMBLES MY OWN IN SOME WAYS...

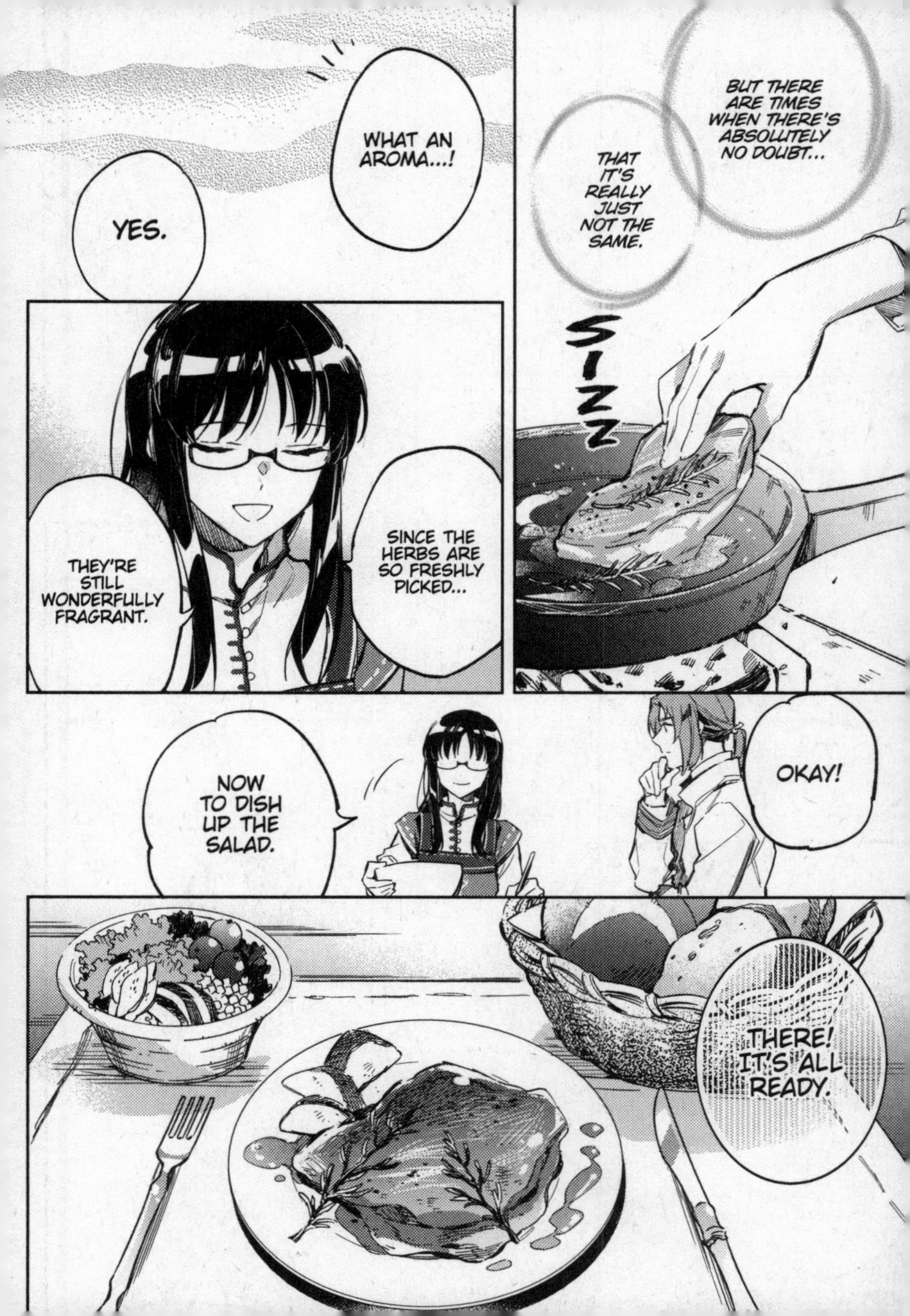
BUT THERE ARE TIMES WHEN THERE'S ABSOLUTELY NO DOUBT...
THAT IT'S REALLY JUST NOT THE SAME.
SIZZ
WHAT AN AROMA...!
YES.
SINCE THE HERBS ARE SO FRESHLY PICKED...
THEY'RE STILL WONDERFULLY FRAGRANT.
OKAY!
NOW TO DISH UP THE SALAD.
THERE! IT'S ALL READY.

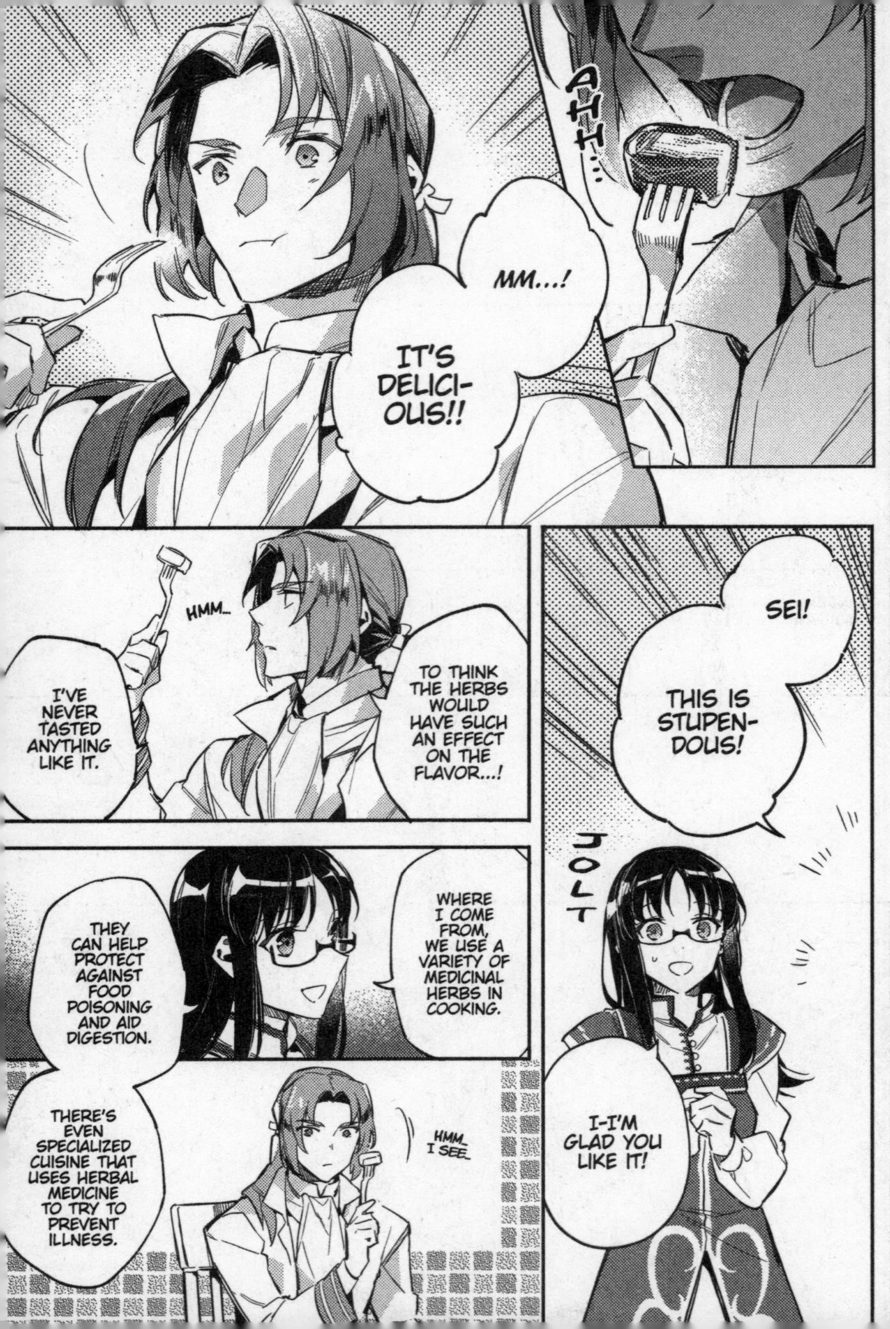
AHHH...
MM...!
IT'S DELICIOUS!!
SEI!
THIS IS STUPENDOUS!
JOLT
I-I'M GLAD YOU LIKE IT!
HMM...
TO THINK THE HERBS WOULD HAVE SUCH AN EFFECT ON THE FLAVOR...!
I'VE NEVER TASTED ANYTHING LIKE IT.
WHERE I COME FROM, WE USE A VARIETY OF MEDICINAL HERBS IN COOKING.
THEY CAN HELP PROTECT AGAINST FOOD POISONING AND AID DIGESTION.
HMM... I SEE...
THERE'S EVEN SPECIALIZED CUISINE THAT USES HERBAL MEDICINE TO TRY TO PREVENT ILLNESS.

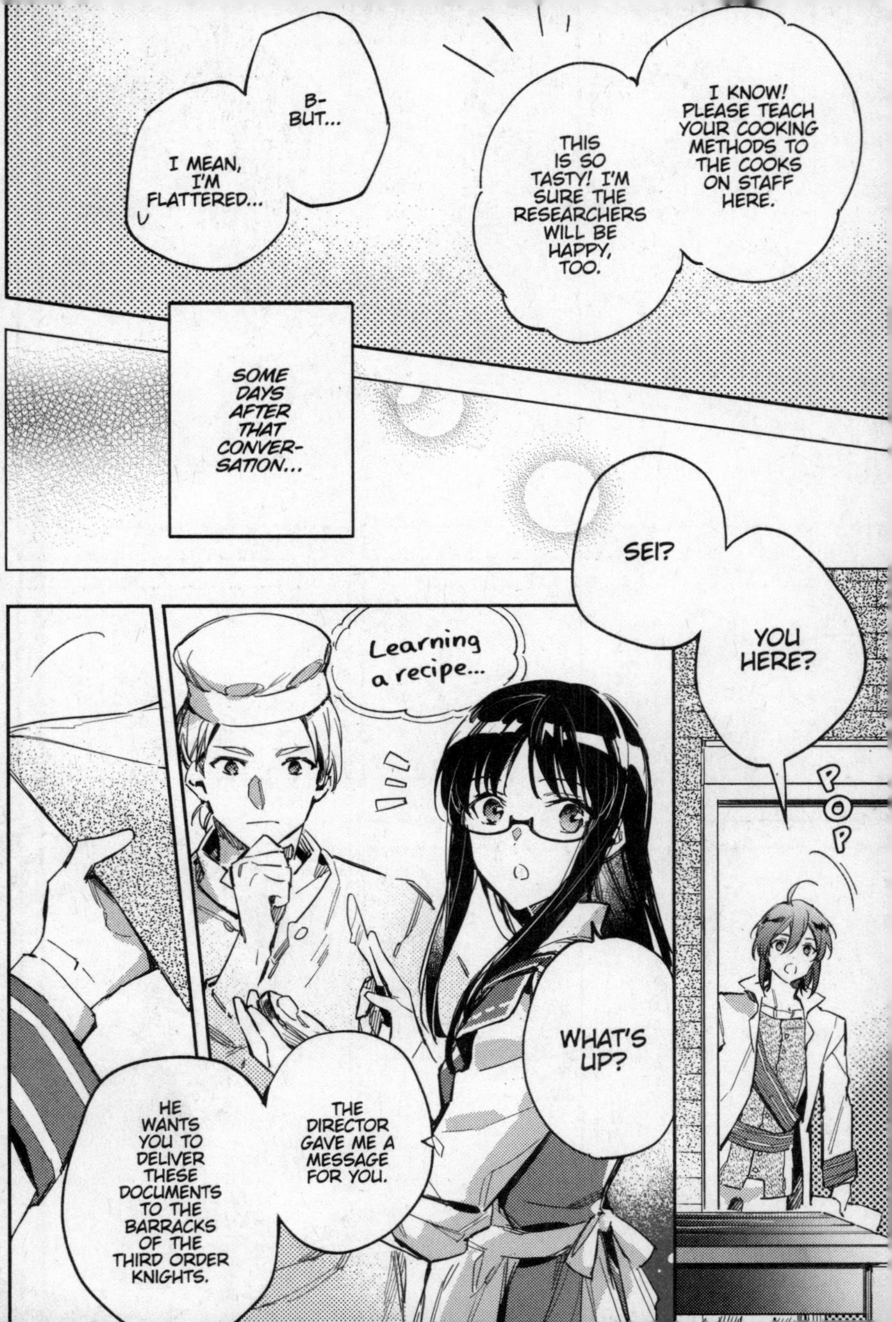
I KNOW! PLEASE TEACH YOUR COOKING METHODS TO THE COOKS ON STAFF HERE.
THIS IS SO TASTY! I'M SURE THE RESEARCHERS WILL BE HAPPY, TOO.
B-BUT...
I MEAN, I'M FLATTERED...
SOME DAYS AFTER THAT CONVERSATION...
SEI?
YOU HERE?
POP
Learning a recipe...
WHAT'S UP?
THE DIRECTOR GAVE ME A MESSAGE FOR YOU.
HE WANTS YOU TO DELIVER THESE DOCUMENTS TO THE BARRACKS OF THE THIRD ORDER KNIGHTS.

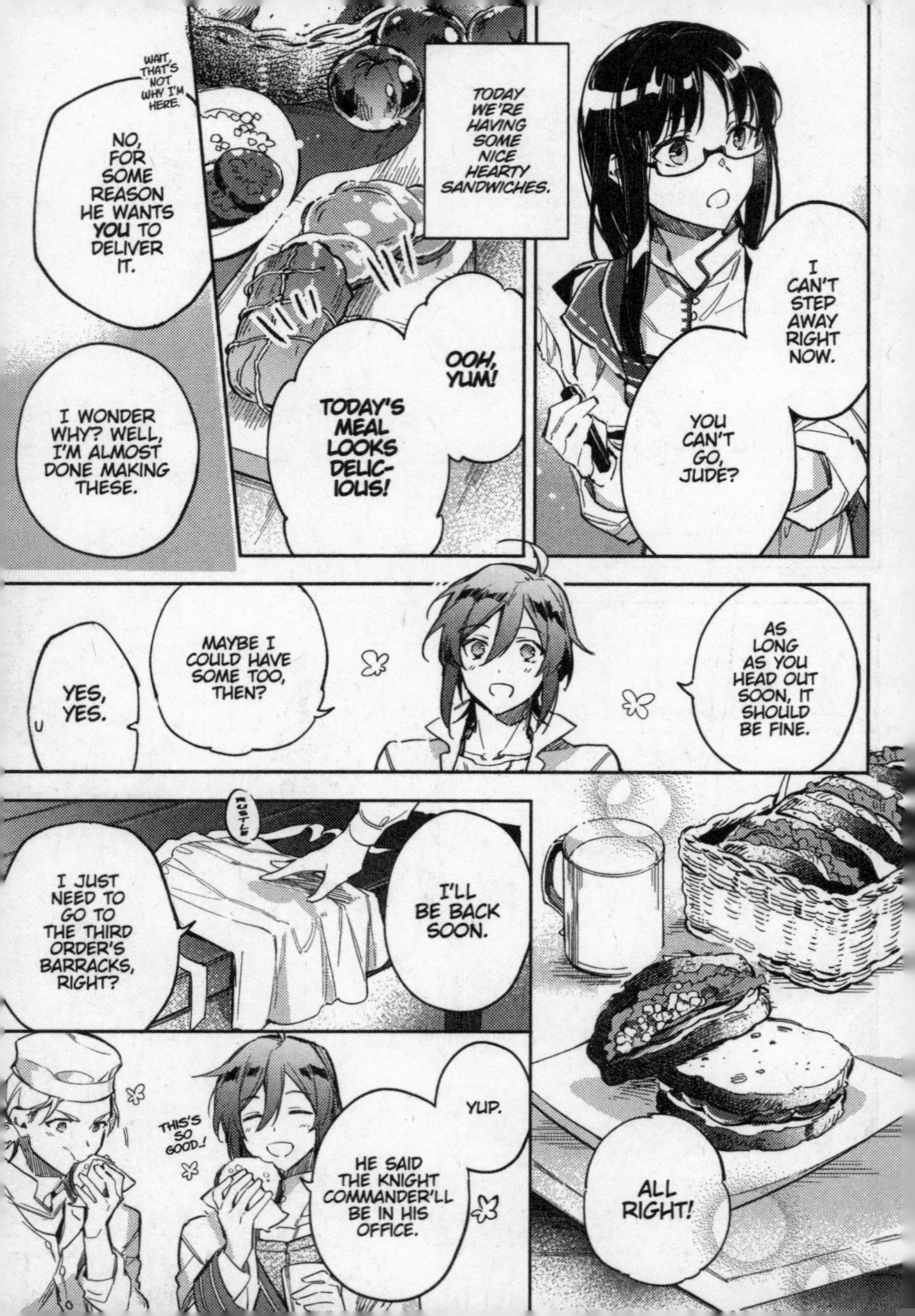
I CAN'T STEP AWAY RIGHT NOW.
YOU CAN'T GO, JUDE?
TODAY WE'RE HAVING SOME NICE HEARTY SANDWICHES.
OOH, YUM!
TODAY'S MEAL LOOKS DELICIOUS!
WAIT, THAT'S NOT WHY I'M HERE.
NO, FOR SOME REASON HE WANTS YOU TO DELIVER IT.
I WONDER WHY? WELL, I'M ALMOST DONE MAKING THESE.
AS LONG AS YOU HEAD OUT SOON, IT SHOULD BE FINE.
MAYBE I COULD HAVE SOME TOO, THEN?
YES, YES.
RUSTLE
I'LL BE BACK SOON.
I JUST NEED TO GO TO THE THIRD ORDER'S BARRACKS, RIGHT?
YUP.
HE SAID THE KNIGHT COMMANDER'LL BE IN HIS OFFICE.
THIS'S SO GOOD♪
ALL RIGHT!

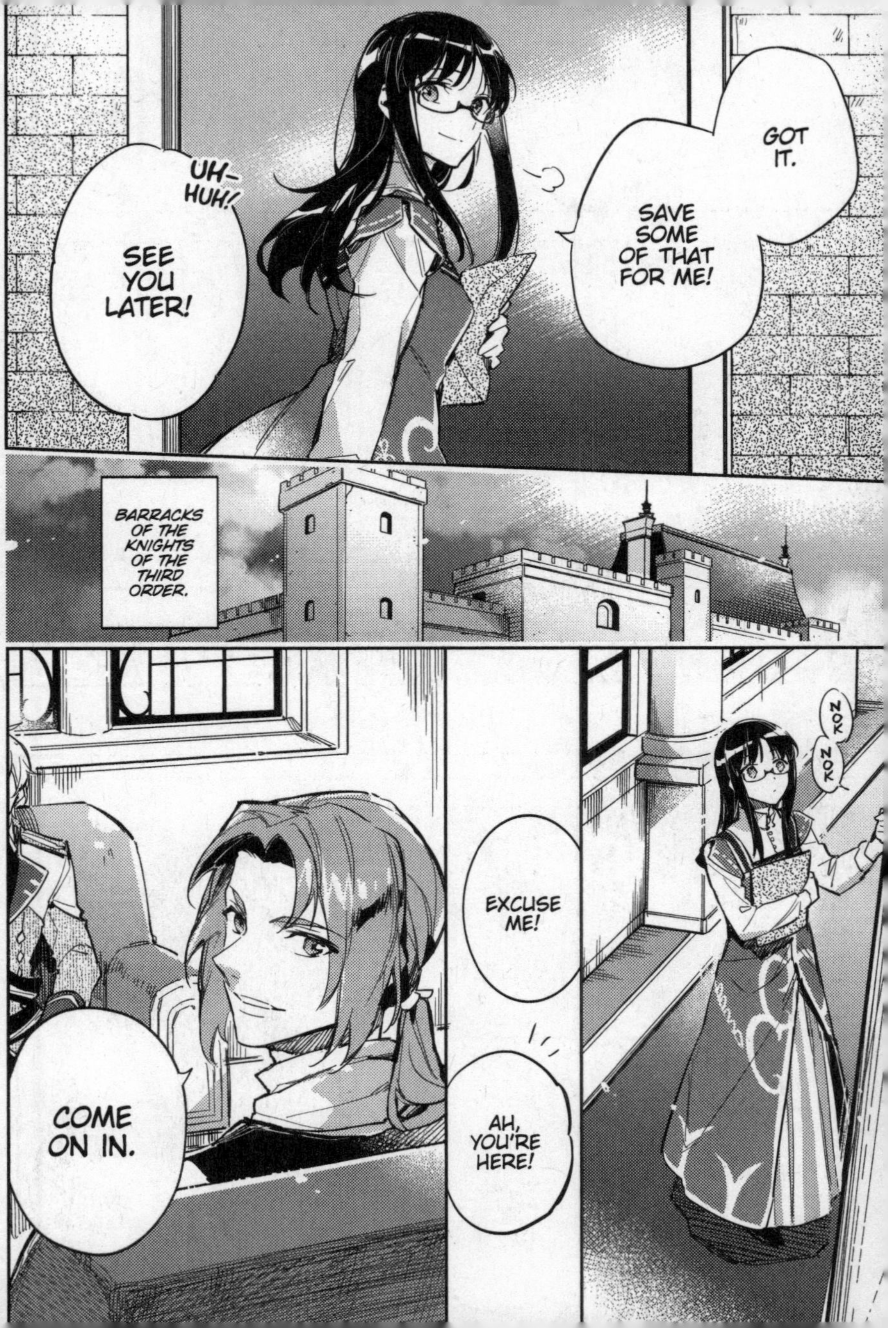
GOT IT.
SAVE SOME OF THAT FOR ME!
UH-HUH!
SEE YOU LATER!
BARRACKS OF THE KNIGHTS OF THE THIRD ORDER.
NOK NOK
EXCUSE ME!
AH, YOU'RE HERE!
COME ON IN.

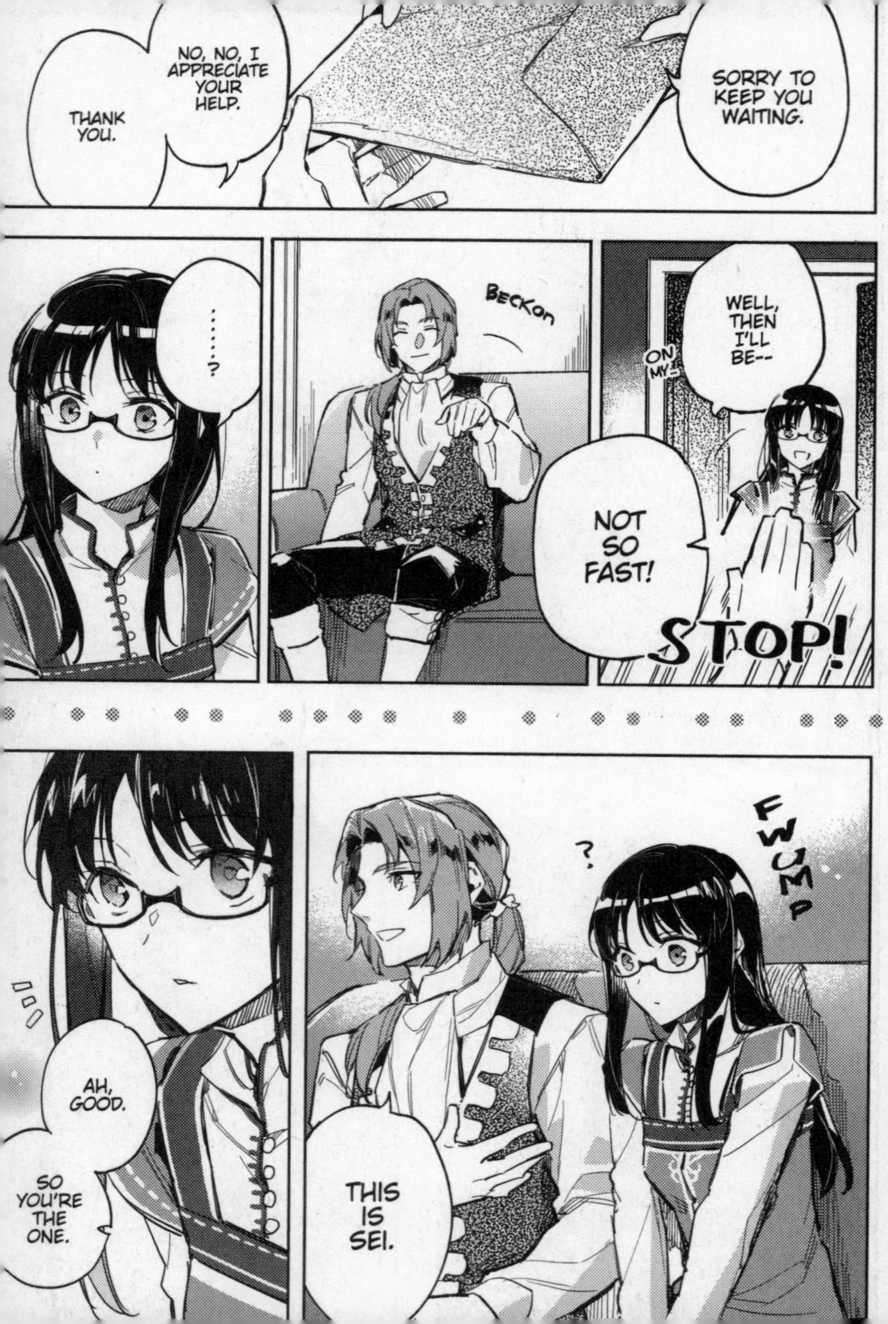
SORRY TO KEEP YOU WAITING.
NO, NO, I APPRECIATE YOUR HELP.
THANK YOU.
WELL, THEN I'LL BE--
ON MY-
NOT SO FAST!
STOP!
BECKON
......?
FWUMP
?
THIS IS SEI.
AH, GOOD.
SO YOU'RE THE ONE.

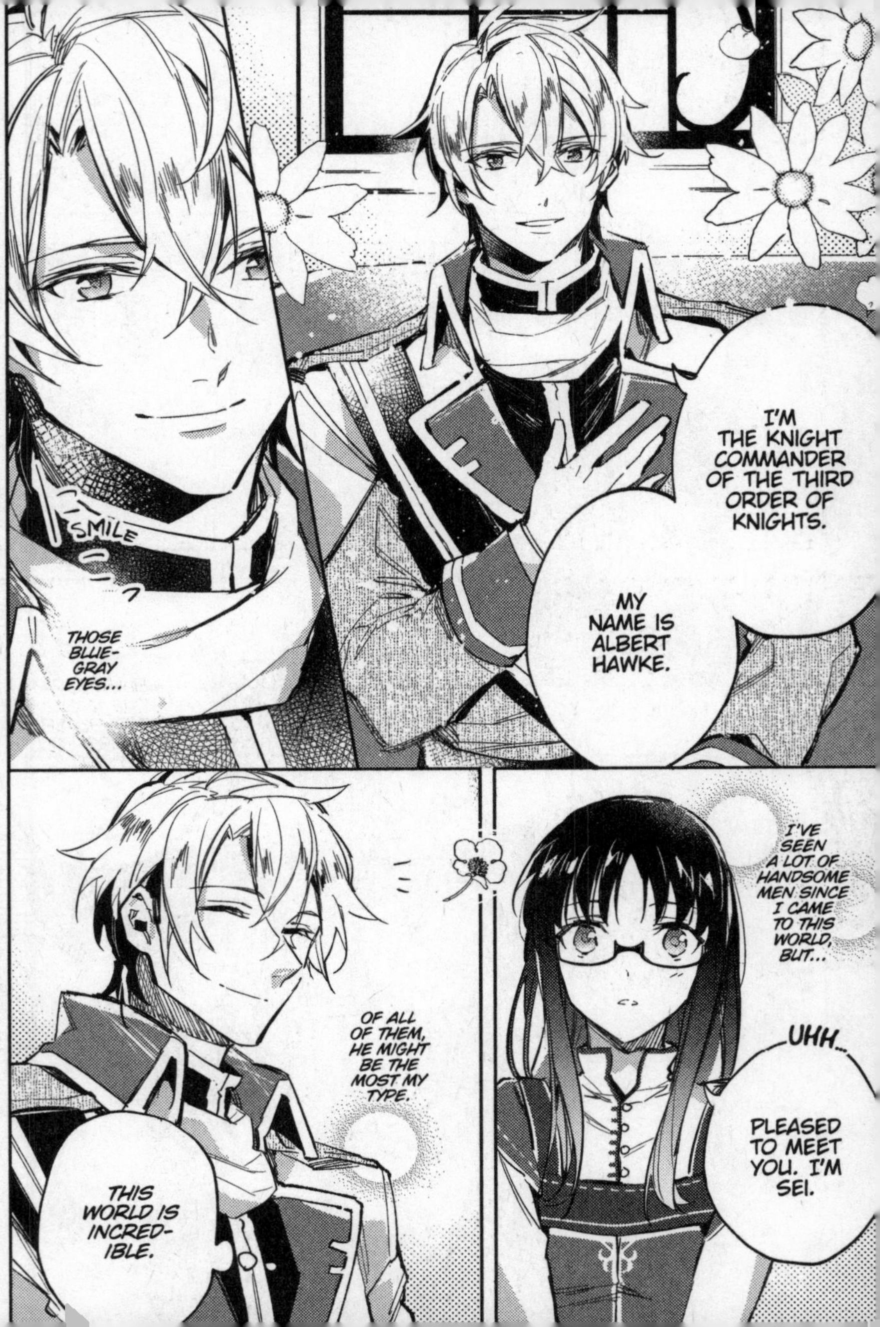
I'M THE KNIGHT COMMANDER OF THE THIRD ORDER OF KNIGHTS.
MY NAME IS ALBERT HAWKE.
SMILE
THOSE BLUE-GRAY EYES...
I'VE SEEN A LOT OF HANDSOME MEN SINCE I CAME TO THIS WORLD, BUT...
UHH...
PLEASED TO MEET YOU. I'M SEI.
OF ALL OF THEM, HE MIGHT BE THE MOST MY TYPE.
THIS WORLD IS INCREDIBLE.

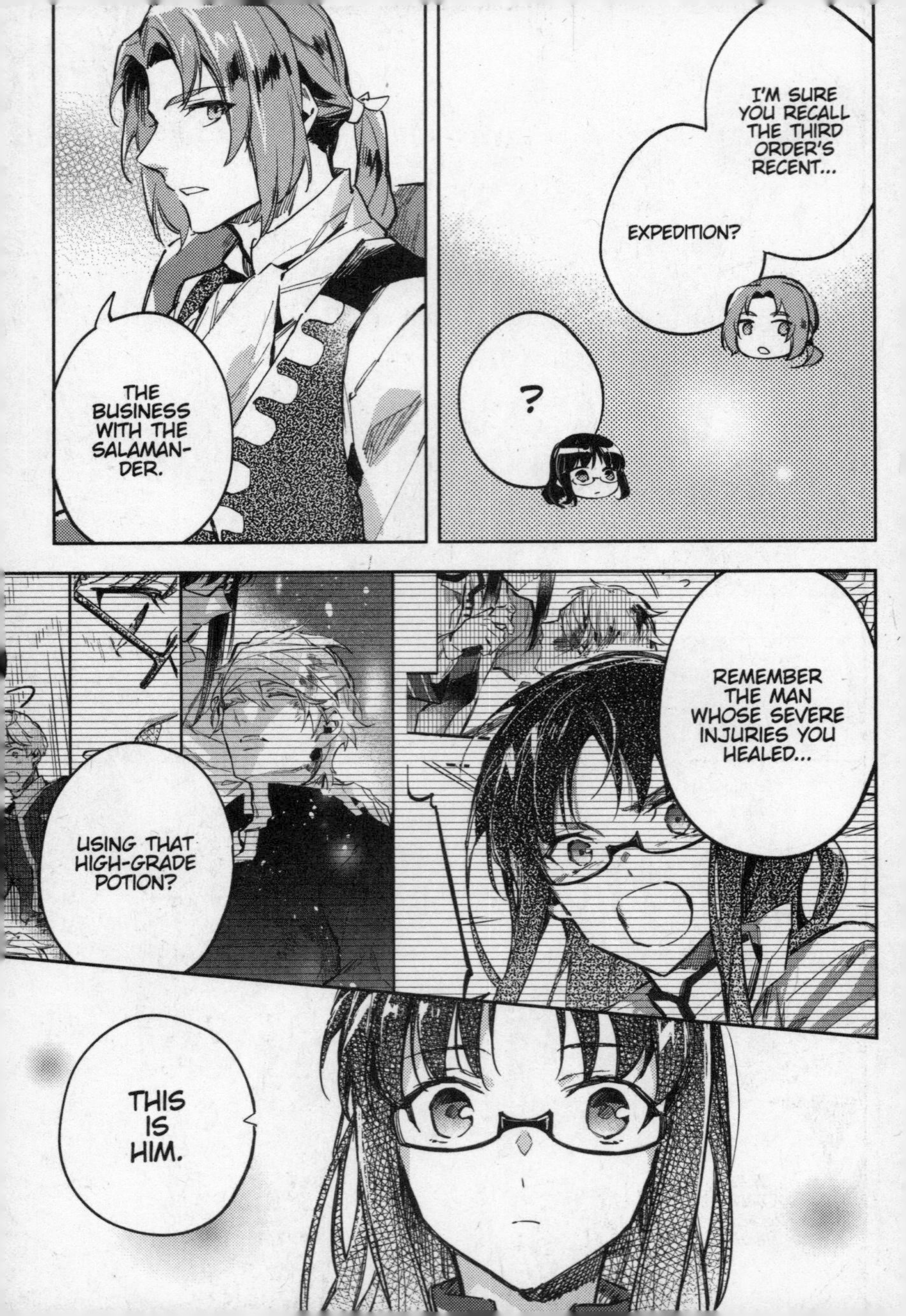
I'M SURE YOU RECALL THE THIRD ORDER'S RECENT...
EXPEDITION?
?
THE BUSINESS WITH THE SALAMANDER.
REMEMBER THE MAN WHOSE SEVERE INJURIES YOU HEALED...
USING THAT HIGH-GRADE POTION?
THIS IS HIM.

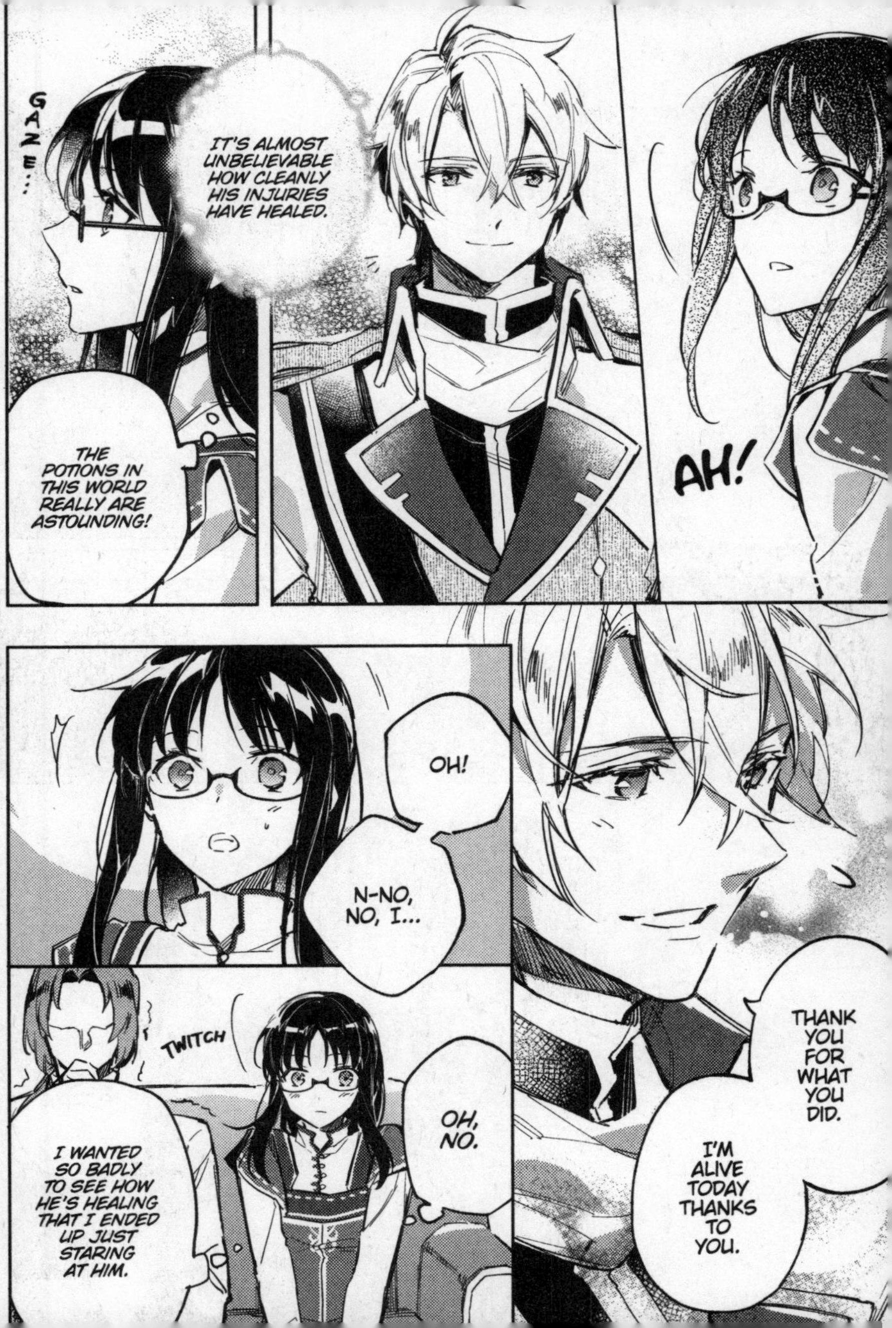
AH!
IT'S ALMOST UNBELIEVABLE HOW CLEANLY HIS INJURIES HAVE HEALED.
GAZE...
THE POTIONS IN THIS WORLD REALLY ARE ASTOUNDING!
THANK YOU FOR WHAT YOU DID.
I'M ALIVE TODAY THANKS TO YOU.
OH!
N-NO, NO, I...
OH, NO.
TWITCH
I WANTED SO BADLY TO SEE HOW HE'S HEALING THAT I ENDED UP JUST STARING AT HIM.

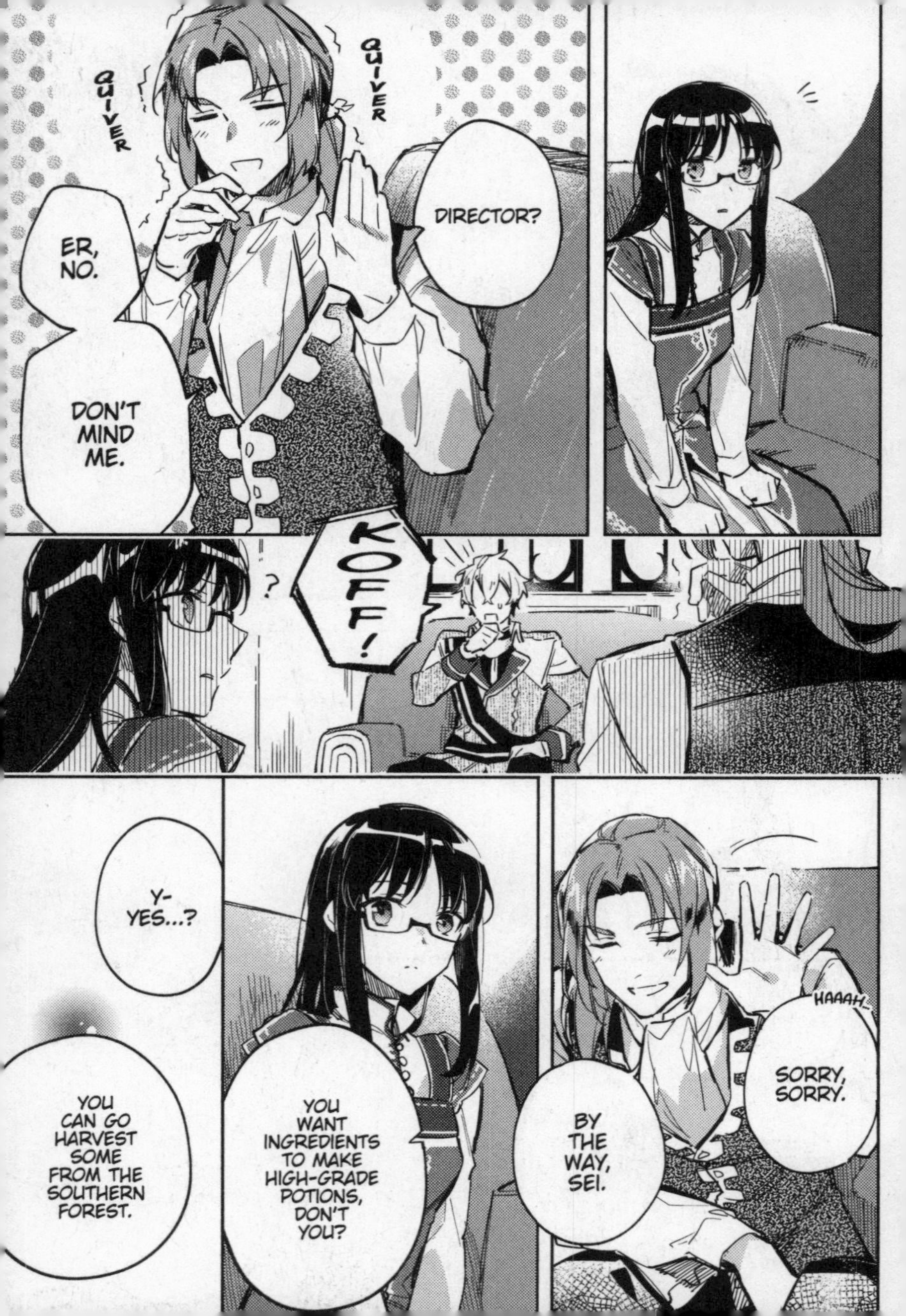
DIRECTOR?
QUIVER
QUIVER
ER, NO.
DON'T MIND ME.
KOFF!
?
HAAAAH
SORRY, SORRY.
BY THE WAY, SEI.
YOU WANT INGREDIENTS TO MAKE HIGH-GRADE POTIONS, DON'T YOU?
Y-YES...?
YOU CAN GO HARVEST SOME FROM THE SOUTHERN FOREST.

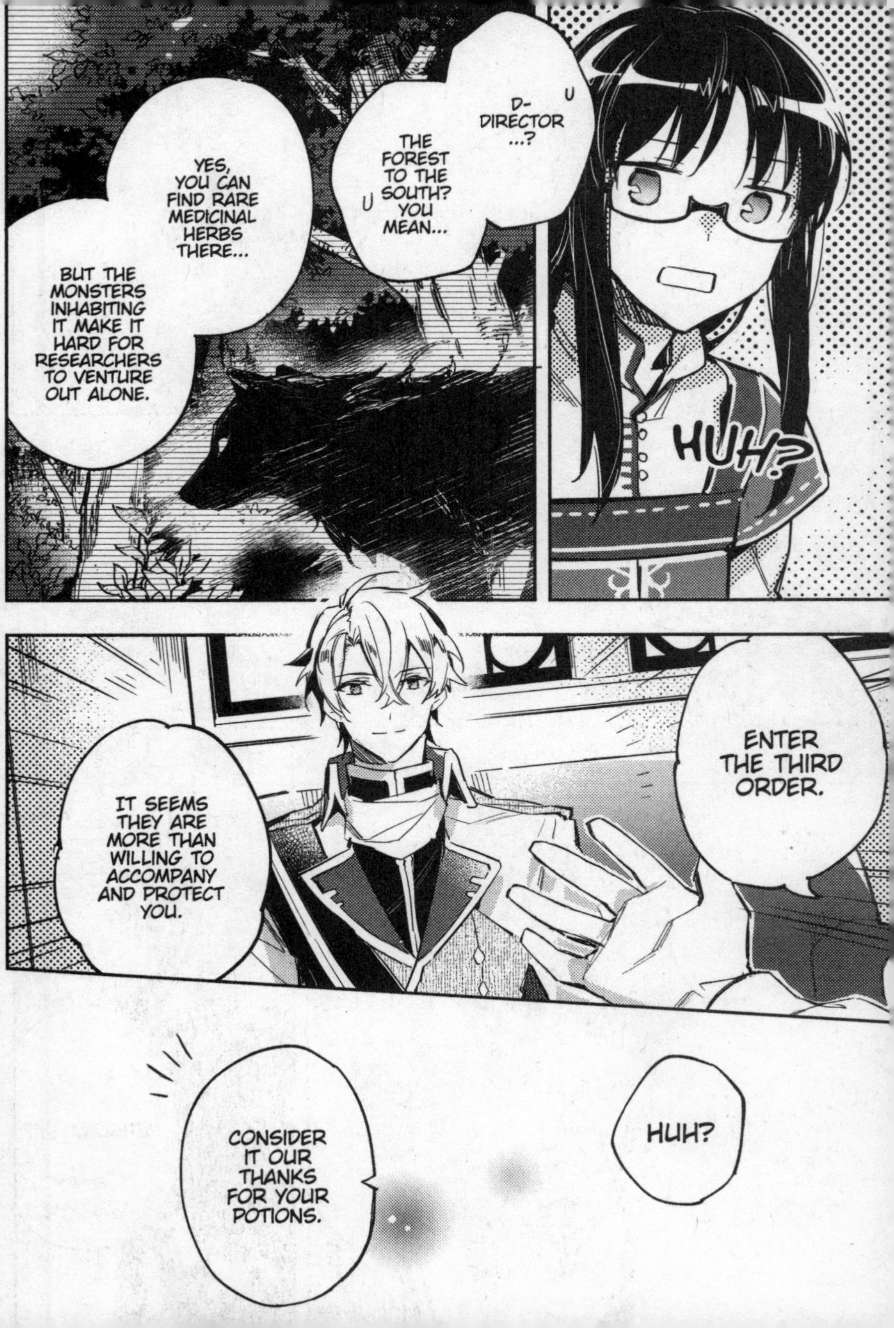
HUH?
D-DIRECTOR ...?
THE FOREST TO THE SOUTH? YOU MEAN...
YES, YOU CAN FIND RARE MEDICINAL HERBS THERE...
BUT THE MONSTERS INHABITING IT MAKE IT HARD FOR RESEARCHERS TO VENTURE OUT ALONE.
ENTER THE THIRD ORDER.
IT SEEMS THEY ARE MORE THAN WILLING TO ACCOMPANY AND PROTECT YOU.
HUH?
CONSIDER IT OUR THANKS FOR YOUR POTIONS.

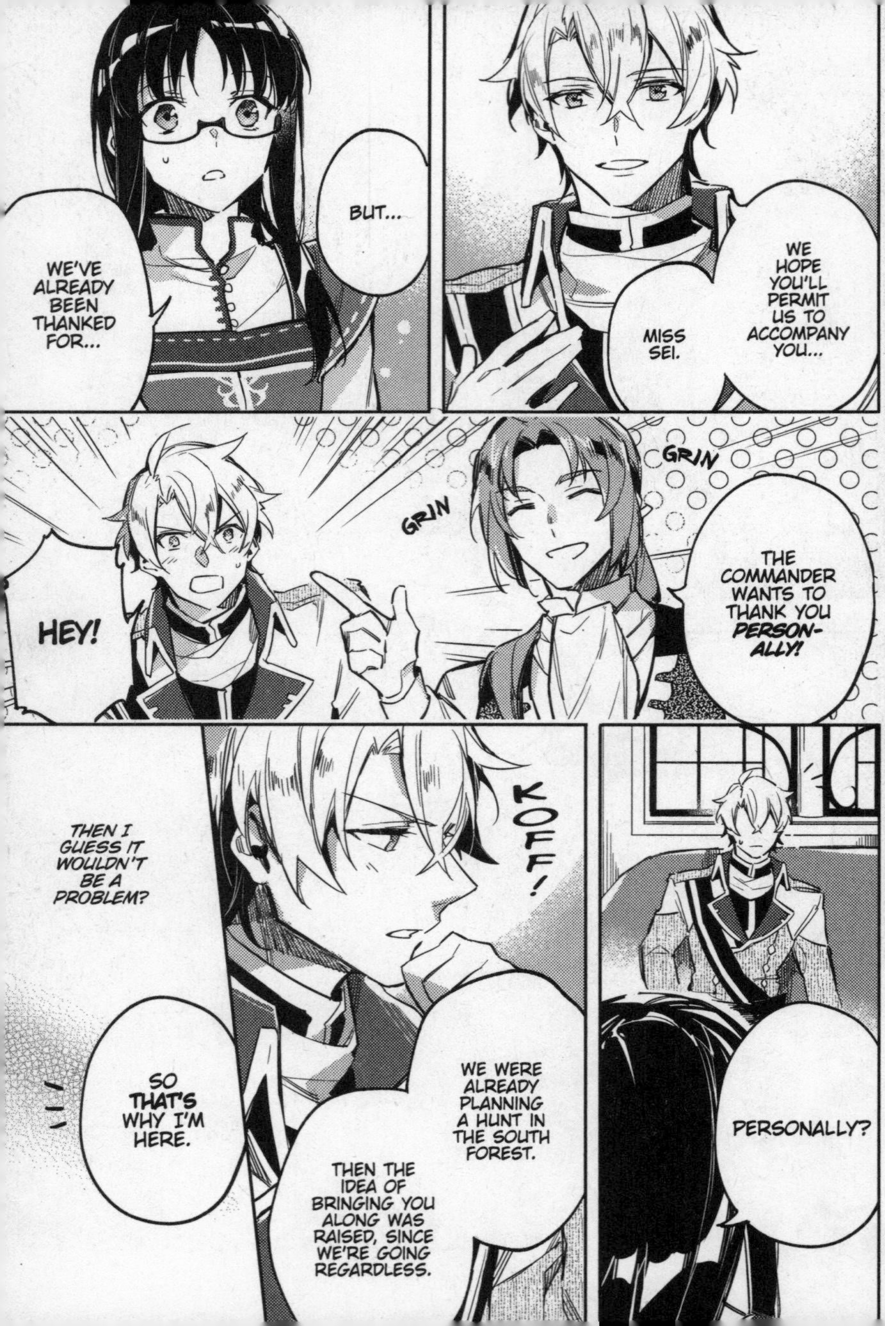
WE HOPE YOU'LL PERMIT US TO ACCOMPANY YOU...
MISS SEI.
BUT...
WE'VE ALREADY BEEN THANKED FOR...
GRIN
THE COMMANDER WANTS TO THANK YOU PERSONALLY!
GRIN
HEY!
PERSONALLY?
KOFF!
WE WERE ALREADY PLANNING A HUNT IN THE SOUTH FOREST.
THEN THE IDEA OF BRINGING YOU ALONG WAS RAISED, SINCE WE'RE GOING REGARDLESS.
THEN I GUESS IT WOULDN'T BE A PROBLEM?
SO THAT'S WHY I'M HERE.

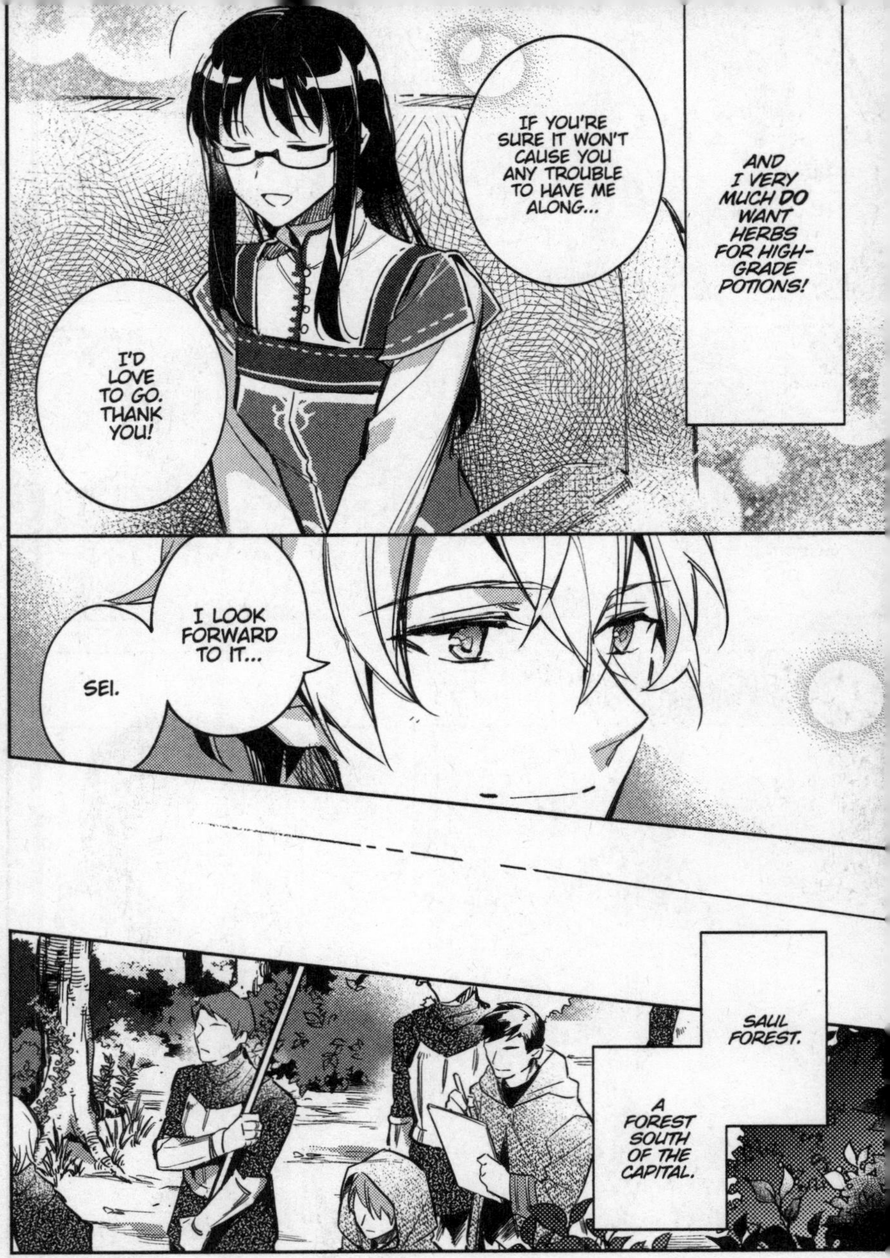
AND I VERY MUCH DO WANT HERBS FOR HIGH-GRADE POTIONS!
IF YOU'RE SURE IT WON'T CAUSE YOU ANY TROUBLE TO HAVE ME ALONG...
I'D LOVE TO GO. THANK YOU!
I LOOK FORWARD TO IT... SEI.
SAUL FOREST.
A FOREST SOUTH OF THE CAPITAL.

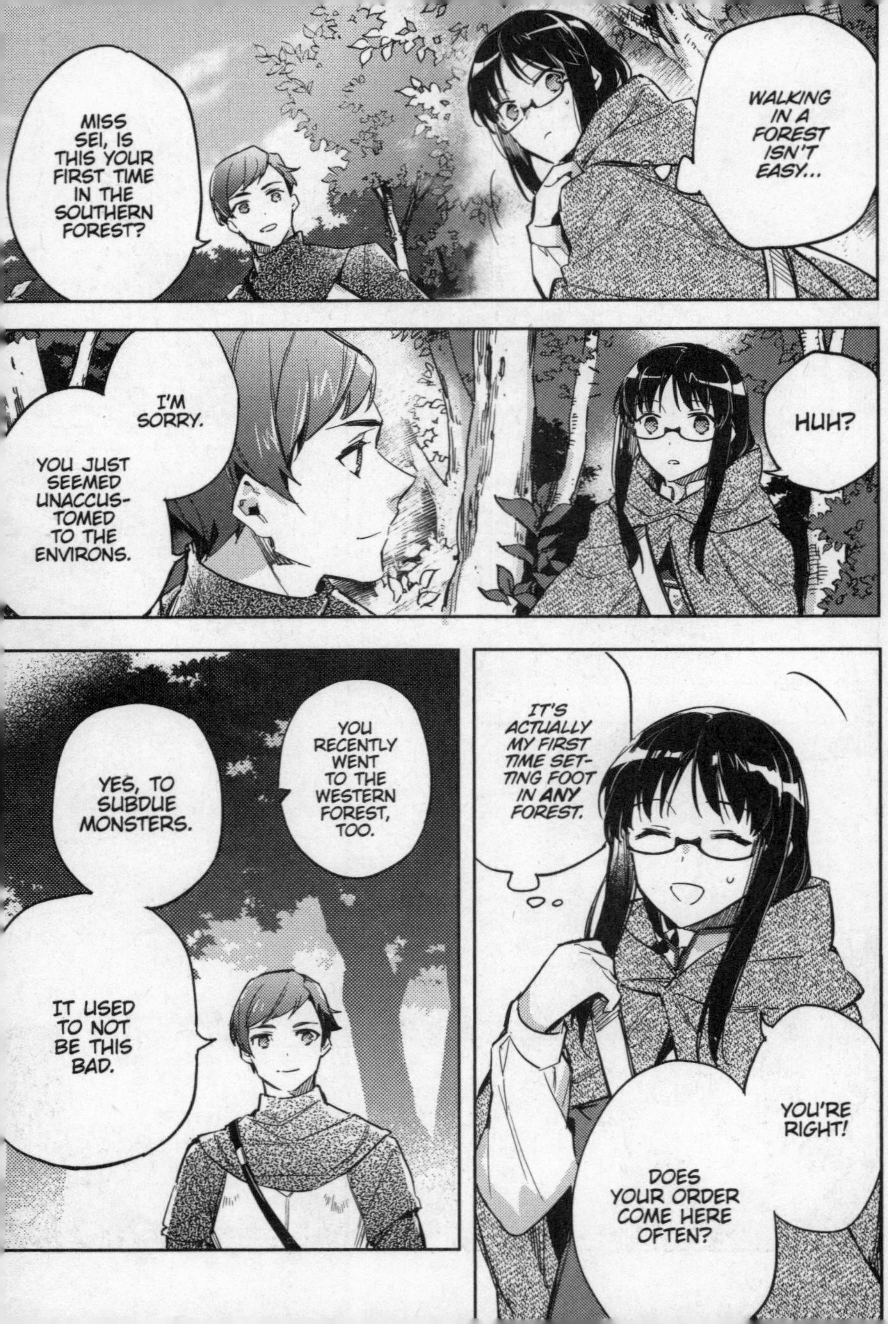
WALKING IN A FOREST ISN'T EASY...
MISS SEI, IS THIS YOUR FIRST TIME IN THE SOUTHERN FOREST?
HUH?
I'M SORRY.
YOU JUST SEEMED UNACCUS-TOMED TO THE ENVIRONS.
IT'S ACTUALLY MY FIRST TIME SET-TING FOOT IN ANY FOREST.
YOU'RE RIGHT!
DOES YOUR ORDER COME HERE OFTEN?
YOU RECENTLY WENT TO THE WESTERN FOREST, TOO.
YES, TO SUBDUE MONSTERS.
IT USED TO NOT BE THIS BAD.

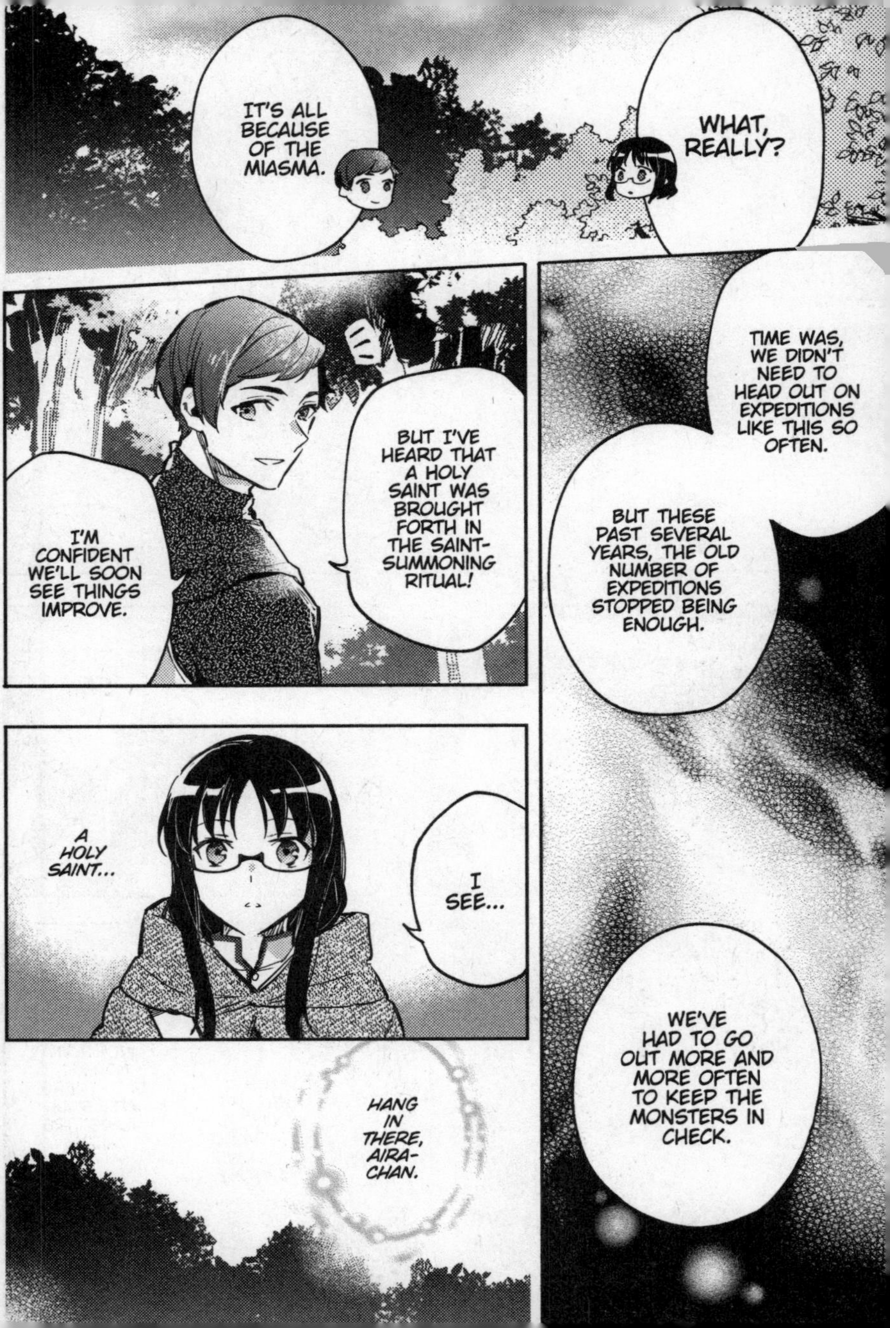
WHAT, REALLY?
IT'S ALL BECAUSE OF THE MIASMA.
TIME WAS, WE DIDN'T NEED TO HEAD OUT ON EXPEDITIONS LIKE THIS SO OFTEN.
BUT THESE PAST SEVERAL YEARS, THE OLD NUMBER OF EXPEDITIONS STOPPED BEING ENOUGH.
WE'VE HAD TO GO OUT MORE AND MORE OFTEN TO KEEP THE MONSTERS IN CHECK.
BUT I'VE HEARD THAT A HOLY SAINT WAS BROUGHT FORTH IN THE SAINT-SUMMONING RITUAL!
I'M CONFIDENT WE'LL SOON SEE THINGS IMPROVE.
I SEE...
A HOLY SAINT...
HANG IN THERE, AIRA-CHAN.

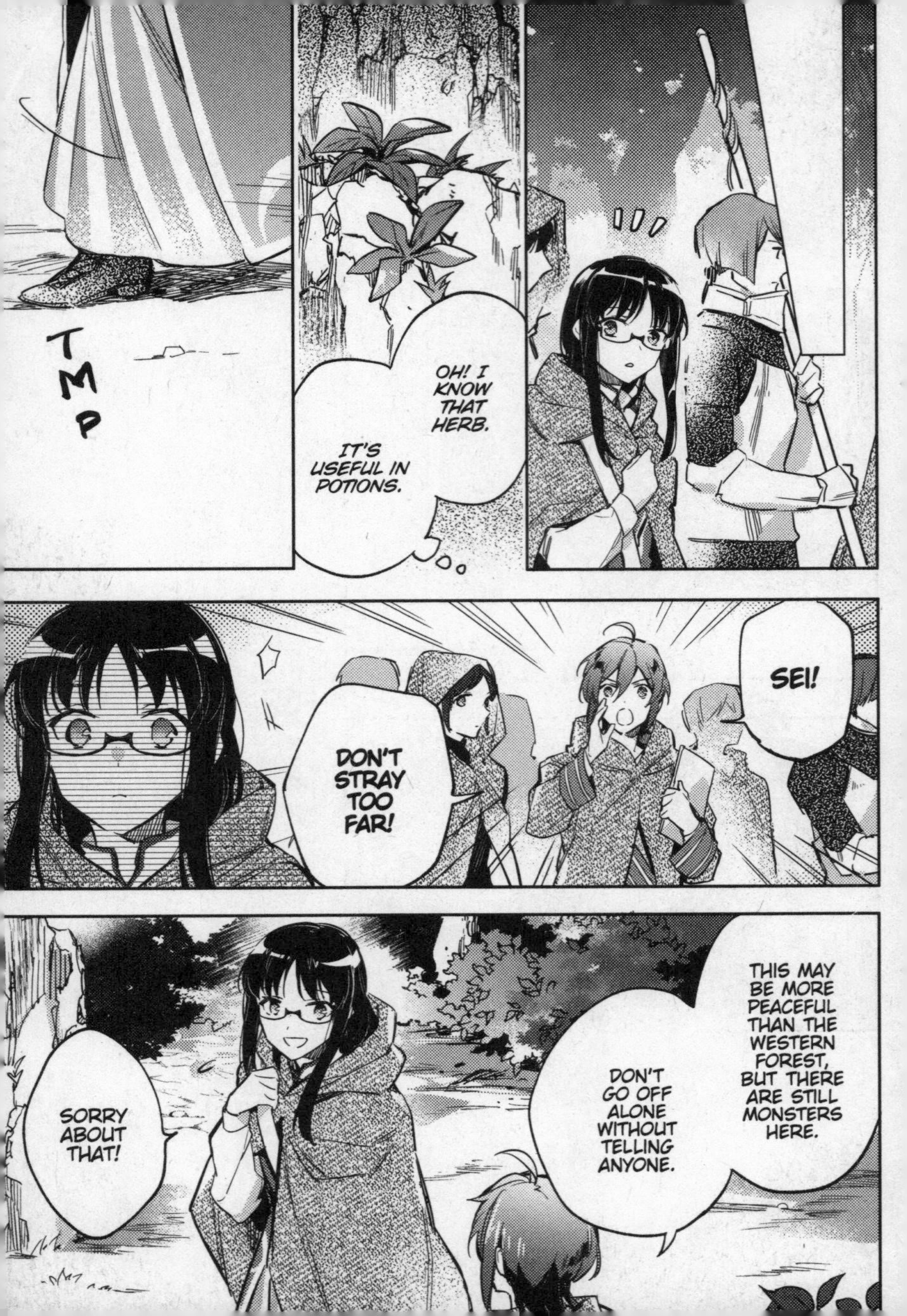

OH! I KNOW THAT HERB.
IT'S USEFUL IN POTIONS.
TMP
SEI!
DON'T STRAY TOO FAR!
THIS MAY BE MORE PEACEFUL THAN THE WESTERN FOREST, BUT THERE ARE STILL MONSTERS HERE.
DON'T GO OFF ALONE WITHOUT TELLING ANYONE.
SORRY ABOUT THAT!

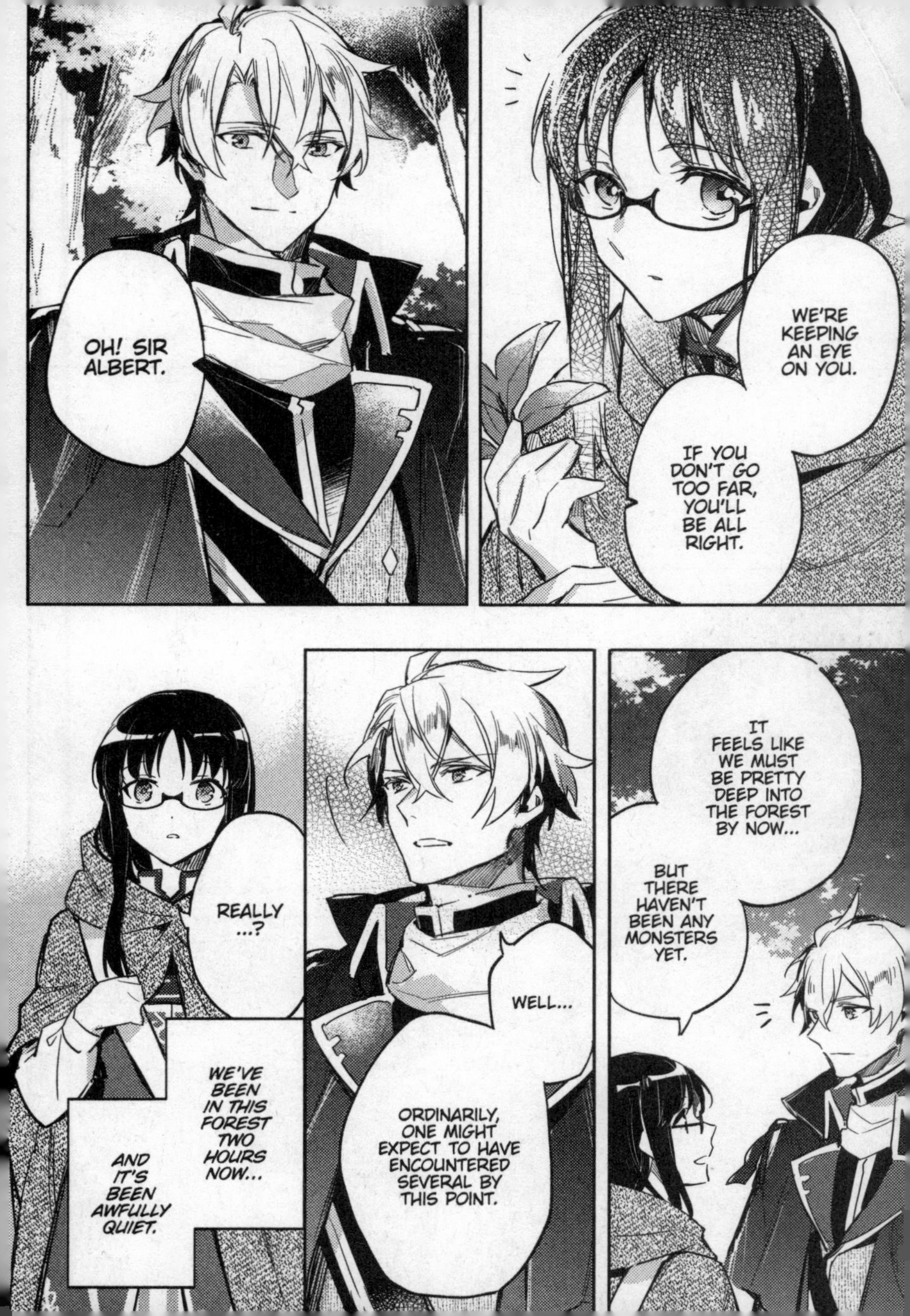
WE'RE KEEPING AN EYE ON YOU.
IF YOU DON'T GO TOO FAR, YOU'LL BE ALL RIGHT.
OH! SIR ALBERT.
IT FEELS LIKE WE MUST BE PRETTY DEEP INTO THE FOREST BY NOW...
BUT THERE HAVEN'T BEEN ANY MONSTERS YET.
WELL...
ORDINARILY, ONE MIGHT EXPECT TO HAVE ENCOUNTERED SEVERAL BY THIS POINT.
REALLY ...?
WE'VE BEEN IN THIS FOREST TWO HOURS NOW...
AND IT'S BEEN AWFULLY QUIET.

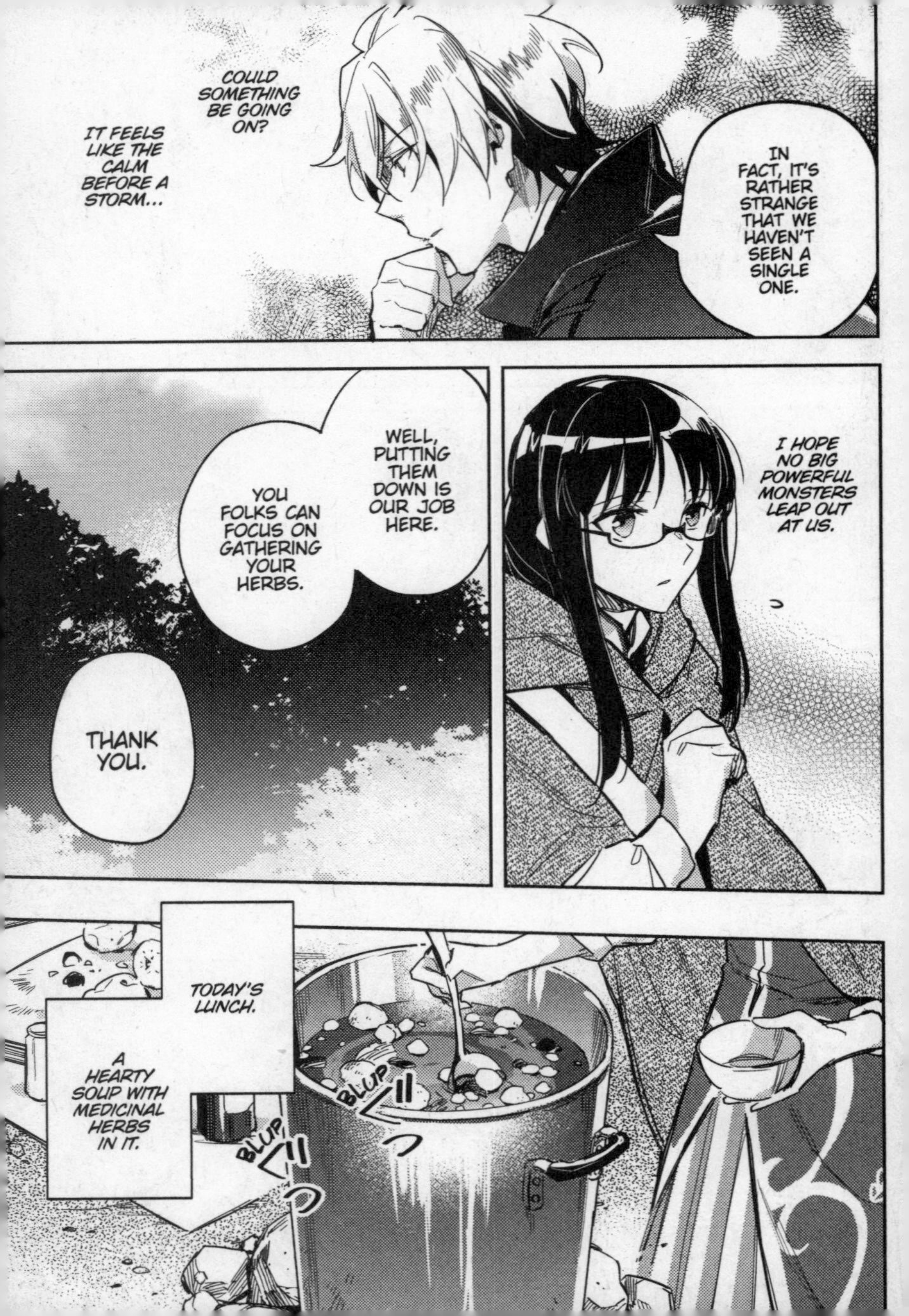
IN FACT, IT'S RATHER STRANGE THAT WE HAVEN'T SEEN A SINGLE ONE.
COULD SOMETHING BE GOING ON?
IT FEELS LIKE THE CALM BEFORE A STORM...
I HOPE NO BIG POWERFUL MONSTERS LEAP OUT AT US.
WELL, PUTTING THEM DOWN IS OUR JOB HERE.
YOU FOLKS CAN FOCUS ON GATHERING YOUR HERBS.
THANK YOU.
TODAY'S LUNCH.
A HEARTY SOUP WITH MEDICINAL HERBS IN IT.
BLUP
BLUP

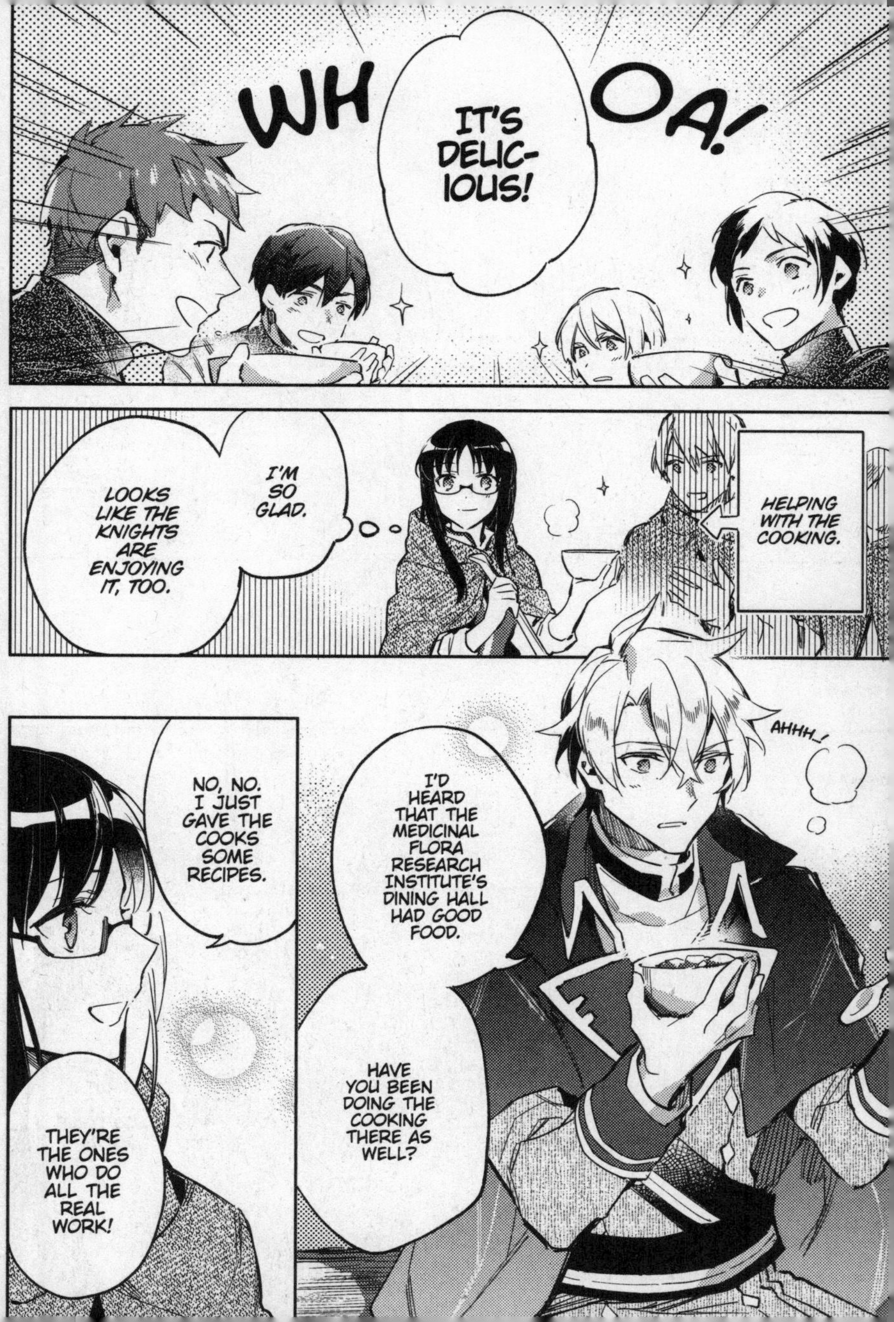
WHOA!
IT'S DELICIOUS!
HELPING WITH THE COOKING.
I'M SO GLAD.
LOOKS LIKE THE KNIGHTS ARE ENJOYING IT, TOO.
AHHH...!
I'D HEARD THAT THE MEDICINAL FLORA RESEARCH INSTITUTE'S DINING HALL HAD GOOD FOOD.
HAVE YOU BEEN DOING THE COOKING THERE AS WELL?
NO, NO. I JUST GAVE THE COOKS SOME RECIPES.
THEY'RE THE ONES WHO DO ALL THE REAL WORK!

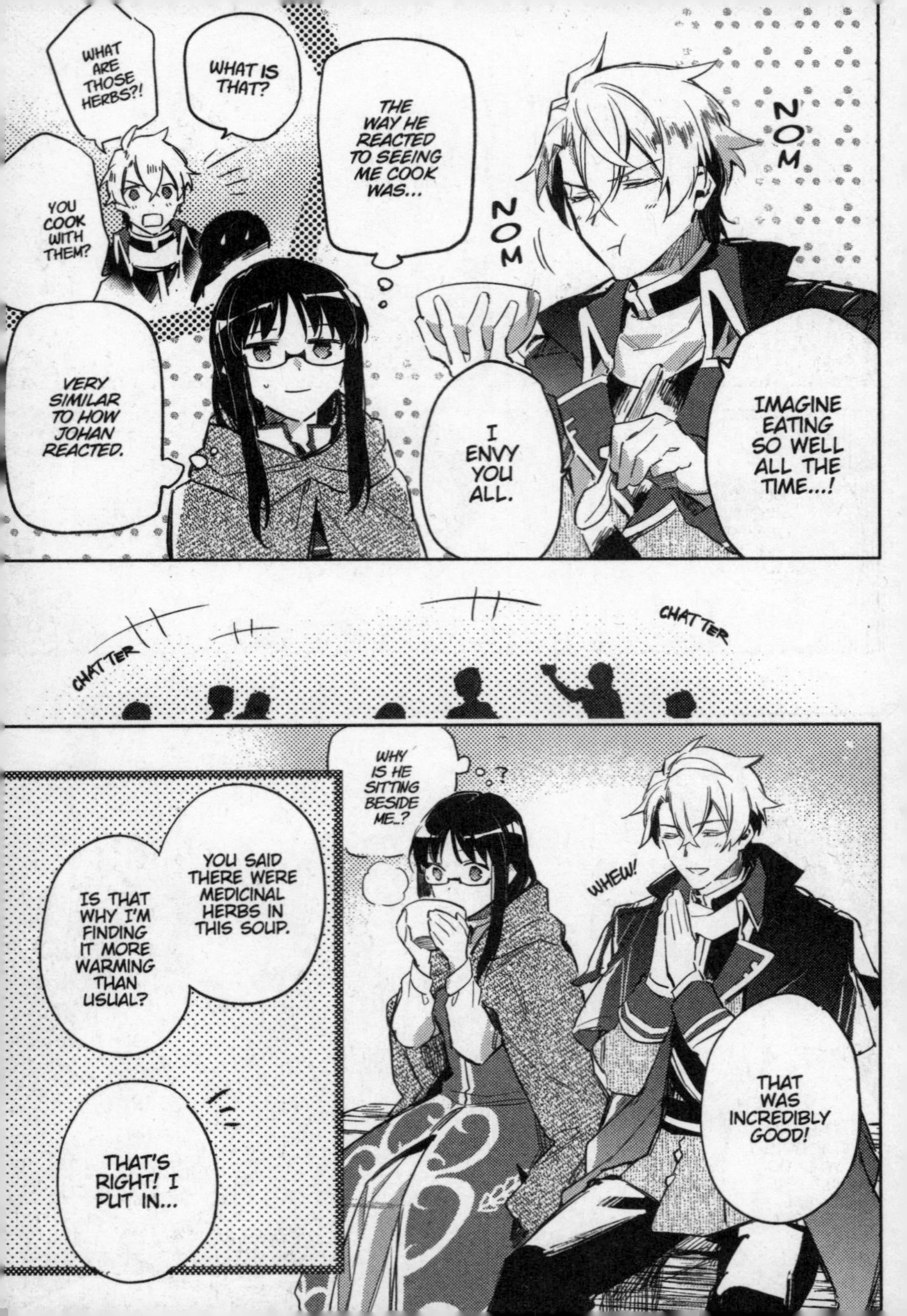
NOM
NOM
IMAGINE EATING SO WELL ALL THE TIME...!
I ENVY YOU ALL.
THE WAY HE REACTED TO SEEING ME COOK WAS...
WHAT IS THAT?
WHAT ARE THOSE HERBS?!
YOU COOK WITH THEM?
VERY SIMILAR TO HOW JOHAN REACTED.
CHATTER
CHATTER
WHY IS HE SITTING BESIDE ME..?
WHEW!
THAT WAS INCREDIBLY GOOD!
YOU SAID THERE WERE MEDICINAL HERBS IN THIS SOUP.
IS THAT WHY I'M FINDING IT MORE WARMING THAN USUAL?
THAT'S RIGHT! I PUT IN...

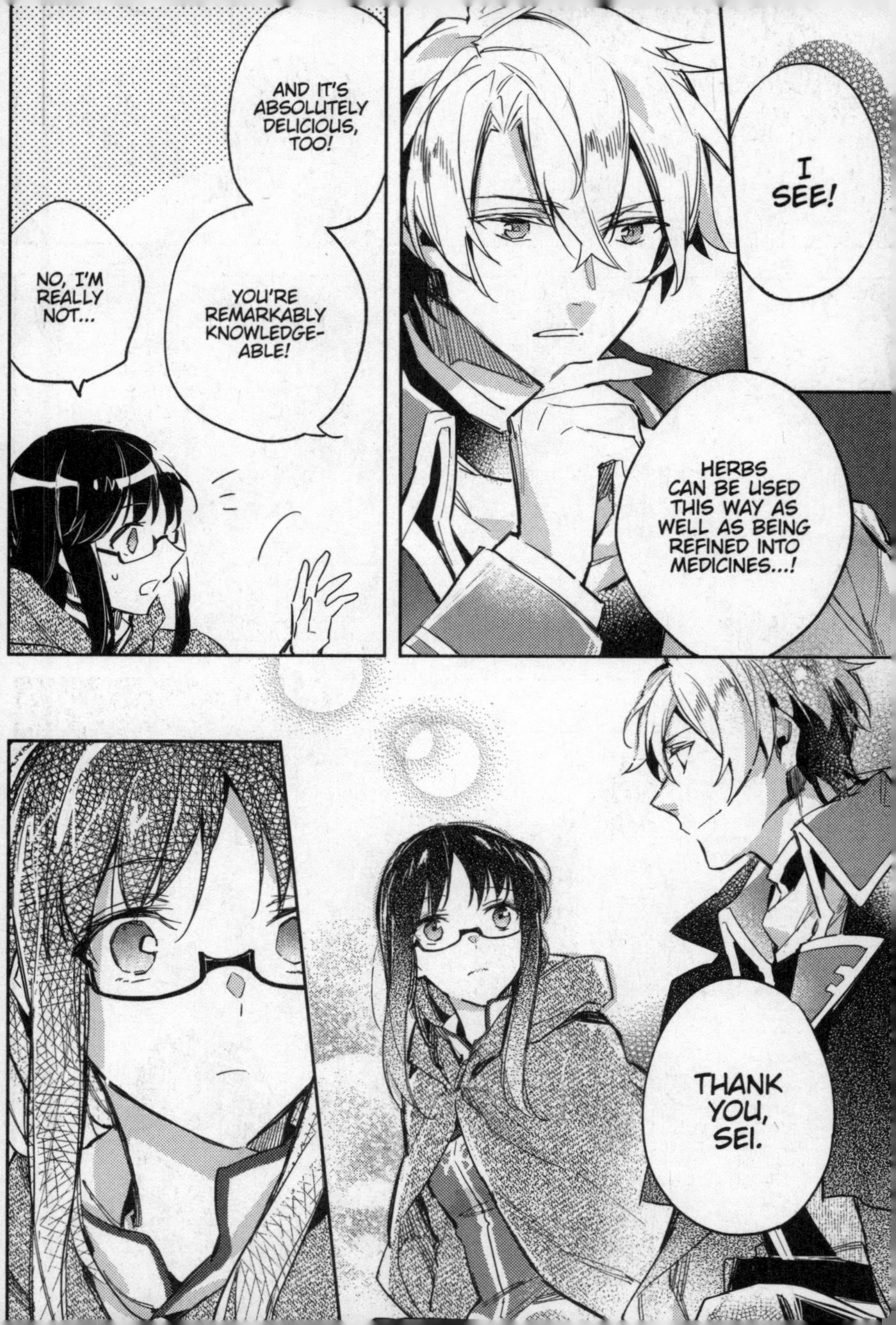
I SEE!
HERBS CAN BE USED THIS WAY AS WELL AS BEING REFINED INTO MEDICINES...!
AND IT'S ABSOLUTELY DELICIOUS, TOO!
YOU'RE REMARKABLY KNOWLEDGE-ABLE!
NO, I'M REALLY NOT...
THANK YOU, SEI.

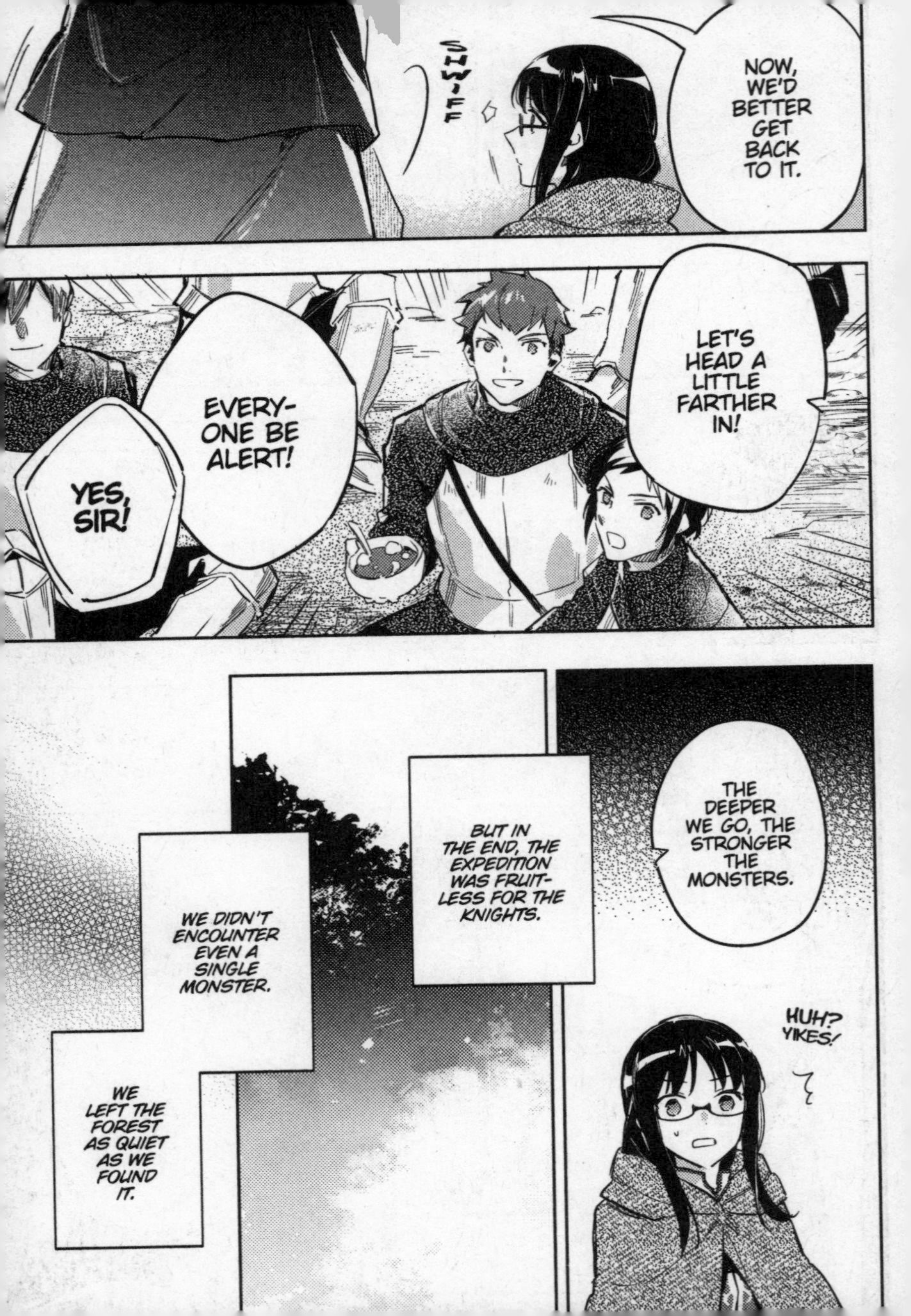
NOW, WE'D BETTER GET BACK TO IT.
SHWIFF
LET'S HEAD A LITTLE FARTHER IN!
EVERY-ONE BE ALERT!
YES, SIR!
THE DEEPER WE GO, THE STRONGER THE MONSTERS.
HUH? YIKES!
BUT IN THE END, THE EXPEDITION WAS FRUIT-LESS FOR THE KNIGHTS.
WE DIDN'T ENCOUNTER EVEN A SINGLE MONSTER.
WE LEFT THE FOREST AS QUIET AS WE FOUND IT.

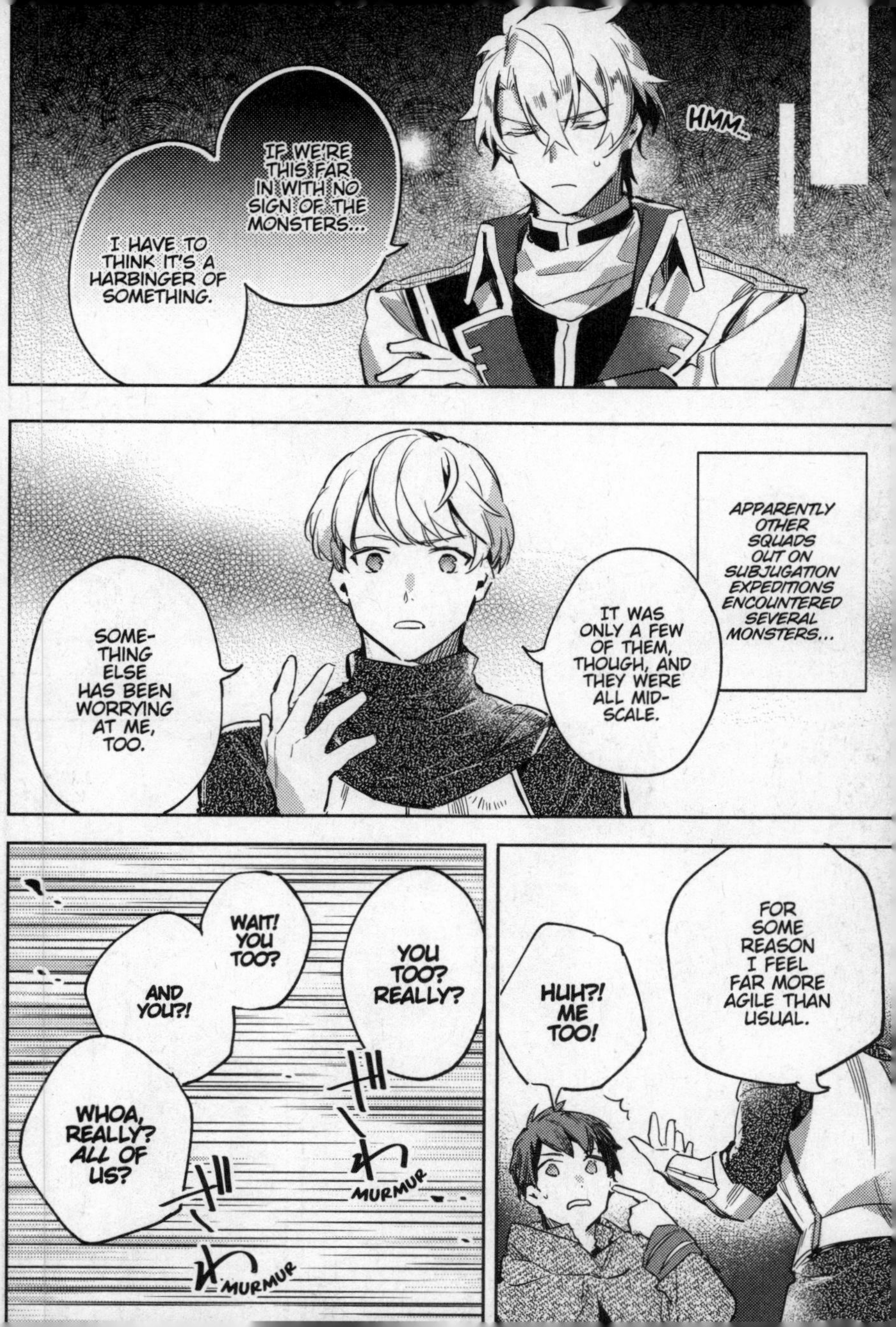
HMM...
IF WE'RE THIS FAR IN WITH NO SIGN OF THE MONSTERS...
I HAVE TO THINK IT'S A HARBINGER OF SOMETHING.
APPARENTLY OTHER SQUADS OUT ON SUBJUGATION EXPEDITIONS ENCOUNTERED SEVERAL MONSTERS...
IT WAS ONLY A FEW OF THEM, THOUGH, AND THEY WERE ALL MID-SCALE.
SOME-THING ELSE HAS BEEN WORRYING AT ME, TOO.
FOR SOME REASON I FEEL FAR MORE AGILE THAN USUAL.
HUH?! ME TOO!
YOU TOO? REALLY?
WAIT! YOU TOO?
AND YOU?!
WHOA, REALLY? ALL OF US?
MURMUR
MURMUR

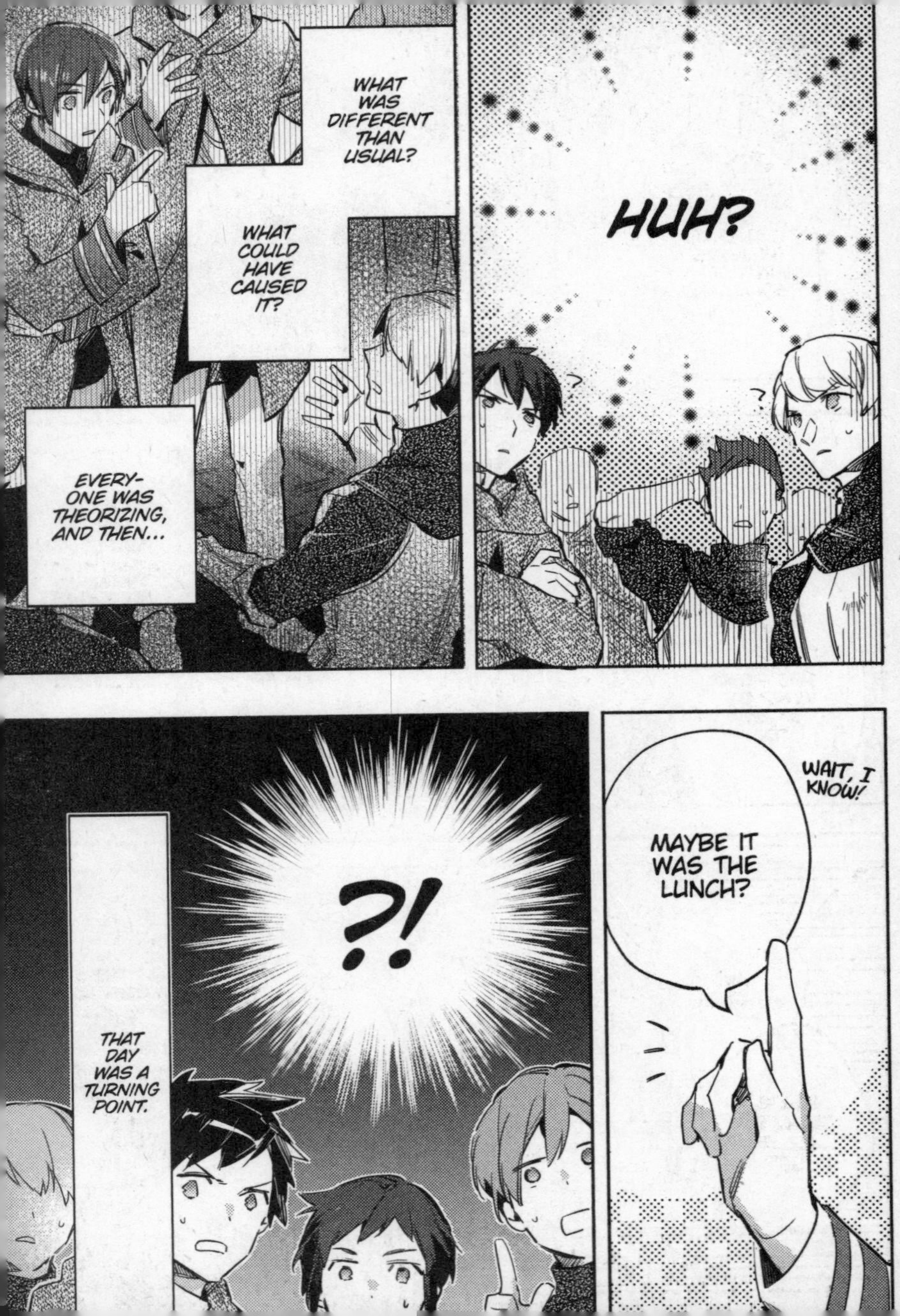
HUH?
WHAT WAS DIFFERENT THAN USUAL?
WHAT COULD HAVE CAUSED IT?
EVERY-ONE WAS THEORIZING, AND THEN...
WAIT, I KNOW!
MAYBE IT WAS THE LUNCH?
?!
THAT DAY WAS A TURNING POINT.

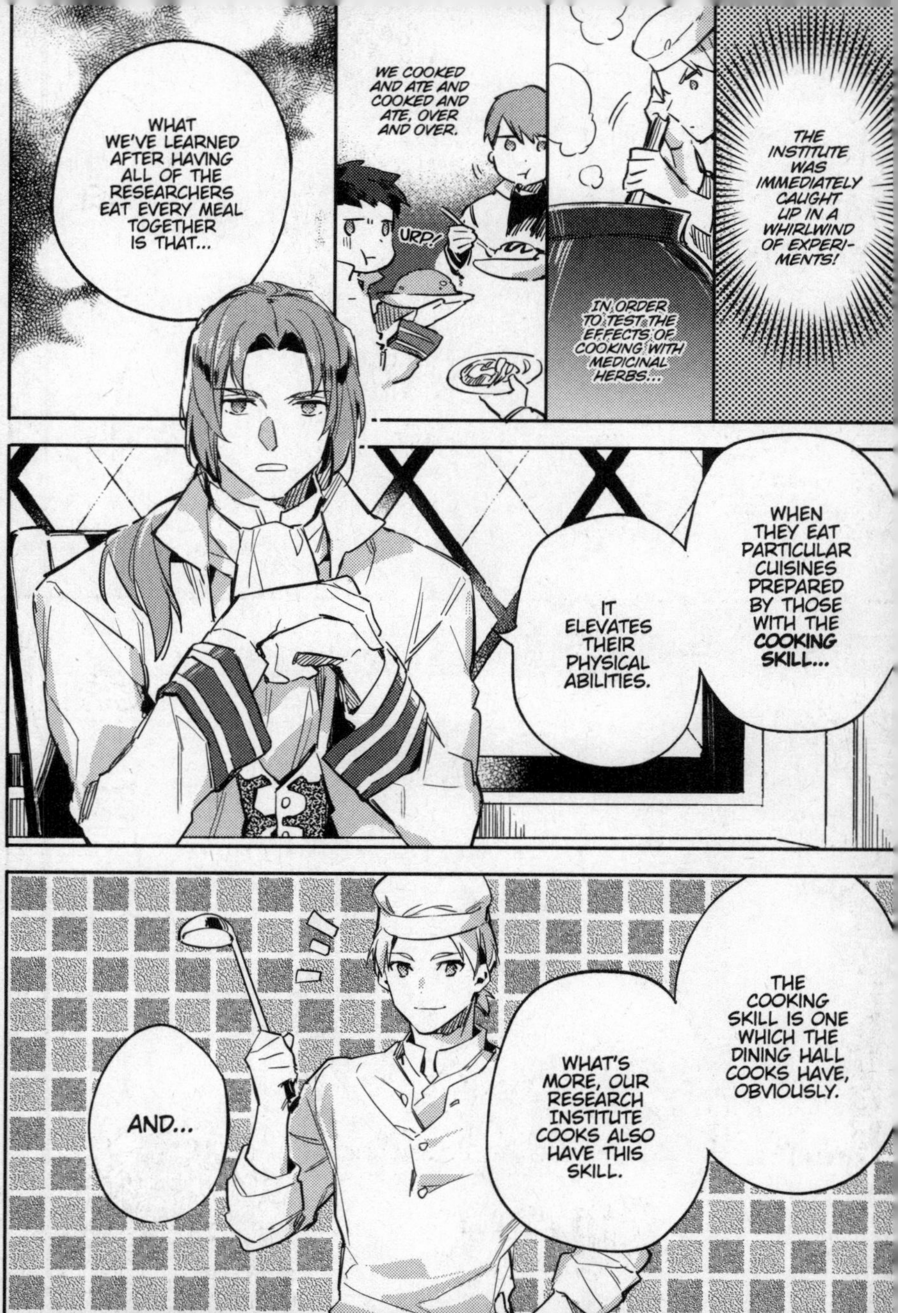
THE INSTITUTE WAS IMMEDIATELY CAUGHT UP IN A WHIRLWIND OF EXPERI-MENTS!
IN ORDER TO TEST THE EFFECTS OF COOKING WITH MEDICINAL HERBS...
WE COOKED AND ATE AND COOKED AND ATE, OVER AND OVER.
URP!
WHAT WE'VE LEARNED AFTER HAVING ALL OF THE RESEARCHERS EAT EVERY MEAL TOGETHER IS THAT...
WHEN THEY EAT PARTICULAR CUISINES PREPARED BY THOSE WITH THE **COOKING SKILL...**
IT ELEVATES THEIR PHYSICAL ABILITIES.
THE COOKING SKILL IS ONE WHICH THE DINING HALL COOKS HAVE, OBVIOUSLY.
WHAT'S MORE, OUR RESEARCH INSTITUTE COOKS ALSO HAVE THIS SKILL.
AND...

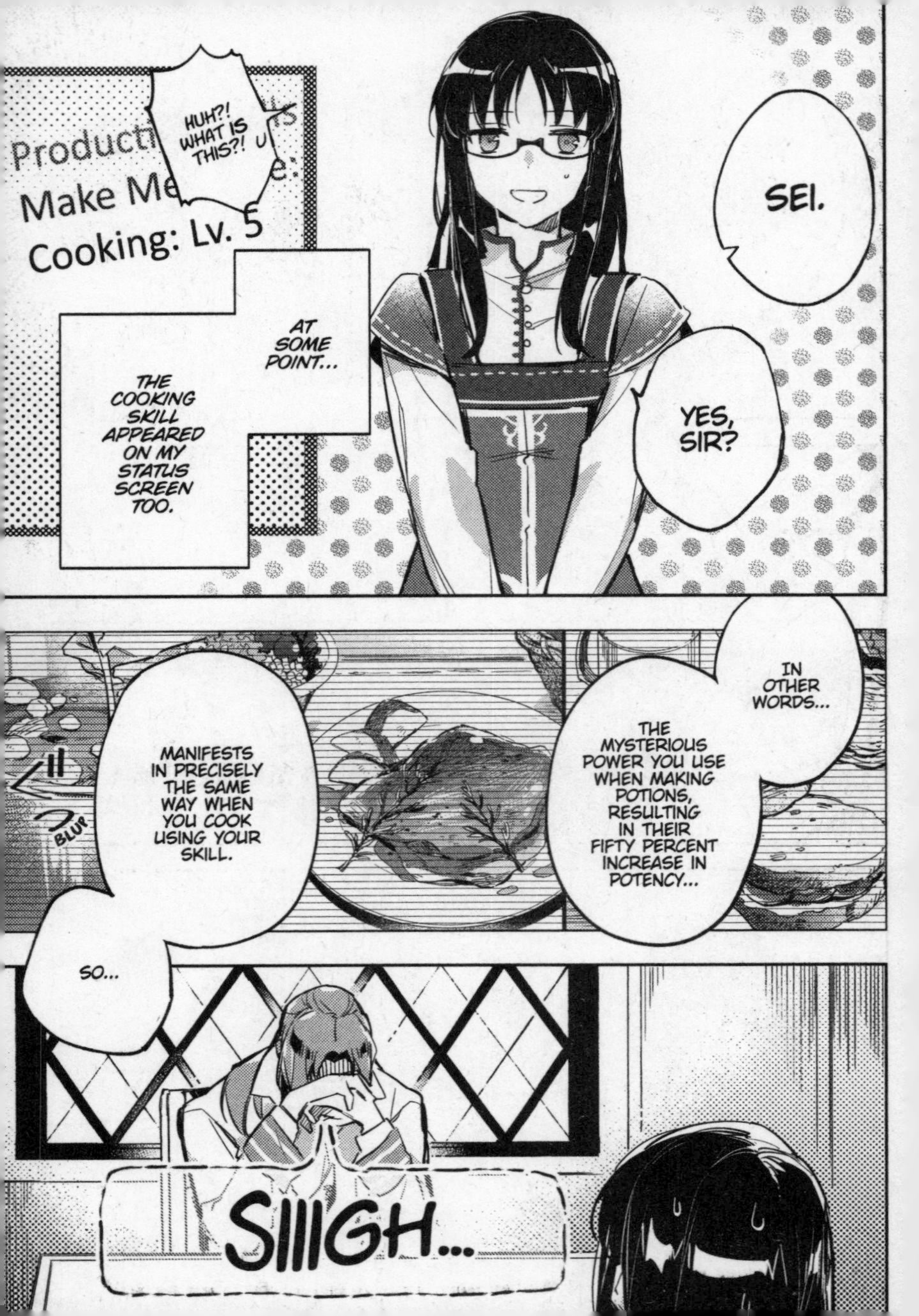
SEI.
YES, SIR?
AT SOME POINT...
THE COOKING SKILL APPEARED ON MY STATUS SCREEN TOO.
HUH?! WHAT IS THIS?!
Producti
Make Me
Cooking: Lv. 5
IN OTHER WORDS...
THE MYSTERIOUS POWER YOU USE WHEN MAKING POTIONS, RESULTING IN THEIR FIFTY PERCENT INCREASE IN POTENCY...
MANIFESTS IN PRECISELY THE SAME WAY WHEN YOU COOK USING YOUR SKILL.
BLUP
SO...
SIIIGH...

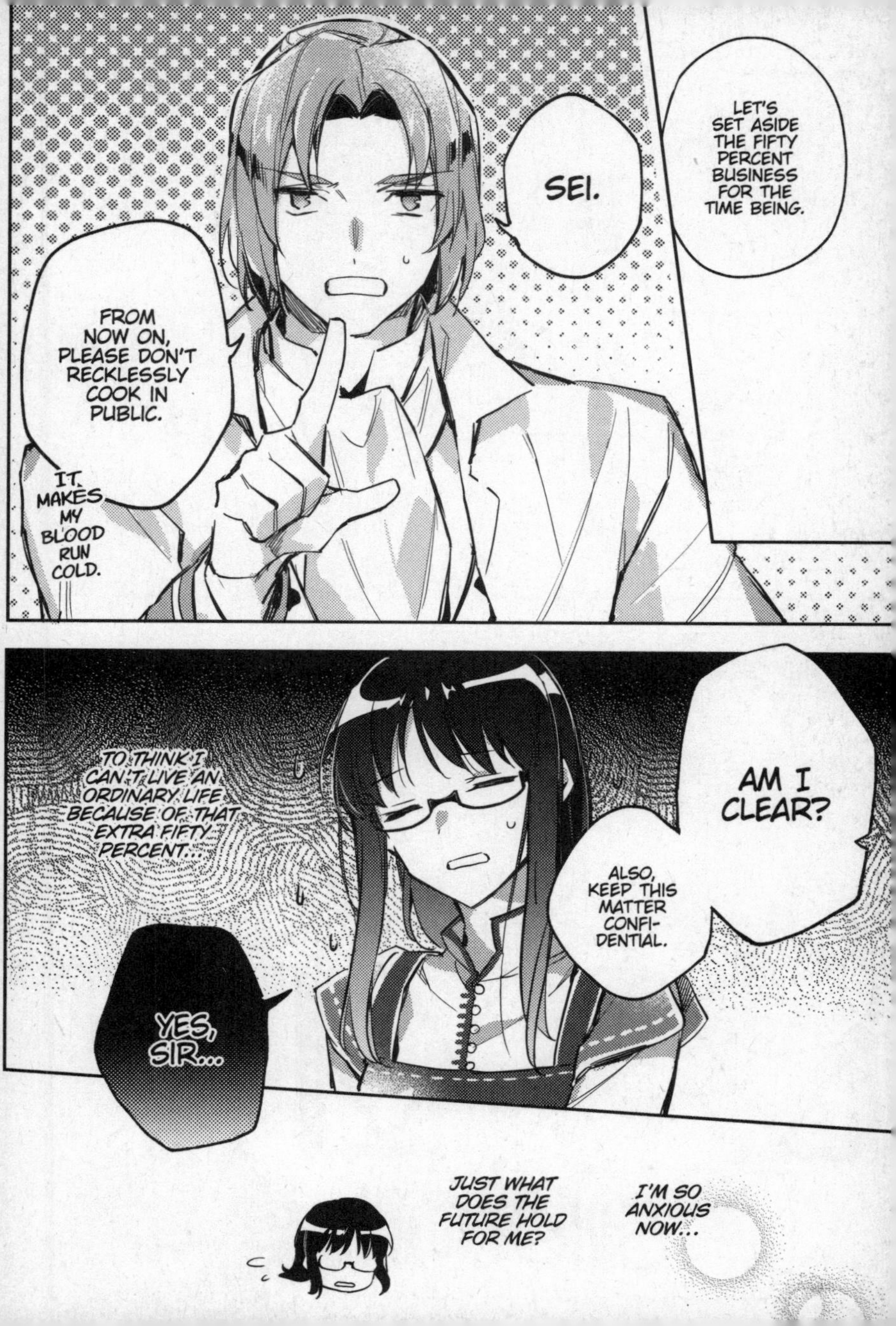
LET'S SET ASIDE THE FIFTY PERCENT BUSINESS FOR THE TIME BEING.
SEI.
FROM NOW ON, PLEASE DON'T RECKLESSLY COOK IN PUBLIC.
IT MAKES MY BLOOD RUN COLD.
AM I CLEAR?
ALSO, KEEP THIS MATTER CONFI-DENTIAL.
TO THINK I CAN'T LIVE AN ORDINARY LIFE BECAUSE OF THAT EXTRA FIFTY PERCENT...
YES, SIR...
I'M SO ANXIOUS NOW...
JUST WHAT DOES THE FUTURE HOLD FOR ME?

The Saint's **Magic Power** is **Omnipotent**

The **Saint's**
Magic Power is
Omnipotent

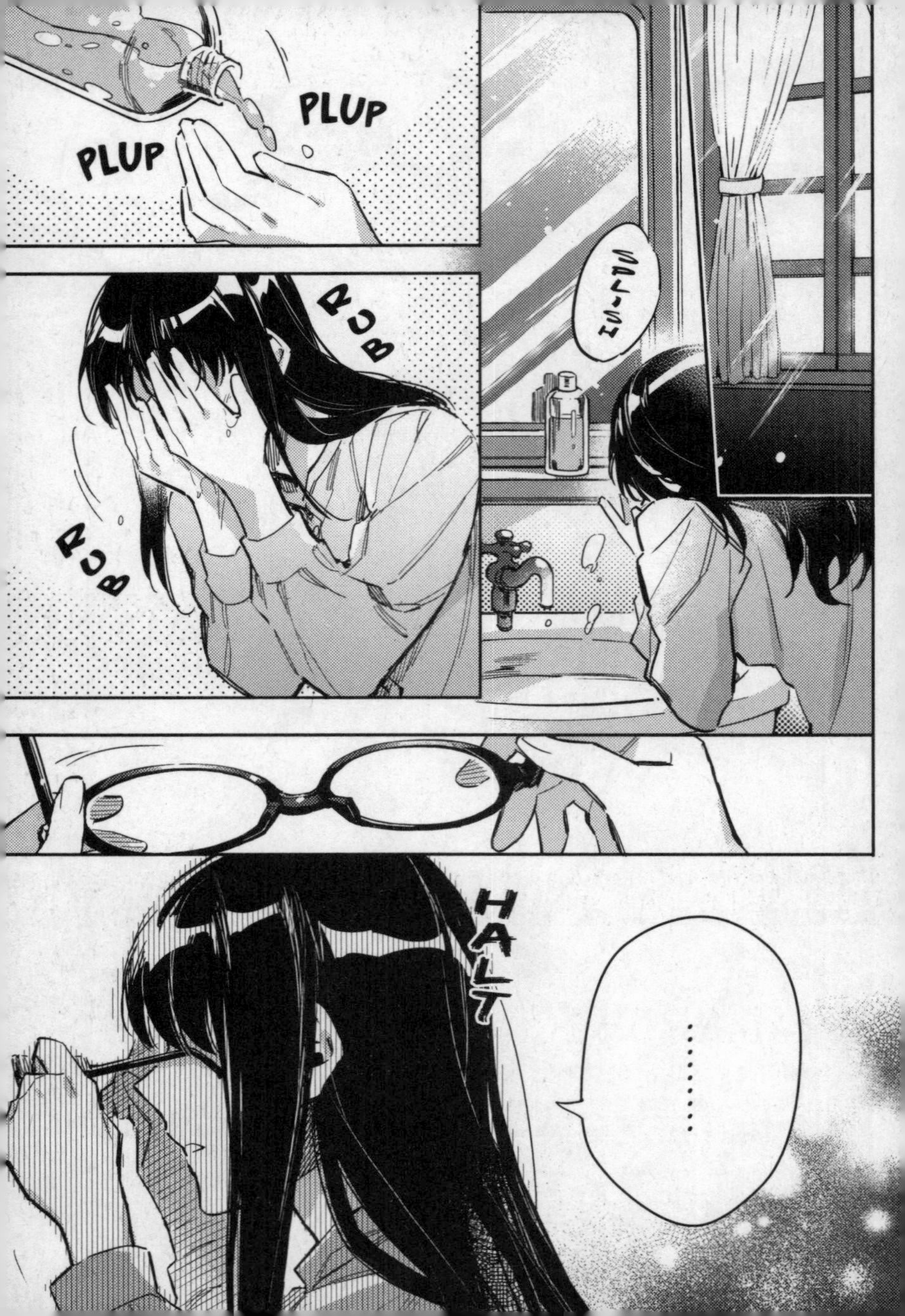
SPLISH
PLUP
PLUP
RUB
RUB
HALT
……

CHAPTER 4
The Library

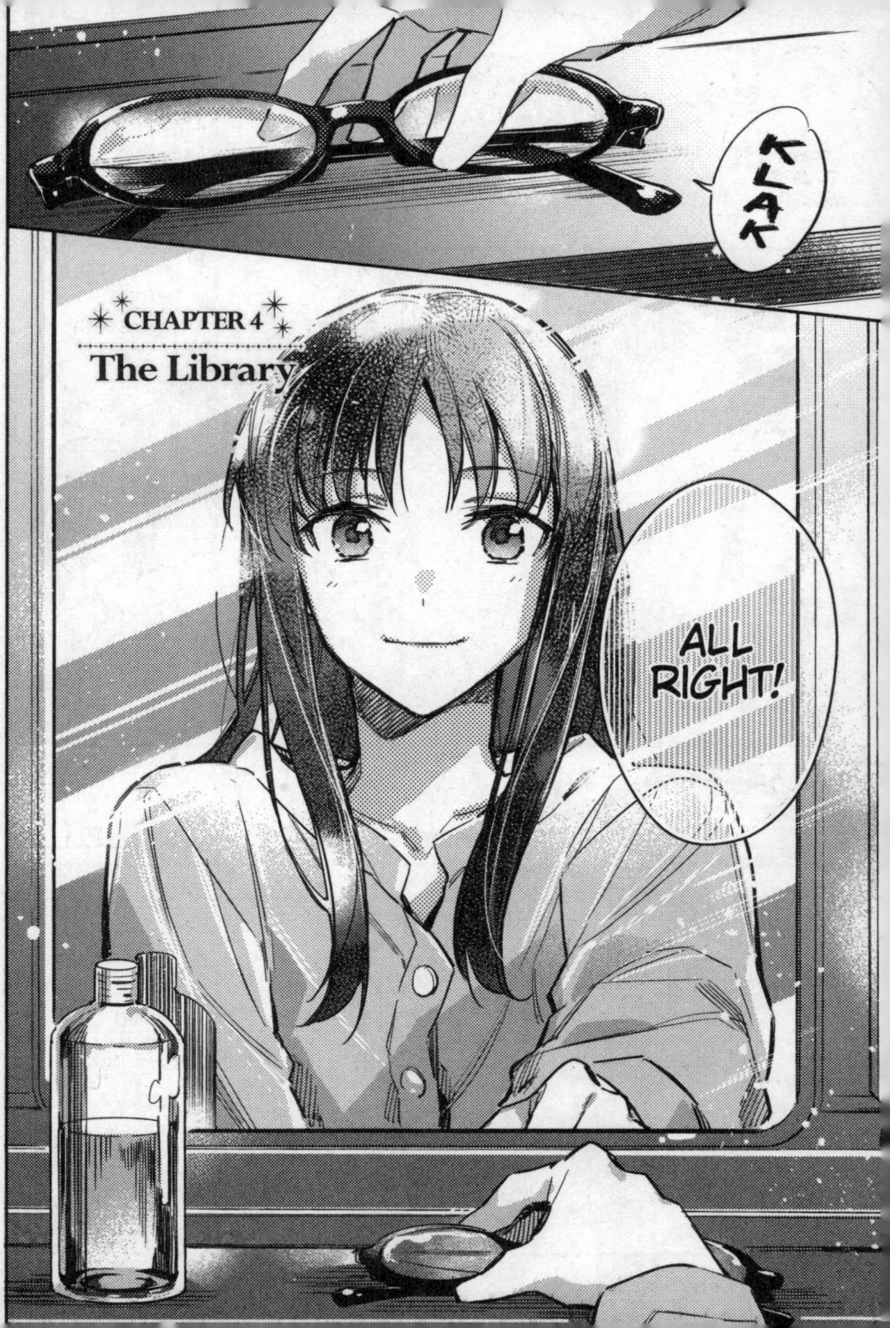
KLAK
ALL RIGHT!

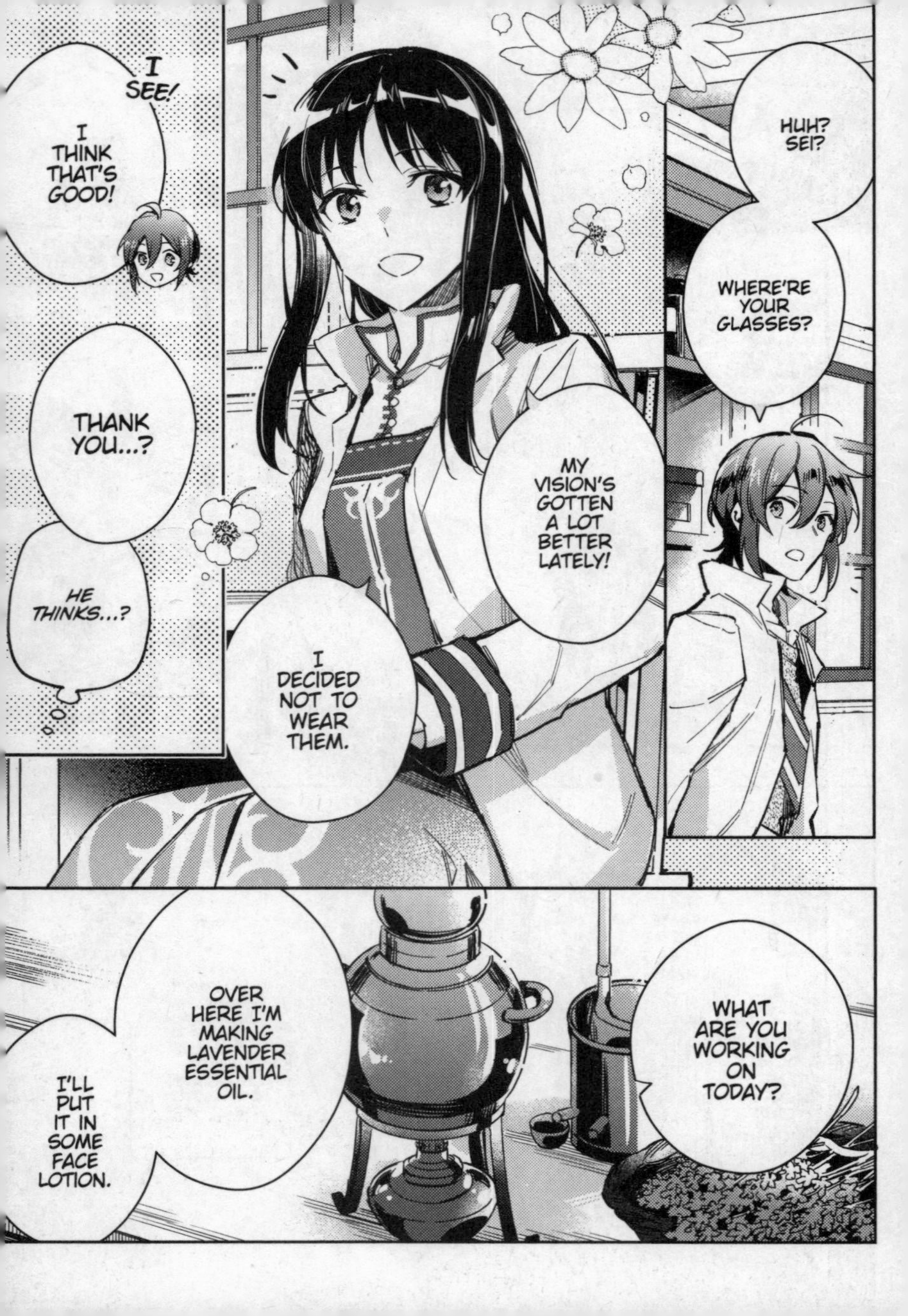
HUH? SEI?
WHERE'RE YOUR GLASSES?
MY VISION'S GOTTEN A LOT BETTER LATELY!
I DECIDED NOT TO WEAR THEM.
I SEE!
I THINK THAT'S GOOD!
THANK YOU...?
HE THINKS...?
WHAT ARE YOU WORKING ON TODAY?
OVER HERE I'M MAKING LAVENDER ESSENTIAL OIL.
I'LL PUT IT IN SOME FACE LOTION.

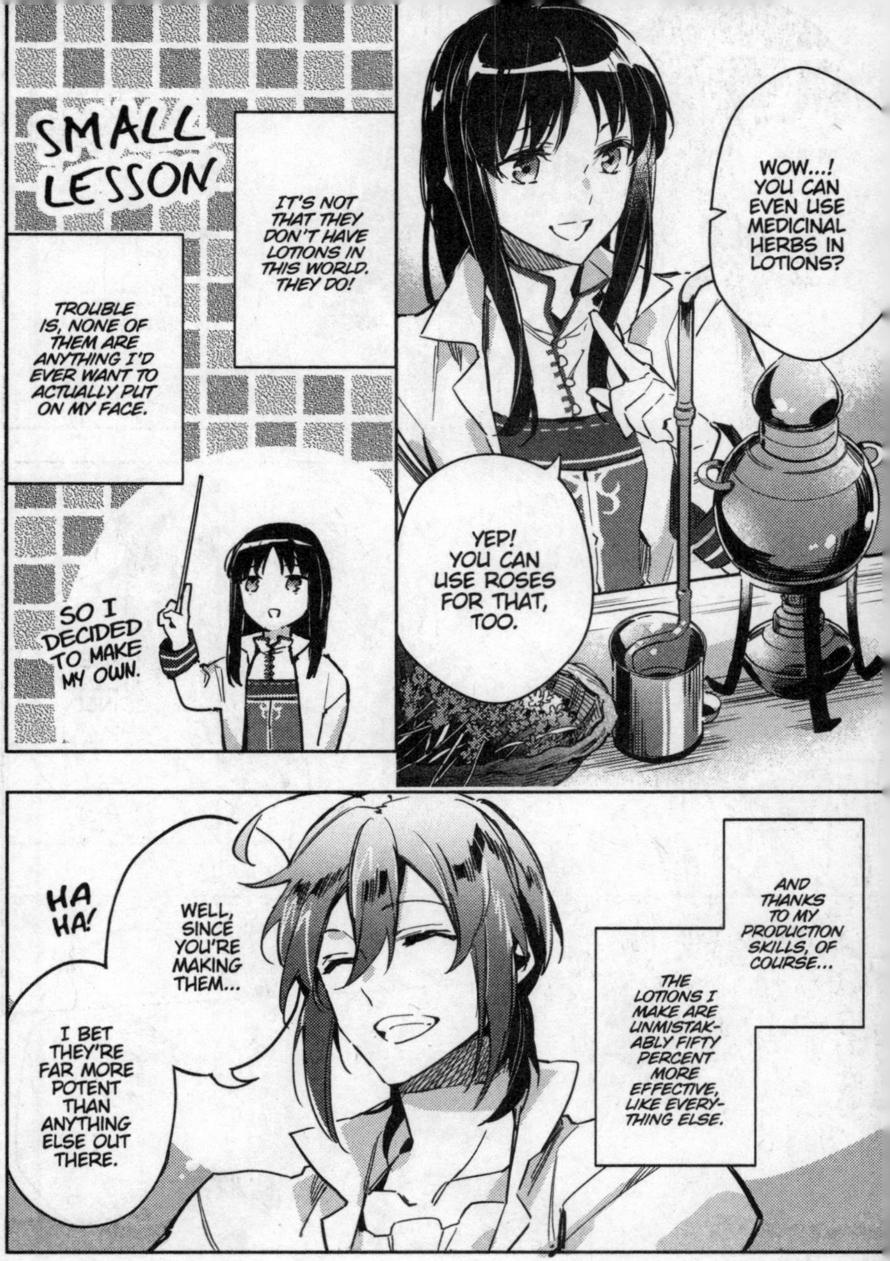
WOW...! YOU CAN EVEN USE MEDICINAL HERBS IN LOTIONS?
YEP! YOU CAN USE ROSES FOR THAT, TOO.
SMALL LESSON
IT'S NOT THAT THEY DON'T HAVE LOTIONS IN THIS WORLD. THEY DO!
TROUBLE IS, NONE OF THEM ARE ANYTHING I'D EVER WANT TO ACTUALLY PUT ON MY FACE.
SO I DECIDED TO MAKE MY OWN.
AND THANKS TO MY PRODUCTION SKILLS, OF COURSE...
THE LOTIONS I MAKE ARE UNMISTAKABLY FIFTY PERCENT MORE EFFECTIVE, LIKE EVERYTHING ELSE.
HA HA!
WELL, SINCE YOU'RE MAKING THEM...
I BET THEY'RE FAR MORE POTENT THAN ANYTHING ELSE OUT THERE.

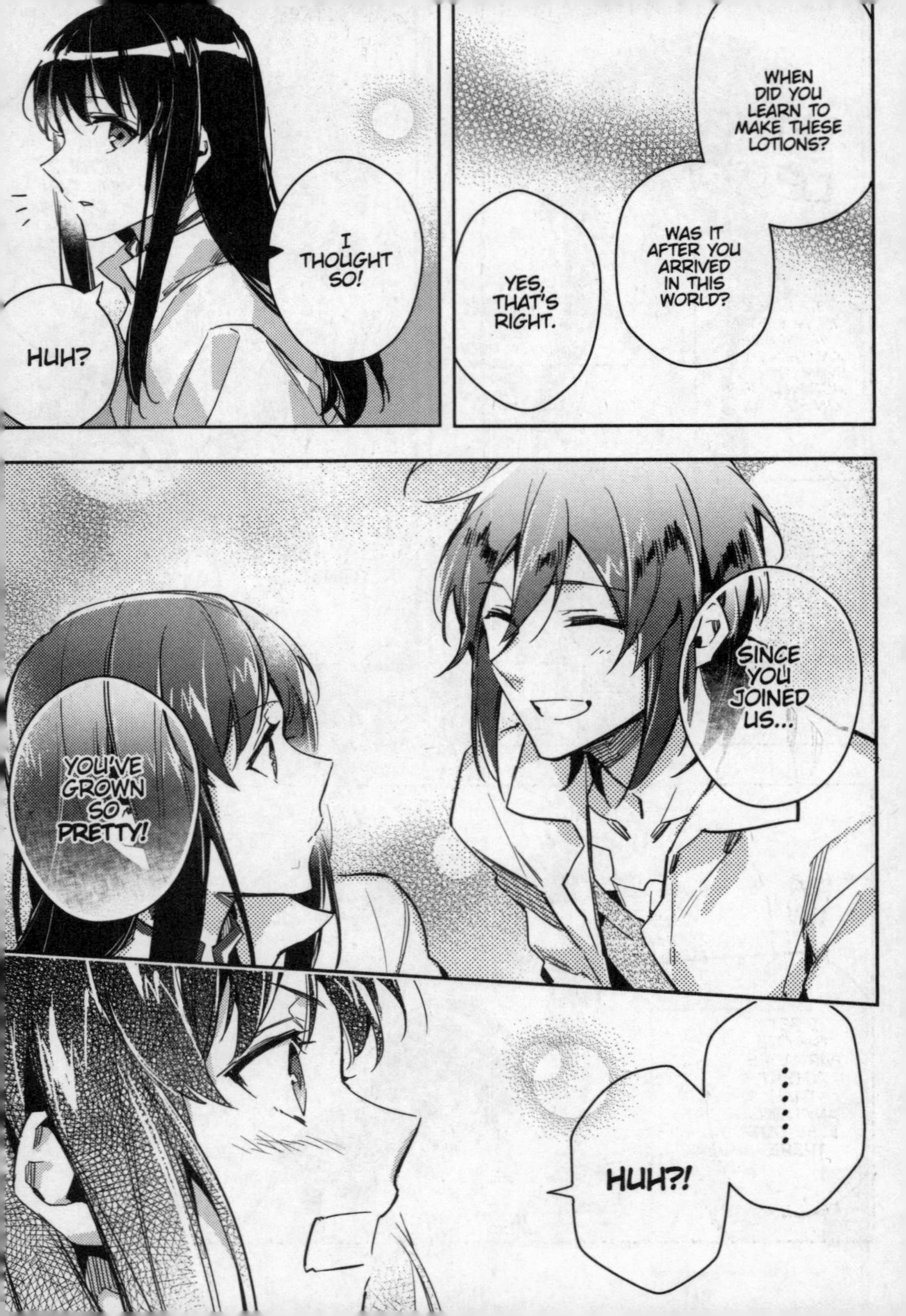
WHEN DID YOU LEARN TO MAKE THESE LOTIONS?
WAS IT AFTER YOU ARRIVED IN THIS WORLD?
YES, THAT'S RIGHT.
I THOUGHT SO!
HUH?
SINCE YOU JOINED US...
YOU'VE GROWN SO PRETTY!
......
HUH?!

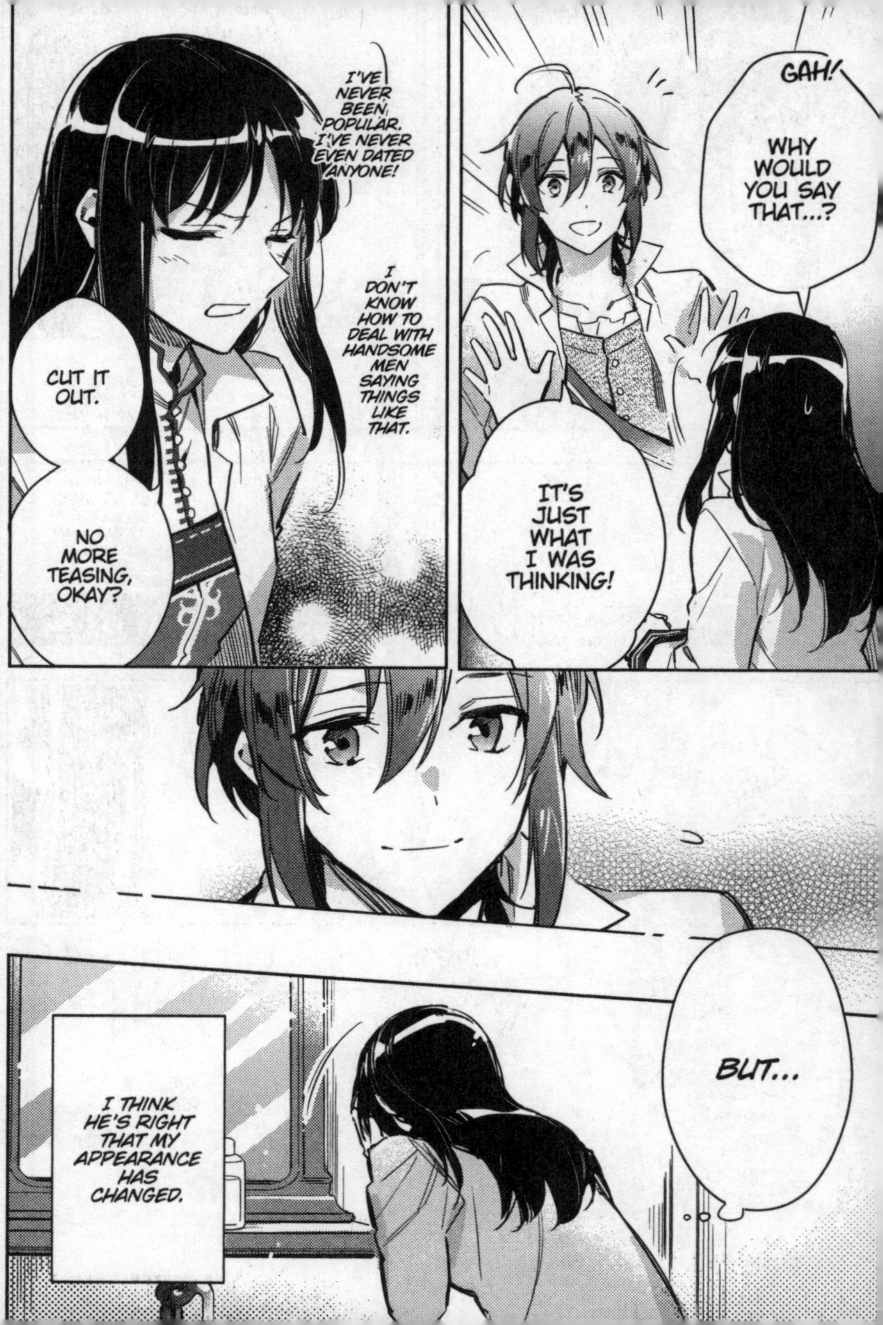
GAH!
WHY WOULD YOU SAY THAT...?
IT'S JUST WHAT I WAS THINKING!
I'VE NEVER BEEN POPULAR. I'VE NEVER EVEN DATED ANYONE!
I DON'T KNOW HOW TO DEAL WITH HANDSOME MEN SAYING THINGS LIKE THAT.
CUT IT OUT.
NO MORE TEASING, OKAY?
BUT...
I THINK HE'S RIGHT THAT MY APPEARANCE HAS CHANGED.

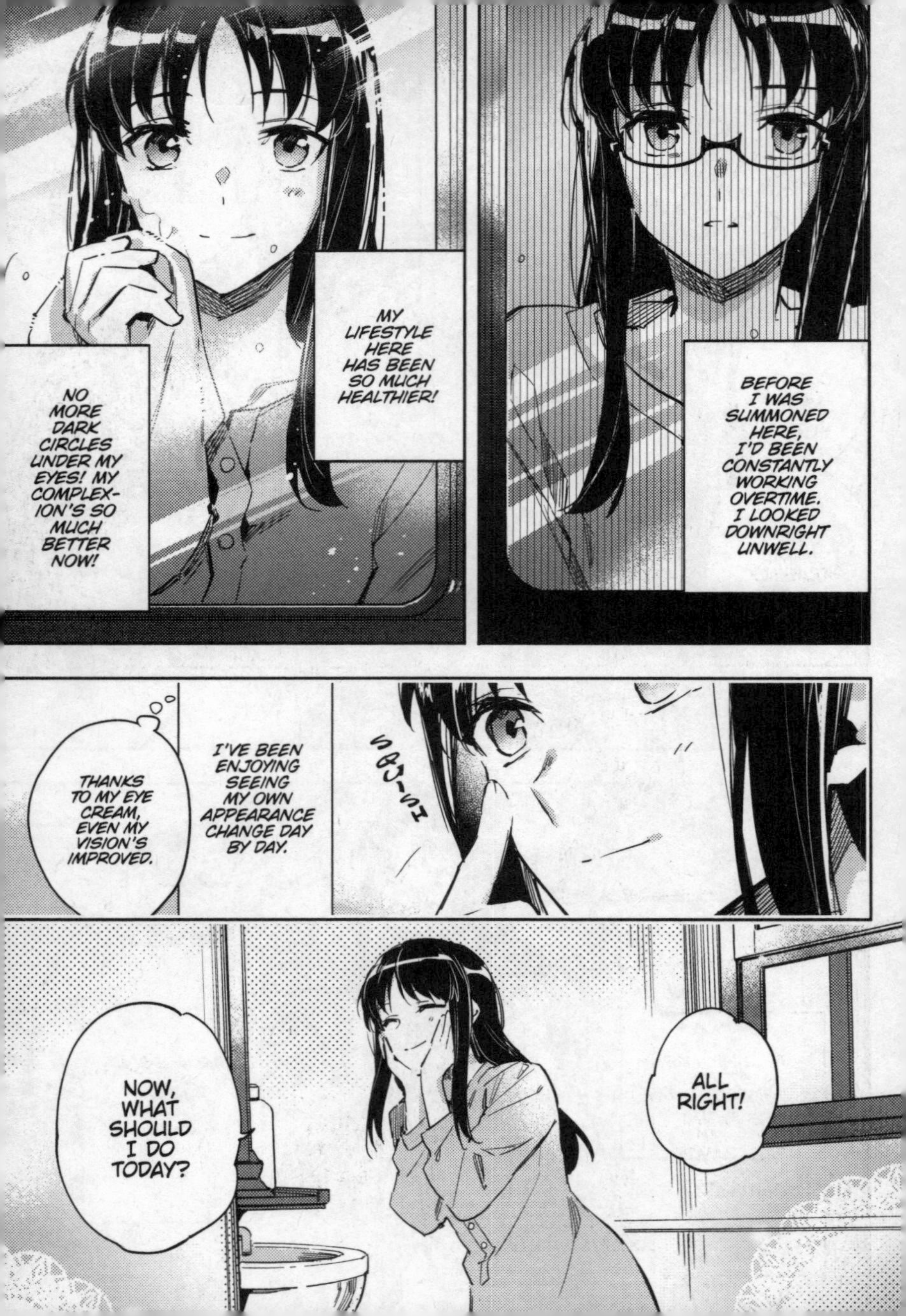
BEFORE I WAS SUMMONED HERE, I'D BEEN CONSTANTLY WORKING OVERTIME. I LOOKED DOWNRIGHT UNWELL.
MY LIFESTYLE HERE HAS BEEN SO MUCH HEALTHIER!
NO MORE DARK CIRCLES UNDER MY EYES! MY COMPLEXION'S SO MUCH BETTER NOW!
SQUISH
I'VE BEEN ENJOYING SEEING MY OWN APPEARANCE CHANGE DAY BY DAY.
THANKS TO MY EYE CREAM, EVEN MY VISION'S IMPROVED.
ALL RIGHT!
NOW, WHAT SHOULD I DO TODAY?

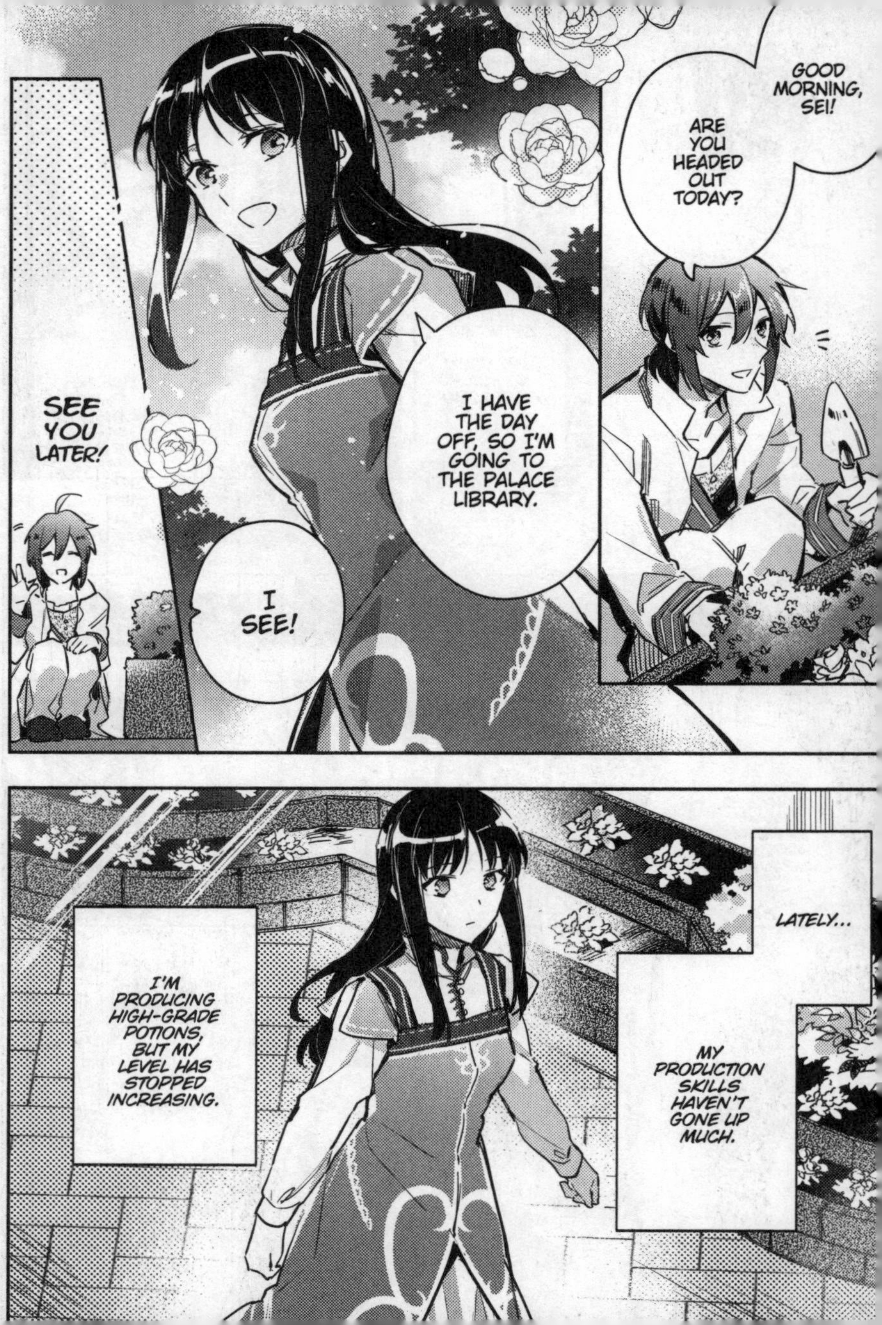
GOOD MORNING, SEI!
ARE YOU HEADED OUT TODAY?
I HAVE THE DAY OFF, SO I'M GOING TO THE PALACE LIBRARY.
I SEE!
SEE YOU LATER!
LATELY...
MY PRODUCTION SKILLS HAVEN'T GONE UP MUCH.
I'M PRODUCING HIGH-GRADE POTIONS, BUT MY LEVEL HAS STOPPED INCREASING.

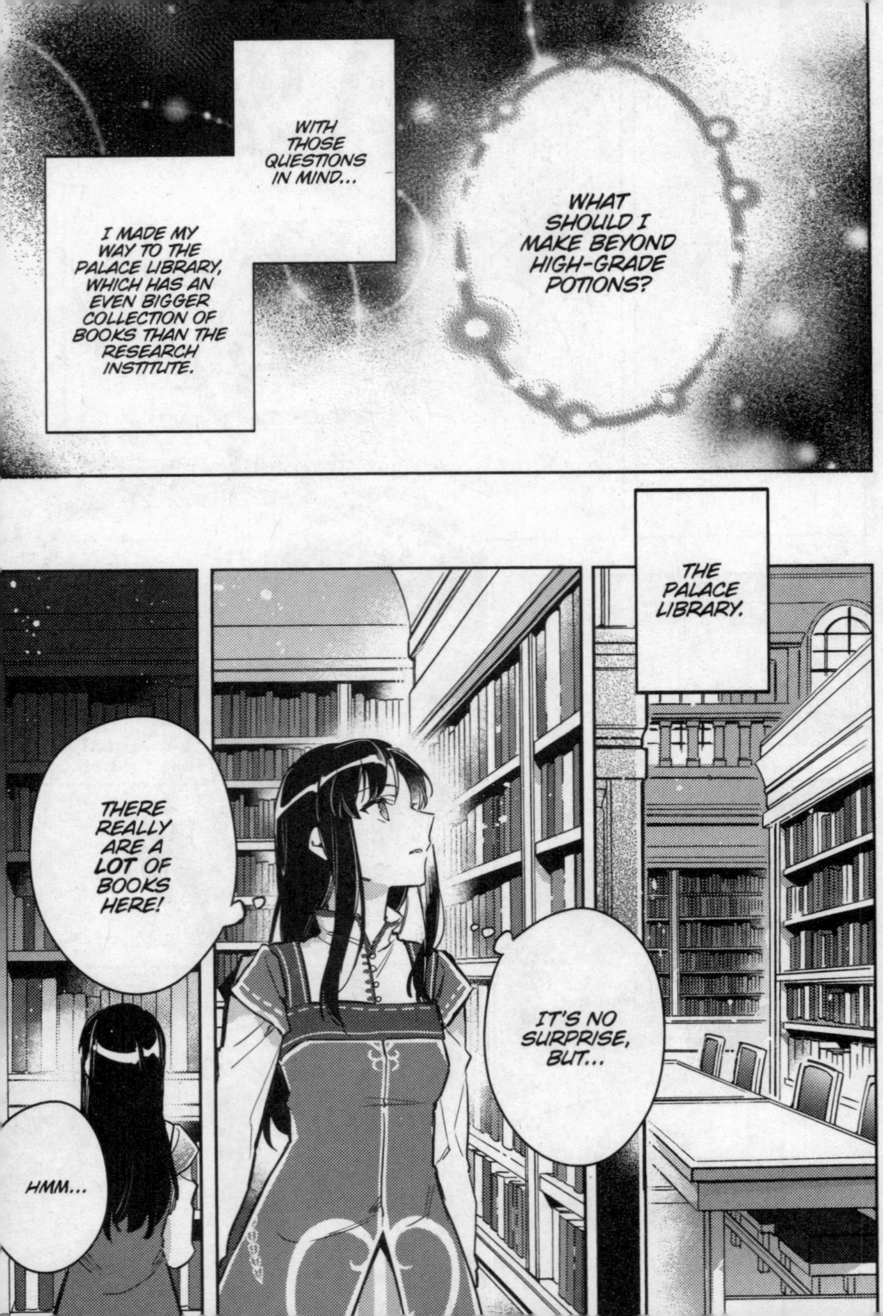
WHAT SHOULD I MAKE BEYOND HIGH-GRADE POTIONS?
WITH THOSE QUESTIONS IN MIND...
I MADE MY WAY TO THE PALACE LIBRARY, WHICH HAS AN EVEN BIGGER COLLECTION OF BOOKS THAN THE RESEARCH INSTITUTE.
THE PALACE LIBRARY.
IT'S NO SURPRISE, BUT...
THERE REALLY ARE A LOT OF BOOKS HERE!
HMM...

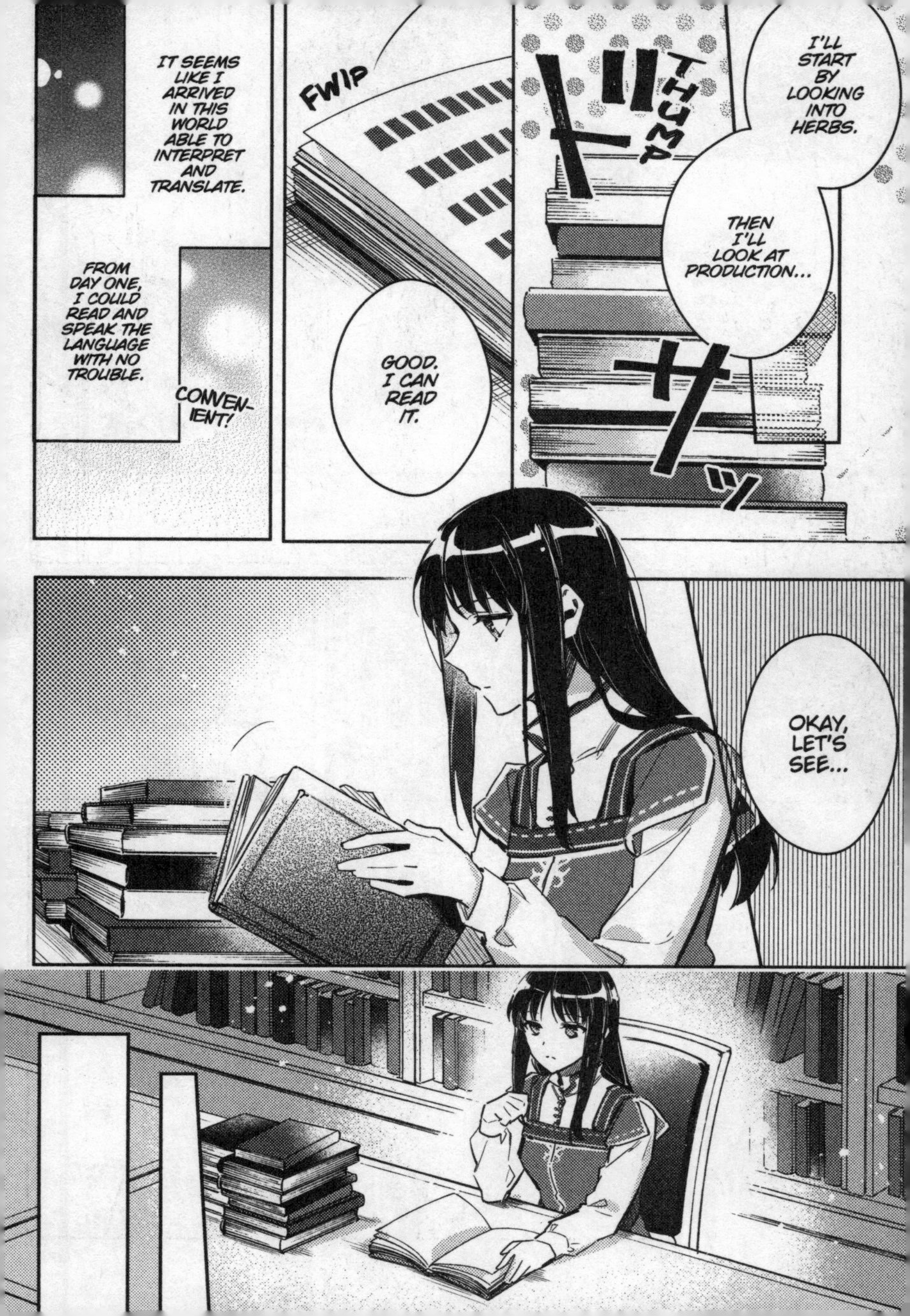
I'LL START BY LOOKING INTO HERBS.
THUMP
THEN I'LL LOOK AT PRODUCTION...
FWIP
GOOD. I CAN READ IT.
IT SEEMS LIKE I ARRIVED IN THIS WORLD ABLE TO INTERPRET AND TRANSLATE.
FROM DAY ONE, I COULD READ AND SPEAK THE LANGUAGE WITH NO TROUBLE.
CONVEN-IENT!
OKAY, LET'S SEE...

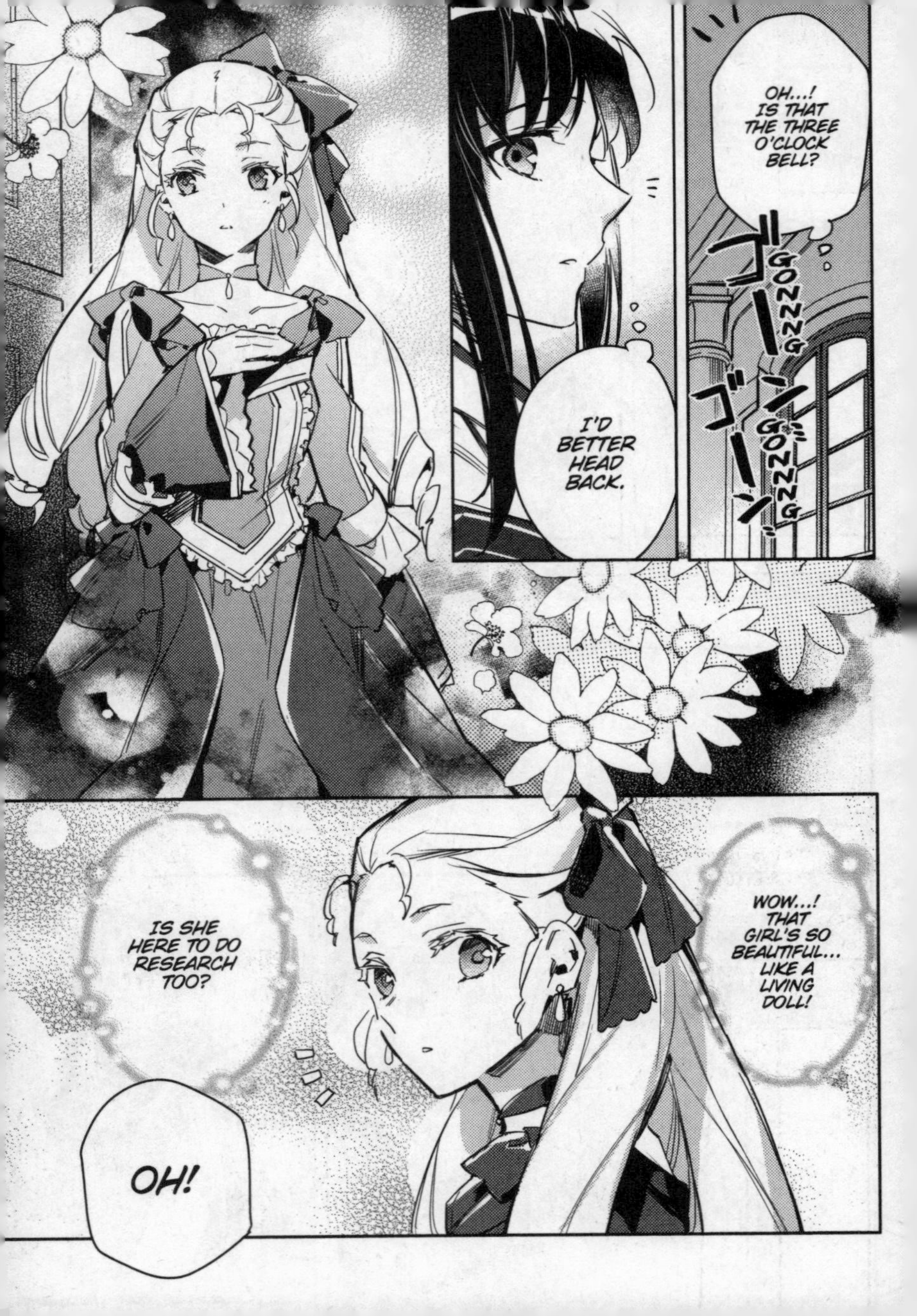
OH...! IS THAT THE THREE O'CLOCK BELL?
GONNNG
GONNNG
I'D BETTER HEAD BACK.
WOW...! THAT GIRL'S SO BEAUTIFUL... LIKE A LIVING DOLL!
IS SHE HERE TO DO RESEARCH TOO?
OH!

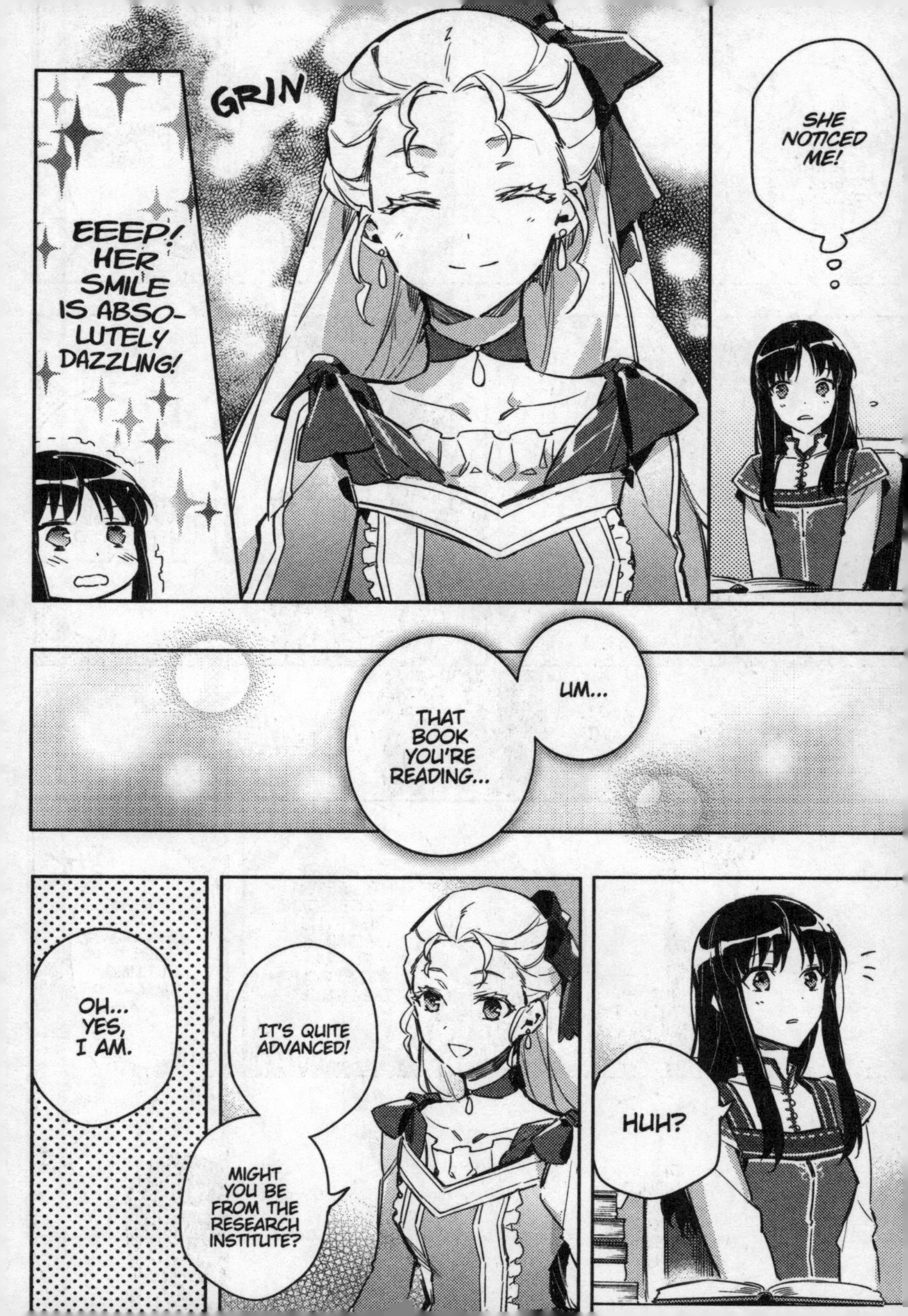
SHE NOTICED ME!
GRIN
EEEP! HER SMILE IS ABSO-LUTELY DAZZLING!
UM...
THAT BOOK YOU'RE READING...
HUH?
IT'S QUITE ADVANCED!
MIGHT YOU BE FROM THE RESEARCH INSTITUTE?
OH... YES, I AM.

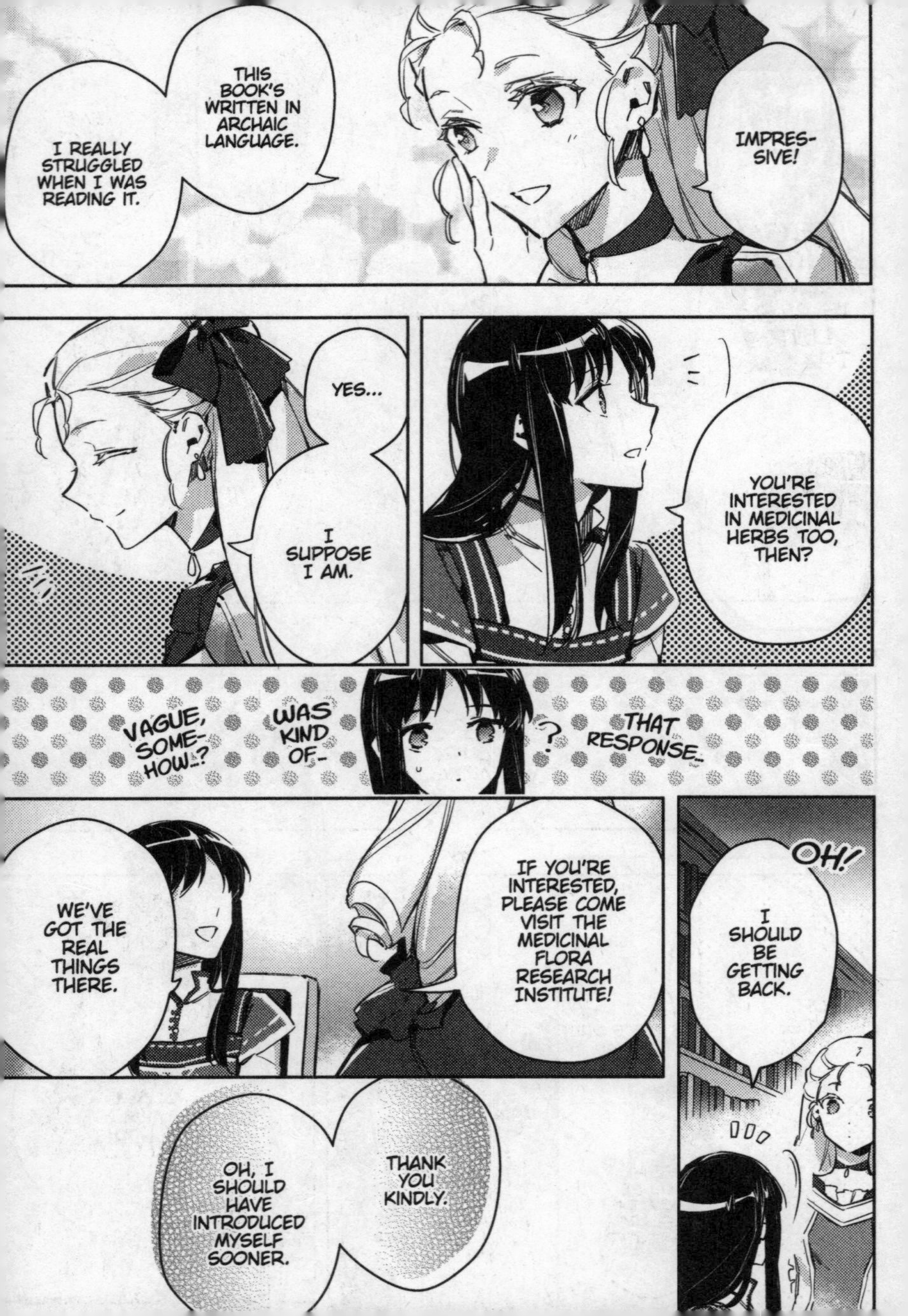
IMPRESSIVE!
THIS BOOK'S WRITTEN IN ARCHAIC LANGUAGE.
I REALLY STRUGGLED WHEN I WAS READING IT.
YOU'RE INTERESTED IN MEDICINAL HERBS TOO, THEN?
YES...
I SUPPOSE I AM.
THAT RESPONSE..
?
WAS KIND OF..
VAGUE, SOMEHOW..?
OH!
I SHOULD BE GETTING BACK.
IF YOU'RE INTERESTED, PLEASE COME VISIT THE MEDICINAL FLORA RESEARCH INSTITUTE!
WE'VE GOT THE REAL THINGS THERE.
THANK YOU KINDLY.
OH, I SHOULD HAVE INTRODUCED MYSELF SOONER.

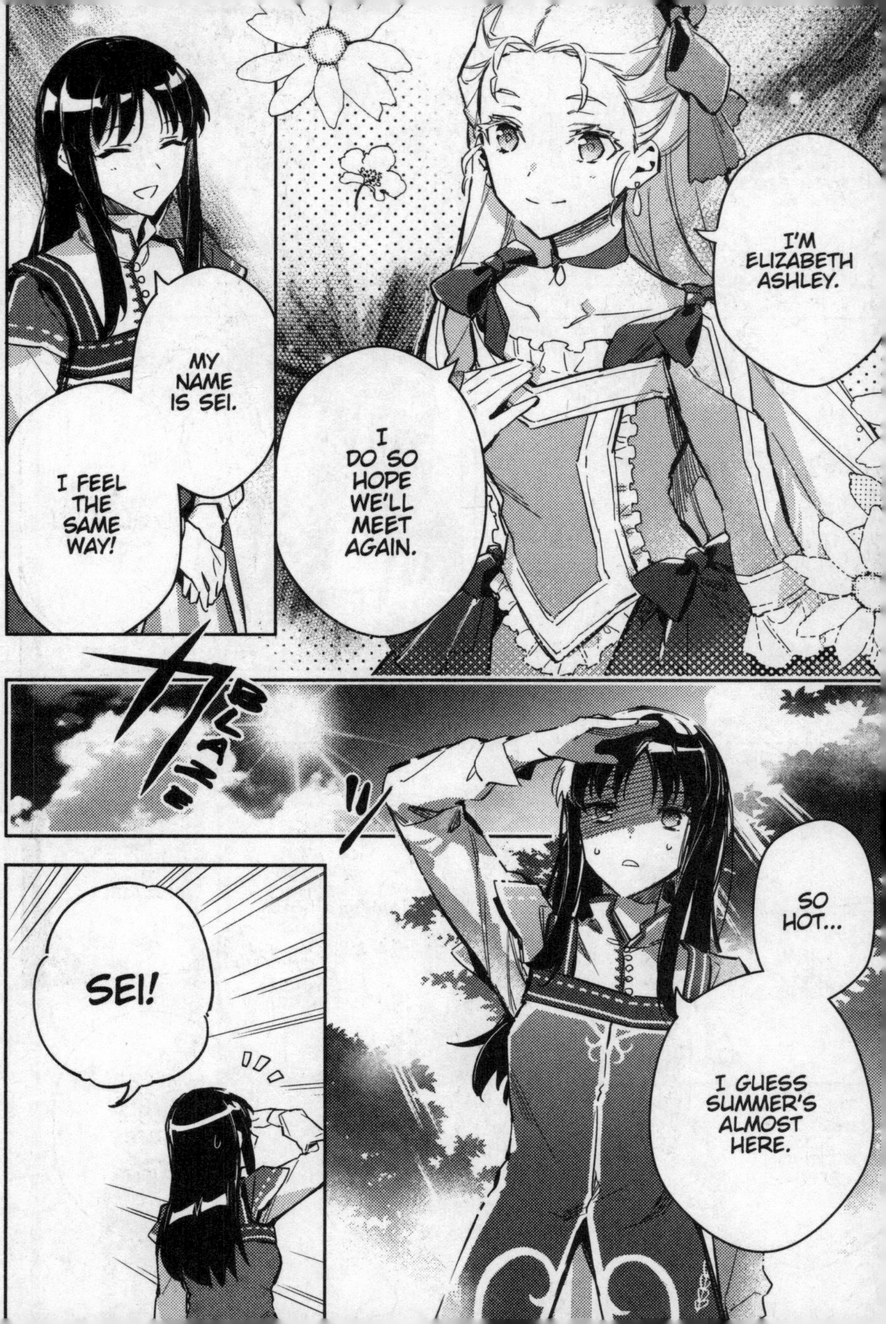
I'M ELIZABETH ASHLEY.
I DO SO HOPE WE'LL MEET AGAIN.
MY NAME IS SEI.
I FEEL THE SAME WAY!
BLAZE
SO HOT...
I GUESS SUMMER'S ALMOST HERE.
SEI!

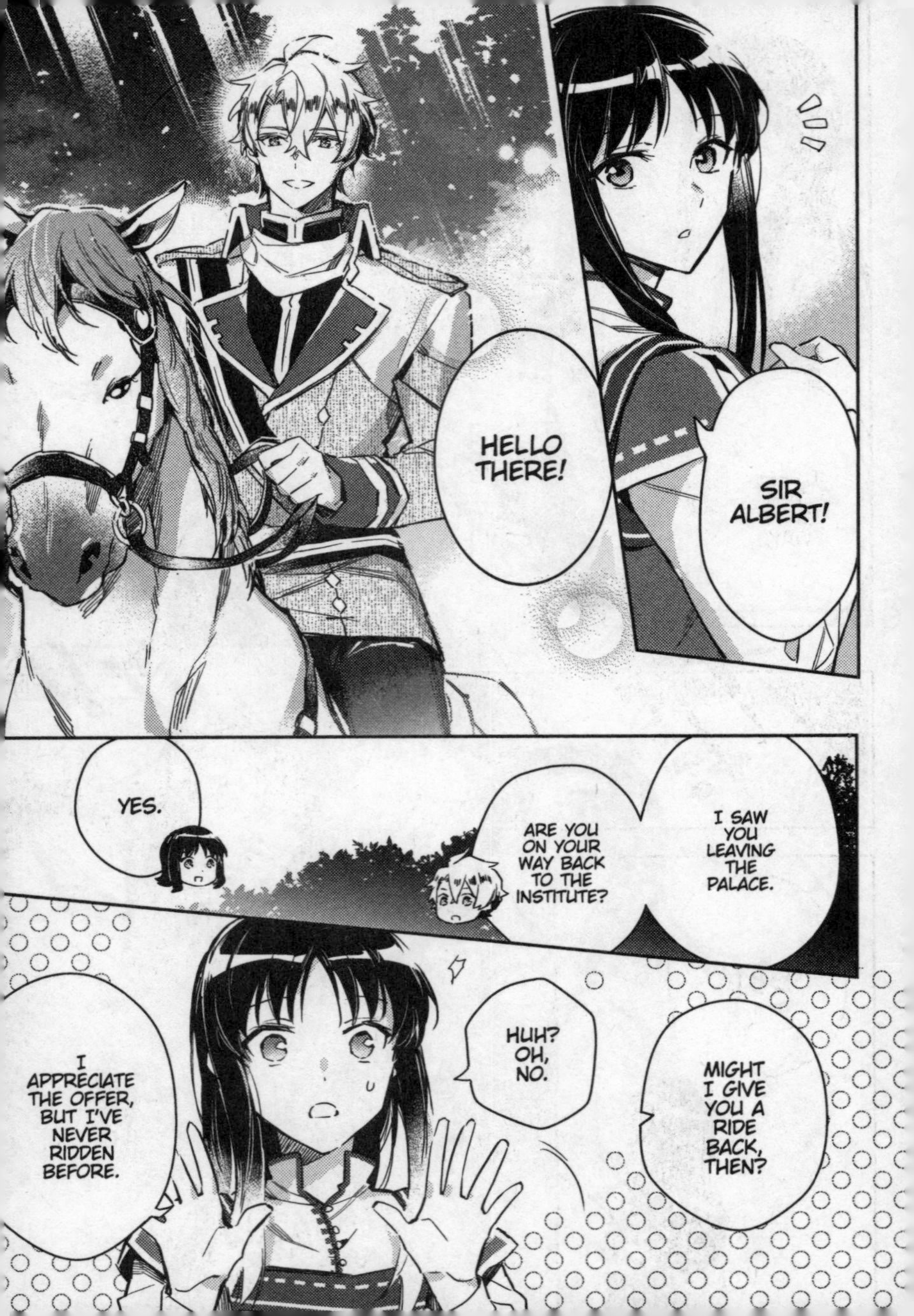
SIR ALBERT!
HELLO THERE!
I SAW YOU LEAVING THE PALACE.
ARE YOU ON YOUR WAY BACK TO THE INSTITUTE?
YES.
MIGHT I GIVE YOU A RIDE BACK, THEN?
HUH? OH, NO.
I APPRECIATE THE OFFER, BUT I'VE NEVER RIDDEN BEFORE.

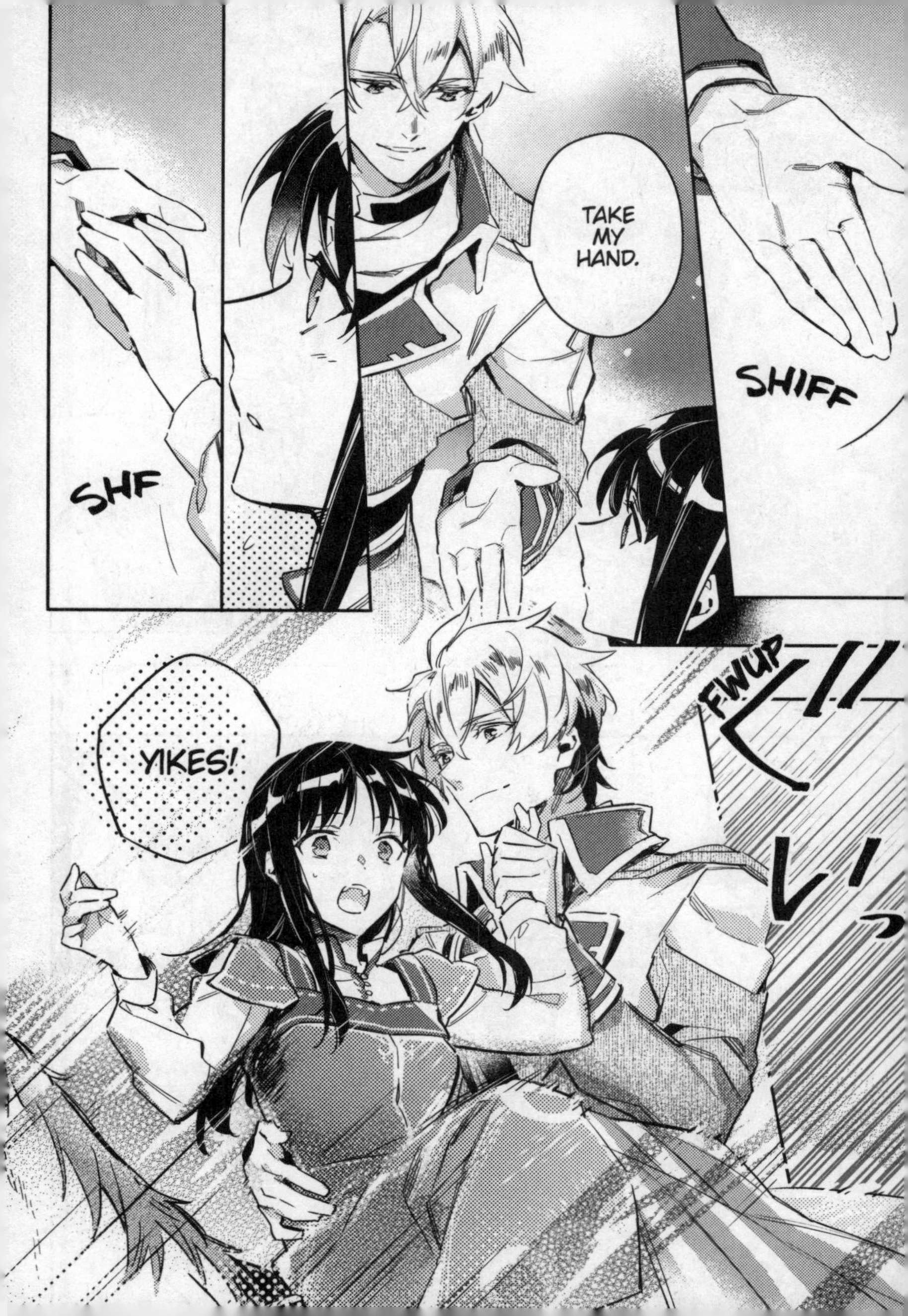
SHIFF
TAKE MY HAND.
SHF
FWUP
YIKES!

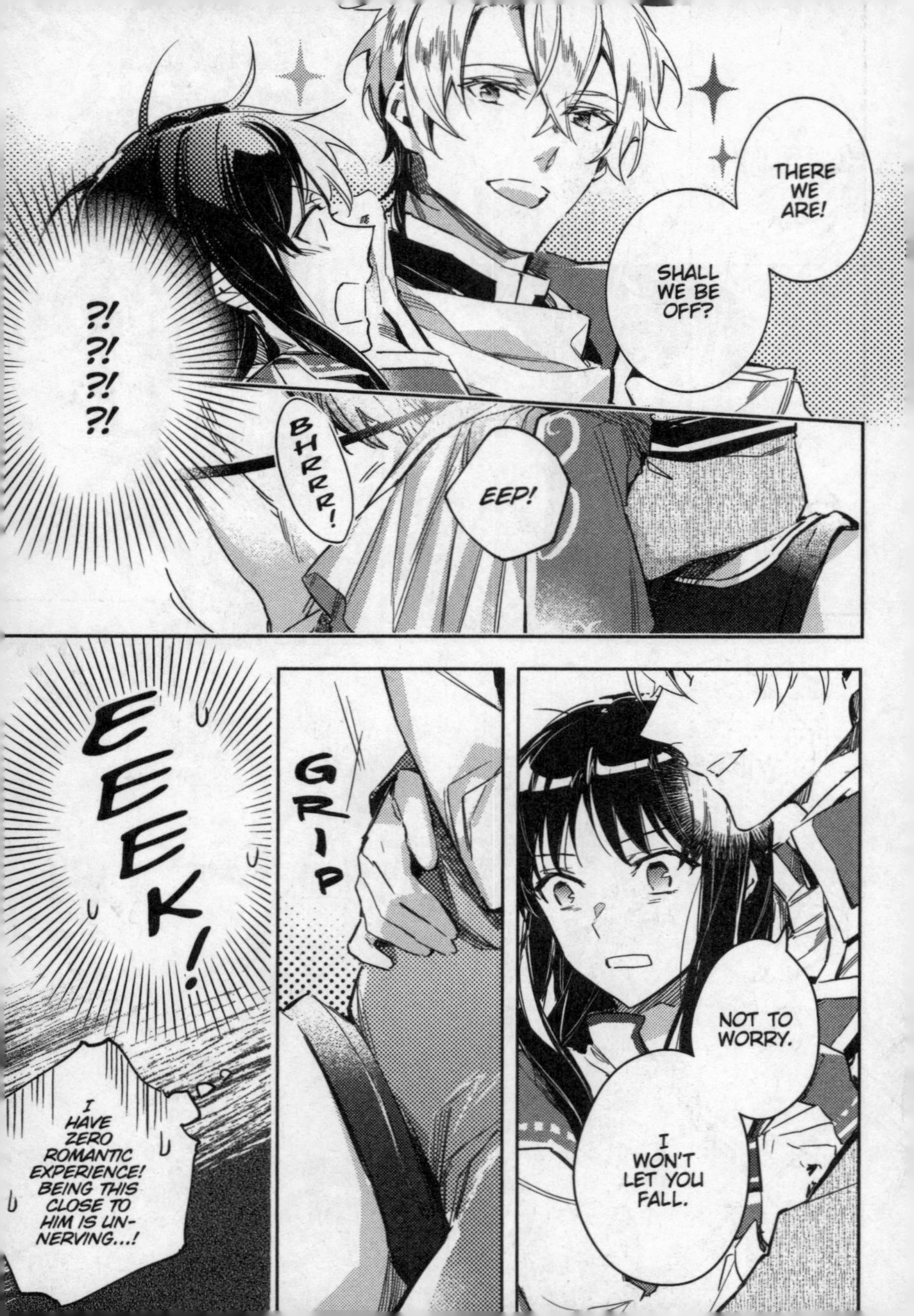
THERE WE ARE!
SHALL WE BE OFF?
?! ?! ?! ?!
EEP!
BHRRR!
NOT TO WORRY.
I WON'T LET YOU FALL.
GRIP
EEEEK!
I HAVE ZERO ROMANTIC EXPERIENCE! BEING THIS CLOSE TO HIM IS UN-NERVING...!

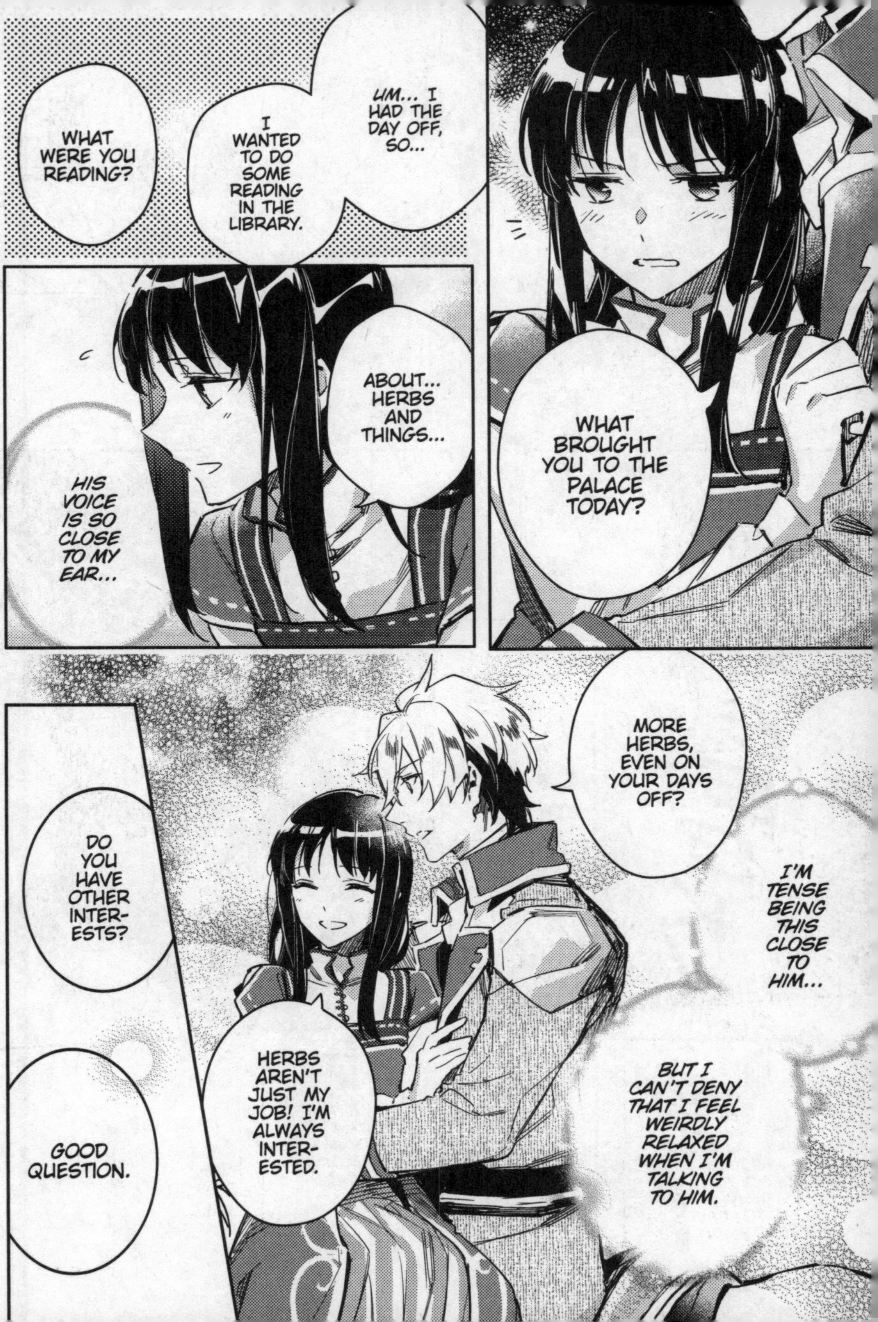
WHAT BROUGHT YOU TO THE PALACE TODAY?
UM... I HAD THE DAY OFF, SO...
I WANTED TO DO SOME READING IN THE LIBRARY.
WHAT WERE YOU READING?
ABOUT... HERBS AND THINGS...
HIS VOICE IS SO CLOSE TO MY EAR...
MORE HERBS, EVEN ON YOUR DAYS OFF?
I'M TENSE BEING THIS CLOSE TO HIM...
BUT I CAN'T DENY THAT I FEEL WEIRDLY RELAXED WHEN I'M TALKING TO HIM.
HERBS AREN'T JUST MY JOB! I'M ALWAYS INTER-ESTED.
DO YOU HAVE OTHER INTER-ESTS?
GOOD QUESTION.

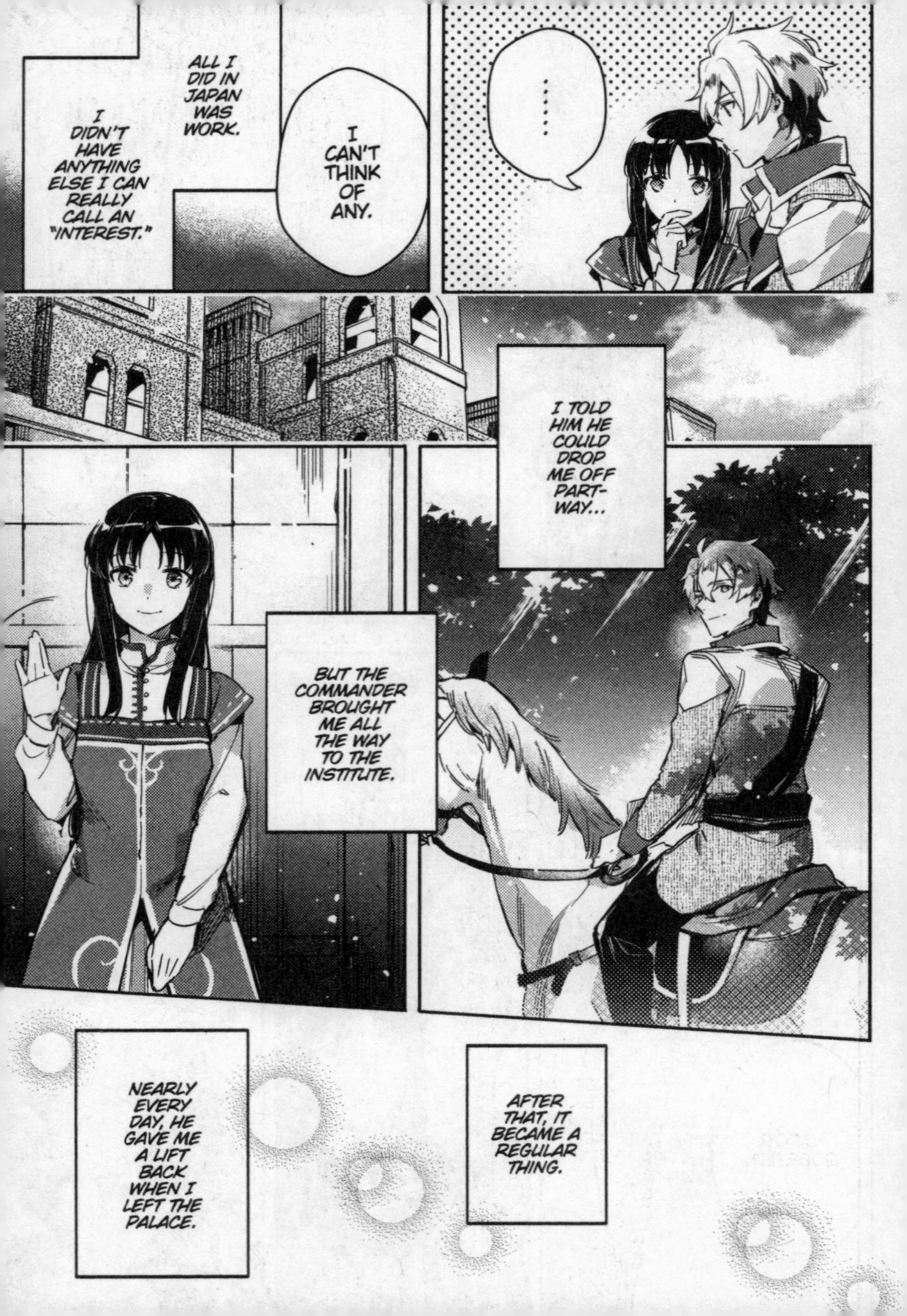
……
I CAN'T THINK OF ANY.
ALL I DID IN JAPAN WAS WORK.
I DIDN'T HAVE ANYTHING ELSE I CAN REALLY CALL AN "INTEREST."
I TOLD HIM HE COULD DROP ME OFF PART-WAY...
BUT THE COMMANDER BROUGHT ME ALL THE WAY TO THE INSTITUTE.
AFTER THAT, IT BECAME A REGULAR THING.
NEARLY EVERY DAY, HE GAVE ME A LIFT BACK WHEN I LEFT THE PALACE.

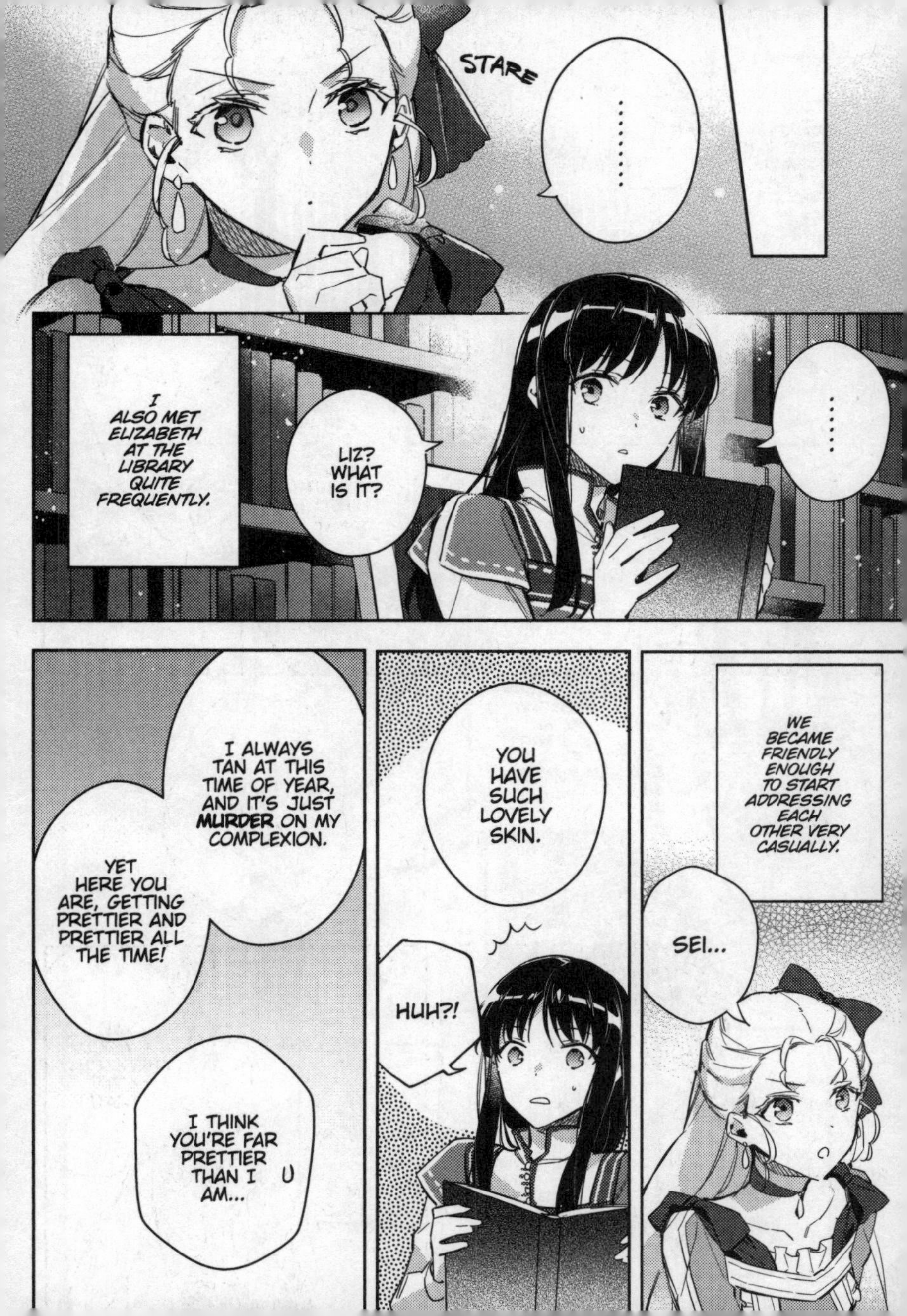
……
STARE
……
LIZ? WHAT IS IT?
I ALSO MET ELIZABETH AT THE LIBRARY QUITE FREQUENTLY.
WE BECAME FRIENDLY ENOUGH TO START ADDRESSING EACH OTHER VERY CASUALLY.
SEI...
YOU HAVE SUCH LOVELY SKIN.
HUH?!
I ALWAYS TAN AT THIS TIME OF YEAR, AND IT'S JUST MURDER ON MY COMPLEXION.
YET HERE YOU ARE, GETTING PRETTIER AND PRETTIER ALL THE TIME!
I THINK YOU'RE FAR PRETTIER THAN I AM...

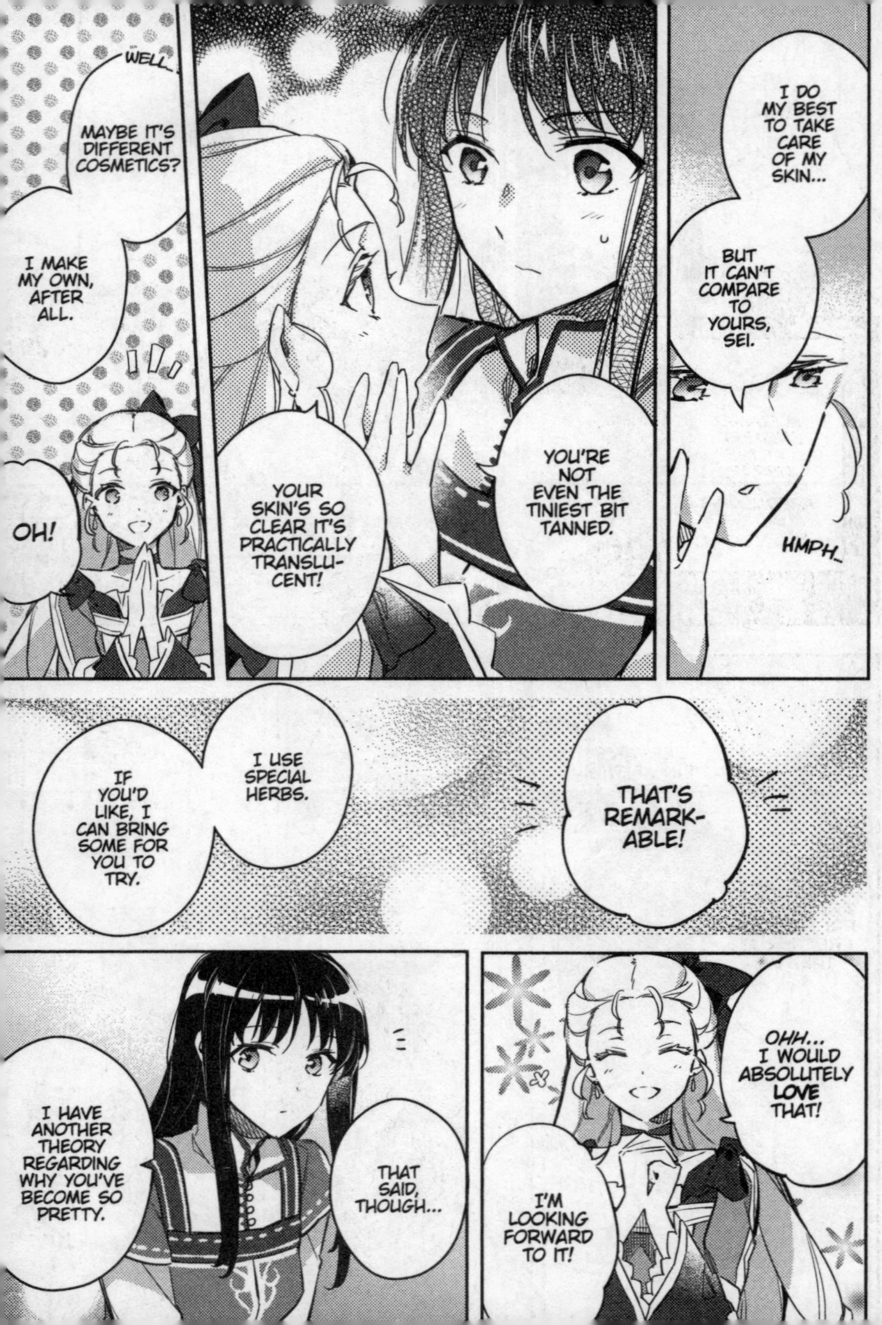
I DO MY BEST TO TAKE CARE OF MY SKIN...
BUT IT CAN'T COMPARE TO YOURS, SEI.
HMPH...
YOU'RE NOT EVEN THE TINIEST BIT TANNED.
YOUR SKIN'S SO CLEAR IT'S PRACTICALLY TRANSLU-CENT!
WELL...
MAYBE IT'S DIFFERENT COSMETICS?
I MAKE MY OWN, AFTER ALL.
OH!
THAT'S REMARK-ABLE!
I USE SPECIAL HERBS.
IF YOU'D LIKE, I CAN BRING SOME FOR YOU TO TRY.
OHH... I WOULD ABSOLUTELY LOVE THAT!
I'M LOOKING FORWARD TO IT!
THAT SAID, THOUGH...
I HAVE ANOTHER THEORY REGARDING WHY YOU'VE BECOME SO PRETTY.

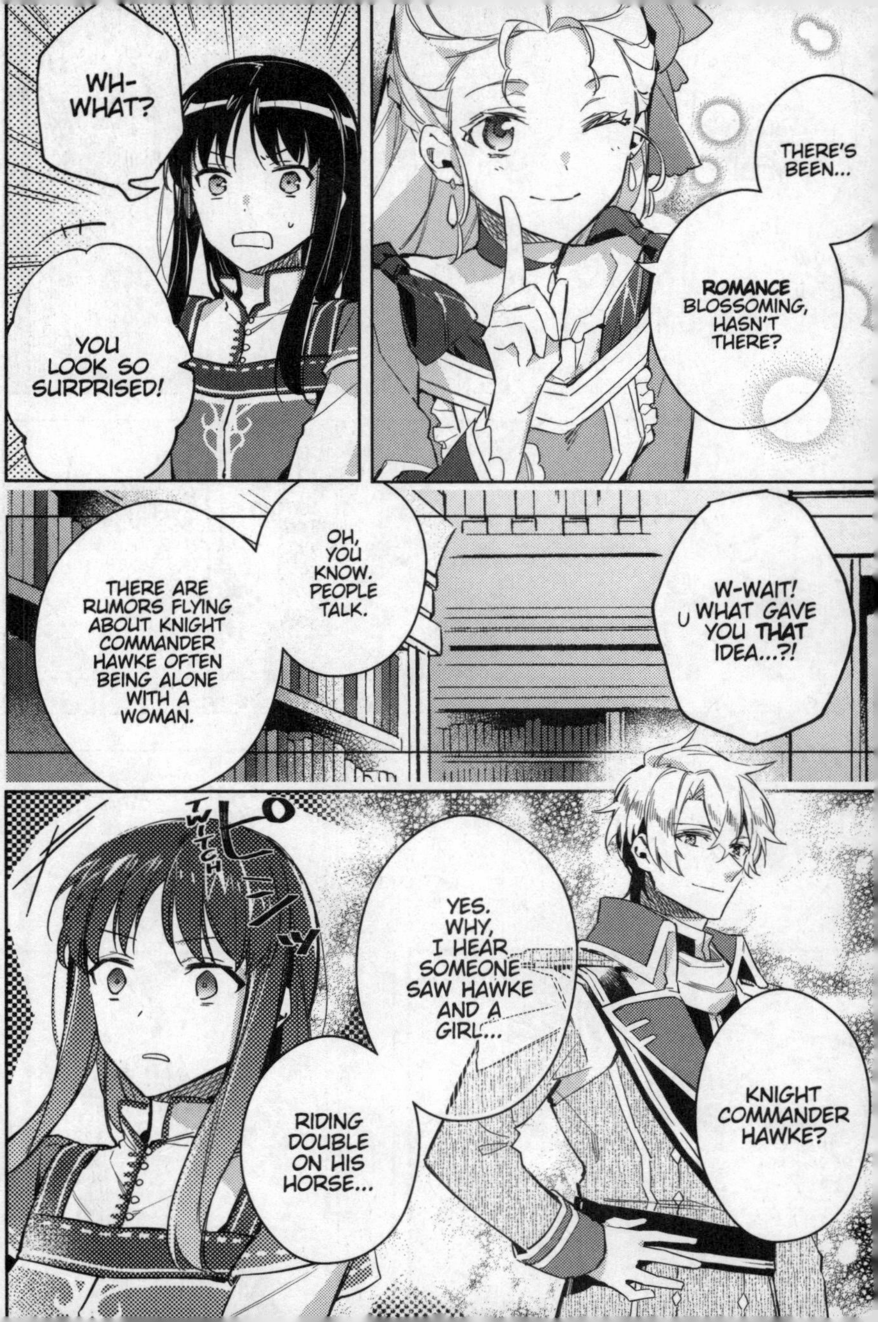
THERE'S BEEN...
ROMANCE BLOSSOMING, HASN'T THERE?
WH- WHAT?
YOU LOOK SO SURPRISED!
W-WAIT! WHAT GAVE YOU THAT IDEA...?!
OH, YOU KNOW. PEOPLE TALK.
THERE ARE RUMORS FLYING ABOUT KNIGHT COMMANDER HAWKE OFTEN BEING ALONE WITH A WOMAN.
KNIGHT COMMANDER HAWKE?
YES. WHY, I HEAR SOMEONE SAW HAWKE AND A GIRL...
RIDING DOUBLE ON HIS HORSE...
TWITCH

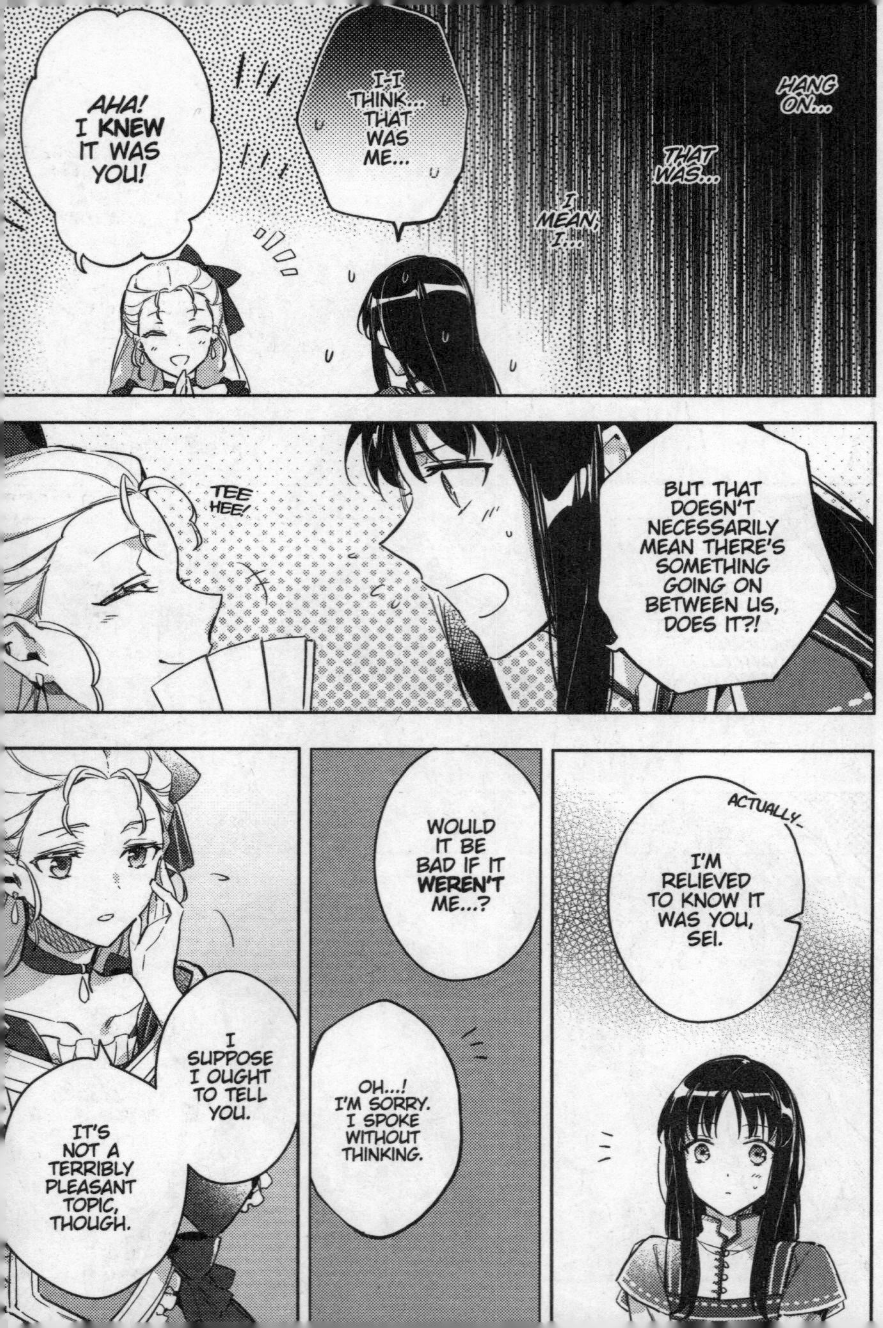
HANG ON...
THAT WAS...
I MEAN, I...
I-I THINK... THAT WAS ME...
AHA! I KNEW IT WAS YOU!
BUT THAT DOESN'T NECESSARILY MEAN THERE'S SOMETHING GOING ON BETWEEN US, DOES IT?!
TEE HEE!
ACTUALLY—
I'M RELIEVED TO KNOW IT WAS YOU, SEI.
WOULD IT BE BAD IF IT WEREN'T ME...?
OH...! I'M SORRY. I SPOKE WITHOUT THINKING.
I SUPPOSE I OUGHT TO TELL YOU.
IT'S NOT A TERRIBLY PLEASANT TOPIC, THOUGH.

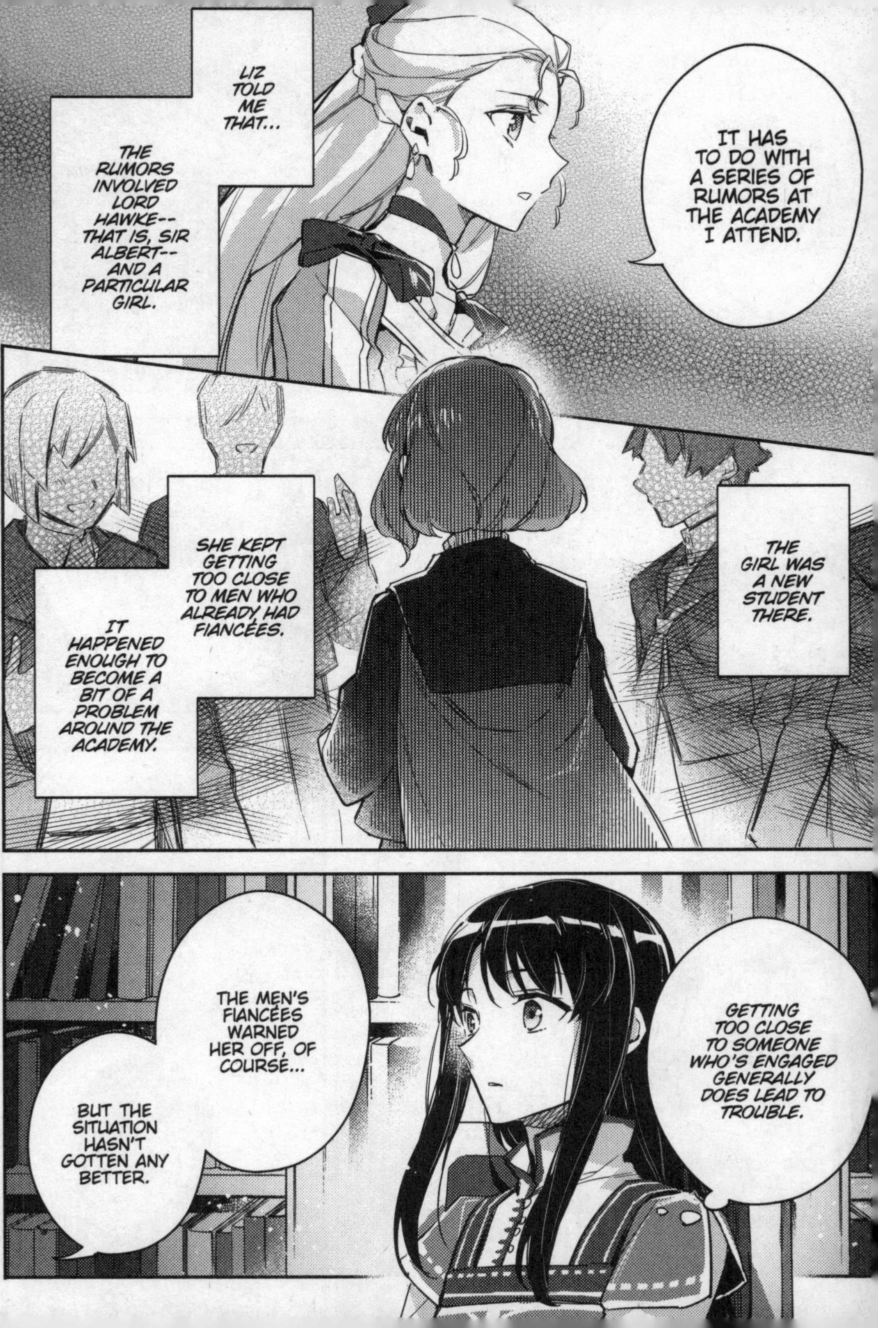
IT HAS TO DO WITH A SERIES OF RUMORS AT THE ACADEMY I ATTEND.
LIZ TOLD ME THAT...
THE RUMORS INVOLVED LORD HAWKE--THAT IS, SIR ALBERT--AND A PARTICULAR GIRL.
THE GIRL WAS A NEW STUDENT THERE.
SHE KEPT GETTING TOO CLOSE TO MEN WHO ALREADY HAD FIANCÉES.
IT HAPPENED ENOUGH TO BECOME A BIT OF A PROBLEM AROUND THE ACADEMY.
GETTING TOO CLOSE TO SOMEONE WHO'S ENGAGED GENERALLY DOES LEAD TO TROUBLE.
THE MEN'S FIANCÉES WARNED HER OFF, OF COURSE...
BUT THE SITUATION HASN'T GOTTEN ANY BETTER.

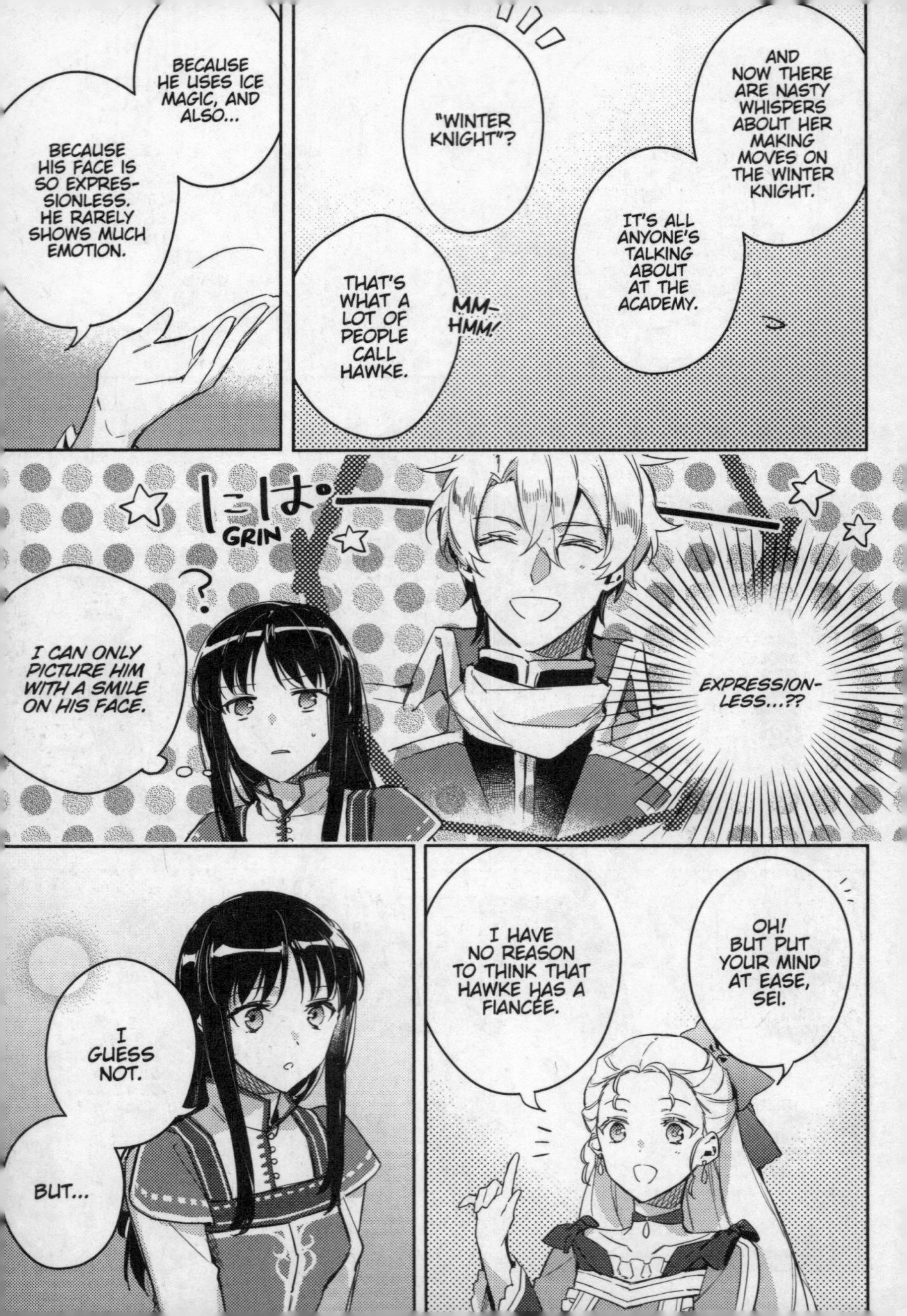
AND NOW THERE ARE NASTY WHISPERS ABOUT HER MAKING MOVES ON THE WINTER KNIGHT.
IT'S ALL ANYONE'S TALKING ABOUT AT THE ACADEMY.
"WINTER KNIGHT"?
MM-HMM!
THAT'S WHAT A LOT OF PEOPLE CALL HAWKE.
BECAUSE HE USES ICE MAGIC, AND ALSO...
BECAUSE HIS FACE IS SO EXPRESSIONLESS. HE RARELY SHOWS MUCH EMOTION.
にぱー
GRIN
EXPRESSIONLESS...??
?
I CAN ONLY PICTURE HIM WITH A SMILE ON HIS FACE.
OH! BUT PUT YOUR MIND AT EASE, SEI.
I HAVE NO REASON TO THINK THAT HAWKE HAS A FIANCÉE.
I GUESS NOT.
BUT...

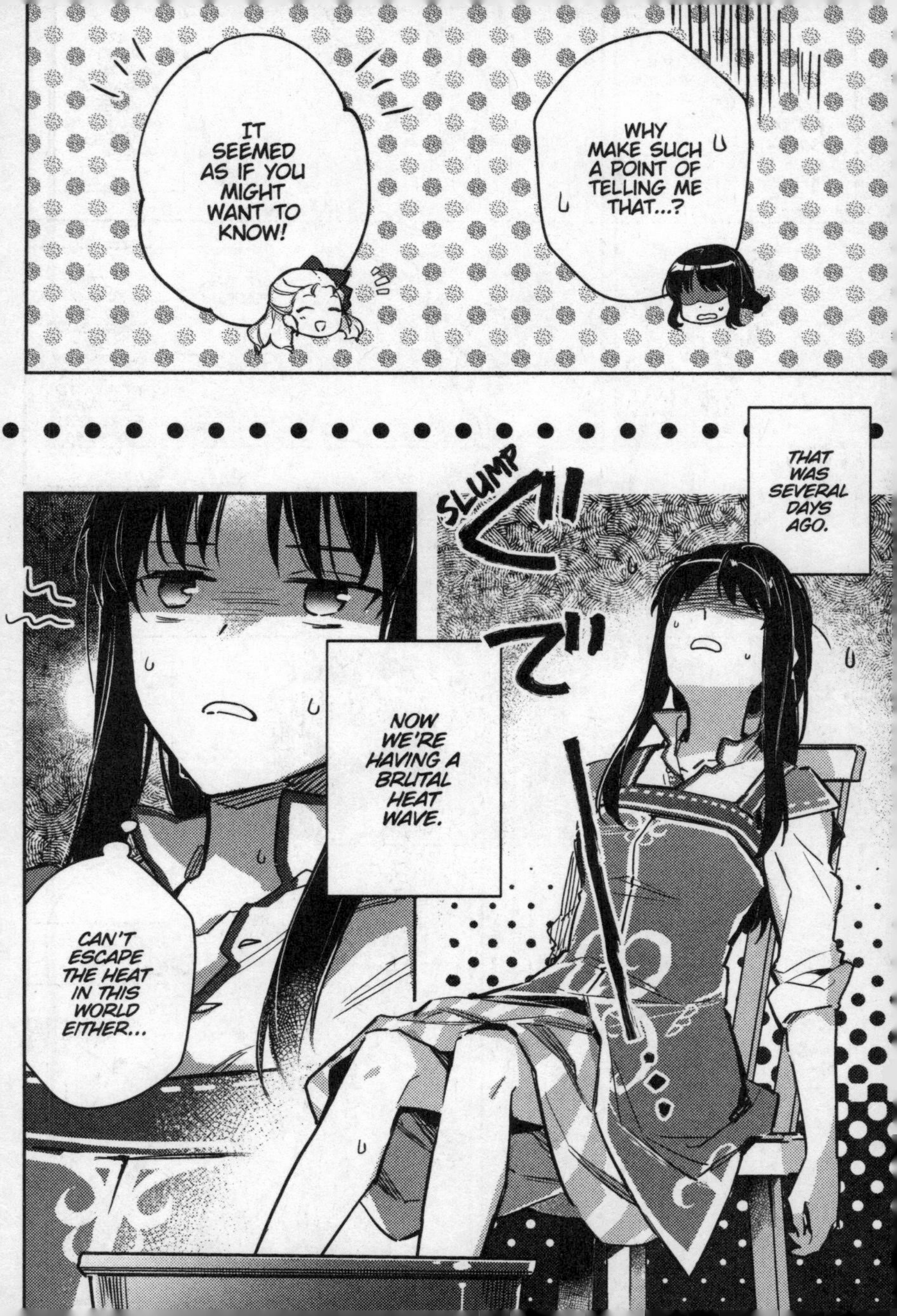
WHY MAKE SUCH A POINT OF TELLING ME THAT...?
IT SEEMED AS IF YOU MIGHT WANT TO KNOW!
THAT WAS SEVERAL DAYS AGO.
SLUMP
NOW WE'RE HAVING A BRUTAL HEAT WAVE.
CAN'T ESCAPE THE HEAT IN THIS WORLD EITHER...

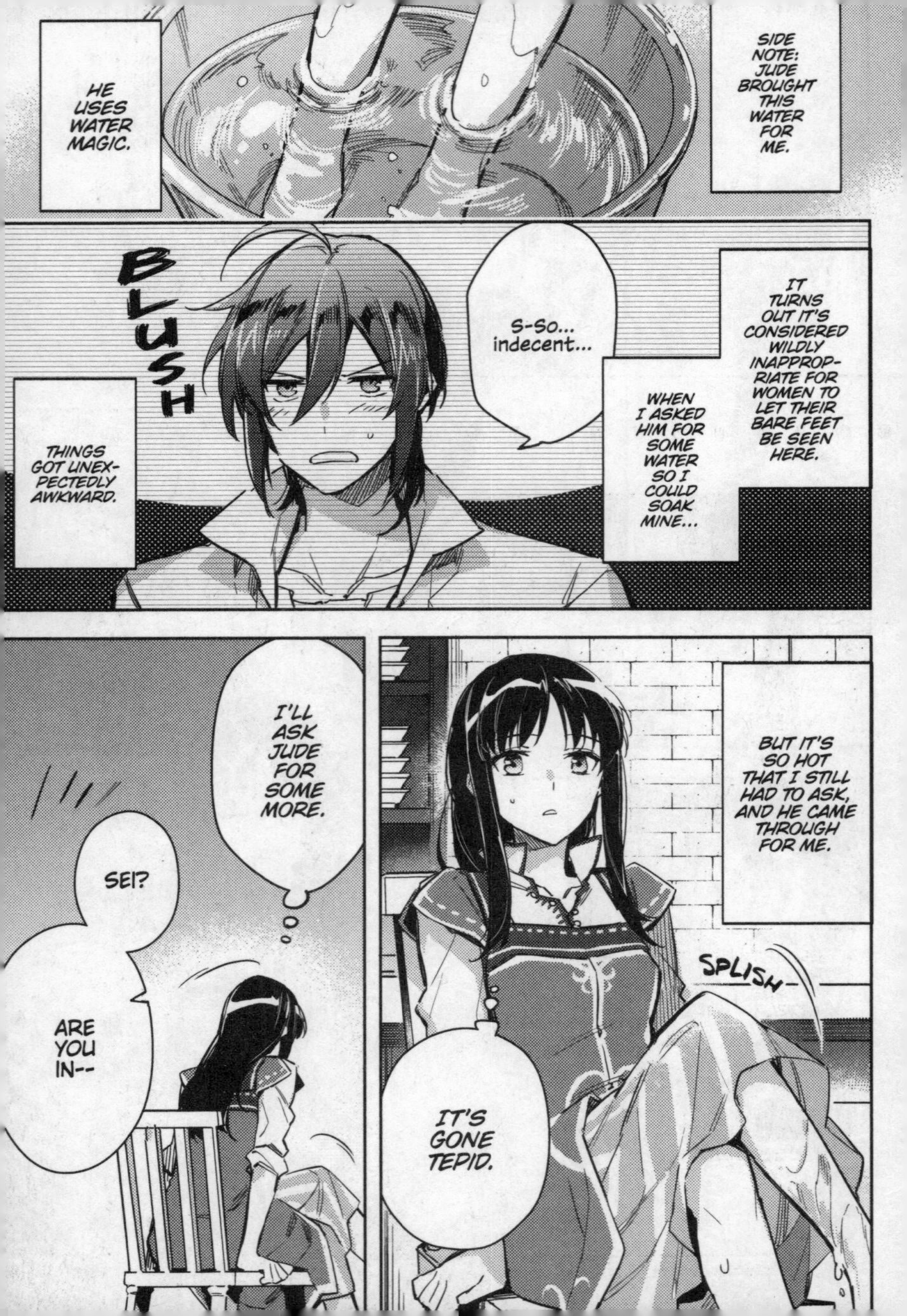
SIDE NOTE: JUDE BROUGHT THIS WATER FOR ME.
HE USES WATER MAGIC.
IT TURNS OUT IT'S CONSIDERED WILDLY INAPPROPRIATE FOR WOMEN TO LET THEIR BARE FEET BE SEEN HERE.
WHEN I ASKED HIM FOR SOME WATER SO I COULD SOAK MINE...
S-So... indecent...
BLUSH
THINGS GOT UNEXPECTEDLY AWKWARD.
BUT IT'S SO HOT THAT I STILL HAD TO ASK, AND HE CAME THROUGH FOR ME.
SPLISH
IT'S GONE TEPID.
I'LL ASK JUDE FOR SOME MORE.
SEI?
ARE YOU IN--

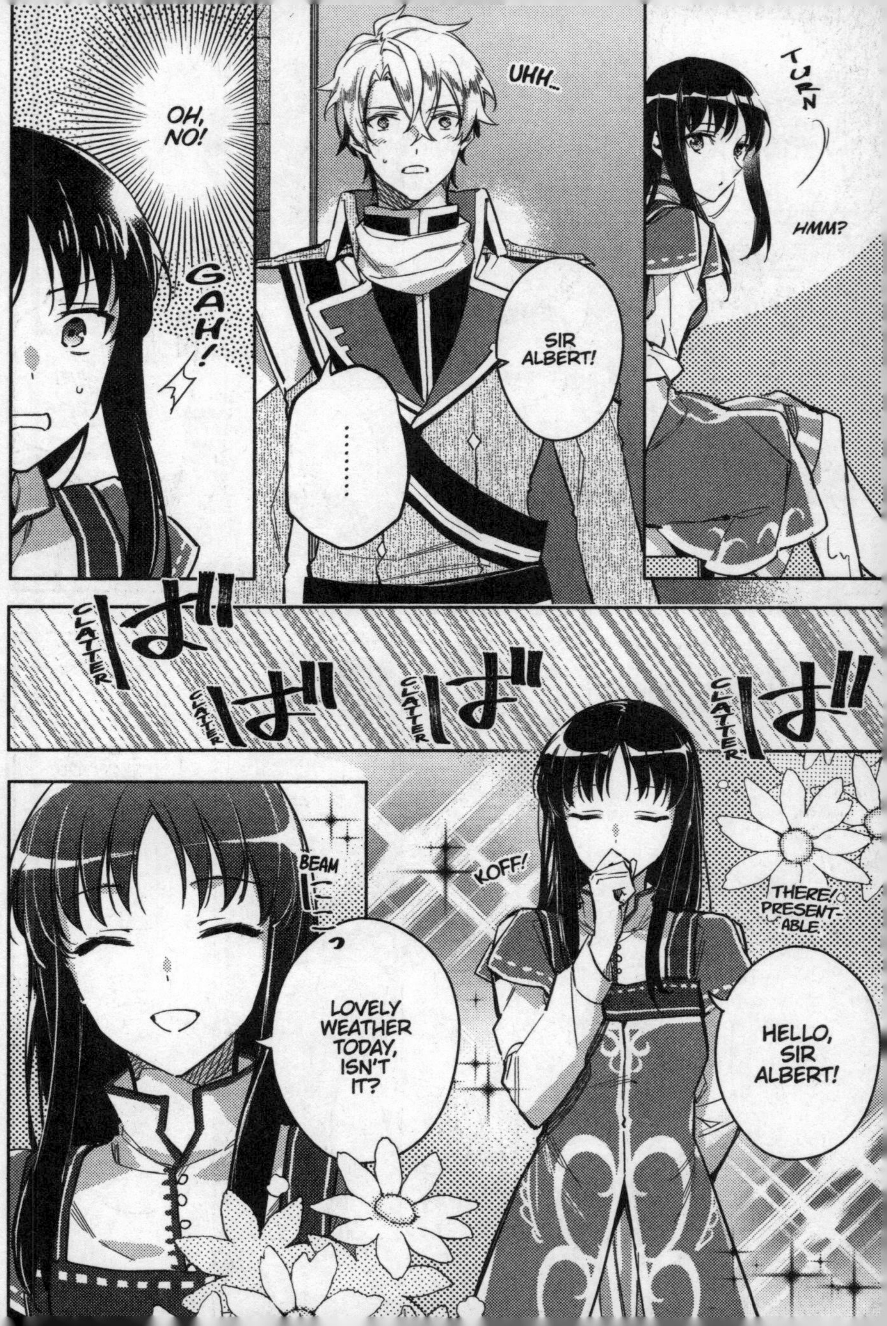
TURN
HMM?
UHH..
SIR ALBERT!
......
OH, NO!
GAH!
CLATTER
CLATTER
CLATTER
CLATTER
THERE! PRESENT-ABLE
KOFF!
HELLO, SIR ALBERT!
BEAM
LOVELY WEATHER TODAY, ISN'T IT?

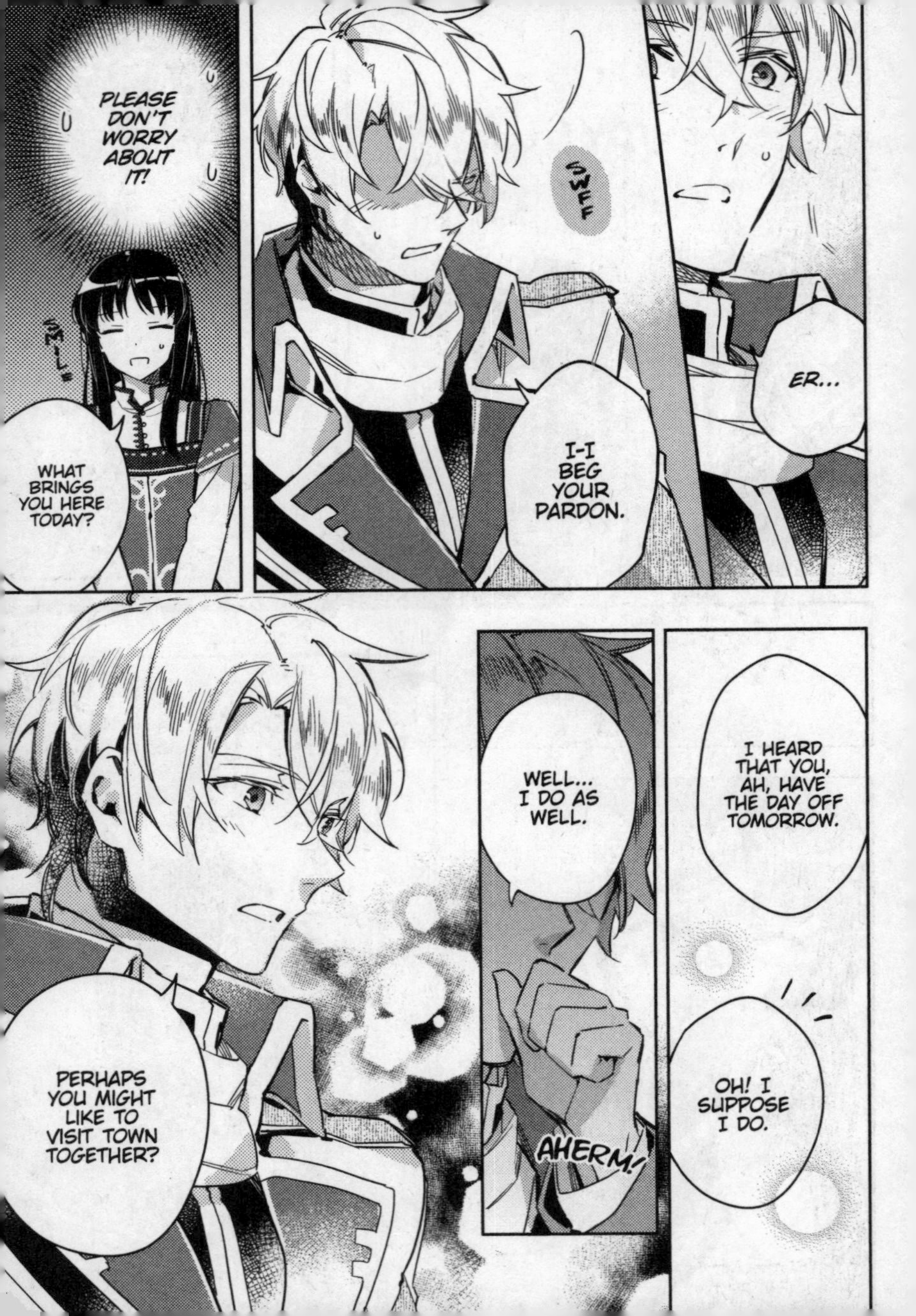
ER...
SWFF
I-I BEG YOUR PARDON.
PLEASE DON'T WORRY ABOUT IT!
SMILE
WHAT BRINGS YOU HERE TODAY?
I HEARD THAT YOU, AH, HAVE THE DAY OFF TOMORROW.
OH! I SUPPOSE I DO.
WELL... I DO AS WELL.
AHERM!
PERHAPS YOU MIGHT LIKE TO VISIT TOWN TOGETHER?

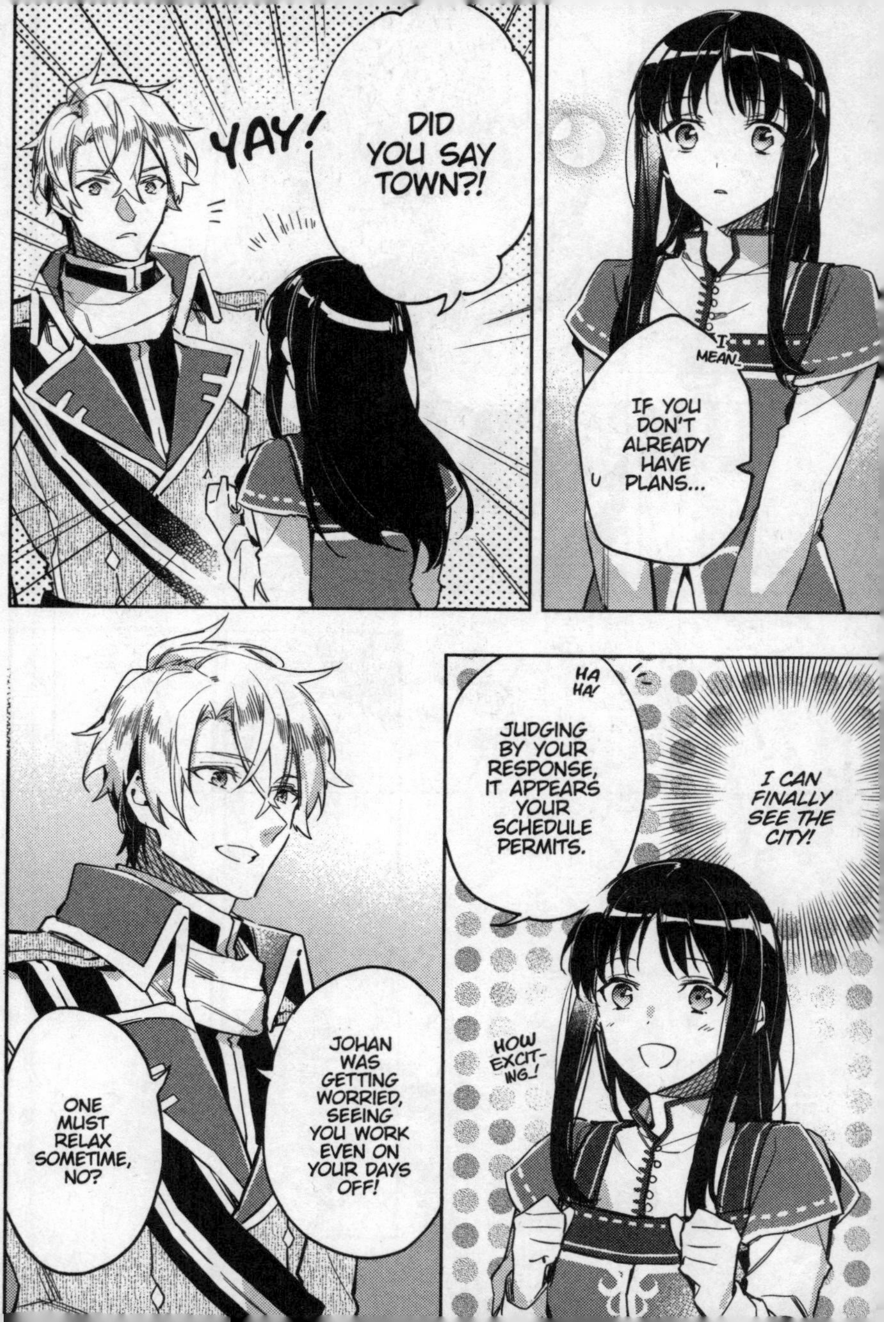
I MEAN...
IF YOU DON'T ALREADY HAVE PLANS...
DID YOU SAY TOWN?!
YAY!
HA HA!
JUDGING BY YOUR RESPONSE, IT APPEARS YOUR SCHEDULE PERMITS.
I CAN FINALLY SEE THE CITY!
HOW EXCITING...!
JOHAN WAS GETTING WORRIED, SEEING YOU WORK EVEN ON YOUR DAYS OFF!
ONE MUST RELAX SOMETIME, NO?

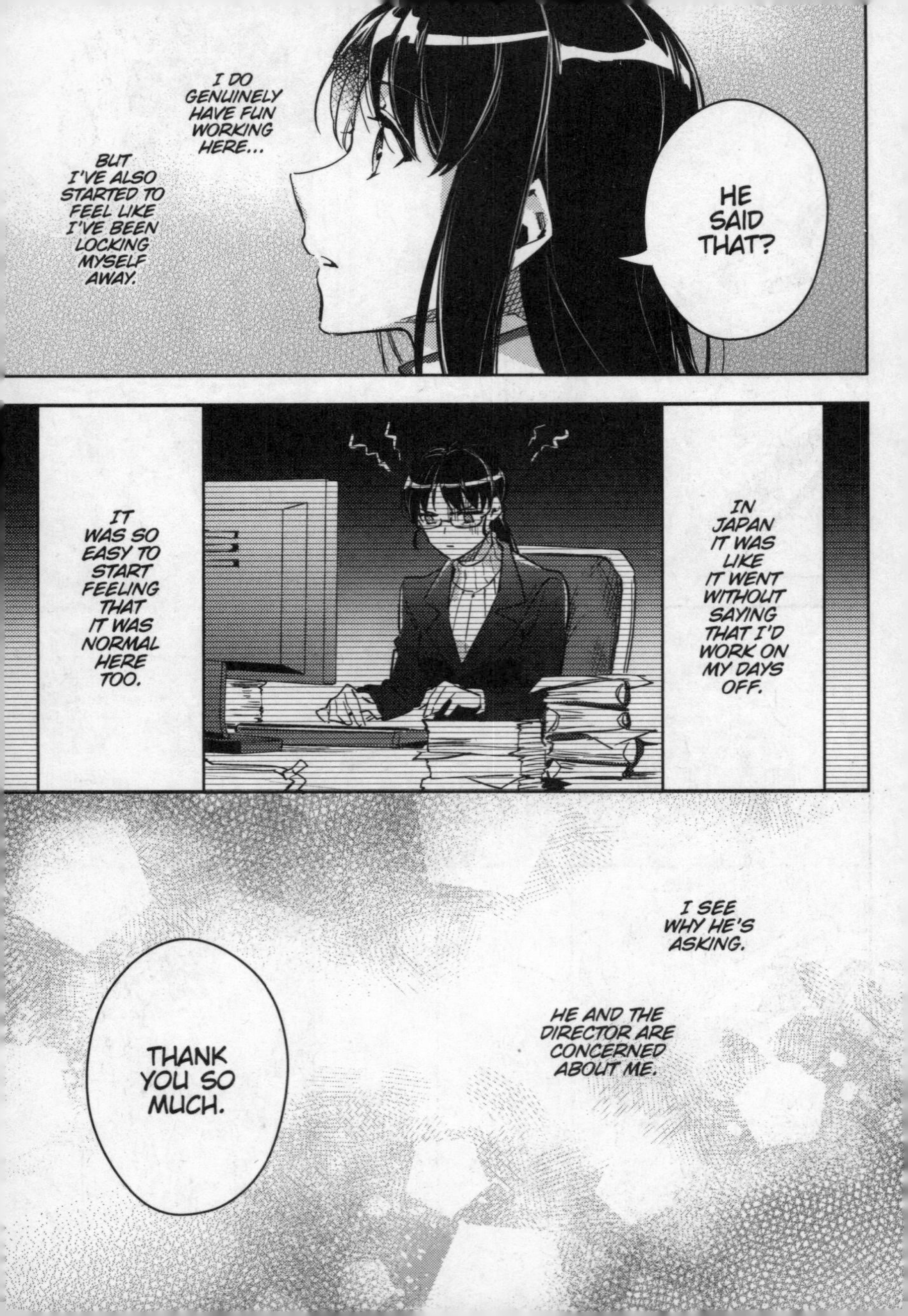
HE SAID THAT?
I DO GENUINELY HAVE FUN WORKING HERE...
BUT I'VE ALSO STARTED TO FEEL LIKE I'VE BEEN LOCKING MYSELF AWAY.
IN JAPAN IT WAS LIKE IT WENT WITHOUT SAYING THAT I'D WORK ON MY DAYS OFF.
IT WAS SO EASY TO START FEELING THAT IT WAS NORMAL HERE TOO.
I SEE WHY HE'S ASKING.
HE AND THE DIRECTOR ARE CONCERNED ABOUT ME.
THANK YOU SO MUCH.

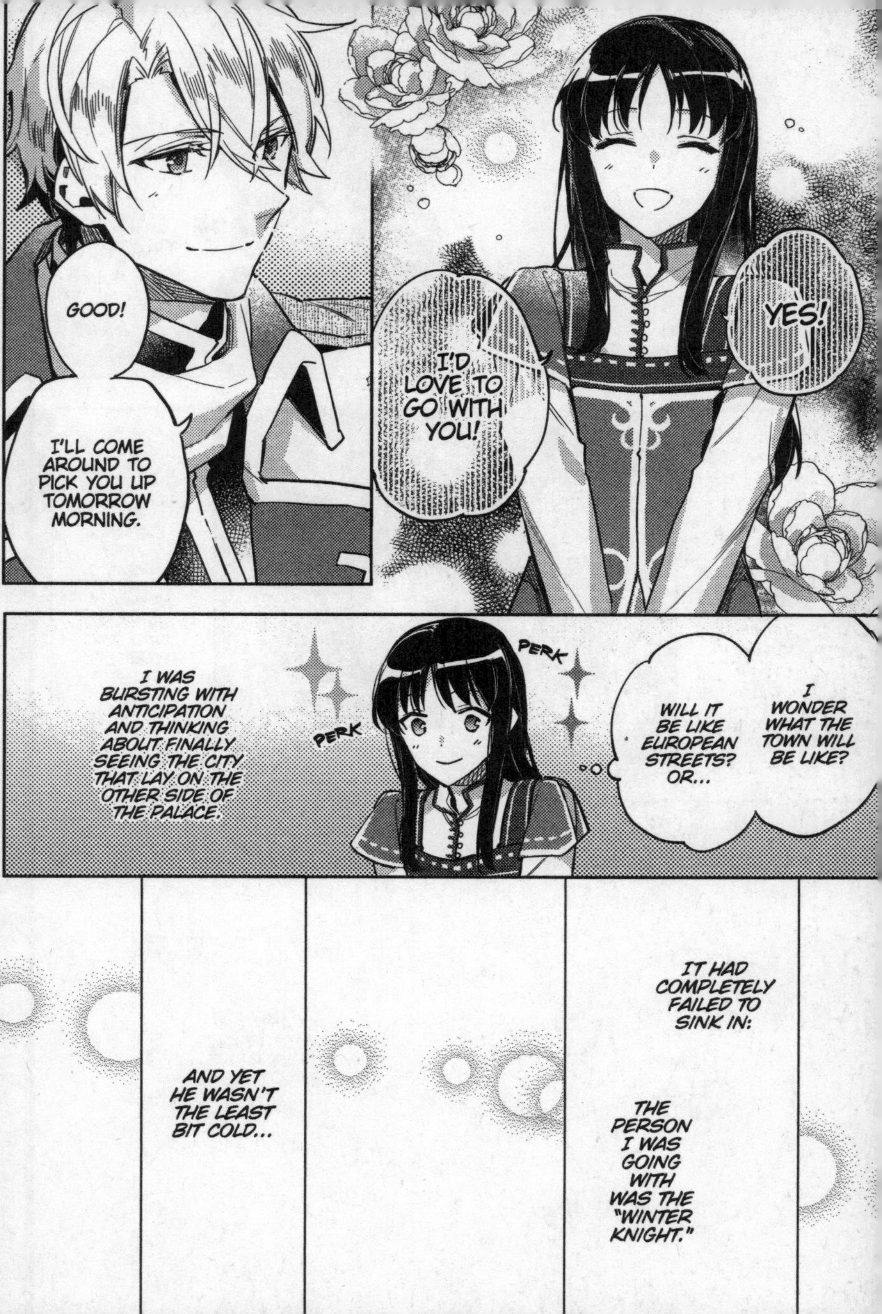
YES!
I'D LOVE TO GO WITH YOU!
GOOD!
I'LL COME AROUND TO PICK YOU UP TOMORROW MORNING.
I WONDER WHAT THE TOWN WILL BE LIKE?
WILL IT BE LIKE EUROPEAN STREETS? OR...
PERK
PERK
I WAS BURSTING WITH ANTICIPATION AND THINKING ABOUT FINALLY SEEING THE CITY THAT LAY ON THE OTHER SIDE OF THE PALACE.
IT HAD COMPLETELY FAILED TO SINK IN:
THE PERSON I WAS GOING WITH WAS THE "WINTER KNIGHT."
AND YET HE WASN'T THE LEAST BIT COLD...

The Saint's*
*Magic Power is *
Omnipotent

The Saint's
Magic Power is
Omnipotent

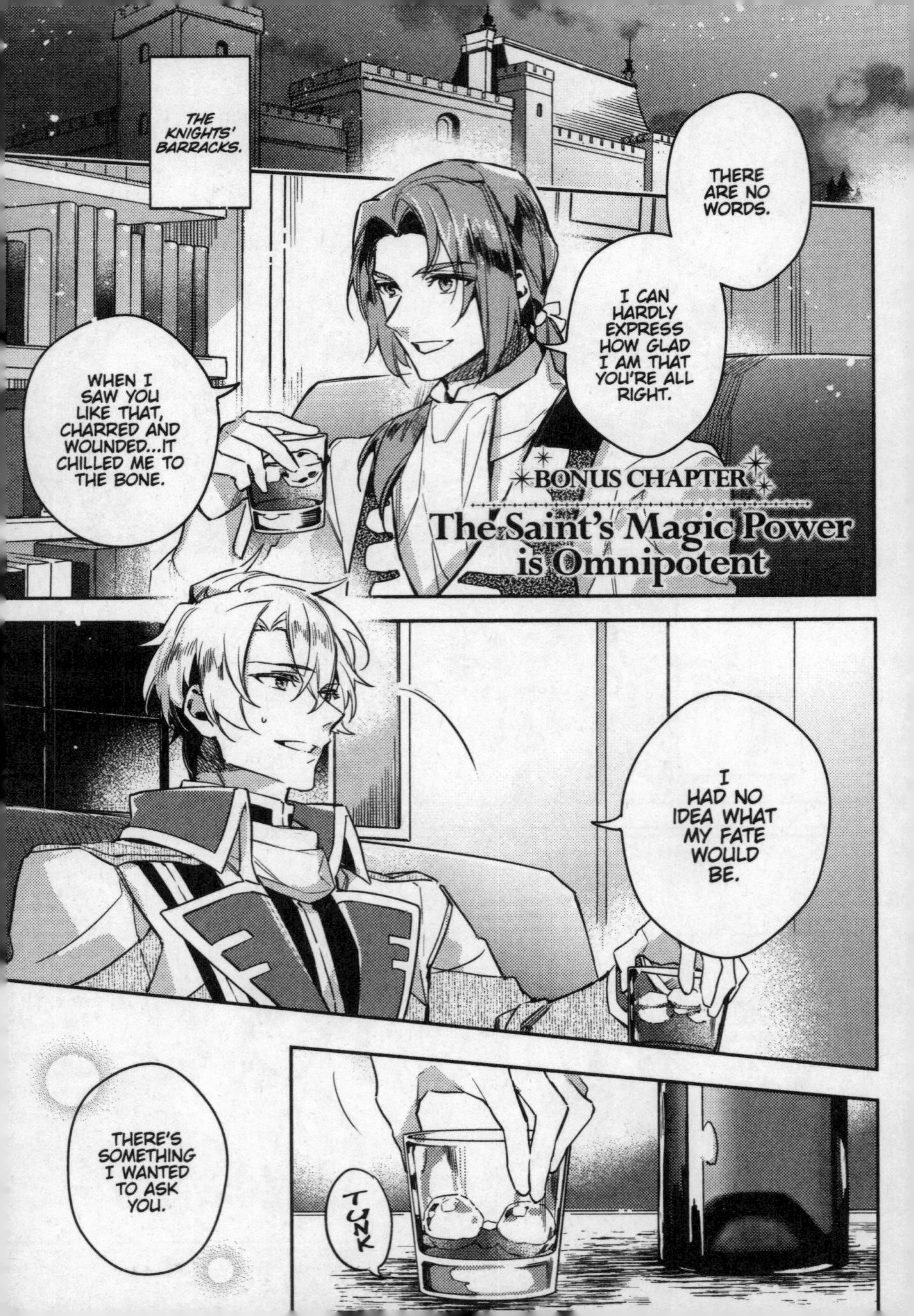
THE KNIGHTS' BARRACKS.
THERE ARE NO WORDS.
I CAN HARDLY EXPRESS HOW GLAD I AM THAT YOU'RE ALL RIGHT.
WHEN I SAW YOU LIKE THAT, CHARRED AND WOUNDED...IT CHILLED ME TO THE BONE.
BONUS CHAPTER
The Saint's Magic Power is Omnipotent
I HAD NO IDEA WHAT MY FATE WOULD BE.
TUNK
THERE'S SOMETHING I WANTED TO ASK YOU.

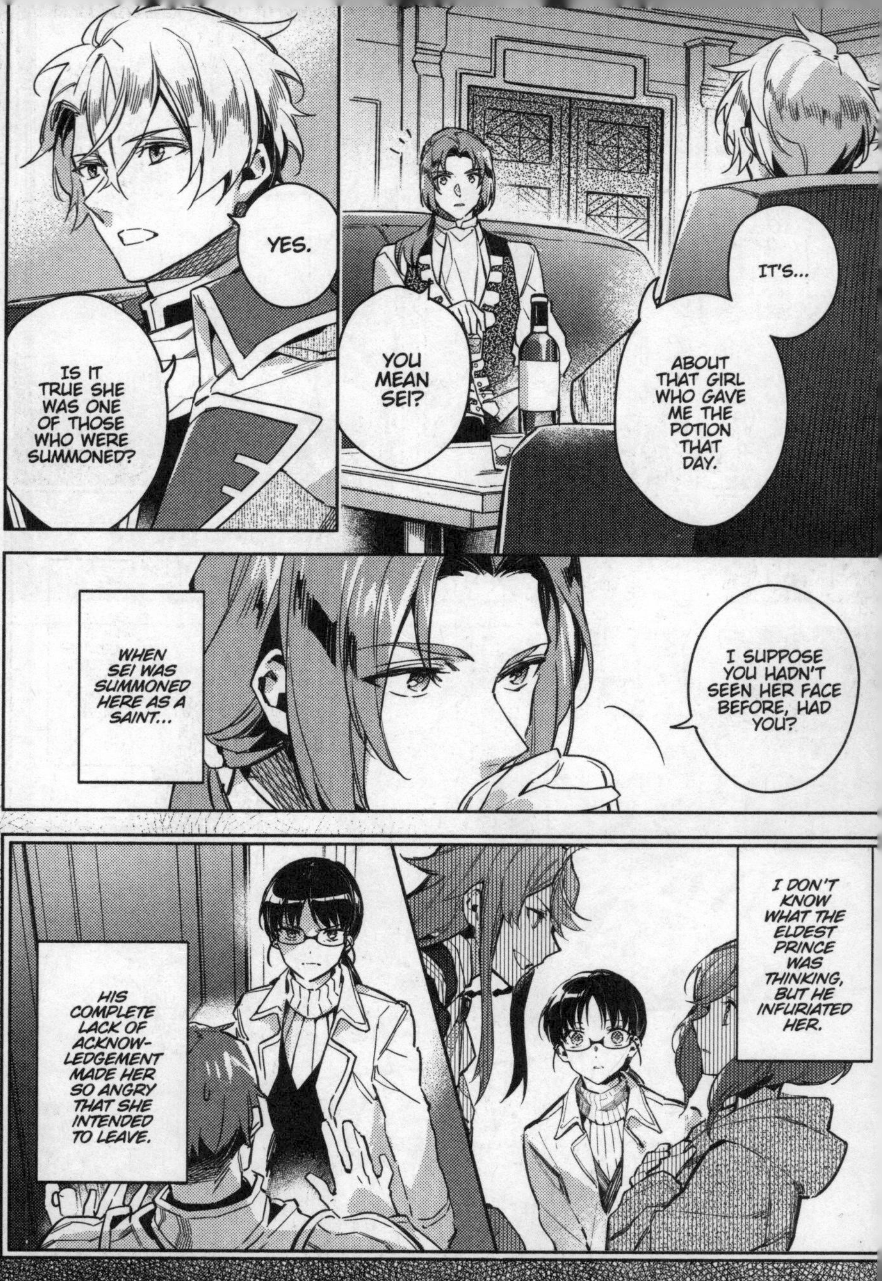
IT'S...
ABOUT THAT GIRL WHO GAVE ME THE POTION THAT DAY.
YOU MEAN SEI?
YES.
IS IT TRUE SHE WAS ONE OF THOSE WHO WERE SUMMONED?
I SUPPOSE YOU HADN'T SEEN HER FACE BEFORE, HAD YOU?
WHEN SEI WAS SUMMONED HERE AS A SAINT...
I DON'T KNOW WHAT THE ELDEST PRINCE WAS THINKING, BUT HE INFURIATED HER.
HIS COMPLETE LACK OF ACKNOW-LEDGEMENT MADE HER SO ANGRY THAT SHE INTENDED TO LEAVE.

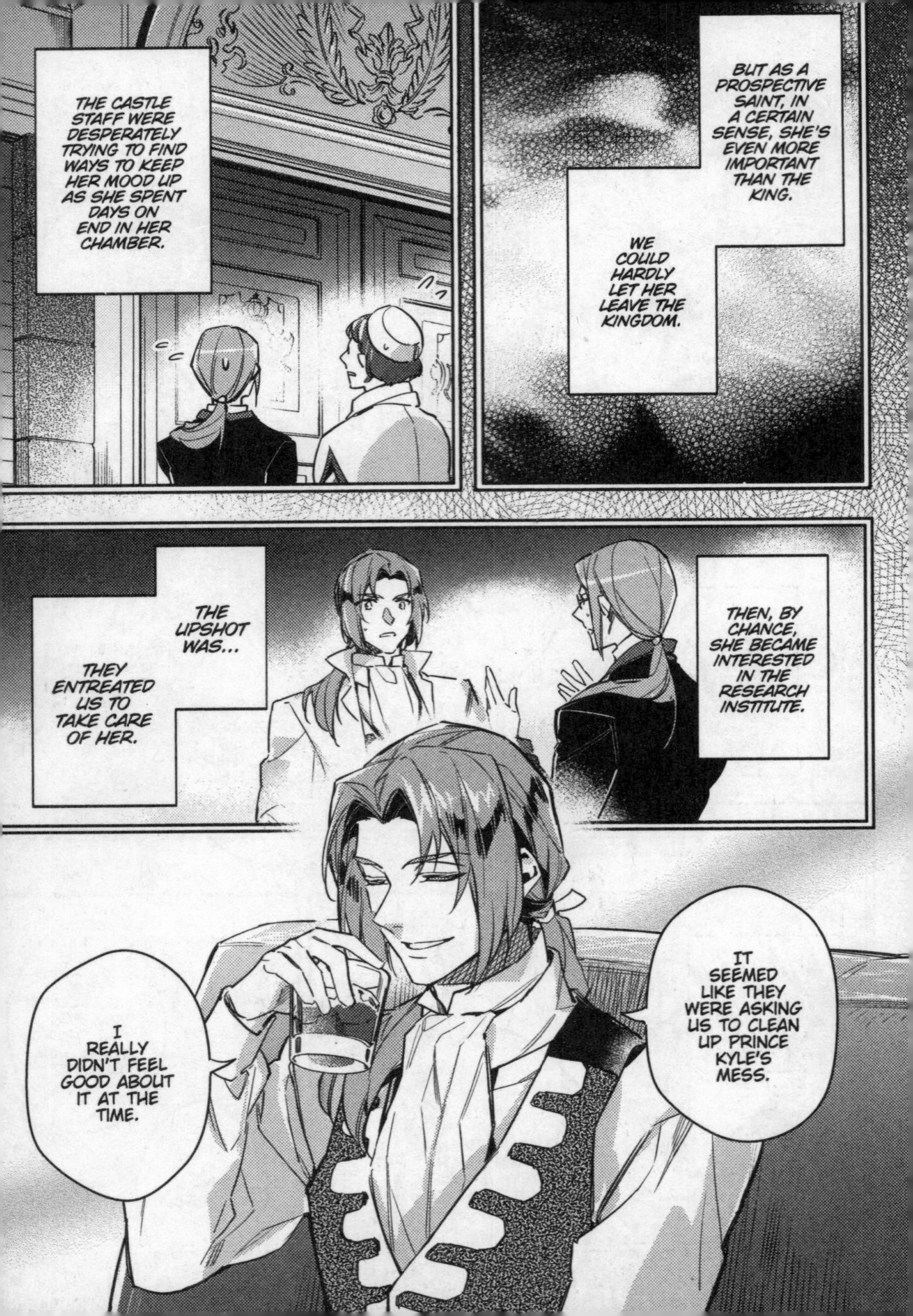
BUT AS A PROSPECTIVE SAINT, IN A CERTAIN SENSE, SHE'S EVEN MORE IMPORTANT THAN THE KING.
WE COULD HARDLY LET HER LEAVE THE KINGDOM.
THE CASTLE STAFF WERE DESPERATELY TRYING TO FIND WAYS TO KEEP HER MOOD UP AS SHE SPENT DAYS ON END IN HER CHAMBER.
THEN, BY CHANCE, SHE BECAME INTERESTED IN THE RESEARCH INSTITUTE.
THE UPSHOT WAS...
THEY ENTREATED US TO TAKE CARE OF HER.
IT SEEMED LIKE THEY WERE ASKING US TO CLEAN UP PRINCE KYLE'S MESS.
I REALLY DIDN'T FEEL GOOD ABOUT IT AT THE TIME.

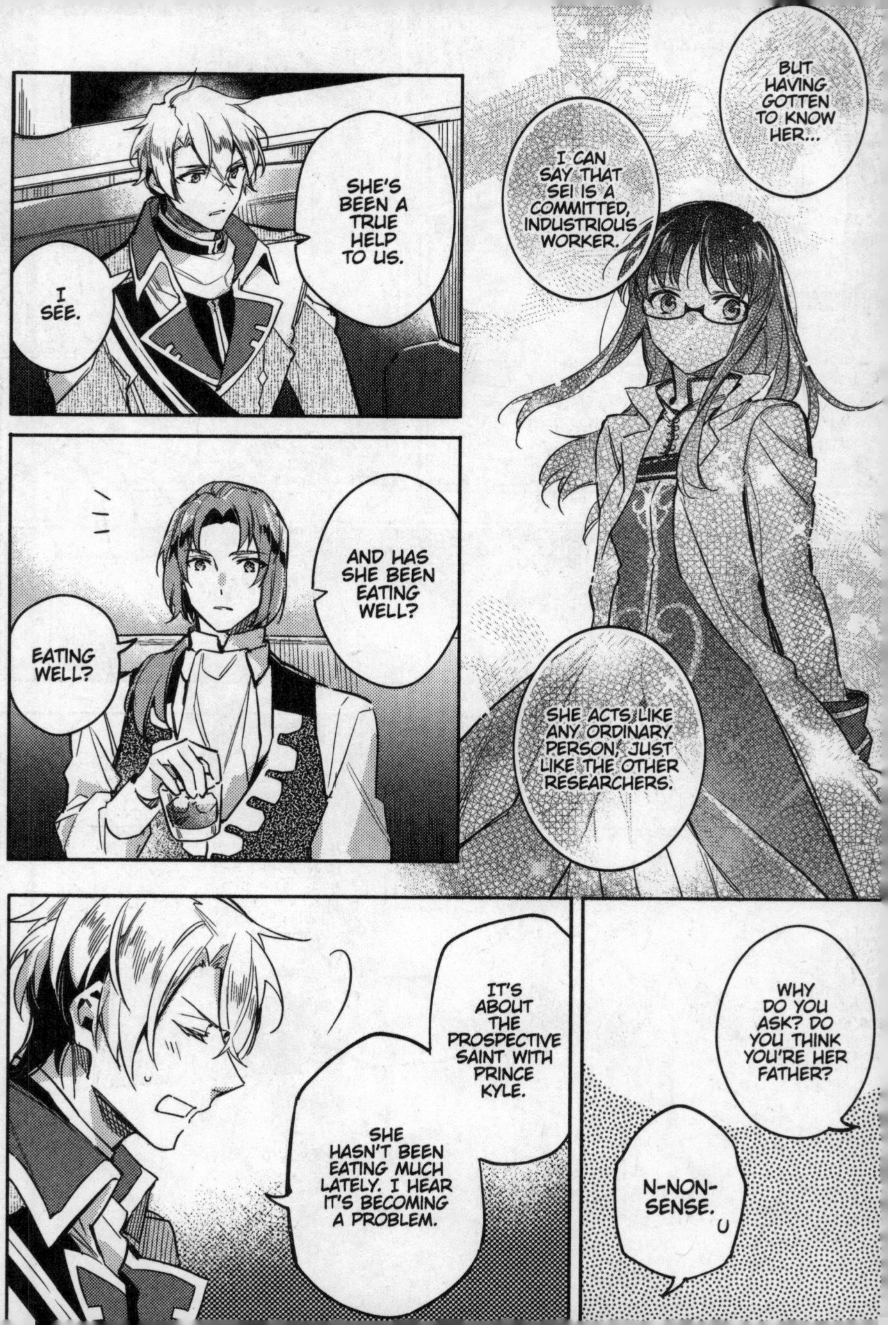

BUT HAVING GOTTEN TO KNOW HER...
I CAN SAY THAT SEI IS A COMMITTED, INDUSTRIOUS WORKER.
SHE ACTS LIKE ANY ORDINARY PERSON, JUST LIKE THE OTHER RESEARCHERS.
SHE'S BEEN A TRUE HELP TO US.
I SEE.
AND HAS SHE BEEN EATING WELL?
EATING WELL?
WHY DO YOU ASK? DO YOU THINK YOU'RE HER FATHER?
N-NON-SENSE.
IT'S ABOUT THE PROSPECTIVE SAINT WITH PRINCE KYLE.
SHE HASN'T BEEN EATING MUCH LATELY. I HEAR IT'S BECOMING A PROBLEM.

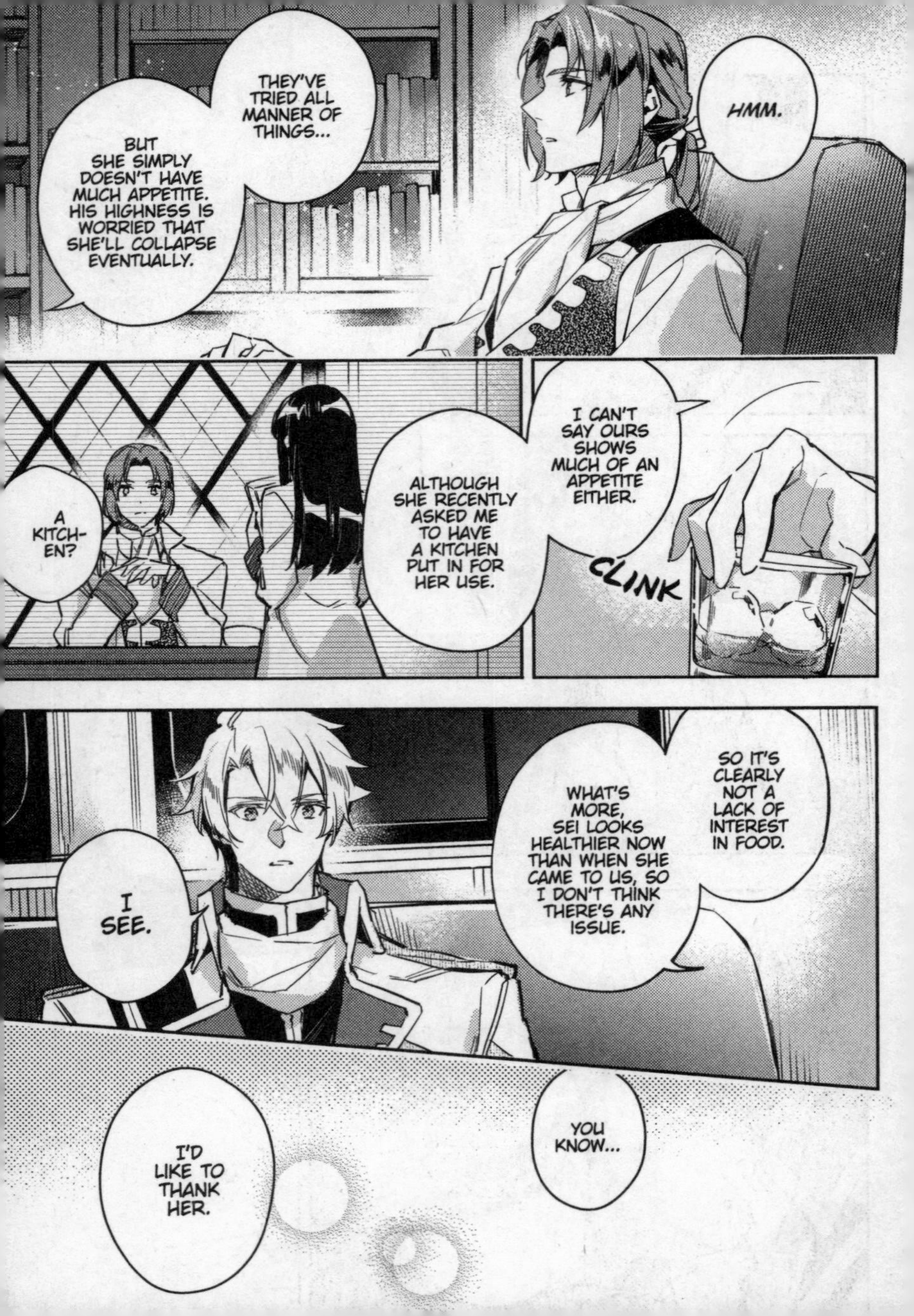
HMM.
THEY'VE TRIED ALL MANNER OF THINGS...
BUT SHE SIMPLY DOESN'T HAVE MUCH APPETITE. HIS HIGHNESS IS WORRIED THAT SHE'LL COLLAPSE EVENTUALLY.
I CAN'T SAY OURS SHOWS MUCH OF AN APPETITE EITHER.
CLINK
ALTHOUGH SHE RECENTLY ASKED ME TO HAVE A KITCHEN PUT IN FOR HER USE.
A KITCH-EN?
SO IT'S CLEARLY NOT A LACK OF INTEREST IN FOOD.
WHAT'S MORE, SEI LOOKS HEALTHIER NOW THAN WHEN SHE CAME TO US, SO I DON'T THINK THERE'S ANY ISSUE.
I SEE.
YOU KNOW...
I'D LIKE TO THANK HER.

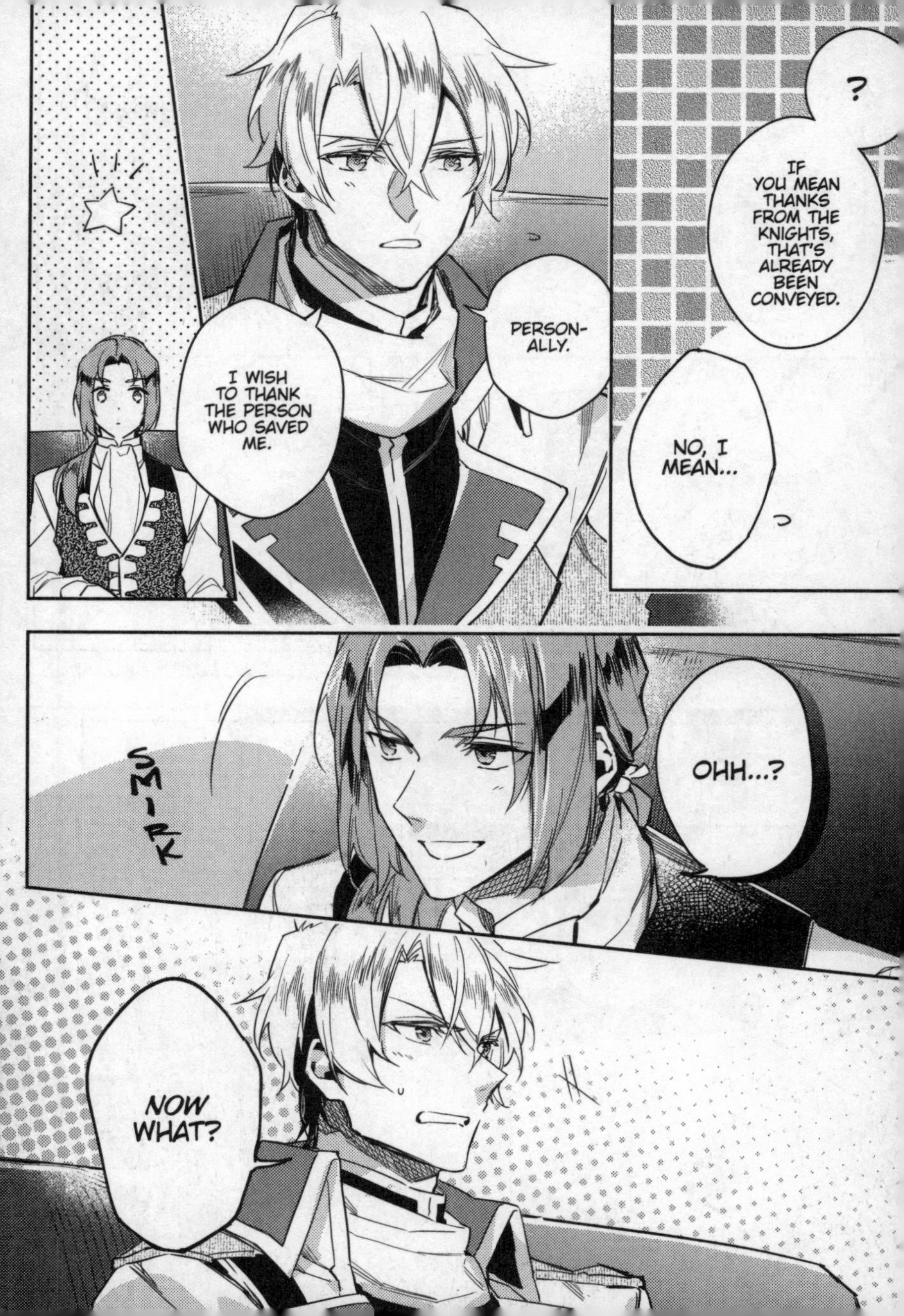
?
IF YOU MEAN THANKS FROM THE KNIGHTS, THAT'S ALREADY BEEN CONVEYED.
NO, I MEAN...
PERSON-ALLY.
I WISH TO THANK THE PERSON WHO SAVED ME.
OHH...?
SMIRK
NOW WHAT?

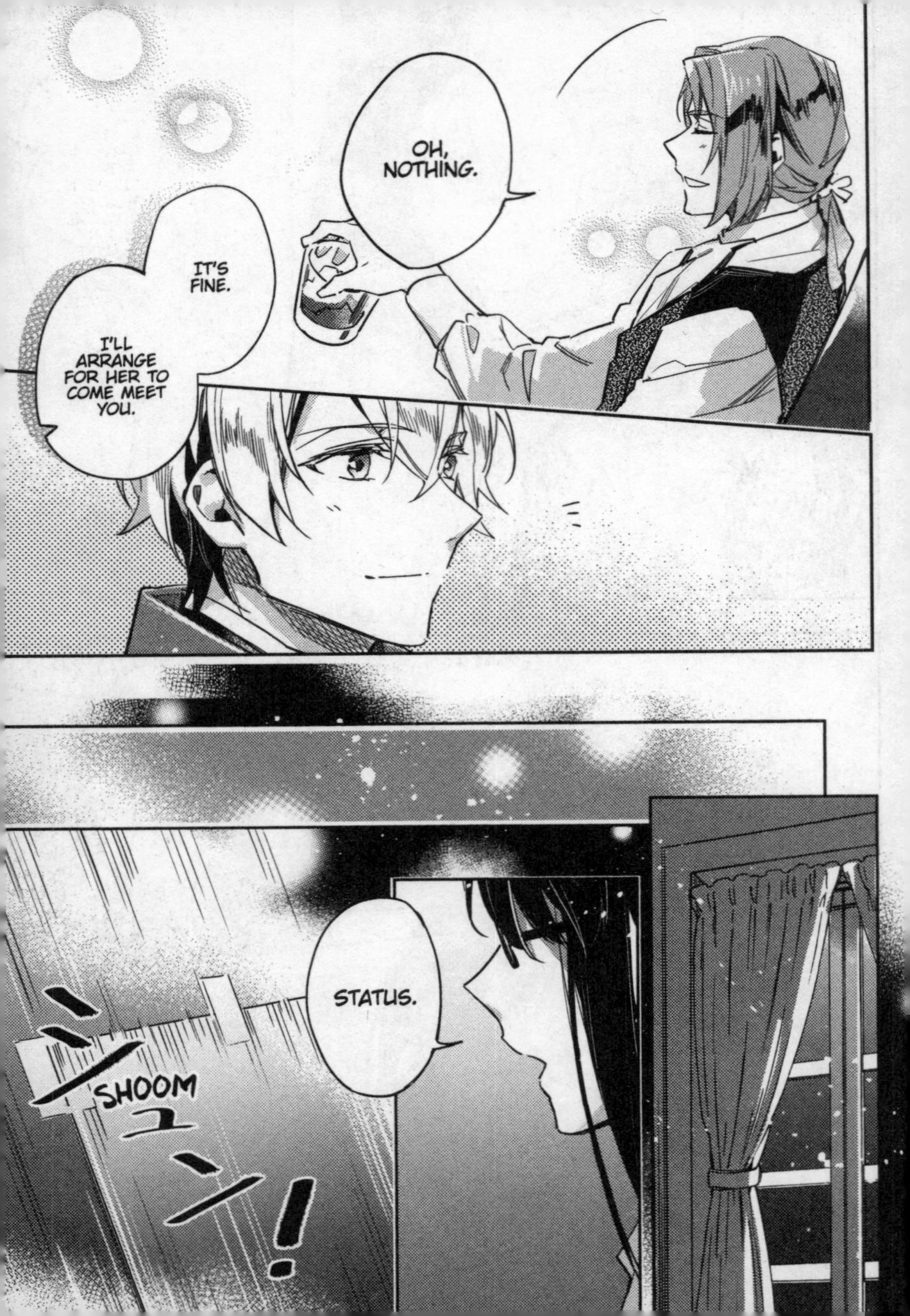
OH, NOTHING.
IT'S FINE.
I'LL ARRANGE FOR HER TO COME MEET YOU.
STATUS.
SHOOM

"HOLY ATTRIBUTE MAGIC..."

"SEI NAKANASHI, LEVEL 55."

"PRODUCTION SKILLS: MAKE MEDICINE, LEVEL 21."

Sei Nakanashi Lv. 55 / Sain

HP: 4,867 / 4,867

LEVEL ∞... M⋅6,067 / 6,067

Combat Skills:
Holy Attribute Magic: Lv. ∞
Production Skills
Make Medicine: Lv. 21

WHAT THE...?

The Saint's
Magic Power is
Omnipotent

The Saint's Magic Power is Omnipotent
Afterword by the Creator

Thank you very much for picking up *The Saint's Magic Power is Omnipotent*. I'm the original creator, Yuka Tachibana. This all began when I submitted my novel to a website called *Let's Be Novelists*, and now, thanks to various twists of fate, it's become a printed manga! I'm deeply grateful to everyone who read it online; to Fujiazuki-sensei, who handled the manga adaptation; to all the editors; and to everyone else involved.

I was really taken aback when talk of a manga adaptation came up. In fact, I was so shocked by it that my emotions were all over the place. At first it felt like they were talking about someone else's work. It didn't feel real at all. Before the first chapter ran in *ComicWalker*, I had a look at the drafts, but it still didn't quite sink in. What finally made it seem real was getting to see the completed pages to check them.

To think it could have this much impact as a manga…!

I was looking at characters and a story that I'd come up with, but as a reader, I was completely sucked in—so much that I'd read the whole thing before I remembered that I was supposed to be checking it over!

This will betray how limited my vocabulary is, but I thought it was simply awesome. When I saw the cover art, I was moved by how beautiful it was, but it was more than that. When a manga adaptation was first being discussed, I heard that a really talented artist was involved, and that truly is exactly what we got. Fuji-sensei, thank you truly for creating such a lovely manga adaptation.

And finally, once again, thank you to everyone who picked up this collected edition. I would be delighted if you look forward to the story at the end of the day and feel warm inside. See you again next time.

Yuka Tachibana

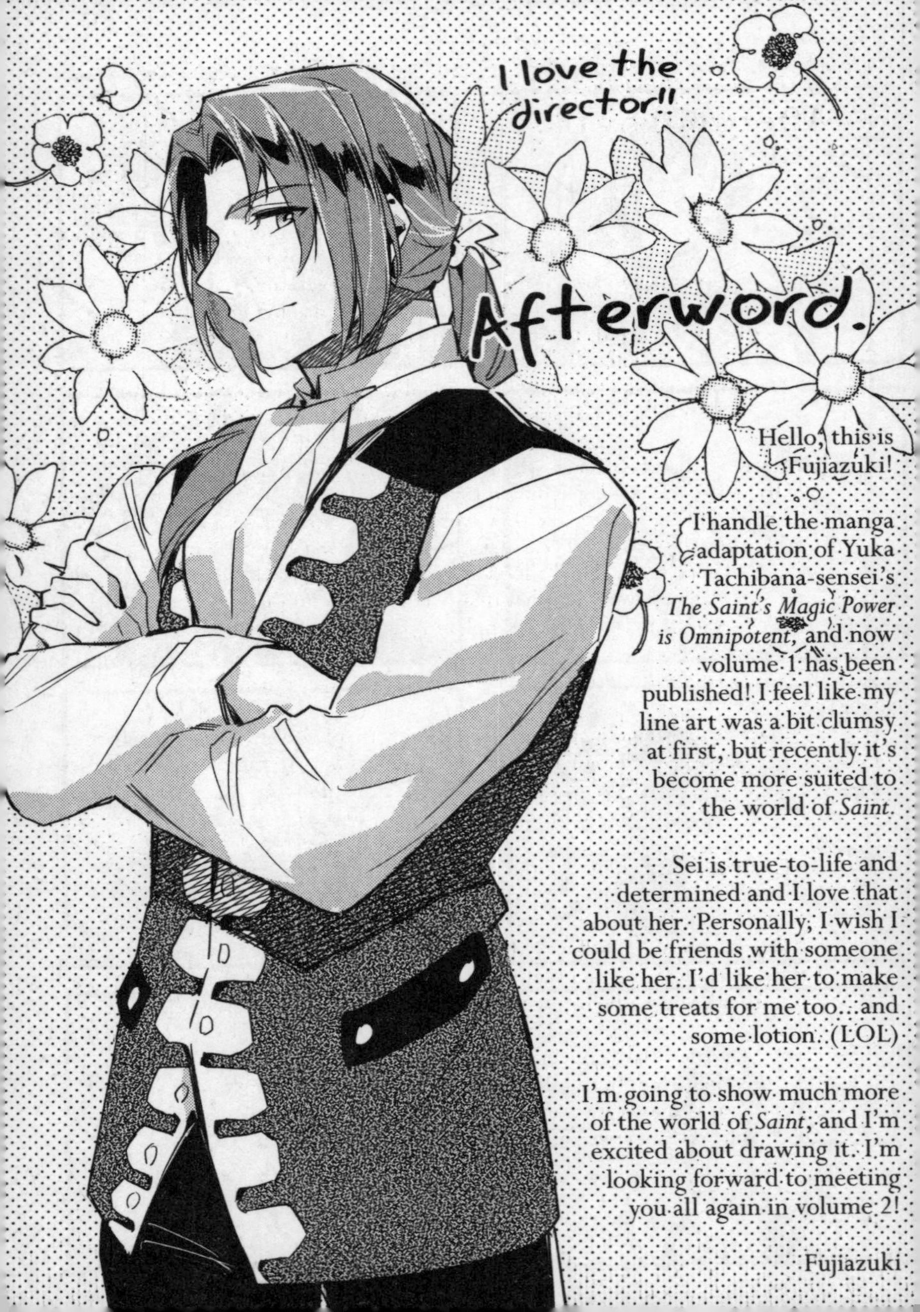
I love the director!!

Afterword.

Hello, this is Fujiazuki!

I handle the manga adaptation of Yuka Tachibana-sensei's *The Saint's Magic Power is Omnipotent*, and now volume 1 has been published! I feel like my line art was a bit clumsy at first, but recently it's become more suited to the world of *Saint*.

Sei is true-to-life and determined and I love that about her. Personally, I wish I could be friends with someone like her. I'd like her to make some treats for me too...and some lotion. (LOL)

I'm going to show much more of the world of *Saint*, and I'm excited about drawing it. I'm looking forward to meeting you all again in volume 2!

Fujiazuki

The Saint's Magic Power is Omnipotent 1 Fujiazuki presents

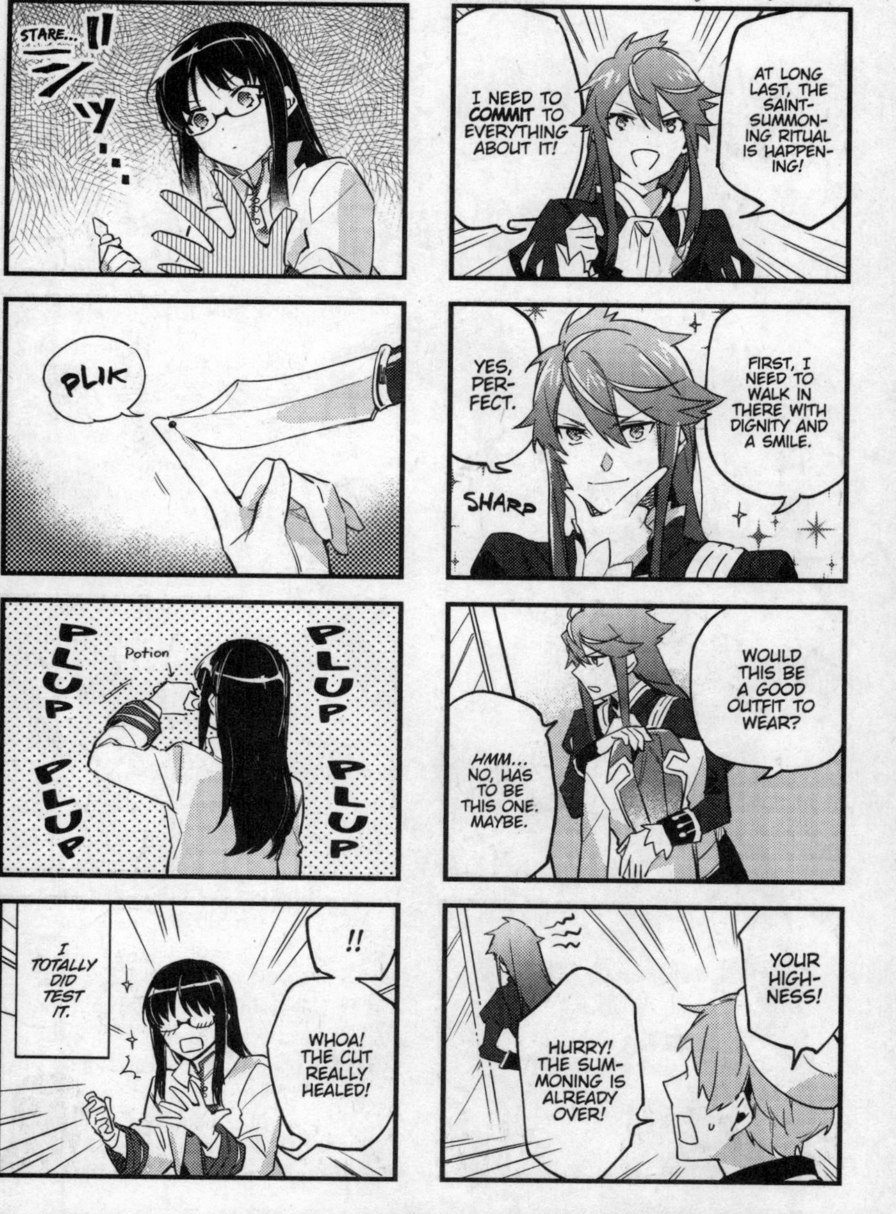
AT LONG LAST, THE SAINT-SUMMONING RITUAL IS HAPPENING!
I NEED TO COMMIT TO EVERYTHING ABOUT IT!
FIRST, I NEED TO WALK IN THERE WITH DIGNITY AND A SMILE.
YES, PERFECT.
SHARP
WOULD THIS BE A GOOD OUTFIT TO WEAR?
HMM... NO, HAS TO BE THIS ONE. MAYBE.
YOUR HIGHNESS!
HURRY! THE SUMMONING IS ALREADY OVER!
STARE...
PLIK
PLUP
PLUP
Potion
PLUP
PLUP
!!
WHOA! THE CUT REALLY HEALED!
I TOTALLY DID TEST IT.